LEAGUE ⬡F ELDER
6TH TURN: KAT

DEMONS, *SPIRALATA* and *COVUS*

REN GARCIA

ST. G   Winter Wolf
PUBLICATIONS

Columbus   Cincinnati

Turns of the Shadow tech Goddess: Kat

Copyright © 2017 by Ren Garcia
Cover Art by © 2017 by Carol Phillips
Listed copyrighted interior image art is
provided in the 'List of Illustrations'
ISBN: 978-1-945039-08-9

Edited by Cas Peace

ST. G

Published by St. G Press, an imprint of Winter Wolf Publications

Printed in the United States of America

First St. G Press edition: July 2017

Visit our website: www.thetempleoftheexplodinghead.com

Table of Contents

Part III

Kat

Part IV

Bellathauser

List of Illustrations

The Known Universe--as seen from Camalopardus

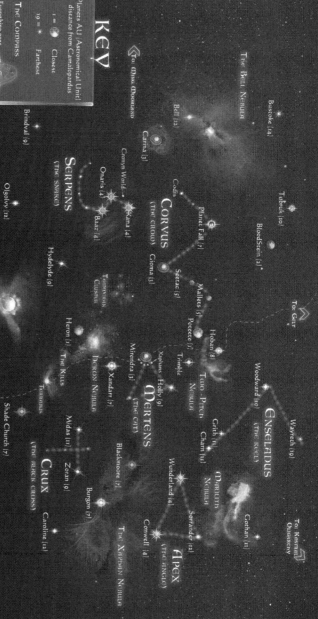

KEY

Planets AU (Astronomical Unit) distance from Camalopardus

1 = ● Closest

19 = ✳ Farthest

The Compass

Everything goes back to the planet Kana.

PU11

AM = East/West longitude.
PM = North/South latitude.

⟨⟨To: Obsis Moonland

The Bell Nebula

Busooke [14]

Tabruk [10]

Bell [12]

BloodStein [2]

Carna [3]

Cestyn World ●

Codis

CORVUS
(The Crow)

Planet Fall [7]

Cisma [3]

Serac [5]

Mallets [5]

Potecte [7]

Hoban [8]

To: Gair

Woodward [10]

ENCELADUS
(The Reef)

Wavech [19]

Onaris [4]
Skana [4]
Baaz [4]

SERPENS
(The Snake)

Trop Pren
Nebula

Grith [4]

Mankrin
Nebula

Gothan [11]

To: Resenati Observatory

Olgolvy [2]

Brindival [9]

Hydelyde [9]

Tombstone
Cluster

Star of Merian
[In Dispute]

Heron [1]

The Kiss

DeKron Nebula

Micridra [3]

Xaphans
Holly [9]

Trambu

Cham [4]

Wunderland [4]

Sorrinder [12]

Xandar [7]

MERTENS
(The City)

Blackmoore [7]

APEX
(The King)

Cosiwell [4]

The Xaphan Nebula

Shade Church [7]

Trinima

Midas [11]

Zoran [9]

CRUX
(The Black Cross)

Burgon [7]

Caroline [12]

LEAGUE
SPACE

XAPHAN
SPACE

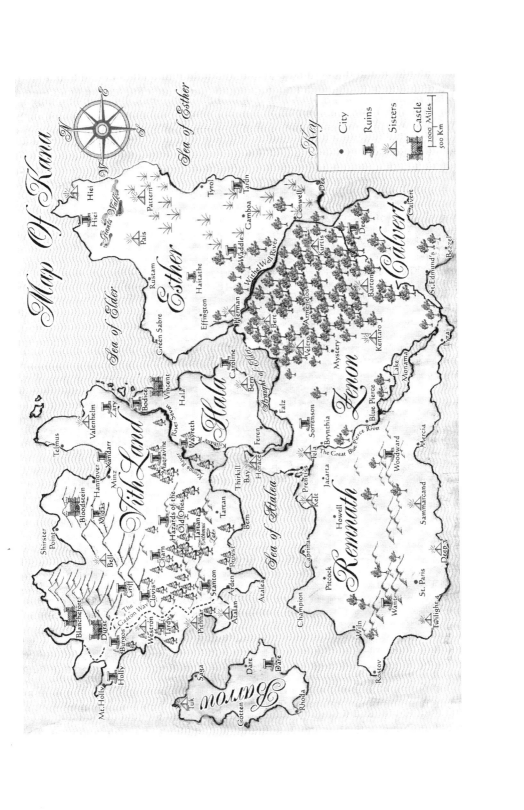

Map Of Kana

Sea of Esther

Key
• City
🏰 Ruins
✳ Sisters
🏰 Castle
1000 Miles
500 Km

Esther

Hiei
Hiei
Hiei
Pattern
Paul's Valley
Pais
Rustam
Green Sabre
Waddle
Gamboa
Conwell
Dee
Dee
Tyrol
Tardn
Effington
Haitathe
Hetman
Wichel Well River
Vedro
Kurtis
Dee
Calvert

Calvert

Bezzel
St. Edmund's
Barton
Bert
Amelelos
Kentaro
Mystery

Zenon

Telmus

Sea of Elder

Nith Land

Valenhelm
Zav
Bodica
Vincent
Xandarr
Hanover
Minz
Rose Seve
Hala
Maqravine

Hala

Caroline
Bern
Vincent
Waymeth
Kilburn
Falz
Lake Monama
Blue Pierce
Straight of Elder

Bloodstein
Midas
Bell
Shirster Point
Hazards of the Old Ones
Cham
Tartan
Tarran
Tolbonne Lake
Feren
Horace
Bay
Thirkill
Sorrenson
Brynthia
Tela
The Great Blue Pierce River
Jacarta
Blue Pierce
Mercia
Woodward

Remnath

Griff
The Gaston Way
Clovis
Stanton
Arden
Provost
Bern
Tartan
Atala
Atalan
Sea of Atalea
Kelt
Capitnan
Piccock
Howell
Sammarcand

Blanchefort
Dust
Burgos
Westron
Pelman
Tardy
Holly
Mt. Holly
Prentiss
Champion
Wiln
Rostov
St. Paris
Wance
Twilight
Deep

Barrow

Tuk
Cotten
Saga
Rhoda
Dare
Dare

Part I
Four Sisters

Black Hat MAUDE-2 "Stealth Missile"

1—Shade Church

The angels warned her against going underground, there is great danger underground, they said, but there she was in a place bereft of wind or sunlight, and she was certain she was dying. Her tail of Shadow tech flicked spatters of warm blood as she stared at the dead body she had just made. The body lay there gushing blood in a pulseless river, its throat torn out. She ran her shaking hand through her matted hair, leaving a trail of blood. Her claws were caked with congealing flesh.

She was alive, the sole survivor, though terribly wounded and bleeding. Her skinny body was soaked with blood from both herself and person she had killed, while her two companions, those who had shared the darkness and the stone pits of the Shade Church for as long as she could remember and whom she considered sisters, were dead. One floated headless in a vat of Shadow tech, the other stabbed to death, over and over.

The horrid image of her sisters, dead, murdered, spun in her thoughts as she lay on the dusty floor, unable to stand from blood loss.

So, this is how she would die, broken, underground, without ever having met her angels and the man they had promised her.

✷　✷　✷　✷　✷

She had lived her whole life in the Shade Church, the underground crucible where Black Hats were trained in the dark. The training consisted of nothing but torment and abuse. Its graduates were those who managed to survive. Like the others crawling in the lightless stone, she was abducted from wherever as a mere infant; stolen from her mother's side, her face bearing the accursed Shadowmark. She had no idea how long she had been there; with no way to mark the time, no way to record it, she really had no conception of time other than the rate at which the others crowded in the dark with her died—which was often. Everything was a long, extended death in the Shade Church.

Huddled in the dark, they told stories.

When you die, angels will come and take you away ... they said. *There is a better place, full of light and color where the gods and their angels live ...*

Angels? Light and color? She had no idea what those things were.

She grew from a child who could stand upright in the dark to an adult who had to stoop to avoid hitting her head on the stony ceiling. The arcane Autocon guards that tormented them were cruel and pitiless.

Either you will live to become a Black Hat, or we will slay you and harvest the Shadow tech within.

Black Hats and Shadow tech. Several concepts were made clear to her by the Autocons. One was that she would, in all probability, not survive the Shade Church; the other, that she was not a person but a worthless bit of property owned by the Black Hats to do with as they saw fit. That was it. The Shadowmark around her eye branded her as their property. The Shadowmark, something she had never seen, bound her into servitude.

At one point in her life, she begged to be saved. Perhaps the angels she had heard of would come and save her.

There are no angels here to save you, the Autocons often said. *There are no angels, there is only Hell.*

* * * * *

The day of her death came at last. They were taken from the pit by the hated Autocon guards, their constant Shadow tech tormentors, and dragged to the surface, the darkness replaced with an overwhelming force that hurt her eyes. She had to squint to block it out. She had heard that outside of the Shade Church was the opposite of darkness. There were 'color' and 'forms'. Daring to open her eyes, she endured the pain and could see what was happening around her. She, and the others with her on the surface, were forced to their knees while a hook was sunk into each of their backs and lodged in place. Then they were all wrenched into midair, dangling from their hooks like pieces of filthy meat. The hook, sunk deep in her back near her shoulder, caused searing agony, but she was used to agony, dealt with it constantly. What she wasn't used to were all the things on the surface she had never seen before. She was dazzled by the light around her, by the color, by the drops of cold water that saturated the rags she wore. She was mesmerized by the others hanging on the hooks beside her; she had never 'seen' them before. She had bumped into them in the dark, felt them, fought them sometimes while the Autocons laughed, but never beheld their images before. Glancing down, she saw her own body; pale, dirty, dangling in midair, looking nothing like what she thought it would look like. They were sometimes given piles of rancid sea creatures to devour, and occasionally they would dimly glow, revealing their forms. That's what she thought she would look like; like a sea creature. Her own body was unimpressive to her. Her fingers twitched as did her feet, vaguely catching her attention.

Now, we shall burn them … came a voice.

Barely aware of what was happening, the hook she hung from began moving, sending her and the others from the depths down the line toward a raging basin of what she thought might be fire—she had heard of fire before, was threatened with it every day by the Autocons.

We will burn your worthless body in fire ...

Look at it. Such light, such color, such warmth. Could this fire be so bad? The end of her life was at hand. She didn't care much about it.

Perhaps the next life wouldn't be so hard.

The line stopped suddenly. She swung back and forth, knocking against those in front of and behind her, the hook in her back digging in, dripping blood.

Two figures came down the line, inspecting those hanging from the hooks. When they got to her, they stopped, standing beneath her dangling feet, looking up at her. They were wearing such amazing things. One of them wore a garment of scintillating color, a shade she could not describe. She couldn't take her eyes off it. It was the color of life, of mercy.

"This one," they said.

She was brought down and taken off the hook. The people touched her, tended her aching wound and washed her body, the fabric of their robes shimmering before her face.

"You have much to live for," one of them said, whispering into her ear.

That was the first time she had ever experienced any sort of kindness. Punches to the face, claws in the dark and lashes across her back were all she knew. Touches created pain, yet here were these people, touching her, healing, enriching, giving her no pain.

Were they angels?

You have much to live for ... they said.

The angels selected several more of those who hung from the hooks, bringing them down as well. She could count on her fingers up to five; anything past that was beyond her. She counted: one, two, three.

Three were brought down, the three who would become her sisters.

After that day, after being touched by the angels in the color of mercy, she and her three new sisters were treated quite differently than the rest at Shade Church. They were removed from the huddled masses in the stony depths and allowed to inhabit a larger area all of their own; still barren, still unbearable, still smothered in darkness, but far better than the cramped pits below. They were given more food, cleaner water, and even frequent baths in silver fluid that cleared their minds of the delirium they had lived in. Still, their treatment was brutal; the hated, arcane Autocon constructs were their daily scourges, dragging them about like worthless meat, beating them sometimes until they were half dead, tormenting them at their whim. The Autocons that terrorized them lived inside their bodies, swimming about like great parasites, and, when hers came out, she felt it wrenching itself from her body in a great wave of sickness. One time, she thought she witnessed an Autocon coming out of her sister's mouth.

She endured the beatings with indifference, the memory of the angels a warm ember in her thoughts:

You have much to live for.

And then there was Shadow tech; the arcane substance growing within their bodies that howled through their souls and followed them into their sleep in a barbed-wire embrace. She could feel it moving about inside her body, and sometimes she could smell it—a primal metallic reek, like dried blood. It came out of her pores, sometimes out of her mouth. When there was too much inside her, it caused her misery unlike anything else, even more than the Autocon could inflict upon her. It was something the Black Hats valued, and they took great pains to cultivate, capture and collect it. *"You are worthless shells protecting a precious treasure ..."* they would hiss. *"The Shadow tech within you is OURS! Understand? You exist to nurture it. Displease us and we shall do a harvest, pulling it from your bodies, sending your souls to Hell and leaving your empty corpses to rot!"*

She and her sisters fully believed what the Black Hats said, that the brackish substance growing inside their bodies causing them pain did indeed belong to the Black Hats.

The Black Hats carefully regulated when and how she and her sisters could make use of Shadow tech. With the Autocons watching, they were permitted to conjure it at select moments, to force it from their bodies like blood that floated, casting until they had a mere basic understanding of it. Other times, they were forcibly bled of it, the odd substance trickling out of their bodies like molten tar. The rest of the time they were forbidden to experiment with Shadow tech, the Autocons inside them ready to kill. To cast Shadow tech without permission meant instant death.

In addition, their bodies were relentlessly trained. Their limbs were stretched into impossible positions and left that way for indeterminate lengths of time; their joints popping, their mouths open, yet unable to scream. During rare moments of peace when the Autocons slunk back inside them, the four sisters sometimes held each other, tending to their wounds, enduring the Shadow tech pain together and whispering what they hoped and dreamed for. She would often count them to make sure they were all there, reaching out and touching their heads in the dark; one, two, three, all there. She could recognize them just by how their faces felt against her hands. Then she would re-tell the story of the two angels that had saved the four of them from the hooks on that strange day. She struggled to describe the color of the robe one of the angels had worn—she had nothing to compare it to in the dark stony world they inhabited. She said it was a color that made her happy, a color of mercy, that it reminded her of a full belly and a soft feeling when the Autocons weren't around. It was their favorite story.

"Tell it again," one sister would often say.

She sometimes wondered if the memory of the angels was simply a kind hallucination amid an ocean of despair. Yet the scar at her back that regularly pained her was proof the angels were real.

2—Sent to Die

They were taken far away from Shade Church and brought before a council of Black Hats, who gazed at them through their featureless masks. Behind them was a writhing cocoon of Shadow tech wherein the Black Abbess herself resided.

"You have been selected from among all others at Shade Church, thus your privileged existence. We are entrusting the four of you with a very important mission. Know you of the Shadow tech Goddess?" the Black Hats asked.

The Shadow tech Goddess; a name she had heard whispered over and over in the stony passes of the Shade Church, a deplored entity who may or may not exist, with the power to destroy the universe. The Shadow tech Goddess was the only person dreaded, feared, and obsessed over by the Black Abbess. She and her three sisters had no concept of the universe; the word meant nothing to them. Could this Shadow tech Goddess destroy the Shade Church? That would be power.

The four of them were to undertake a perilous mission deep inside enemy territory, deep inside the hated League itself, and the prospects for their survival were minimal at best—the Black Hats were quite clear about that. If they survived the trip, which was in no way assured, and if they managed to elude the ever-watchful eye of the League's mighty Sisterhood of Light, to the *one* trainee who brought the Black Abbess information on the whereabouts or the identity of the Shadow tech Goddess would be granted freedom from the Shade Church and all the horrors within. She would be granted great power, be given a name by the Black Abbess herself and presented with a temple of her own; allowed to become a full Black Hat, at last ready to unleash Hell.

"We have it on good authority that information regarding the Shadow tech Goddess may be gathered in a remote area of the League ... The four of you shall go there and procure this information; we will send Autocons to monitor your activities and ensure you do your duty. Only one of you shall return to us, to great riches. The others will die in the heart of the hated League."

Only one? Counting on her fingers, she realized one, two, three ... of them would die.

She wasn't afraid of death, or was she?

You have much to live for, the angels had said.

✱ ✱ ✱ ✱ ✱

Shortly thereafter, they were taken aloft under guard into the void of space in a Xaphan warship. They were pumped full of calories to sustain them on their long journey, sealed deep inside bulky, impossibly tight atmosphere suits, unable to move, barely able to breathe, and loaded one by one into the sparse, machinery-filled interior of a Black Hat stealth missile and bolted in. Without word or ceremony, the missile with the four of them entombed inside, was fired into space toward the League.

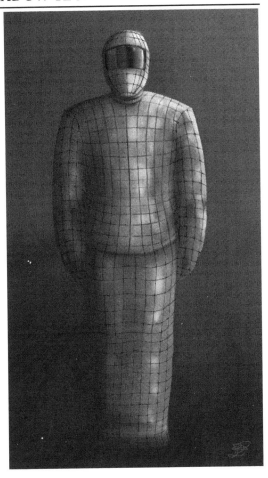

Like everything else she had ever experienced, the confinement in the missile was pure torture. She could barely move a muscle, her arms bound at her side. The bulky atmosphere suit furnished her with enough diluted oxygen to remain conscious, but only just. Her lungs thirsted for air in an unending roar; a roar that followed her into her fitful bouts of sleep. Panic, closed in, buried alive—got to get out! Unable to move, she couldn't scratch or stretch, and she had no choice but to soil herself. The suit soon stank of waste and ammonia. Hallucinations danced before her eyes. The uninsulated circuitry inside the suit seared her bare skin, and when she wasn't being burned, the dank cold of the missile froze her nearly to death. Though she was given an injection of calories to sustain her, her stomach cried out for food. Nearby, buried in layers of smothering metal, she could hear her sisters muffled cries, each moaning for relief.

For what seemed like an eternity, none came.

The Autocon inside her body swam through her Shadow tech like a giant parasite. It cajoled her along the way with its icy Shadow tech voice:

"Do not die! The Black Abbess is invested in your success. Die, waste our training in you and we will reclaim our Shadow tech and cast your soul

to Hell where it will be devoured for the remainder of eternity ... Do not die, you worthless female!"

Through this buried-alive Hell and the constant cajoling, a kind voice from the past rose up from the wellspring of her memories to calm her: *"You have much to live for ..."*

The angels had spoken it to her, and she clung to the silent voice and the memory of the garment the color of mercy; barely alive in the dank cold of her atmosphere suit.

✶ ✶ ✶ ✶ ✶

Eventually, the missile seemed to come to a stop, change course and plunge into the atmosphere of some fertile world, presumably deep in the League. Pre-programmed with precision, the four of them were ejected, tumbling away in a free-fall as the burning missile screeched down like a comet and burrowed deep into the rocky earth.

She plummeted, hitting the ground with a terrific commotion, the bulky suit shielding her from the brunt of the impact. The pounding nearly shook the teeth out of her mouth.

The Black Hats' technology survived, the latches turned and the suit opened, releasing her from its wretched embrace. Stinking, barely alive, she crawled nude from the suit, leaving behind the bare metal to emerge into a place of wonder. There was blessed open space and cool breezes, all free of pain. Weak from her ordeal, she fell to the ground and lay there for a long time, reveling in the openness, watching fingers of smoke from the suit drift away. Drift away to where? Over her head, instead of a stone vault, was a vast openness veiled in mist and tiny, soft lights. The emptiness frightened her for a moment; she felt as though she might fall upwards into an endless abyss and be lost. And what was she lying on? Not stone, it was soft and yielding to the touch; she could tear it away with her fingers.

She felt she was dying, the confinement in the suit too much. She lay there on soft ground, looking up into a great dark vastness, open and mysterious, dappled with a tapestry of twinkling lights.

So beautiful. She would die having witnessed such wonders.

✶ ✶ ✶ ✶ ✶

Still alive, she lay there, partially out of her head with delirium. She felt something holding her, gently cradling her head and neck in a warm embrace. Being held in such a compromised position wasn't something she was used to. There were few warm embraces in Shade Church. She felt a heart beating and soft flesh, smelt sweet scents. Lengths of braided hair danced over her face. Opening her eyes, she saw nothing but a blur.

"Kat? Can you hear me?" came a soft voice. "Kat?"

What was Kat?

The figure leaning over her spoke. "Drink this. It will restore your strength. Drink." A vessel came to her lips, providing nourishing liquid. She felt a hand caress her cheek. She lay there and drank the liquid. The liquid was delicious, she had never tasted such a thing. She felt strength return to her.

A voice whispered into her ear. "We've watched over you. We've wept as you suffered at the hands of the Black Hats and prayed the Fates would grant you strength. But all that is over now; here your life, your true life, will begin. Be strong for a little longer. Be bold. Such things await you, I promise. Not far from here is a group of ruins. These ruins are your salvation. Seek them out. The habitations above ground are safe; however, there is danger, and you must listen. First, the Sisters might come if they detect your Shadow tech, and if they discover you, their judgment will be swift. You cannot stand against the Sisters, their power is much too great."

The figure held up a pouch of soft material and shook it. Metallic objects clinked within. "In this pouch are three *Sentrils*. They will protect you from Shadow tech and will hide your presence from the Sisters' gaze."

She felt a hand come into hers. "You place one *Sentril* to your left, and the other to your right. The final you place before you. Stand between them and you shall have protection. Understand?"

She couldn't respond.

"Secondly, do not under any circumstances go underground. There is great danger there. I don't have time to explain why. Stay above ground and you shall be safe."

The voice continued. "We have more gifts for you. The Autocons that have tormented you can be of some help when properly managed. You may capture one with this device, here." A cold metallic capsule came into her hand. "Remove the lid and an Autocon will be captured within. The device has only room for one Autocon though; if you try to capture more than one, the second will be destroyed. Once captured, the Autocon will not be able to escape, and you will be able to compel it to provide the knowledge you will need. We have also left you with clothes, food, and other essentials."

She received a odd, slightly wet touch on the cheek.

"You are not alone, Kat. You are loved. Never forget that."

A thick mist fell over her. When the mist departed, she was alone at the foot of her open atmosphere suit, the figure gone. She wondered if she had merely dreamed the encounter; it must have been a dream. Yet she tasted the nourishment at her lips and held the metallic device given to her in her hand. She felt life flowing back into her.

Who had been there with her? Who fed and held her? Who was Kat? Was she Kat? Was that her name?

The angels, from her dreams! It must be them, it had to be! Her heart beat with excitement. Where were they? Why did they go? Was this place their home?

In her hand was a large silver device that was smooth and round. At her side was a pouch of soft, wondrous material. All gifts from the angels. The angel promised the device would capture an Autocon should one arrive, and the items in the pouch would protect her from Shadow tech and from the 'Sisters', whoever they were. She opened the pouch; inside were several bits of shiny metal formed into cubes. How many?

One … two … three. Three cubes.

She could see odd inscriptions scratched into the metal surface of the cubes. They clinked together in her palm.

How did they work? The angel had told her how to correctly place them. She oriented herself by the location of the scar on her back. Her hand nearest the scar was her 'Scar hand', while her other hand was the 'Not Scar hand'. She placed a cube on the ground next to her Scar hand, and the other one near her Not Scar hand. The final one she placed in front of her.

Nothing happened. No lights, no noise, no smoke. She wondered what was supposed to take place. The other device the angel had given her was much larger and heavier than the cubes. Turning it about, it felt like a solid piece of metal, cold and smooth in her hand.

Not far away, she saw yet another object in the dark, larger still than the cubes and the metal device. More gifts from the angels! She was excited, she burned to know what it was. She stepped around the cubes and wobbled to the object to inspect it.

Her reverie was quickly broken. Raw agony blasted up from within as the vat of Shadow tech in her body violently thrashed about. She knew what it meant; the Autocon inside her was stirring, prodding at her insides with its claws, ready to crawl out. In terrible pain, she fell to her knees, her muscles tightened, her throat constricted. She heaved, vomiting gouts of Shadow tech that coalesced into shallow pools of choking black tar. It stank, it fumed. It thickened and rose up into a pillar of dense smoke. From the smoke, the Autocon took shape, twisting, gloating, its glittering eyes forming in the darkness.

"*Get up!*" it said in a wiry voice full of contempt. "*Your mission is before you, two miles to the west, the abandoned Ruins of Clovis await. The information we require is there, underground. The missile is ten point two-four miles to the southwest. There is a return stage that is pre-programmed to bring you back to the Shade Church. Get the data and go to the missile. The return stage has room for only one. If you are not on it, you shall be left behind. The Sisters that rule over this place will soon detect your presence here and execute you. Obey us! Get up and get moving or I will wring the*

Shadow tech from your dying body and leave you here!"

Nude, she sat up, her skin blackened, her old scar from the hook aching. In the inky blackness of Shade Church, she had never before seen what an Autocon looked like—they were denizens of the dark, just the floating gleam of malevolent eyes and the hard feeling of clawed hands. But, here, she could see it plainly. It was a teetering column of black smoke bearing the tell-tale primal smell of Shadow tech. It had a slender body and a vaguely formed, mouthless head dotted with two points of cold light where eyes should be. It had a set of skinny, overly long arms, knobby elbows  and wrists, and a pair of hands studded with smooth, curved claws. It had no legs, just a twisting wisp of curled smoke.

She was frightened, but the angel had promised she could capture the Autocon. She looked to the device in her hand, uncertain how to use it. She held it up and shook it, hoping something favorable would happen.

"I gave you an order!" The Autocon swiped at her, raking its claws across her shoulders and chest. *"Obey me!"* it cried.

The pain, the terrible withering pain! She fell to her knees. All the helplessness and smothering of Shade Church returned in full. She felt like a slave all over again.

"What is that in your hand? Give it to me!"

The angel's device. She clutched it tightly. The angel said it would capture the Autocon, but it didn't seem to be working. "This is mine ..." she managed to stammer.

It lashed her across the face. *"Nothing you have is yours. Everything belongs to us. You have no family, no identity, no standing, no possessions and no name. You don't deserve a name. I said give the device to me!"* It reached out with its claws.

She rebelled. For the first time ever, she acted against her Autocon tormentor, and, by extension, her Black Hat masters as well.

"I have a name! My name is Kat!" She darted past it, displaying a great deal of speed in the process, trying desperately to return to the cubes placed on the ground a short distance away.

"You will die for your disobedience!" it roared in pursuit. *"Die! Die!"*

She placed her entire trust in the angel. Either the cubes would work as promised, or the Autocon would kill her. She wanted to live! The angel promised her!

You are loved ... the angel had said.

What was love?

In a few desperate bounds, she was there within the perimeter of the cubes. Heart pounding, she waited for the Autocon to fall upon her.

The Autocon approached, roaring, claws raised. To her shock and relief, it no longer appeared to see her. It whirled around, swiping at nothing with its claws. Its claws passed into the cubes' perimeter and collapsed into whirling smoke and a wave of cinders. It was enraged. *"Come out of there! Obey me!"*

The angel's gift worked! Now to decipher how the other gift functioned and capture the Autocon. Moving it about in her hands, she found the device had a lid that she could grip and twist off. After several twists, it came away, revealing a sturdy and smooth hollow interior.

"What are you doing, you worthless slave?"

"I told you, my name is Kat! The angels gave it to me!" Moments later, the Autocon was caught in an ethereal wind, and pulled inside the device with relentless fury, filling it like a dense patch of evil smoke. It roared in helpless, shocked dismay."I have standing, I have possessions, I have a name, and I am ... 'loved'!" she yelled as the Autocon swirled into the depths of the device.

From above, she heard a torrent of horrid noise, like the wailing of a demon coming to tear her soul out. She saw several balls of darkness shooting across the openness overhead, coming down fast directly toward her. In a storm of smoke and agonized curses, the muddled forms of ...one ... two ... three ...

... Autocons whirled about her, tumbling, tangled together, all being drawn into the device. Watching in horror, she realized these Autocons must have come from her sisters, all one, two, three of them. Her sisters must have survived to the ground and been released from their atmosphere suits just as she was. The angel's device must have pulled their Autocons away from them even though they might be a great distance away, and now they jostled to enter.

Only one Autocon will fit in the device, the angel had said.

Strange light and horrid noises came from the device. The Autocons swirled in apparent agony, shedding Shadow tech in a sooty geyser.

...the rest will be destroyed, the angel had also said. She watched as the brutal process unfolded around her, the Autocons slowly being dashed into nothingness until, at last, they were gone, leaving her holding the device in blessed silence. Giving thanks to the angel for her deliverance, she placed the lid back on and cast the device aside. It clinked and rolled on the ground, the Autocons gone. Victorious, she reveled in the moment; the angel had given her the tools she needed to best her age-old tormentors. "Kat, Kat, Kat!" she cried, jumping up and down. "Named by the gods, freed by the gods, loved by the gods. I am KAT!"

Seething with excitement, she took in her surroundings. Before her was a great rolling land covered in material that was soft beneath her feet, marked at intervals by great mounds of stone rising up to a vast inviting veil of mist draped in blinking lights and a large roundness of greater light, like a floating, glowing stone that cast everything in a soft light. She had never seen such wonders. Her heart pounded. Alone, she took it all in, trying to understand what she was seeing.

She tested the device imprisoning the Autocon, to make certain it was sound and that it couldn't get out. She carefully picked it up and shook it. The device was ominously quiet. She wondered if the Autocon within was dead—good riddance if it was. She gathered the cubes, held them in her hand and returned them to the pouch.

Now, to the angels' remaining gift. She went to it, wondering what it was, eager to see what other things they had given her. The gift was made of fibrous, flexible components, meshed together to form a capsule of some sort. She picked it up; it was fairly light. She shook it; something rattled within, she could hear items moving about. "What is this?" she asked herself with wonder.

She received a reply. *"That is a basket made of wicker, or some other type of dry, flexible wood."*

She dropped the basket. "Who spoke?"

"I spoke," came a dry voice from the device imprisoning the Autocon. She went to it, picked it up; its metallic surface was slightly warm. Closely examining it in the light cast by the round stone overhead, it was a metal capsule about the same length as her hand to her elbow. It was smooth, composed of a glinting metal that reminded her of the lights from above. At either end it had some sort of intricate decoration cut into the metal with great workmanship. In the center was a window filled with swirling smoke, and, though dim, the shining eyes of the Autocon shone through.

"You are the Black Hats' beast, created to torment me?" she asked.

"My mission is to train you to become a Black Hat. The training is hard by necessity. You have a duty to perform. Release me from this prison and I

shall consider forgiving you this trespass."

A lifetime of conditioning dictated her actions—she automatically made to obey, to open the lid and release the Autocon. A growing bit of resistance stayed her hand. "I will not. This device is now your home. Be thankful you aren't one of the ones who came later and are now dead."

"You are a Black Hat in the service of the Black Abbess. You will obey us."

"I am not a Black Hat! I hate the Black Hats! I serve none but myself and my sisters, wherever they might be."

"Release me, or we shall harvest your Shadow tech."

"Then do it. Take it from me if you can. I await my punishment."

She waited a few moments, wondering if the Autocon would make good on its threat and kill her, ripping the Shadow tech from her body.

Nothing happened. *"Release me,"* it said again, somewhat deflated. *"This prison is a torment."*

"Then you know how I felt in the darkness of the Shade Church and the missile. I will consider destroying you—that shall be your release. First, I have questions. What is this?" She pointed at the basket the angel had left.

"As I said, it is a basket. A primitive contrivance for carrying light objects. I realize your exposure to simple items is limited. I can assist you, guide you, add to your knowledge if you promise to release me."

She considered her response. "As I said, when I release you, I shall kill you. What do I do with this 'basket'?"

"It is hollow. It has a lid you may open, or you may destroy it as you will."

"I will not damage this gift. This is a gift from the gods." She flopped to the ground and carefully manipulated the basket, having a bit of trouble with the lid. Soon, she found a latch and opened it. Inside was a trove of wonders. She sucked in her breath as she sorted through them. She pulled out a wondrous container sealed with a lid. She toyed with it, turning it over in her hands. She tried biting it, pulling on it with her teeth—nothing. Ah look, the container seemed to have a top similar to the device imprisoning the Autocon.

"That is a jar with a removable lid," it said. She worked the lid until she managed to twist it off. She held the lid aloft in triumph—she had mastered its operation. Inside the 'jar' was a terrible-smelling substance. She got some of it on her fingers. It was cold and slippery. "What is this?" she asked with disgust, wiping her fingers clean.

"That is an alkaline surfactant of fatty acids scented with various perfumes and essential oils. It's commonly known as 'soap'."

"The soap is vile-smelling," she said.

"It's meant to cleanse your filthy body. Had you not been such a knobby

slag, had you the occasion to have been presented to a Warlord while in the Shade Church, you would have been thoroughly cleansed with a similar surfactant, minus the perfumes, of course."

After some doing, she twisted the lid to the 'soap' back on, essentially reversing what she had done to get the lid off, proud of her mastery of twisting and untwisting things. "Then I shall keep it in trust for the gods and present it to them when they arrive."

She put the jar back into the basket and pulled out a strange device. It was lightweight and hollow with a pair of curved stems. She turned it about in her hands. She had no idea what to make of it.

"That is a pair of goggles with a heavily tinted lens," the Autocon said. *"To protect your tender eyes."*

"From what?" Kat asked.

"From sunlight."

Sunlight? She had no idea what that was. Moving the 'goggles' about, she found they were contoured in such a way as to fit over her eyes, the stems going behind her ears and the main part of the goggles resting on her nose. With them on, she couldn't see a thing. She took them off and returned them to the basket.

The next thing she came across was a set of neatly folded fine fabrics. She showed the fabrics to the Autocon.

"Those are clothes. That is a body suit of fine material. That is a tunic, a cloak and a pair of slippers for your feet." Clothes! She was eager to put the clothes on, to cover her naked body, but then stopped herself.

"I am dirty from that horrid suit. I wish to be clean before putting these clothes on."

"You stink of filth," the Autocon said. *"Use the soap, you are in great need of it."*

"Nonsense. I wish to be clean, to cleanse the filth of the Shade Church from my body, but I shall not use the soap. Where may I cleanse myself?"

"A fresh water stream is available 1.2 miles to the northeast."

"Show me. I am now your master. You will guide me."

Following the Autocon's instructions, she returned the fabrics to the basket and moved fast from the smoking remains of her suit, running with great speed, reveling in the soft feeling of the loose ground beneath her feet. She carried the basket with both arms as she ran.

Every step she took yielded a new revelation. It was too much for her to take in. The course to the stream led her into a copse of what she thought at first might be giant people standing still with their arms lifted high into the air. There were a great number of these figures standing about, unmoving, and they had not just two arms but many, swaying slightly, chanting in an odd sound. Burning with curiosity, she approached one and found them not to be giant people as she first thought, but legless columns driven into the ground. They were much bigger than she was, and must be very powerful. She touched one; it wasn't stone or flesh, it wasn't fabric or Shadow tech; it was unlike anything she had ever experienced. It was knobby and slightly squashy. She thought it smelt good. "What is this?" she asked.

"That is a coniferous tree. A tree is a long-lived perennial plant. As in this case, where there are many trees grouped closely together, this is a forest."

"I see. I see! A forest!" she said. She continued on into the forest until she reached a spillage of water moving along the ground with a steady rumbling noise.

"We have arrived. This is the stream. The water comes from the mountains and is quite cold."

She set everything down and splashed in the water with abandon, reveling in the cold crispness of it. She cleansed herself with a smooth stone she found at the bottom of the stream, rubbing it against her skin, washing away the filth and pain of all she had endured—her confined life in Shade Church, the trip in the missile, all of it. Refreshed, she emerged from the stream and opened the basket, pulling the clothes out. Eagerly, she put them on, savoring the luxurious feel of the fabric on her damp skin, all except for the slippers, which she rejected. She liked the feeling of the ground beneath her feet. Drunk with excitement, feeling like a queen showered with gifts, she dug further into the basket. She found a container that smelled wondrous. The container had a lid similar to the device imprisoning the Autocon. She was now an expert at opening these lids—she proudly twisted it off. Inside, she found a cache of food. Food! Several chunks of flesh in thick liquid that fumed with delightful smells.

"That is some sort of baked fowl in an unknown culinary sauce," the Autocon said. *"I detect high levels of salt and fats and other components that will not furnish your body with useful calories. Do not eat this food. We have strived to regulate your intake of salts and fats."*

"We were starved."

"You were given exactly the daily caloric amount you required. We were training your bodies to be optimally conditioned to encourage the growth of Shadow tech. Eating this food will hinder growth and fatten you in the process."

Scowling, Kat smacked her lips, grabbed several pieces and devoured them. The food had such taste, she had no words for it; it was like being tickled on the inside. She had no idea food could taste like this. It felt delightful in her mouth, it felt amazing chewing it, swallowing it, feeling it settle into her belly where it continued to give her pleasure like a glowing ember. The whole experience of eating one's fill was unknown to her. It sent her into rapture, for she had been given only tiny amounts of bland, taste-less, uninspiring food at Shade Church. Licking her fingers, barely control-ling herself, she decided to save the rest for later. With supreme effort, she closed the container, once again proud of her newly acquired skills at open-ing and closing the lid. She belched with delight.

"Now that you have over-indulged in fats and salts, we should continue to the ruins to immediately commence your mission," the Autocon said.

Kat belched again. Ignoring the Autocon gave her almost as much plea-sure as eating the food. She banged the Autocon against a tree and tossed it aside. Digging through the basket, she found one final thing: an odd piece of parchment that shone in the dim light.

"What is this?" she asked the Autocon, holding the parchment up.

"Your mission is at hand. The Black Hats will not tolerate your insub-ordination."

"Frag the mission, and the Black Hats, and you as well! There is no mis-sion. What is this? Answer!"

"That is a photograph," it replied with a sigh. *"For capturing images."*

Capturing images? Was such a thing possible? She stared at the 'pho-tograph', seeing the likeness of a person captured on it, but couldn't see it clearly. Whoever's image was captured on the photograph must be impor-tant, for the angel had given it to her. She placed the photograph carefully back into the basket. She would examine it later.

There was much to see, much to experience. She decided to climb a tall tree to see what was around—the angel had warned her of danger, and she was mindful of that. She tried climbing one to see what was about. She slipped and fell back down to the ground, trying and failing a few more times. She needed to dig into the tree to gain a secure purchase.

She thought a moment.

The Shadow tech within her, she had been told it could do many things. To use Shadow tech at Shade Church was forbidden, but here ...

"Forbidden, what you are doing is forbidden. The Shadow tech does not belong to you," the Autocon said.

She concentrated, feeling it moving within her, feeling it slowly con-dense on her hands in a warm sludge. She felt it near, following her will. She smelt it, like blood, like hot metal. It came according to her bidding, pooling in her hands. Now to shape it, to mold it into a useful form. She imagined she needed hooks of some sort to climb the tree, and the Shadow tech responded, flowing across her hands, forming at her fingertips into stout claws. Now, holding the Autocon in one hand, she climbed, her new claws digging in, supporting her weight with ease. The trees were jealous of her clothes and her Autocon; they picked at her clothes, catching the fabric, trying to take them from her. Her limber body scrabbled up the length of the tree until she reached the top. Nestled in the heights, she could see all around. Down below, past the edge of the forest, she saw the silent remains of her atmosphere suit, its panels open like a wilting flower, the cavity she had occupied impossibly small. In the other direction, basking beneath the great stone of light overhead, was a fold of land easily traversable. She had many questions for the Autocon.

"What are those stone mounds I see?"

"Mountains, specifically the Westron Mountains of the Great Vithland Range."

She gazed at them in awe. "And above, those lights?"

"Enough! Your mission is at hand."

"Answer the question!" She banged the device against the tree. "Answer!"

With considerable irritation, the Autocon answered. *"That is the sky, the lights you see are stars, one of which you just now journeyed from. There are two moons out this evening: Solon and Elyria. Elyria is the larger and more reflective of the two. It will be daybreak in several hours. I suggest we proceed to the ruins immediately. The Sisters have no doubt detected the entry of the stealth missile into the atmosphere and will be investigating this area soon. We must have completed our mission and be gone before that happens."*

She saw a huddle of structures far off in the distance, the towering mountains looming over them—those structures were what she had been sent to investigate. She no longer cared much about the Black Hats' mission, or the Shadow tech Goddess for that matter, but the angel had told her the structures, the 'ruins', were her salvation. Perhaps the gods were there waiting for her. She was eager to see them.

She saw movement. She saw a great many large creatures moving at great speed through the forest, creating a breathtaking amount of noise.

"What are those creatures?"

The Autocon sighed. *"Those are Vithland Wapiti, otherwise known as Common Elk."*

Kat watched the elk depart, admiring their apparent speed and strength. "We will now go to the ruins," she announced with authority, relishing her new-found power over the Autocon. Standing there in her gorgeous new clothes, with a full belly and the enslaved Autocon, she felt as if she ruled the world. She was Kat, beloved of the angels and the gods. Kat God-loved. She opened the lid to the basket and tossed the Autocon in, shutting it tight as it protested. As the Autocon once inhabited her body, now it would inhabit her basket.

She set off, running through the trees, her feet crunching through loose materials on the ground.

She quickly found herself in a bit of a dilemma; carrying the basket was tiresome and difficult, slowing her down. She needed a better method for carrying the basket and she needed to move faster. She had no thought of leaving the basket behind, for the angels had given it to her. She pulled the Autocon back out. "I require assistance, for I cannot carry the basket and cover the ground."

The Autocon laughed at her. *"Hehehehehe ... You call yourself Kat. Kat, a worthless feline creature crawling about on four legs with a little tail. Frolic on the ground, little Kat, and wave your fluffy tail."*

Kat thought about it. Despite the Autocon's chiding, running on the ground might give her more speed. She recalled the elk and how fast they were. She dropped to all fours, her limbs limber and stretchy. Stirring the Shadow tech within her, her use of it steadily improving, she decided to put it to further use. She coaxed it out of her body in waves of dense, foul-smelling mist, forming it into a sturdy framework of black linkages around her arms and legs, forcing her into a crouching position, augmenting her strength and agility. Using the Shadow tech framework, she could move with great speed along the ground, loping like an animal, covering vast distances in only a short time. Shadow tech was truly a wonder; with it at her command, what couldn't she accomplish? Carrying the basket, though, was even more of an issue now that she was on all fours. It was impossible, actually.

A fluffy tail ... the Autocon said. Struck with inspiration, she sprouted a tail of Shadow tech from the base of her spine. Far from being 'fluffy', the meaning of which she didn't quite understand, her tail was hard and strong, flexible and dexterous like a third hand. The tail easily took the basket and held it over her head.

Proud of her ingenuity, she tore along the ground, loping along at amazing speed, the basket held securely by her tail.

3—The Ruins

The Home of the Gods

Under a veil of glittering stars, she arrived not long later, tearing fast along the ground. The Shadow tech framework she had created pained her terribly, her back and joints ached for release, but that didn't matter.

She had arrived. She tried to release herself from the grip of her own Shadow tech, but it wouldn't budge. She was stuck in this painful crouching position.

Gah! She would deal with it later.

She came into a vast clearing free of giant trees, where the ground was cold and stony, only a few weedy plants struggling for purchase. Around her, like a herd of animals, were the sprawling hulks of wondrous boxlike 'things' with many holes cut into them, huddled about on a flat bit of ground between the mountains as if grazing in a remote pasture.

"Behold, the Ruins of Clovis and the end of our adventure," the Autocon announced. *"These buildings are the old habitations of the House of Clovis before they left the League three thousand years ago. The buildings have lain abandoned ever since."*

Kat gazed at the buildings in wonder. In Shade Church, there was Skull Charnel City; a collection of underground structures where the strongest of crawlers lived and fought. She wasn't strong enough to fight for such a place, so she avoided it. But here—look at it. There were many buildings, more than three, more than five, many more, and all to herself. The buildings were arranged in some sort of divine plan, though she couldn't determine what it was. She had never seen structures like these, built with skill and craftsmanship, huddled in the dark; places gods would live.

Her heart pounded. Where were the angels and the gods? She appeared to be the only person about. Why weren't they out to greet her?

Pathways ran through the structures; some clear, others littered with debris and ragged vegetation. She tore down the pathways on all fours, clattering through the loose stones, shouting for the angels, shouting for the gods to come out. She did the grand tour, seeing everything two and three times. Some of the structures had fallen in, mere skeletons of stone and masonry, reminding her of the bones of a giant beast she had once seen, while others seemed fairly intact, their stony faces dotted with empty holes.

She fetched the Autocon from her basket and pummeled it with questions. "Tell me what these buildings are."

The Autocon complied. *"That is the Wheelhouse, and over there is the cistern. The largest structure is the main habitation, once the grand manor of Clovis. The smaller are ancillary buildings: work houses, dormitories for the staff and so on. Enough! We are not interested in these structures above ground, or in the sordid history of this woe-begotten place. We are looking for an underground catacomb. The catacomb is our destination. Evidence of the Shadow tech Goddess is there to be found. The Black Abbess must have it."*

"I told you I don't care about that!"

Ahead, in a stand of trees, she saw a group of people. The angels? The gods! She skittered to a stop before them.

At last!

They towered over her, standing on a lofty platform. They seemed pristine people, wearing clothes, which was very impressive to her. They seemed to be in command of the vegetation, for it appeared to sprout from their very bodies. There were more than five on the platform. Counting, she counted to five twice. Five, two-times.

"I am here. I have come as you requested," she said.

The angels said nothing, they didn't even move.

"I have clothes! I have a basket! I am Kat!"

Nothing.

She had a thought: perhaps her Shadow tech claws and armature was frightening them, or, perhaps, they couldn't see her because she was locked into place on all fours at the base of their platform. She again attempted to get rid of the Shadow tech and stand up to face them but, try as she might, she could not dispel it. She groaned and stretched, rolling in the dirt, her legs sticking up in the air, trying to free herself of her own Shadow tech construction. The Autocon laughed at her lack of skill.

"Ha, ha, ha! You look like a turtle on its back roasting in the sun, ha, ha, ha!"

She gave up. She was unable to stand erect, but was not overly put off. She was used to crawling. She would work on the problem later, though the gods must certainly be unimpressed by her lack of skill.

"Speak to me, I wish to hear your voices!" she cried, flopping about on her back, struggling to stand.

The Autocon laughed again. *"These figures before you are not people, nor are they gods. They are statues, mere effigies in stone. These are images of the Clovis, who once lived here before fleeing the League long ago. They cannot answer, and even if they could, why would they speak to you?"*

"The angel told me I am 'loved'. That must mean something! If I am loved, why would they not speak to me?"

"Love?" the Autocon choked. *"Love? Love is a thing for painted dandies, for League fools. Love has no place in the Black Hats!"*

"I am loved! If love is despised in the Black Hats, then I accept it all the more, for I despise the Black Hats."

"Love will be your death. Seek you a suicide, then seek love."

Perturbed, she set the Autocon aside and climbed up the platform, scrabbling about at the feet of the statues. She rummaged through the vegetation, pushing it aside, feeling the cold stony faces of the figures. The Autocon was correct; the people were made of carved stone, standing together in lofty grace wearing carved clothes. She was empty with disappointment. She jumped down to the ground. The ruins were utterly still and quiet.

"Where are the gods?"

"There are no gods other than the Black Hats," the Autocon answered.

"Ha! Wait! I hear something."

Listening hard, she heard a faint set of grunting, guttural sounds drifting through the ruins. She also saw momentary snatches of dim light. At the edge of the ruins where the forest began, up a steep path leading toward the roots of the mountains, she saw the source of the light and the sounds. A set of heavy-looking doors were built into the ground, the light passing through the cracks highlighting the texture of the stone. She rubbed her head—everything she saw was new to her. She had little if any reference, nothing to compare it to.

"These doors?" she asked the Autocon.

The Autocon chirped with excitement. *"This is what we seek! The entrance to the catacombs!"* It was jubilant. The device imprisoning it shook.

The catacombs. The doors were built into the pathway side by side, fitting loosely together, quite like the fastened doors in Shade Church that led to places unknown. A large latch was built into each door, meeting in the center. Dim light flashed through cracks, highlighting the long, straight edges of the doors.

"Enter! Enter now, you useless slag!" the Autocon demanded. She wouldn't be intimidated or rushed. Listening carefully, the sounds pulsed up from behind the doors in a steady note loud enough to make them minutely vibrate. She put her ear to the doors. There were chaotic bangings, like beating drums mixed with bits of moaning or chanting that she used to hear in Shade Church. She also heard voices speaking; passing words she didn't understand back and forth.

Here were the catacombs, the objective of the mission the Black Hats had sent her and her far-flung sisters on, and a place the angel had specifically told her to avoid. Somewhere down there were hints of the Shadow tech Goddess. None of her sisters were around; she seemed to be the first. She could go down, collect the information, locate the stealth missile and return to the Black Hats and become one herself.

She wanted none of it.

More banging. Something blocked the light for a moment. She was certain someone was just on the other side of the doors. She saw the heavy latches turn of their own accord, and the doors rattle slightly in the frame.

The Shadow tech Goddess is in the catacombs, rattling the door.

"You will enter the catacombs now, or I will kill you. Kill you!" the Autocon raved.

Don't go underground the angel had said to her.

"KILL YOU!" the Autocon roared in a demonic voice.

In its fury, a great energy built up in the Autocon's prison. It jolted, shaking itself loose from Kat's grasp. It tumbled to the ground, bounced once and rattled through the crack between the doors. It was gone. She heard the fading sound of it clattering away.

TINK! Tink! Tink! ... tink! ...

She stood there incredulous. She had lost the Autocon to the one place she was told not to go.

Don't go underground. The Shadow tech Goddess awaits.

Though she hated the Autocon, loathed it, she needed its knowledge, and now it was gone. She had to have it back, and the only way to get it was to open the doors and go in.

The doors ...

Part of her daily training in Shade Church was meant to purge her of fear: Black Hats did not feel fear. Yet Kat was not a Black Hat. She felt her stomach clench, like it did when the Autocon was trying to come out. Her mouth went dry, her limbs felt heavy, drawing breath became a labor and her matted hair stood on end. She was terrified. She checked her claws: small, black, curved to a deadly point. She added more Shadow tech to their making and they grew, well past the ends of her fingertips, making her hands as deadly as a great beast. She would go in, get the Autocon, and hurry back. She took hold of the latches, her claws sparking on the metal, readied herself, and pulled the doors open.

The Shadow tech Goddess ...

A dusty stairwell lit in a collage of blinking lights went down at a sharp angle, biting deep into the ground. She took a breath in relief.

Nobody there.

She had expected a demon, a destroyer feared by the Black Abbess herself to come bounding out; instead, she was met with a haphazard set of stone stairs that went down a considerable distance before flattening out to a bumpy landing ending in an arch far below. The light blared through the archway. A vast underground space waited beyond, she could see hints of it, hear the vast echoes of nothing, smell the dankness. It reminded her of the confused underground world of the Shade Church; stony, bare, eternally soaked in darkness. It was as if she had gone nowhere, hadn't traveled the heavens and come to the home of the gods. Here was Shade Church again, beckoning her to come and be swallowed. Bits of debris lay strewn about in the space beyond the arch as if a subterranean battle had taken place; crushed stone, displaced items, taken lives, and nobody had ever cleaned up the aftermath.

There was the Autocon, lying innocently at the bottom in the flickering light just waiting for her to come down and get it.

Bel ...

A whispered voice like a puff of wind came up from below. Steeling herself, Kat skittered down the stairs, feeling the old grit under her hands and feet, stepping in the same depressions the Old Clovis once had as they descended the stairs.

To worship the Shadow tech Goddess. To pray for the end of all things ...

Down she went, claws furrowing the stone. Halfway down, she slipped and tumbled, feeling the stone wrench into her flesh. Out of control, she slammed to the bottom of the stairs and came to a stop. Ahead was the arch. Through it, she saw a long disused space thrown into hard relief by the flickering on and off of light that had been dim and difficult to see on the surface but which was blinding in the depths. She saw slabs of stone tossed about, overturned masonry, relics in metal and glassy gems arranged around an altar before a stone wall. The light came from something sitting atop the altar, something that burned with light, its power warming her flesh.

Lying on the stony floor near the altar was a body; shoulders flat against the ground, arms and legs splayed. The body seemed deflated, and was quite dead. She had experienced enough death in Shade Church to know it from a distance. She didn't have to see, she could feel it was dead. The body, which appeared to be a female like herself, wore a magnificent set of clothes; fine, well-made garments covering her arms and chest, with more garments over her legs down to the knees. The corpse had something on her feet, something heavy-looking and uncomfortable. Some sort of object, perhaps a weapon, lay nearby, glinting in the light. She had a fleeting thought of running up and stealing the clothes, except for the things on the female's feet. She didn't want the feet garments at all.

Wait! The body stirred, metal rattled.

Who are you? came a ghastly voice.

She was overwhelmed with fear as the body stirred. Never in all her dark days in Shade Church had she been so afraid. Unable to move, pinned to the floor with overwhelming fear, she watched as the body, with deliberate slowness, sat up, leaned on its metal weapon and turned its head in her direction. She saw the peeling, parchment flesh and bits of dead bone, felt hollow eyes gazing at her with malice. Bones grinded. Teeth chattered.

WHO ARE YOU?

She forced herself to act. She reached out with her tail, seizing the Autocon. The Autocon felt like it was pinned to the ground. She struggled to lift it and be gone.

The figure stood. It shambled in her direction, dragging its weapon behind it, each step a monumental struggle.

She pulled, forcing the Autocon off the ground. She turned and fled up the stairs, claws sparking. Reaching the top, she closed the doors, rattling them in their frame. The last thing she saw as the doors slammed shut was a quick glimpse of the arch and the shadow of the dead woman approaching.

She didn't wait around. Hardly able to breathe, she tore down the path, past the statues, convinced whatever was down there would be hot on her heels. She stopped and waited, ready for the doors to burst open. The Autocon lay before her. It seemed dead, as if its energy had been consumed.

She waited, crouching, breath ragged, claws dug into the ground.

Was that the Shadow tech Goddess she had seen? A dead body?

Time passed. Nothing happened. The sounds issuing from the doors faded; the light leaking through the cracks stopped. Whatever was down there seemed to have no power on the surface. The angel had said so and her body agreed. The fear that had nearly debilitated her was gone; she felt command of her own body returning.

The angel said the surface was safe, and she believed the angel. The Autocon began to stir, the glow of its eyes through the window returned. *"Did you collect the evidence?"* it asked, its voice a distant whisper.

"I did not."

It shouted. *"Then get back down there!"*

"I am not going back down there!"

"You're a coward!"

"Most likely."

She had no intention of ever returning to those accursed doors. Best give them plenty of space and never go back there again. She bounded back into the central ruins and immediately felt better, occasionally scaring off beasts and their young lurking in the shadows. She had hoped the gods would present themselves, but they did not appear to be there at the moment. Near the center of the structures she found a building with no roof, the interior filled with debris-strewn standing water. She wandered into one of the habitations, an old dormitory according to the Autocon—a place for sleeping. She found it suitable for dwelling. Amid the fallen masonry, her footprints in the dust, she located a place to safely hide her basket. Taking the Autocon with her, she scrabbled up to the highest point in the ruins and had a look around. The doors were far away up the path nearing the base of the mountains, silent and dark. She was not entirely certain what her next move would be, perhaps she might set out and search for the angels and the gods, or discover what happened to her sisters. They must be about someplace; their Autocons had been here, they must be too.

What did it matter? Here, she was free. The idea of freedom, to live her life as she would in the blissful open was just dawning on her, the smothering darkness and pain of the Shade Church with its Autocons and atmosphere suits far behind. To be free.

To be loved?

What was love? Was love here in the dark? Could she unearth it? Could she wear it? Could she eat it? Would it protect her from the Black Hats and the Shadow tech Goddess?

She suddenly felt extremely tired, her claws, the armature and her Shadow tech tail ached. She needed sleep, she needed to process all she had seen. She would search for love and the gods later. She returned to her newly claimed abode and shuttled about on the floor in rapid circles, trying to free herself. There would be no sleeping with the Shadow tech fastened to her body.

No luck.

She took a moment. In the Shade Church she would have struck out, attacked, inflicted pain on any near enough to feel it; that's how things were dealt with. Here, in the home of the gods, it was time to take a new approach, to think and puzzle this out.

She had a thought.

She removed the *Sentril* cubes from their pouch and laid them out in the correct positioning on the floor: one by the Scar hand, one by the Not Scar hand and the final before her. She left plenty of room inside the perimeter of the cubes for her body. Perhaps the cubes could destroy her Shadow tech. She bounded into the perimeter. Instantly, her Shadow tech claws, tail and framework fell apart into sooty smoke that drifted out the window. Relief! She was free to stand. She felt like dancing. She removed her clothes, and carefully placed them back in the basket. She marveled at the clean smell of her body; it still smelled like the water of the stream. She rubbed her aching skin where the Shadow tech had dug in. It left a deep impression and lacerated her skin at several points. It hurt, but she had felt much worse. Sleep was coming up on her fast, no fighting it. She removed the photograph from the basket and placed it nearby. She could see a figure captured in the photograph. She could see a head and shoulders, a pair of arms, and it seemed to be wearing fine clothing. She was too tired to concentrate on it. She would sleep and inspect it fully later. She went to the window and, one more time, checked the doors lurking ominously up the hillside.

Nothing. Doors closed. Quiet. No lights. No dead woman. No goddesses. No Sisters.

The feeling of sleep taking her was luxurious. To sleep without being knocked unconscious or smothered into oblivion by an Autocon's hand was a true gift of the gods. Stretching out on the gritty floor within the cubes, used to the feel of bare rock against her equally bare skin, she closed her eyes and, for the first time as a newly free woman with a washed body and a full belly, slept in comfort, thoughts of the underground and what might lurk there far from her mind.

This must be love.

*   *   *   *   *

When she awoke, the world seemed to be on fire. A great fiery ball had risen from the ground and hung over the mountains, filling her habitation with shafts of blinding light. In a panic, shielding her eyes, she hid in the shadows and consulted with the Autocon, ready to flee into the forest at any moment.

The Autocon chided her. *"It is daytime, you stupid woman, and that bright object in the sky is the sun, a star, specifically Beta Terragrin, furnishing this world with light and warmth. You truly are a simpleton, knowing absolutely nothing. Every world has a dawn and a dusk, day and night."*

Sunlight. Impossibly bright. The angels had given her a gift regarding sunlight. She rooted around in her basket, locating the goggles. She fumbled with them, situating them until they rested over her eyes. With the goggles on, she could see, she could see all around. She went to the window and gasped.

"And what world is this? Tell me!"

"Kana. The stronghold of the League. The fastness of the Sisterhood of Light."

"And this is sunlight?"

"Yes, it's sunlight. It's daybreak, early morning."

Kana, Home of the Gods, flush with light. Though afraid at first, with her goggles she was greater than the daylight. She soon became fascinated by the 'sun' and its light and the vivid colors that came with it, few of which she had ever seen before. When she pulled her clothes out of the basket to put them on, she had a terrific surprise. The color of her clothes was the same color as the angel's robe—that same wonderful color of mercy that filled her memories with comfort and warmth.

"What color is this?" she asked.

"Green," the Autocon replied in a dry manner. *"It's green."*

She was joyous. "Green, green, green! The best of all colors!" She donned her clothes with pride, grabbed the Autocon, holding it like a great baton, and went outside into the light.

Look, there was green everywhere! The trees were green, the ground was green in long patches. This was the land of mercy! Full of questions, she pummeled the Autocon: what was this, what was that? She learned the sky was blue and the 'clouds' running across it were white. The statues that had disappointed her so were gray, and so were the doors she refused to approach. There were reds and browns, ochres, and bits of yellow and orange. She learned so much her head began to hurt. She learned about 'deer' and 'birds', 'wolves' and 'bears'. This place, this Kana, was truly the home of the angels and the gods themselves, if only they would present themselves. She found a great room in the habitations, larger, loftier than the others. She found the open space inviting. Ancient debris of small size and amazing color lay scattered about; wreckage from a past age. Putting her new knowledge of colors to the test, she saw lovely reds and soft blues, flawless greens and tawny browns. She was fascinated by the debris. What was it? The debris was composed of many small objects, dirty, but each of perfect, mesmerizing symmetry. The objects weren't masonry and, after careful consideration, she determined they weren't wood or earth either. They were hard, but slightly squashy. They were small and lightweight. When she held one of the objects in her hands, it opened and closed, revealing thin flexible sheets within. The sheets smelled incredible. Taking several whose colors she favored, she sped back, showing them to the Autocon.

"That is a book," it said. *"The sheets within are pages."*

The 'pages' were covered with black lines and symbols. *"Writing,"* the Autocon told her. *"Captured words."* She marveled at it, not fully comprehending. Words, snatched out of the air and placed on a page. She demanded the Autocon tell her what the writing said.

The Autocon refused. *"You know my price."*

The depths. The catacombs. Kat had no intention of returning to the depths. She brought the 'books' to her habitation, placing them near her photograph.

After some of her excitement diminished, she felt her stomach growling. Hunger—she knew it well. Reveling in her new freedom and ample spare time, she decided she would eat. Taking her food container from the basket, along with the photograph, she scrabbled up to the top of the ruins, set her things out in the sunshine, and ate like an empress, wearing her goggles, relishing the food, sticking her hands in, scooping up the liquid, licking them clean. In the light of the sun, she could, at last, clearly see the image in the photograph as she ate.

It was a man.

There were only females at the Shade Church, female company was all she had ever known, though she had seen men a few times; walking in the galleries near the surface, reviewing the females with a calculating eye. Mostly, they came as guests of the Black Hats, and were allowed to pick out some of their number and take them away. She didn't know what the men did with the females they took.

The man in the photograph wore something on his head. The Autocon called it a 'hat'.

"A Hat? Is he a Black Hat?"

"No, bloody woman. He is not a Black Hat. That's simply a hat he's wearing, a triangular Vith hat by the look of it. You do not have to be a Black Hat to wear a hat."

"I see, I see." Looking further, the man wore clothes—a green garment, like hers, ample with fasteners and bits of metal. The garment he wore was magnificent and she feasted her eyes. She longed to touch it. She was full of questions as she looked at the photograph. Who was he? Was this man an angel? Was he a god? Was he a gift to her, like the clothes and the devices? The angel had given her this photograph, so he and his garments must be gifts to her too. Like the clothes, like the cubes and the Autocon device, he must belong to her, to Kat.

"Who is this man?" she asked the Autocon.

The Autocon did not answer.

"Speak!" she demanded.

"I'm certain I have no idea. Some League man, look at his clothes," it finally responded. *"The League is the enemy, you are in enemy territory. If you see this man, you should kill him, for he is the enemy."*

"Kill him? Why? He is not an enemy. He is a gift to me. He might be a god."

"A gift? A god? And what are you going to do with this man once you have him? You have no idea, do you?"

Good question. She puzzled. What would she do with this League man? What could she do with him? She couldn't wear him like clothes or eat him like food. "What do men and women do together?"

The Autocon scoffed. *"Ha! What indeed? Xaphan men come to Shade Church, pay a fee to the Black Abbess, and pick out crawler trainees, like you, to abuse and do with as they please."*

"They abuse us? What does that mean?" She had a flash of inspiration. "Is that love?"

"Ha! Love? Love means nothing. That is what men and women do— they abuse each other's flesh."

After some contemplation, she arrived at a monumental conclusion."Then, I am going to 'abuse' him. That's what I'm going to do with him. I will abuse him to the best of my ability. I will abuse him all day long, and … and if he pleases me, I will, in turn, allow him to abuse me. See, that is how people should treat each other—abusing each other all the time in the name of love."

"Why would this League man want you?" the Autocon asked. *"He appears to be a man of some means, of wealth. You are a faceless denizen of the Shade Church, a crawler who probably wouldn't have survived to become a full Black Hat ever. Who are you? What do you have to offer? You can't even read a book."*

"I am Kat. I am ..." She wondered. She had never seen herself. She bounded down to the cistern and beheld herself in the surface of the water. She saw a crouching, rail-thin woman staring back at her; pale skin, unkempt hair, and small, unsmiling face wearing a pair of goggles that blotted out her eyes. Her hair was a tangled mess of hopeless snarls, like the leaves in the trees, but less proud, more disheveled. What color was it, her hair? She considered it, puzzled over it. Her hair reminded her of the color of the clouds, the big fluffy ones, white, mixed with a bit of yellow from the sun. She touched her hair, burred and ratty, never given a second thought. The man's hair in the picture was orderly and short. She removed her goggles to see her face without them. The sunlight was blaring, impossible. She squinted, opening her eyes on occasion only to go blind with the light. She managed to briefly catch a glimpse of herself. There was a discoloration near one of her eyes. She tried to wipe it away, but it wouldn't go.

"That is the Shadowmark. It brands you as a bearer of Shadow tech," the Autocon said. *"The mark proves you belong to the Black Hats."*

She put her goggles back on. She didn't like the Shadowmark. She wondered if the man would like her. Would he want to abuse her? She would be crushed if he didn't.

"I want to impress him," she said. "I will impress him with my clothes and my knowledge of the surroundings and with opening and closing things and with eating food, and with my skill with Shadow tech. And I shall learn to read."

"That Shadow tech is not yours!"

"It is mine and so is he, and so are you! Everything is mine! Everything is Kat's!"

She shook the Autocon. "Teach me to read the captured words on the page!"

"You wish to read, then get your ungrateful carcass into the depths!"

She tossed the Autocon aside. She tried to summon Shadow tech, to make the Shadow tech within her obey her commands; it rumbled within her and did nothing more. The Autocon laughed at her. After another few tries, it emerged from her body. She managed to re-create her Shadow tech claws, tail and armature that forced her into a crouching position. She would need to practice with her Shadow tech, so she could properly abuse the man. She couldn't wait to see him and his beautiful garment in person for the first time, and abuse him. She would abuse him as the Autocon watched, so that it could see how proper people should act.

She returned to her habitation, put the Autocon in its hiding spot, removed her goggles and went to sleep, lying on the floor, her brain buzzing with all the things she had learned and dreaming of abusing the man.

★ ★ ★ ★ ★

"Woman! Wake up!"

She roused from her sleep and became aware of movement outside. She automatically suspected the doors in the ground, that perhaps the Shadow tech Goddess was loose, doors thrown open and on the prowl. From her vantage point, she could see that the doors beyond the ruins were as she had left them: closed, their light muted by the sun. Instead, something large with great sails moved overhead—it moved as a dark patch across the sky, blotting out a vast portion of it, plowing through the clouds, dissipating them as it passed. It cast an immense shadow across the mountains.

"Avast!" the Autocon called out. *"It's the Sisters in their Venera ships! The enemy has detected us!"*

The Sisters' ship looked like a great spiral floating effortlessly on air, giant-sized, rivaling the great mountains; shadowy white like the clouds. It looked more like a living creature than a vessel. At the front of the ship was a great mass of tentacles that reached about in tentative jabs, probing the air, collecting information. As it approached, she felt the ground tremble. The angels had warned her of the Sisters and what they could do to her. She felt no particular fear as the ship came in, only a bit of anger. These ruins were hers, she had just arrived, and here were the League's Sisters, whoever they were, to take what was hers. She thought to stand, allow the Sisters to detect her, and fight them. This place was given to her by the gods and she ought to fight for it, but the angels had implored her to hide from the Sisters; perhaps they were greater than she was? Perhaps they had better clothes and better food? Perhaps their skill at opening things was better. Perhaps they would kill her?

To locate the angels, meet the gods, abuse the man and be taught the wonders of love, she must thwart the Sisters and survive. She threw the Autocon into the basket, deployed her *Sentril* cubes and stepped inside, her Shadow tech claws instantly turning to smoke.

"The Sentrils will protect you," the angel had said.

Outside, a shadow fell as the vessel passed overhead, the brightness of day turning to more familiar night. The habitation shook. She thought she could hear the whisper of mental voices flashing back and forth, the Sisters chattering amongst themselves, questioning, wondering what was here. Through the window, a tentacle from their vessel came wandering in, floating with weightless grace, tentatively probing the old stone of the room. She stared at it, unable to determine if it was stone or metal; it seemed to shrink and expand as if it were breathing. It moved without sound as it floated about the room. Kat stood within the cubes, waiting, wondering if the tentacle, guided by the Sisters in their vessel high above, would discover her. She had to duck once or twice as it swept past her position.

After a time, the tentacle retreated through the window and the vessel moved on, floating across the sky, getting lost in the clouds, the light of day returning. She breathed easy. Once again, the angels' gift worked as they had promised.

"How is it you are not dead?" the Autocon asked as she retrieved it from the basket.

"I am too great for the Sisters," she replied. The Autocon groaned in disappointment.

4—Bird, Walker, Wheel and Kat

As the days passed, she settled into a routine. As she washed in the cistern, she would ask the Autocon the same question. "Tell me, what is 'love'?"

The Autocon despised the question. Every day it would offer a different answer.

"Something that has no relevance."

What is love?

"Love is a sudden kick in the teeth and a stab in the back."

What is love?

"Love is a rotten piece of devoured fruit that will not digest and will not be expelled without assistance."

What is love?

"A fatal envenomation that leads to hallucinations, nausea, insanity and then death."

Kat laughed. "I believe you have no idea what love is. You've answered all my other questions or demanded I venture into the depths; why not this one? Love must be truly grand if it's unknown to you."

Later, the sun turned red and disappeared behind the mountains. Darkness came, stars returned. As always, she lamented the sun's passing.

As she gazed at the emerging stars, she sensed the approach of others. She saw something move across the starry sky—not the Sisters in their great ships, but something small with wings. From a different direction, something strode over the lofty tops of the mountains, moving fast. Finally, from yet another direction, something large moved along the ground. Her Shadow tech tail flicking with interest, feeling no fear, she crouched and watched the objects approach.

The angels? The gods? The man, perhaps?

"Avast! Black Hats approach," the Autocon said.

It was her sisters, all three of them converging on this place.

Her sisters, alive and well!

One came down from the sky, nude, wearing a Shadow tech harness around her chest that allowed her to move effortlessly through the air. *"She has created wings like a bird,"* the Autocon said.

Another sister came in, this time wearing a harness that mimicked her legs, only on a grand scale; her Shadow tech legs expanding and contracting, allowing her to step over the mountains in great strides. In one hand she carried a large weapon, also made of Shadow tech.

The Autocon was enraged. *"She has fashioned a bladed weapon of*

Shadow tech. That is a killing offense and I demand you slay her for such folly, or release me and I shall do it. Now!"

"Be silent," she said.

The final sister moved along the ground in a construct that rotated around her, rolling like a pebble, carrying her along at great speeds. Behind her contrivance was some sort of basket-like construct that smoked. *"She has created a wheel-like vehicle in Shadow tech, along with a large cart in tow. I admire the ingenuity."*

Held inside the cart was some sort of large, smoking object. *"The stealth missile!"* the Autocon cried in dismay. *"She has claimed the return stage!"*

Her sister got out of her Shadow tech wheel and stood proudly before it, her filthy nude body plain in the shimmering starlight.

Kat was overjoyed to see them. She bounded down from the top of the ruins, crouching on all fours, claws digging in, her tail waving about her head in excitement. "Welcome, sisters, welcome to this place of wonders! We have arrived at last!"

They saw her and came forward. The sister wearing the bird harness spoke. "Hail, sister! Where is your Autocon? Mine wrenched itself from my body and thought to torment me as I emerged from the atmosphere suit, to continue the treatment we suffered at Shade Church. I attempted to flee, but it turned into a ball of smoke and flew away."

"Your Autocon came to me. I watched it be destroyed, fear it no longer. What is the harness you created?" Kat asked.

Her sister proudly unfurled her Shadow tech wings and held them up for all to behold. "I once snuck to the surface at Shade Church and witnessed creatures moving across the air with great speed. I took inspiration from that and copied the creatures. When the blinding light comes, I hide. When it goes, I can move across the air as they do."

"I saw that," Kat said. "The blinding light is called 'daytime'. Those creatures are called 'birds' and the great open space above is the 'sky'. We are no longer denizens of the dark. Here, in the light and open spaces, we must have names fitting our new station. All these wonders around us have names, and we must as well. We will call you 'Bird', for you are the master of the sky, mistress of the birds. I am glad you are here."

"How do you possess this knowledge?" Bird asked with no small measure of wonder.

"I have come to know it."

The sister in the leg suit lifted her weapon and spoke. "Then I shall have a name as well. I too was accosted by my Autocon, demanding I submit. I made this mighty weapon in defiance of it. And, like Bird's, it turned into a ball and was wrenched from our place of battle. I know not what came of it."

"It came to me and was also destroyed." Kat admired her sister's masterful Shadow tech weapon. "How did you create such a wonder?"

"I was once given to a warlord to please his primal fires, and he had a weapon like this. I copied it. After my Autocon vanished, I created this harness of Shadow tech and strode across the pillars of stone. Give me a name, sister, to celebrate my victory and liberation! I must also have a name."

"The pillars of stone are called 'mountains', sister. We will call you 'Mountain Walker', or simply 'Walker' as you walk across the great mountains with ease, becoming their master."

Walker was pleased.

Their sister who rode in on the great circle with the missile in tow stepped forward, her nude body proud in the dark. She looked Kat over. "What are you wearing?"

"Clothes, given to me by the gods."

Her sister considered this. "Are you certain those clothes weren't meant for me instead of you?"

"I do not believe so," Kat said. "Why?"

"Because I should have clothes. Only Black Hats wear clothes, and I wish to be a Black Hat."

"Then pray to the gods and perhaps they will offer you some."

Her sister rubbed her chin. "The gods ought to pray to me. I also require a name, the greatest name of all, for I am strong. I fell to earth and went deep underground. I should be dead, but I am too great to die. I emerged triumphant from the atmosphere suit and crawled to the surface. There I was met with a terrifying emptiness."

"That is the sky. Do not fear it."

"Did you name it?"

"I did not. I have come to know its name."

"Under the 'sky', my Autocon came. We did battle. I killed it with my Shadow tech. I twisted its neck until it was dead and I was alone. I must be a Black Hat to have accomplished such a feat."

Kat thought back; she remembered that one, two, three Autocons came from the sky and were destroyed. One for Bird, one for Walker, and the last for this sister.

Perhaps she wasn't remembering correctly.

Her sister went on. "I saw a tower of smoke in the distance and went there, though the smoke was far away. Running on foot was too slow, so I devised this mighty Shadow tech machine. It is called a 'wheel'. I know this for I was once hand-selected to pull a cart of dignitaries across the Lebon Salt Plains. The pulling was hard, we labored to pull. I was the lone survivor; the others pulling the cart died along the way and I pulled their carcasses along with the cart through the salt. I recreated the cart and the wheel.

The wheel took me to the smoke, which came from the Black Hats' missile and its return stage. I dug it from the ground and lifted it with Shadow tech. The missile shall return me and me alone to the Black Hats." She looked about in a threatening manner. "I am afraid I shall have to destroy the lot of you, for we all seek the same thing."

Bird shook her head. "We do not. I wish nothing further to do with the Black Hats and their missile. You may have it, sister. Return to the Xaphans and wreak terror amongst them if you must. I wish to stay here and discover all that there is to see."

"As do I," Walker said.

"And me as well," Kat said. "This is a place of angels and I have been promised gifts."

"More gifts?" Bird asked.

"Yes."

The final sister shook her fist. "Good, then I will not have to kill you. I wish to be a Black Hat and hold dominion over all. I wish to inflict upon others what was inflicted upon us. I want that power. I long for it."

"Then I will help you to get it," Kat said from her perch atop the ruin, her tail flicking. "First, we will call you 'Wheel, the Black Hat', for you travel in a great wheel."

"And what will we call you?" Wheel asked. "You are a wearer of clothes, a teller of stories and believer in the angels and the gods. I do not believe in them."

"But they are real. The angels saved us years ago and hand-selected us to live, saved us from the Black Hats' fires. They came to me as I emerged from my suit, half dead. They gave me nutrition to revive me and wondrous clothes to wear, and goggles that I may see in the daylight."

"You can see in the daylight?" Bird asked, awe in her voice.

"I can. As for my Autocon, it came to me and I defeated it using the angel's gifts, and forced it to provide me with information."

"Your Autocon lives?" Wheel asked.

"By my leave. It has provided me with information. My name is 'Kat', given to me by the gods. Kat is my name."

✶   ✶   ✶   ✶   ✶

First, Kat insisted they wash and be civilized. She led them to the cistern, where they splashed into the water. Bird and Walker laughed, submerging and jumping back up. Wheel appeared dour at first, but even she enjoyed the bath.

"Tell me again why you have clothes and goggles and I do not," Wheel asked several times as she bobbed in the water.

After washing in the cistern, Kat led them up the hill to the location of the doors leading into the ground. They walked the pathways leading out of the ruins, their freshly-washed bare feet crunching on the stones. Kat stopped at the statues, admiring them. Ahead, up the hillside, lay the doors sunk into the ground; silent and innocent in the starlight, covering the face of evil.

Walker hesitated. "Something festers up ahead, I feel it."

"There is great danger there," Kat said. "The angels told me, and I have witnessed it. A ghost haunts below. I shall go no further."

"A ghost?" Wheel asked. "Was it the Shadow tech Goddess?"

"Possibly."

Wheel came forward, proud and naked, walking on the balls of her feet with flair. She stared at the doors built into the ground. The doors silently dared her to enter. She was impassive as she studied them. "I am not afraid of doors or ghosts. Black Hats feel no fear."

Bird spoke up. "I'm afraid. I want nothing to do with them."

Walker stepped back. "There is something wrong with this area. Can you not feel it?"

"What is wrong?" Wheel asked. "I feel nothing."

"I cannot be more specific. Something is not right here."

Wheel scoffed at Walker. She brazenly strode up the steep path and put her hands on the latches, pulling the doors open with aplomb. Kat felt a moment of terror as the doors opened. She watched, half expecting Wheel to die suddenly, or have the ghost woman at her throat, but none of that happened. The doors were thrown open, revealing a quiet inky darkness plunging precipitously down into the hillside.

No ghost, no lights, no cacophonous sound, nothing. What happened to the light and the sounds, Kat wondered? What happened to the terrifying figure lurking below? It was a bit of a disappointment.

Wheel peered down into the open doorway. She looked back. "I could command you all to come with me."

"Then I would laugh at you, for you do not command me," Kat said.

"I am a Black Hat. I am not afraid," Wheel said.

"You are not a Black Hat. You are a crawler, like us."

"I am the most powerful of all crawlers. I held Skull Charnel City in my grasp. None dared challenge me for it."

"Then become a Black Hat; your prize awaits you in the depths. And we are not afraid either," Kat said. "There simply is nothing we want in that hole."

Wheel scowled a bit, then went down the long flight of steps, her feet crunching on the grit, her head ratcheting down one step at a time, her hair the color of night. Kat and Walker came forward to close the doors. When they arrived, Wheel was standing far below at the bottom by the archway, staring in. There was no blinding light as Kat had seen before; just seething darkness veiling the mystery and emptiness within. Wheel hesitated, trying to see what awaited her in the dark, then, as proudly as she could, passed through the arch, her naked body disappearing from the light. Kat and Walker closed the doors behind her with a dramatic clank, sealing her in. They retreated back down the hill past the statues. Bird, nervous, was thankful to leave the area, as was Kat.

"I hope she finds what she's looking for down there," Bird said.

"As do I," Kat replied.

"Do you think she needs our help?" Bird asked.

"Yes," Walker said. "However, she went down there of her own free will. I will not go."

They returned down the path to the safety of the ruins, the horrid feel of the doors gone. Bird and Walker claimed habitations near to Kat's. Kat showed them her Shadow tech defeating *Sentril* cubes, her books, her basket and the device constraining the Autocon. They marveled at the shiny metal baton with its glowing eyes in the center.

The Autocon was noisy. It pleaded with them to kill Kat and proceed with their mission, essentially to join Wheel underground.

"Kill her! Kill her at once! I command it!"

They laughed at it and enjoyed picking it up and dropping it to the floor.

"Why are you so favored of the gods?" Bird asked Kat as she beat the Autocon against the floor.

"I do not know."

"Perhaps the gods will come for us as well and shower us with gifts," Walker said.

"Let us hope so."

And then Kat showed them her photograph. They huddled around and gazed at it. "Who is this?" Walker asked.

"A man. A gift to me from the angels and the gods, like my clothes and my cubes."

"The gods are kind. He is a handsome man," Walker said, looking at the picture. "Where is he?"

"I do not know. The angels said he is somewhere nearby. I intend to find him at once."

"Very inviting," Walker said. "I was given to men by our Black Hat masters many times, but none were as handsome as your man."

Kat burned with curiosity and questions. She had never been around a man. "You were? And what did you do? What was done with this man? Did he abuse you?"

"Abuse me?" Walker thought a moment. "I do not know. The Black Hats took me and several others into the light. They washed us, clothed us, scented us, fattened us up and put us on display before roving groups of men. I was selected several times. I do not know if they abused me or not. We often wrestled. They put their bodies all over me and tore my clothes off. And we wrestled. They grunted like beasts declaring victory in some guttural language. Considering all we had suffered in Shade Church crawling in the dark, getting washed and fed and wrestling with the men was a pleasant afternoon by comparison. I did not mind it so much."

Kat listened and closed her eyes. She couldn't wait to find the man and abuse him, which, apparently, consisted of eating, washing and wrestling. She already knew how to eat and wash. She would ask Walker to teach her how to wrestle.

"What about love?" Kat asked.

"Love?" Walker frowned. "I do not know what that is."

Over the next few days, Kat, Bird and Walker woke every morning and bathed in the cistern, laughing and splashing in the water. Kat shared her goggles with them, so they could walk about in the daylight. Kat discovered her eyes were becoming accustomed to the light; she didn't need the goggles as much. Incredibly, Walker liked the gods' soap. She washed herself with it, the water turning to an odd froth, her skin smelling like the wind.

Bird also liked the soap, but she didn't wash with it; instead, she molded the soap into little shapes and figures. She was becoming quite skilled.

Without fail, every day when the sun climbed to its highest point, Kat would return to their habitation and find more gifts from the angels waiting for her; usually a few more pieces of clothing and a large container full of delicious hot food which she shared with her sisters. She was always careful to set some food aside for Wheel, should she return from below and be hungry. After a few days, Bird and Walker were fully clothed with pieced-together items, though they both shunned the slippers, as Kat did. The Gods began leaving them odd bits of clothing that bewildered them: thin and shapeless squares of cloth along with light-weight bulbous cubes that seemed to be filled with air.

"Those are blankets and pillows, to warm your worthless bodies and support your tender, empty heads," the Autocon said. They had no idea what to do with them. Kat was astonished and rather annoyed when Bird took the blankets and pillows and ripped them into narrow strips, wrapping them around her forearms and calves—though Kat liked the look and copied it, destroying all the blankets and pillows. Walker too, though Bird had to help them get it right. Kat never saw the angels leave the food or the clothes, and if she waited in the habitation to greet the angels, nothing would come. Every so often, she would catch glimpses of smoke drifting away from the habitation, marking the angels' passing, but that was all.

Walker taught Kat how to wrestle, the two of them rolling in the grass, twisting their limbs into strange positions. Bird eventually joined in, all three of them wrestling, usually Kat and Bird versus Walker. Walker was skilled enough to wrestle them both and still win. Bird wasn't very good at wrestling, getting in the way and hanging on most often. She was much better with her hands, taking things she found in the habitation and twisting them into amazing decorations which she hung around her neck. She loved the disgusting soap the angels had given her, creating fascinating little statues with it. She eventually created so many, she shared.

Walker was a goddess to Kat. Big, solid, very beautiful. Walker allowed Kat and Bird to examine her naked body. Having been raised in the dark, they barely knew or understood the landscape of their own bodies, save what they could easily see. Lying back in the grass, Walker allowed them to look. Kat was amazed by what she saw, and saddened a little too. Walker was much larger and fuller than Kat was. Her legs were longer and meatier. Her backside was much bigger and her breasts were gigantic compared to Kat's. Kat thought she was beautiful in comparison to her own skinny body. The Autocon tormented her on the subject.

"You see, proper men value a great posterior and a lovely set of breasts. They worship them."

"But why?" Kat asked.

"Because they can grab them, toy with them, decorate them, offer them in barter and trade. Such a pity YOU have NOTHING to grab with your insignificant breasts—your puny little titties—and unacceptable posterior."

Even Bird's body was of greater proportions than hers. Kat wondered why she was favored of the gods over Walker, and was secretly terrified that her man, once he arrived, would choose Walker, with her breasts and her massive rear end, over her.

And then they would discuss love, trying to wrap their heads around it, trying to determine what it was.

Bird thought love might be the wind in her hair as she flew. Walker was certain love was a place one could visit. She thought love must be a temple in the mountains.

And Kat? She had a thought love might be how she felt when she looked at her man's picture, and how she felt as she waited for him.

Those were their days. They ate, they washed, they played, they discovered each other, they contemplated love and they slept.

5—The Ghost

Kat tore across the ruins, running like an animal, spine flexing, her Shadow tech claws biting into the earth and kicking up grass and bits of stone, her tail following like a sail. Overhead, black wings flapping, Bird came down in a graceful dive, her goggles seated on her face. She reached out, trying to grab hold of Kat's tail on the fly. Kat darted to her right, effortlessly changing directions, and Bird missed, soaring back into the sky. Walker followed in huge strides, covering the ground fast, her giant Shadow tech legs moving like massive pendulums. Kat moved between Walker's giant legs, cutting in and out, running rings around her. Though Bird flew across the sky and Walker was strong and beautiful, neither was as fast as Kat.

They reached the outskirts of the ruins near the now-familiar statues, where the dreaded doors beyond spoiled the sunshine. Kat skidded to a stop. She rolled over on her back, laughing and panting. She looked up at the statues and fancied the notion that one of the male statues resembled the man from her photo. She sat next to the statue sometimes, leaning against it. She cleaned the vegetation from its stand. Bird even caught her talking to it once.

"Why do you talk to the statue?" Bird asked as she landed. She lounged in the tall grass and absently twisted its long blades together, her goggles glorious on her face. She didn't need them much anymore for protection against the sun; she simply favored them.

"I ask him why he is not yet here. The gods promised him to me. I tell him I want him here now. I tell him to obey me, for he is mine. I think love is with him."

Walker was curious. "Love is with the man? Do you understand men?"

"No."

Walker laughed. "Men are difficult to understand and impossible to make sense of. If love is with this man, then it is something that will make no sense. Perhaps this man lives in the City of Love. Here is some knowledge: all men can be controlled if you determine what they want. All men want something, and when you know what it is, you shall command them."

Kat was burning for more of this knowledge. "How do you learn what they want?"

"Ask questions. Ask many questions. Force them to answer. Eventually, you shall know."

Kat was amazed. She would never forget what Walker had shared with her. Bird toyed with her decorations, her hair brown like the trees, her neck obscured with self-made decorations, her hands smelling of soap. Walker's hair was blue like the sky, long and flowing. Kat liked it much better than her own cloud/sun-like color. Bird had managed to remove all the snarls and kinks from her hair. It now moved and flowed unvexed, like Walker's. All of them laughed, casting their Shadow tech aside, their skill with it having grown by the day. They practiced all the time, concentrating, forcing the river of it within their bodies to move at their command. All trial and error, all by guesswork and happenstance, each sharing their new-found knowledge. To their amazement, their skill appeared to grow, to become more precise—controlling Shadow tech got a little easier with each session. Kat could soon form her claws and tail at will, and get rid of them just as quickly. Bird could form her dark wings and Walker could lift herself nearly to the clouds on her Shadow tech stilts.

"You are so fast, sister!" Bird said, lounging on the ground, searching through the grass for interesting stones and other bits with which to fashion a new decoration. "I can barely keep up with you, even in flight."

Kat laughed. "I feel at home running along on the ground. I enjoy it."

"I will try that," Walker said. Kat opened the latest container of food given to her by the angels. They ate, taking turns dipping their hands in and pulling out succulent bits of steaming food. Bird wanted the last piece. Kat pulled the piece out of the container to give it to her, but then put it back. "I must save a piece of food for Wheel."

"Why? She is not coming out of the depths. No backsies, Kat," Bird said.

"No what? What is a 'backsie'?"

"No givebacks. I made the word up. I would like the last piece of food."

"That's a funny word, I will remember it. But I'm sorry, sister. This piece is for Wheel."

Bird relented and wiped her hands on her green tunic, leaving two saucy streaks. "So, how long are we to stay here, sister? I have traveled far; there is so much to see beyond these forlorn ruins. In the direction of the setting sun, I discovered a great body of water going out to the end of the world where the sun goes to take its rest. I want to cross it, to discover what is on the other side, but it's a long trip and I want my sisters with me when I do it."

"What if there's nothing where the sun sets but more water?" Kat asked.

"Then, I will know that."

Walker spoke up. "I too wish to branch out and explore farther. There is indeed so much to see. I have a belief that the sun does not live in the water, but rather in a shrine over the mountains. I wished to see it for myself. The other day, I ventured far in the direction of the rising sun to locate this shrine. I found more mountains there, much larger than these we have come to know, much crueler, covered with white frozen powder."

Kat thought a moment. "I think the Autocon called that 'snow'."

"Snow. There is much snow in the direction of the rising sun; though, after walking a day and enduring the snow's bite, I came across smaller mountains with no snow, and many trees of delicious colors I cannot describe. You are the giver of names, Kat, not I. I did not locate the sun's shrine as I had hoped, but I did discover what I believe is a habitation. A living habitation, not a ruin like this one. Many people are there. I saw vehicles cavorting in the sky above the clouds—not the Sisters' giant white ships we hide from; these were smaller, sleeker, flown with deft hands, higher and faster than even Bird can fly. I saw lights in the habitation, like the stars. I smelled food being prepared—my mouth watered smelling it. I thought I heard people talking. I wanted to let the people see me, to welcome me." Walker closed her eyes and put her hands to her heart. "I longed for it, sisters."

"You would not be welcome. We are considered the enemy in this place," Kat said.

"Why are we the enemy? We have done nothing."

"The Autocon says Black Hats are the enemy here."

"We are not Black Hats. We are victims of the Black Hats. Perhaps they would welcome us for that? Perhaps they can tell us where the City of Love may be found. I want to go to the city."

Kat shook her head. "The gods told me to stay here. I shall do so until they appear."

Walker looked around and hugged herself. "But this place is not safe for us, Kat, becoming less so by the day. It is cursed. Please hear me. Several nights ago, I awoke. I did not feel well; it was a strange sensation. I saw lights and heard strange sounds. I thought I heard screaming." Walker pointed at the ominous doors built into the hillside. "Coming from there."

"Perhaps you imagined it," Bird offered hopefully.

"No, no," Walker continued. "I have more to tell. Later, I again awoke; this time my body was in agony. I rose, certain I was in my death throes. There was much light outside the windows, and I peered out. I saw great lines of light traveling along the ground, going off in many directions. The light was like the moon, only it was in the ground."

"Blue light?" Kat asked.

"Yes. Let me show you." Walker swiveled her head about, looking for a flat bit of ground. She held out her hand, breathed deep and summoned her Shadow tech from within, the great black fountain of it flowing from her hand. She formed it into a long spike. Using the spike, she drew a picture on the ground.

"The lights started at the door." Walker scratched a circle into the ground, representing the door. She drew a series of concentric lines radiating away from the circle. "This is what I saw. All that is unsettled and unclean comes from those doors. There were lines, here, and here, all glowing in the living earth. And I saw the statues—those ones right over there—moving, just as we move. They walked among the ruins. I felt they were looking for us, looking to take us to their place of death and sacrifice us. I returned within the *Sentrils*. I wished to die with my sisters." Walker paused a moment, shuddering. "Then the sun came up, I awoke, and all was as normal. No lights. No spirits."

"Why didn't you tell us of this sooner?" Kat asked.

Walker allowed her Shadow tech spike to fall apart into cinders. "Because I know you enjoy this place. I did not wish to ruin it for you. Now, will you not leave with me, escape the evil that will certainly overtake us?"

Kat thought about it. "The gods said to stay here and that is what I will do until they come for me. Above the ground is safe."

* * * * *

That evening, as they disrobed and went to bed, Kat was unsettled. Walker's words stayed with her.

The evil here will certainly overtake us ...

The angel had promised her that the ruins above ground were safe, while below ground was dangerous. Kat watched her sisters sleep. She would not allow anything to happen to them. Touching them both on the face, Kat dressed and sped out of the ruins ... to the waiting doors built into the ground.

The angels had warned her. She had no intention of ever going down there again, yet there she was, going down into the depths to face whatever was there, for her sisters. It occurred to her as she approached the doors up the hillside—could what she felt for her sisters, the kinship, the laughter, the daily discoveries, the sharing of their innermost thoughts, the care ...

Was that love?

The doors were shut and dark. Heart beating, she gripped the handles and threw them open.

Stairs going down into a murderous dark. No sign of Wheel. No sign of the ghost she had seen before. It had been days since Wheel disappeared into the dark. She must be dead. She must be. The Black Hats' mission had cost Wheel her life before it had even begun. Wheel should have been up in the sunlight discovering herself with her sisters. Yet she couldn't get the Shade Church and the Black Hats out of her heart. Kat had done it. Bird and Walker had done it. Why couldn't Wheel?

Summoning her courage, Kat went down, claws at the ready. Her Shadow tech felt solid and deadly. Her tail flickered, ready to strike. She could defend herself should she have to.

She reached the bottom, staring into the darkened archway, seeing nothing. She listened: silence.

"Wheel!" she called out, her voice vanishing into the dark.

No reply.

Listening to the surging of her own heart, she clattered in, bumping into bits of junk lying on the floor. Occasionally, her claws would spark, touching off a bluish bit of light.

Something tugged at her clothes on her Scar side. She spun and slashed with her claws.

CLANG!

A protruding piece of stone shattered under her claws, falling to the ground in dust. She continued on.

Feeling her way in, she felt the ground with her hands and probed about with her tail. Her tail bumped into something tall and thin sticking up from the floor. She had reached a column of stone; this was it. She remembered seeing a column of stone previously ... *near to where the ghost had lain.*

Before her, a plume of blue light appeared. It didn't seem real to her at first, light in this lightless place, but, certain enough, a smoky column of light bloomed before her, twisting, moving like the clouds moved across the sky. She thought she caught glimpses of people moving about in the light, many people; she had no idea who they might be. A figure came into focus, floating in the blue light. She saw a slender form, and she saw metal as well, studded with dots of light. The metal reminded her of the atmosphere suit, and its memory repulsed her. She couldn't see the figure's face, it was obscured by the light. She was confused, light brought things into clarity; yet in this case, the light obscured and hid detail.

"You're here!" the figure said in a surprisingly cheerful voice. "I was hoping you would come. Wheel told me all about you."

Kat held onto the column. She wanted to flee, to be away. She had never been so terrified, but she managed to calm herself and stay where she was.

"I have your man, the one you've been waiting for. He's here. Wheel wanted him, but he preferred you. I'll take you to him. Come, he's not far."

"The man?" Kat asked. "Are you the Shadow tech Goddess?"

"No."

"Are you a god?"

"Of course. Of course I am. We are pleased with you. Come. He's waiting."

Kat held fast. "But why did you ask the angels to tell me to remain above ground? They said below the ground was dangerous."

"They erred. There's nothing to be afraid of here in the depths. You're so powerful with your Shadow tech. Come, he will not wait much longer. If you make him wait, he'll abandon you and select your friend, the one with the blue hair. You wouldn't want that, would you?"

Abandon her and go to Walker? That was one of her many fears, that Walker would take the man. Walker was bigger than she, stronger than she, prettier than she. Why wouldn't he prefer Walker to Kat? She tentatively stepped forward, to go to the figure. The figure in the blue light held its hand out, a soft, thin hand. Its body bobbed in excitement. "Yes, come to me."

Kat returned to where she had been and held onto the column. "If you are a god, then show me the color of mercy. Then I will believe you."

"We've no time for that, child. Come … You're running out of time."

"Show me the color of mercy."

The figure floated in the blue light. It raised its hands: one soft and delicate, the other metal, like the atmosphere suit. The blue light changed to a darker blue, an angrier blue.

"You cannot, can you? You are not the gods," Kat said.

She saw the figure's face for the first time; part flesh, part metal. Diabolical eyes fixed on her. Its voice changed from a pleasant note to an evil drone. "I am going to take great pleasure in … killing you, you stinking, worthless little cow. I would have made it quick for you, but now … now …"

The figure lunged, but seemed to be stopped by some sort of barrier. The blue light faded, the figure faded with it. "I have a nice present I wish to give you. Soon, very soon …"

The blue light and the figure were gone. Kat's heart pounded. It hadn't known what the color of mercy was; therefore, there was no mercy in it. She prayed to the angels for her deliverance, as no doubt death would have awaited her had she gone to the thing in the light. Wheel must have also encountered that creature. Had it taken her, killed her?

She wanted nothing more to do with the underground. She turned to make her way back to the surface. She and her sisters would have to leave, strike out and discover another place to reside. This place was too evil for them to remain. When they got to the place they were going, wherever that was, she hoped the gods would tell the man.

She froze. Noise …

Kat heard scraping in the dark. She couldn't pinpoint where it came from; it seemed to be everywhere. She felt infernal eyes upon her. Kat again felt a welling of fear form deep within her.

The ghost is near.

It spoke. *Did you see it? The demon? It took your companion. It offered her power and riches and she accepted. I assumed it would take you too.*

"It said it was a god and it was not a god," Kat replied.

More scraping, nearer this time. She thought she saw a hint of a bent passing outline and the glint of a weapon being dragged behind.

Who are you? came a breathless, dead voice.

She managed to speak. "Kat. Who are you?"

I am all that is left of Gwendolyn, Lady of Prentiss, murdered by the demon, just as you almost were. The demon took my body and wears it, defiling my flesh. I see the demon, even now, laughing at me with my own face. Why are you here?

"The gods told me to be here."

Silence. Finally:

The Gods?

More silence.

Why?

"What are you asking me? I do not understand."

Why have you been picked? You look like a Black Hat to me, you and your friends. I have watched you.

"We are not Black Hats," Kat replied. "I have come here to protect my sisters and make this place safe."

And is that all?

"To protect the man when he comes."

The man?

"The man wearing the magnificent garments. The gods promised him to me. I have washed for him, and eaten food for him, and taught myself for him. For the man, and my sisters, I have come here in the dark. For ... love ... I have come here."

The man was mine. My love. But I am dead now. Killed by the demon in the blue light, just as it wanted to kill you. In other places, I carry on. I see them here, where the universes meet. I see other, still-living versions of myself with him. You live, I am dead, I must accept that. I will go, to other places where he needs me still.

In the blackness, Kat saw the weary form of the ghost approach, a glinting of sunken eyes and a flashing of lipless teeth.

Know this: after the demon killed me and stole my flesh, it went to an accursed place and began weaving itself a web of nightmares. This web will be your undoing one day. You will have to go there and face it. That is the role of my man, to face the arcane—in death, I have come to know this. If you wish to stand at his side, you will have to face it as well. You will most likely be killed by it if you face it again. Farewell.

The ghost walked away into the dark. Gone, gone to other places.

6—Wheel

The next morning, Kat informed her sisters of what she had encountered underground; the demon in the blue light, and that the ruins were not safe for them to remain. Walker and Bird were quite pleased.

A problem quickly arose: where should they go?

Bird wanted to go in the direction of the setting sun, to the water. Walker wanted to go the opposite way, in the direction of the rising sun.

"We shall be guests in the sun's temple, and then we shall set out to the habitation beyond the mountains."

And Kat, she had no idea where she wanted to go. Leaving the ruins was heartbreaking for her. She felt she was failing the gods. What of her man? Would he locate her in the wilderness?

They bandied it around all morning, as they ate, as they washed in the cistern. Eventually, they decided to settle the matter with wrestling. The winner would decide where they went. Walker made quick work of Bird. Bird was not a great wrestler.

Kat was eager to wrestle Walker. It was a rough match, both of them discolored, bloody, hair torn out in places, Bird gasping as she watched. Eventually, Walker's strength won out. Kat was beaten.

"We shall go that way!" Walker, torn and bleeding, cried, pointing at the mountains.

Kat wiped the blood from her mouth. "And what of the man? He will not know where to find me."

Walker tended to Kat's wounds. "If he is a gift of the gods, then they will instruct him where to go."

They returned to the habitation to dress, gather their things and go. Walker wanted to get started before midday.

Wheel was waiting for them in the habitation when they arrived; filthy and naked, standing somewhat bent on the dusty floor. A new basket of gifts from the angels lay before her, opened, rummaged through.

"Sister! You have returned!" Kat said. "We thought you lost! There is a demon roaming the depths. It is not safe here."

Wheel regarded Kat with disgust. "You have stolen from me!" she replied, pointing at Kat, her voice quivering with anger.

"What have I stolen from you?" Kat asked.

Wheel stepped forward. "This!" She held out a piece of parchment.

Kat took the paper and looked at it. There were numerous black lines on the paper, all familiar in their mystery. "That is writing," she announced.

"I have books full of writing. I cannot read it, and the Autocon refuses to divulge what it says."

"The writing proves you have stolen from me," Wheel said. Kat stared at the paper, marveling at the writing. "It says that all these things here are gifts from the gods to me, to Wheel, and you have stolen them. The gods say you must die for that."

Kat stared at the paper in Wheel's hand. "That cannot be what the paper says."

"Yes, it is."

Kat was stunned. Could it be that Wheel had deciphered the mysterious letters Kat could only marvel at? Wheel stood triumphant, while Kat was heartbroken. Never in all her entombed days in Shade Church or during the harrowing trip through space in the stealth missile had her spirit been so completely crushed; all she had thought, all she had hoped for, was gone. She had dared to believe she was special. That had meant everything to her.

Wheel cuffed Kat across the face, sending her to one knee. "Now, give me your clothes, all of you. And the food too. Everything is mine! Mine! Then, we shall proceed to the cistern and execute Kat for her trespass against my property."

The three of them stood there, stunned.

"Now! I said seize her!" Wheel screamed.

Walker found her voice. "I refuse, and I do not believe you are being truthful regarding what the paper says. Kat believes what you say, but I do not. What did the men I was given to once tell me of lying, of deceit? Are you a liar, Wheel? Who are you? You are a crawler, just as we are, and there are one, two, three of us and only one of you. We are powerful with Shadow tech. If you wish to fight us with your wheels and your lying mouth, then let us fight, and you will be destroyed."

Wheel laughed, her eyes were livid with delirium. "Get them," she said.

Behind Wheel rose a great shadow in smoke and ash, reeking of Shadow tech. It was the Autocon, tiny eyes gleaming amid the smoke, holding the sundered pieces of the silver device that once imprisoned it.

"What have you done?" Kat cried.

The Autocon dropped the pieces and lunged, seizing both Kat and Walker, its claws sinking in deep. They writhed in agony.

Bird stood helplessly, the decorations she had made clinking at her throat. "Sister, why are you doing this? We nurtured each other in the darkness. We took comfort in each other," she implored.

"Because you have stolen from me, taken things that were meant to be mine! The gods favor me, not you, and as a Black Hat, these two will be my first victims for your arrogance!" Wheel roared, ripping the decorations from Bird's neck and casting them aside.

Bird, always the most timid and gentle of the three, found her courage and attacked the Autocon, trying to assist her sisters. The Autocon dashed her aside with a shattering smack. Bird rocketed into the floor and didn't move.

Wheel picked Bird up by the neck; she was limp in her grasp. "Finish these two. I will take this one below as a sacrifice." Wheel walked away, dragging Bird behind her.

The Autocon exalted in its freedom. It ruffled its wings, and soared through the window to the cistern waiting below. It was giddy with excitement, quivering as it flew, knocking Kat and Walker together like a pair of hated dolls. It landed near the water *"And now, my dears ... "* it said.

It forced them to the ground and rammed its clawed fingertips further into Kat and Walker's ribs. Never had Kat felt such unendurable pain. She could do nothing but writhe on the ground and pray for death, hoping it would be swift. She felt a torrent move inside her; her muscles clenched and a gusher of Shadow tech issued forth from her mouth in a projectile of black, plunging into the depths of the cistern, the water quickly turning brackish. The process seemed to last forever as the Shadow tech gushed from Kat's mouth, displacing the water in the cistern. Shadow tech shot from Walker's mouth as well, though it also came out of her nose and her eyes, black rivulets tailing down her face.

The both of them drained, the Autocon dashed Walker aside and seized Kat by the neck.

"And you, for your temerity, I sentence you to immediate death!" The Autocon roared, rearing back and sending his claws whistling for Kat's throat.

Walker summoned her strength and sprang, forming a great spike of Shadow tech. She parried the blow meant to kill Kat.

CLANG!

She was knocked off her feet. She righted herself, pushing an impressive blade from her Shadow tech spike.

"Another bladed weapon!" the Autocon hissed in rage.

"To seal my fate," Walker said.

"Well then!" the Autocon cried, turning to her. *"Come with your bladed Shadow tech weapon all so that I might savor your death all the more!"* As Kat struggled to recover, the Autocon attacked Walker, its wings flapping in excitement. She again met its claws with her Shadow tech blade, swinging, clashing, locking in a horrid dance. Walker was the strongest of them, the most beautiful, the most skilled, the best fighter. She must be able to meet, and defeat, the Autocon. If not she, then who?

CLHANG!

Her blade rent asunder, falling to the ground in jagged pieces. The Autocon's claws then found their mark, cutting deep into Walker's shoulder, dashing her to the ground near the edge of the cistern. Blood pulsed from the wound. Her remaining Shadow tech spent, Walker lay there, helpless. With no defense, the Autocon swiped her head off clean with a single blow and cast her headless body into the cistern.

"Walker!" Kat cried, her voice clotted with emotion. Shadow tech bubbled from Walker's neck. She bobbed at the surface for a moment, then sank beneath the black.

The Autocon turned to Kat. *"And now ... It's your turn, woman who would imprison me, enslave me, pummel me with your witless questions! How will you die? What fitting end do you deserve? You shall join your foolish comrade in the depths, buried under a living sea of Shadow tech, never to be found."*

Never to be found?

Never to see the angels, the gods or her man? To be dead here in the wilderness unmourned, unsung, undiscovered? The thought terrified her.

The Autocon attacked, bringing the claws that had just killed Walker down in a dreadful arc. Though low on Shadow tech, Kat wasn't fully drained of it. In an instant, she formed Shadow tech claws of her own and met the Autocon's in mid-swing, wondering if this would be the last act of her life.

CLANG!

Shadow tech screamed. Sparks fell to the ground. Kat was spun around in mid-air with the force of the blow, her arm wrenched back in pain. Yet, beyond hope, her claws held, matching the Autocon's. They wrenched their weapons apart, Kat panting, arm on fire. The Autocon came again, savoring the moment, swinging with its claws, aiming for Kat's throat.

CLANG! CLANG!

She met the blows, her body suffering with each hit, their claws notching and holding together.

Kat struggled for breath, exhausted. Raising her arm to defend herself was agony, her limbs heavy like stone. She fell to the ground. The Autocon hovered over her. It wrung its hands together in triumph. It raised its claws and attacked.

Miss!

Kat managed to recover her strength, darted to her Not Scar side and scampered away, the Autocon finding nothing but churned earth. Kat forced her limbs to move, to demonstrate the speed that had so impressed her sisters.

Her sisters!

Walker!

Walker dead!

And where was Bird?

Taken by Wheel.

She had to save Bird.

She forced the last little bit of Shadow tech within and formed her armature, allowing her run on all fours. She tore across the ruins toward their habitation. Tears streamed down her face for her sisters.

The Autocon followed in quick pursuit, floating just above the ground. Kat was fast enough to open some distance. Without hesitation, she bolted up the side of the ruin and clambered into the window of her habitation, the Autocon following.

"I have waited to kill you! I have thought of little else as you subjected me to one humiliation after the next! All your insignificant questions as you squandered the Black Abbess' Shadow tech," it hissed.

Kat skidded to a stop. The Autocon drifted in, its body rippling, eager for the kill. It took a chunk out of the stone with its claws to display its power, then it fell on Kat, ready to tear her throat out and be done with her.

CLANG! Shadow tech hit Shadow tech, Kat's claws holding, screaming. Before the Autocon could attack again, Kat darted around it.

Sentrils appeared around its body, one, two, three ... thrown to the floor as the angels had taught her. Wheel hadn't taken the *Sentrils*, hadn't known what they were. She had left them in their pouch in Kat's basket.

Now it would be the evil of the Black Hats' Autocon against the angels' gifts. Which would be greater? Kat watched with fascinated horror.

The Autocon shrieked as Shadow tech sloughed away from its body in smoky chunks, rapidly diminishing it in size. Cinders littered the floor as the *Sentrils* did their work. The Autocon thrashed, trying to escape, but the *Sentrils* held it in place. In misery, it tried to swipe at Kat. She chopped its arm off, releasing fire.

The Autocon collapsed into a well of billowing smoke. *"Free me, I beg you!"* it cried, its voice a dying, heated whisper.

"This is for my sister, Walker," Kat said. "I will see you dead!"

The Autocon whimpered. *"Wait! I can continue to serve you, good Kat, devoted Kat ... I'll go back into the device and be your slave again! I wish it!"*

The device was destroyed. Kat ignored it. She watched the Autocon bubble and smoke. It was no match for the angels' gifts. Moments from destruction, the Autocon was desperate. *"Don't you want to know what the paper actually said?"*

Kat hesitated. Yes, she wanted to know—she was desperate to know, but she would not free the Autocon.

She had to be strong.

"I will wait for my angels and they will tell me what it says."

The Autocon shrieked one final time and fell apart into aimless drifting smoke.

Gone.

Dead.

Walker avenged.

Kat quickly dressed and pocketed the *Sentrils*, just in case she needed them again.

Now, to save Bird.

7—Bellathauser

Kat tore out of the ruins, loping along as fast as she could, leaving a cloud of dust in her wake; focusing on the doors built into the ground, bright in the sunshine, decorated with intricate carvings that she had, grudgingly, come to appreciate.

The doors laughed at her from the hillside like a set of closed shutters hiding a world of horrors.

Here comes the little girl. Didn't scare her off the first or second time ...

She had never been so afraid in all her life. The doors. The depths. The things she had seen there.

The demon in blue light.

Her task was clear: save Bird. She had just lost Walker; she could not bear to lose Bird too. Her black claws, proven in battle, clattered on the stony ground as she dashed ahead, her tail flicking at her back. She cleared the bulk of the ruins, entering the grassy area leading up to the nearby mountains.

The doors awaited, eagerly chattering.

Kat forced herself ever closer, running on all fours at top speed.

Come to us ... they seemed to say with their mismatched mouths; *we're waiting for you.*

Loping down the path, she passed the stand of vegetation where the statues held vigil. She glanced at them once and nearly skidded to a stop.

The statues were gone from their pedestal, just as Walker described them days earlier. Where were they?

There they were, up ahead, arranged in front of the doors, blocking her entry. They stood there with their arms raised in a threatening manner. Their bodies had been split apart right down the center and put back together again, unlike statues attached to each other.

Let us hug you ... they seemed to say.

Kat was determined. She had to save Bird. She darted through the ranks of statues, hearing them utter horrid, ephemeral roars.

There were the doors, built into the ground, ready to swallow her.

Come to us, child ... they seemed to say. *Come and see what we have for you ...*

Kat wrenched the doors open, rocking them on their hinges, revealing the steps going deep into the ground. She plunged down the stairs at a gallop, barely under control, her claws barely touching the steps, reaching the bottom in just a few clattering strides. Snatches of blue light blared through the archway. All the lights and sounds she had witnessed prior to Wheel entering the depths were back with even greater force; lighting the cave-like interior with an ominous shimmering wave that made the place seem unreal and phantasmal. Seeing the dazzling lights shook Kat to her core, but she went through the arch anyway, entering the ruined chamber beyond. She was determined to save Bird, and if that meant treading in the dark and killing Wheel, then so be it.

The air was dank in the chamber; it felt heavy, like being in the cistern deep under the water. The place was very wide, going off in either direction as far as she could see, but it wasn't very high. If she stood up and reached, she could easily touch the ceiling with the tips of her fingers. The ground was littered with bits of jagged masonry, both big and small.

She heard the flapping of wings.

Ahead was Wheel, standing near the column where Kat had previously seen the demon. Bird lay at her feet, her Shadow tech wings slumped to the floor. The blue lights had returned, the wall lit up in blue. Wheel beat her fists against the wall.

"I have what you asked! Blood and sacrifice!" Wheel cried. "Now give me what you promised!"

"Wheel!"

Wheel turned. Her malice-filled face was lit up in blue light.

"Let Bird go!" Kat said.

Wheel grit her teeth. She formed a wheel of Shadow tech and attacked Bird with it, bringing it up and down over and over. "Blood and sacrifice for you!"

Blood covered the stones. Blood dripped from Wheel's hand.

"Bird!" Kat cried.

Bird lay still on the ground.

Kat was enraged. "I loved you, sister!" she cried. "I saved you food and prayed the gods would protect you, and this is what you've done? Taken Bird's life for no reason! You claimed I stole from you—it is you who have stolen from me! Taken my sisters! Unleashed the Autocon! Lied to me about the paper! You will never see the light of day again!"

Wheel formed a second formidable disk of Shadow tech to match the first; sharp and deadly. Kat flexed her claws and showed them to Wheel.

Wheel struck, launching the disks at Kat. She leapt aside, bouncing off the masonry and posts. CLANG! CLANG! Both misses, Kat too swift to be targeted. The Shadow tech disks dug into the stony floor with a spray of sparks. Forming more disks, Wheel threw them one after the other, seeking Kat's flesh. Dodging the disks like a tiger, Kat bounded forward and closed the distance. She sprang, coming to grips with Wheel, reaching with her claws, her feet slipping on Bird's still-warm blood. They struggled, each trying to end the life of the other, their feet skidding on the gritty floor. Wheel was strong, like Walker had been; she got the upper hand and drove Kat into the ground.

"Bellathauser, here is your sacrifice!" Wheel cried. "Come and take it and give me what you promised!"

Kat put her hands around Wheel's throat and sank her claws in deep, drawing blood. Wheel screamed in searing agony. She lifted Kat's tiny body into the air and slammed her to the floor, trying to pry her hands free.

"I am a Black Hat!" Wheel gurgled, blood coming out of her mouth. *"Black Haaaaaaaat!"*

Kat refused to let go; she sank her claws in farther, hot blood pulsed from the wounds. Wheel grimaced in torment.

As Kat readied to take Wheel's head off, there came a meaty ripping of flesh. Kat felt untold agony plow into her chest. Blood pulsed. Wheel had scored a hit with her disks on Kat's Scar Hand side; the disk biting deep into her flesh below her ribs, draped in sheets of dark blood. Wheel wrenched herself free of Kat's grip and delivered a crushing kick to Kat's face, sending her sprawling. Bleeding but still standing, Wheel dragged both Kat and Bird to the glowing wall and beat on the stones.

"Bellathauser! Blood and souls for you!" she gurgled, coughing up blood. "BLOOD AND SOULS FOR BELLATHAUSER!"

This time, Wheel received a response. Something appeared in the distance; a solitary figure striding through the blue light, lean and diabolical. Soon, it was just a step away on the other side of the wall.

The demon had returned.

The demon reached through the wall and seized Bird. In jerking stages, it dragged her through to the other side; Kat seeing a tangle of limbs and Shadow tech feathers mixed with floating drops of blood.

"Give me the other one. I want the other one!" the demon shrieked, casting Bird aside. Wheel slammed Kat's face into the wall, hoping to push her through too. Kat struggled, but Wheel was too strong, she was held in place. The demon turned its attentions to her. She felt cold metal clamp onto her neck, slowly pulling her through the wall, just as it had done with Bird. Wheel pressed her foot against Kat's back. Kat's arm went through. In a final effort, Kat twisted about and wrapped her tail around Wheel's waist, holding fast. She drove her claws into the demon's metal arm. Lights flickered and went out. The demon seemed to go dead for a moment.

Kat didn't waste a second. She pulled her arm back through, and before Wheel could react, ripped her throat out in one smooth motion, holding it warm in her hand. Blood pulsed in spurts, staining the walls. Eyes wide in shock, Wheel fell to the floor.

In terrible pain, having lost a great deal of blood, Kat fell next to Wheel's twitching body, her tail going limp. Trembling, she stretched out her hand for Bird, but couldn't reach her mangled body. Instead, she found Wheel nearby and touched her head with her hands. She remembered the shape of her head, the contours of her face, from their time together in the darkness at the Shade Church.

"Tell me the story again," Wheel would often ask in the dark.

Now she was dead.

✶ ✶ ✶ ✶ ✶

She might have passed out; she thought she might have died. She lay there for an indeterminate length of time, feeling Wheel's body grow cold, feeling the blood around her congeal. Figures in the dark leaned over her. She felt herself lifted into the air and carried back to the light. Before she knew what was happening, she was back in her habitation.

Kat lay there, unable to move or speak, the darkness swirling around her.

Here she is ... came a soft voice. *We must help her.*

Another voice, harder, more skeptical. *This ... this is the one you picked? She's mostly dead. Can you save her?*

Why should I? You willing to die for the terrible choices you've made?

I am.

Don't you turn your back on her!

I'm going to blank bits of her memory; we don't need all this unpleasantness today messing her up.

Forms leaned over her. Hands on her face.

It's time for our girl here to get to saving the universe.

✶ ✶ ✶ ✶ ✶

When will he come?

Kat ruled the silent places in the mountains alone, never seeing a soul. She inhabited this great, silent place alone, running the great open passes unfettered. So much room and space for just Kat.

She had dreams of sharing this place with others like herself, of laughing, of sharing food, of rolling in the grass, but they were just dreams. There was no one here but Kat. She had no idea as to where she might have come from, or how long she had been here. Perhaps she had always been here, alone in a place made for many.

Every day she looked to the skies, waiting for the man to come, the man the gods promised to her. She often saw small vessels passing overhead, very high, above the clouds, heading beyond the mountains to points unknown. She often wondered where the vessels were going; perhaps to a place where there were many. She longed to see those places, to see other people, like her. The gods told her to remain, and remain she would, for as long as it took.

Today, though, seemed a different day.

Today, Kat crouched on the wheelhouse stone. She watched as a small vessel came down from the sky to land in the clearing outside of the ruins. It was a beautiful blue vessel, like the sky, like the waters. She watched a man get out—a man in a magnificent green garment.

Her heart raced, her dagger-like claws flexed and bit into the stone. Hurriedly she put on the cumbersome harness over her shoulders and around her waist. Buried deep in her thoughts a voice told her:

Hey cutie pie, wear the harness when the Man comes. You can thank me later...

Her man had come at last—the gods be praised. Now it was time to abuse him!

She was ready.

Part ll

Demons, *Spiralata* and *Covus*

Lady Alesta & Lord A-Ram

1—Mons Eagle

All of this astral plane nonsense was for their mutual friend, Bel …

Lord A-Ram and Lady Alesta of Dare came through the gateway in a sizzle of harsh light and grating noise. Alesta stumbled; moving through the gateway was always a sickening task for her. She felt dizzy, the room around her spinning, her guts in a twist. It was so unlike her Road; the Road was so calm and tranquil, like stepping outdoors to a fresh new morning.

A-Ram assisted her, gently taking her by the shoulders and guiding her. Coming through the gateway was like being transformed into a piece of superheated metal sparking on an anvil awaiting the blacksmith's hammer.

CLANG!

And they were through.

A smallish man, the runt of his family, A-Ram wore a dark blue Calvert suit and string tie. He appeared as any businessman from Dee or St. Edmunds might look. His hair was bright blonde and styled as well as it could be. A pair of Dragon lenses from Onaris sat on his nose. His eyesight, uncorrectable, was virtually nil without them.

Lady Alesta was dressed in homespun. She wore a hooded robe of shimmering forest green brocade, sleeved in golden fabric that went down to her ankles. She had made the robe herself on a simple loom in an equally simple Merian barn. The brocade, despite its humble origins, was lovely. If Alesta had an interest in such things, she could sell her fabrics and most probably earn a fair income. She could hire a number of workers to loom for her, to turn out her fabrics in volume and retire a wealthy woman. But Alesta wanted none of that; she was a Pilgrim of Merian, impoverished, listening to the call of her lonely Star that no one outside her order could see—not even her love, Lord A-Ram.

Beneath the brocade, Alesta wore the standard garb of her order: a white smock that went down to her knees, a belt of red and green beads, and a number of tangled red and green necklaces made of tiny dyed shells around her neck. Her hair was thick and dark brown, held back with various pins and combs; several of which A-Ram had given to her. On her feet she wore a pair of button-up traveling boots, though they suffocated her with every step. A hundred plus years of living as a Merian and rarely wearing shoes had given her a distinct dislike for them.

The room around them unfolded as the light of the gateway faded. It was a crucible of thick stone; the walls and gritty floor felt warm to the touch. There was no visible way out of the room and it always unsettled Alesta; though she and A-Ram had passed through it many times now. Alesta fell into A-Ram's small but reassuring embrace. There was a great familiarity between the two, an easy rhythm and a simple loving flow they shared that went beyond mere love or adoration; they were simply 'right' together, complete and whole, and neither could have gone on this adventure far from their home into the unknown without the other. Together, though, they could endure anything.

"I hate this part," Alesta said, holding onto him. "I feel buried alive in here."

"She'll let us out. She always has," A-Ram replied.

They waited in the dark, feeling smothered in the small, hot room. Soon, a glowing outline formed in the wall, tracing out the rectangular shape of a door. The stone swung out with a rocky fuss and A-Ram and Alesta gladly passed through. Outside in the vast lavender sunshine was a grand portico of polished jewels of blues and purples, and smooth cool marble columns rising up to misty heights leading off a long way in either direction. Behind them was no trace of the crucible room they had just left. They were completely alone in a vast, magnificent city.

The portico was familiar to them; they had walked down it together many times. As always, Alesta leaned against A-Ram and unbuttoned her boots, kicking them aside and rejoicing at her freedom. A-Ram picked them up and placed them into a small traveling bag he carried. The boots spent more time in the bag than out of it. Hand in hand, they started down the column-lined passage. The polished floor of the portico was spotlessly clean, not a trace of dust, grit, dirt, imperfection or anything else. It was flawlessly smooth, like warm porcelain. It felt good on Alesta's feet.

This walk was probably A-Ram's favorite part, just a bit of private time with Alesta amid fabulous finery, like having a grand castle all to themselves; no chatter, no staring eyes, no hustle and bump, just the two of them in glorious silence and open sun-washed space. He once convinced her to stop and make love right there on the immaculate floor in the center of the portico. It was an old fantasy he wished to indulge, to have bold sex in a public place, and, as they were alone, Alesta shook her head and complied. 'Rammy' just loved experimenting with sex, trying different things in different places, developing novel situations and scenarios and making them happen. She had to admit he was quite creative in his selection process.

They could now check-off the 'Sex in a Public Setting' scenario.

Farther down the passage was a small table set in an outcropping overlooking a quiet inlet of water. The table was always crowded with fine foods: steaming mutton, roast fowl, braised beef and other savory entrees along with plates of fresh, sweating fruits, baskets of bread, fine ales and wines and a tankard of clear cold water. The table was always set for two, the food always fresh, piping hot and ready to be eaten. A-Ram seated Alesta and they dined alone. The table afforded them a wondrous view. Beyond the portico there was a causeway spanning a harbor of calm water. The sky past the edge of the portico was an amazing color; soft azure mixed with hints of lavender and dancing with a cosmic arrangement of bright stars. There were two moons so large that when they were in the correct positions, they created a sort of roof, blotting out the stars. Today, the moons weren't out yet and they enjoyed the gallery of twinkling stars in full color as they dined.

This was Alesta's favorite moment, dining alone with her love under the stars and enjoying the delicious foods, feeling like she was the queen of the universe.

Across the causeway and looming over the water was a great palace built in a spiky, god-like architectural style neither of them was familiar with. Alesta liked to gaze at it as she ate her meal; it was very pretty and somewhat imposing to look on.

The place had a name, she and A-Ram were told: Ansara, Mons Eagle, Court of the Gods of Cammara.

This wondrous yet empty place was Cammara; a place of lore and riches far away from their home in the League. Cammara, the long lost home of their ancestors 200,000 years prior, abandoned by the Elders save for those select god-like people who chose to remain. A-Ram and Alesta were, without question, the first modern Leaguers to see Cammara since it had been abandoned. One day, when she and A-Ram had children, Alesta wondered if she would come up with the words to adequately describe this place to them.

Guarding the entrance to the court was a great twisting vortex that rose high into the sky, past the point where they could see, like a great rope hanging from the heavens. It undulated slowly back and forth and, if they listened closely, it generated a grinding, scouring sound. The vortex used to frighten Alesta; it was elemental and terrible, and she didn't like to look at it. But now she had become accustomed to the thing and didn't pay it much attention.

They finished their meal and continued on, their bellies full. The food they had just eaten would be put to good use; they had a long way to walk. On and on they walked, passing boulevards and causeways, not encountering a soul. Their passage along the portico was soundless save for the dull thuds of their footfalls. They came to a grand square cut flawlessly into the center of several intersecting streets. In the center of the square was a large fountain in the shape of a plain round bowl filled with calm, pearly water. A-Ram and Alesta approached the fountain—like they had done so many times before. From this mystical fountain, they could see far into the past, into the future, into other places populated by other people. From there, they could see all, like cosmic voyeurs.

They gazed into the water.

"How many times have we done this now, Rammy—five or six?" Alesta asked.

"Six. I wonder what Bel will be like in this universe? The farther we get from home, the stranger he becomes."

"He's still Bel, our friend, no matter how far we travel," Alesta said.

A-Ram laughed. "Remember him as a woman a few universes back, Bear-Bear? That was something else, wasn't it?"

"She was a fine lady."

"She certainly was," A-Ram said with a bit of nostalgia.

As they stood by the basin, the water came up in a great, controlled cascade, like a mound of clay under the precise control of a potter's hand. The water shaped itself, adding form, texture and color. As A-Ram and Alesta watched, the image of their friend, Stenstrom, Lord of Belmont- South Tyrol, came into clarity, towering over them in his usual long HRN coat and his metal Tyrol boots. He was standing on a lofty rooftop overlooking a city by the sea.

"Well, he looks fairly normal in this universe, I must say," A-Ram said heartily. "He's wearing his usual uniform and such. He looks trim and healthy, as always."

Alesta looked up at the image. "Yes, but look, is he wearing his old mask again? He is—I see it. And why is he walking about on the rooftops like a prowler? What's he doing up there? And where's Gwen? She's usually never far from his side."

A-Ram took Alesta by the hand and led her away from the fountain. "I suppose we'll find out in short order." As they walked away, the water collapsed back into the basin.

Ahead was the causeway spanning the harbor and the great castle of Mons Eagle. A figure approached from the opposite direction, walking toward them at a brisk pace. "A-Ram, Alesta!" came a pleasing feminine voice. In the silence around them, hearing another voice was somewhat shocking.

"We're here," A-Ram answered, waving.

Beyond, in the bluish light, the vortex had vanished.

A smiling woman came toward them. She was tall and thin, much taller than either A-Ram or Alesta, and she loomed over them. She wore, as always, an odd, rather utilitarian outfit resembling a pilot's flight suit, though they had never seen any sort of flight vehicle associated with her in the dozen or so times they had met her here before. They had never seen her get out of a Ripcar or Sub-Orbital; they had never witnessed her flying a vehicle or anything of the sort. She had a life-support harness complete with tubes and dangling hoses that she might connect to an oxygen system on a de-ventilated ship. The hoses clinked and knocked together as she walked. Her boots were heavy and thick-treaded. She wore a compartmented belt and at her shoulder was a holstered gun. Despite her workman-like clothing and conspicuous sidearm, her blonde hair was styled up and set into place, as if she were expecting a cultured evening on the town.

This was the Woman with the Gun. They knew her by no other name. In the beginning, they often asked what her name was and she never replied with a direct answer, so they stopped asking.

She had come to them one night in A-Ram's quarters aboard the *Seeker*, watching them sleep in the dark. When they became aware of her presence, she said she was the wife of their mutual friend, Stenstrom, Lord of Belmont-South Tyrol. She said she was desperate, claiming that both she and Lord Belmont needed their help. Alesta wanted to call for security. The woman was clearly lying, clearly an intruder. Their friend, Lord Belmont, was not married, and the long-standing favorite to claim his hand was certainly not this woman; it was either Gwendolyn, Lady of Prentiss, or the flamboyant Morgan-Jeterix of the Grand Order of Hospitalers. Alesta's bet had always been that the studious Lady Gwendolyn would win out, while A-Ram was certain it would be the passionate Morgan-Jeterix.

But here was this woman with a gun at her shoulder, a stranger, claiming she was Lord Stenstrom's wife. And then she made the most outlandish claim of all: she told them she was a *Wvulgrom*, a person from another universe. In another universe, in an alternate place and time, she said, she was the wife of Lord Belmont.

By rights, they should have fled from her or called the ship's security as Alesta had wanted, but she had a genuine if rather tragic air about her that captivated A-Ram. She seemed sincere, she had an arresting and calming effect on them, and they listened. A-Ram thought she might be a goddess disguised as a mortal woman. He continued to believe that.

She said Lord Belmont had come under the influence of an arcane device known as the Anatameter and, if proper steps were not taken, he would lose his soul to it.

A ridiculous story, truly, but she proved her claims. She predicted the coming of certain events and she was right time and time again.

She knew the true nature of their friend Morgan-Jeterix, and it was horrible.

She had access to odd technology. She had taken them far away to the place of Mons Eagle on Cammara where they now stood, a place no one from the League had seen in 200,000 years.

Always, she told them Lord Belmont's soul was at risk. The Woman with the Gun begged their help. For the soul of their friend they decided to delay their wedding and help her. They had visited five odd universes so far where they witnessed strange things, but were delighted as well, for their friend Lord Belmont, no matter what guise he took, was always the same at heart.

The Woman with the Gun had promised them wondrous stories that they could tell to their children, of adventure in far-away places, and she had been correct in that too.

Now, smiling, she placed her gloved hands on both A-Ram and Alesta at once. "It is so good to see you again, my friends." Like the crucible room they had come from, her touch was warm and energetic.

"And you," A-Ram replied, looking up at her beautiful face.

"Did you eat? I left the table out for you again."

"We did. It was very good."

The Woman with the Gun smiled. "I'm glad, I'm glad."

She led them out across the causeway toward the waiting, silent castle. Alesta glanced skyward, looking for the vortex. "Where has the cyclone gone?" she asked.

"You two need never fear it," the Woman with the Gun answered. "It is your friend. It is your protector."

They stepped off the causeway and proceeded into the waiting castle. Alesta glanced back: there, on the other side of the harbor, was the great columned portico, the vanguard of the massive city of Mons Eagle beyond. In the center was the little table where they had dined.

"Come, we have much to discuss," the Woman with the Gun said.

The interior of the castle was a sumptuous gullet of polished stone, wrought metals in clashing colors, all dizzying and difficult to take in all at once. At the end was a vast chamber of lofty proportions and mysterious in drifting stained lighting. There was a small passage to the left; the Woman with the Gun led them in that direction. For a brief moment, A-Ram and Alesta could see into the great chamber. Inside, seated high atop thrones of riven gold, were a man and a woman; both elegant, both of royal bearing.

Both were still and unmoving, as if wax figures cast in state. A-Ram and Alesta had caught glimpses of them many times—always still, always silent, always in the same position. Aside from the Woman with the Gun, they were the only other people they had ever seen in the city.

"Who are those people?" Alesta once asked.

The Woman with the Gun answered. "Those are the Gods of Cammara."

"Why do they not move?"

"They do move, you simply cannot perceive it. It's all a matter of time."

They went deep into the castle. The veneer of fine stones and sheathing of impossible color gave away to bare, unfinished rock in drab grays. They came upon a great stone door. The Woman with the Gun opened it and they stepped into a cramped work area. The area consisted several small rooms; one leading out to a terrace over the water. The walls and floors were covered with a chaotic topcoat of parchments and scrawled drawings, all scattered about. Every available surface was covered with tacked-up or piled-up papers.

"Please make yourselves at home," the Woman said. It was impossible to take an unguarded step or a casual seat without first having to be mindful of papers and crinkled scrolls.

The Woman with the Gun sorted through the papers, picking them up and setting them back down, going over important details in her head, puzzling over them; one moment confused, one moment elated and another moment frustrated. As they waited, Alesta went out and stood on the terrace, admiring the view. A-Ram watched the Woman with the Gun work. She did not settle in and make herself comfortable. She didn't remove her harness or unlace her boots. She didn't let her hair down or even remove her gun.

She was restless; her concentration riveted on the papers.

"We have made remarkable progress," she said, still fishing through papers, holding several in her hand. "With your help, things are progressing as we hoped. We have opened the way to great Cammara, as we are standing here. We have established a dialogue with the Gods of Cammara in the court of Mons Eagle. Not the ones frozen in time in the Great Hall, mind you, but different ones in a different time. There are many such places here in this city; it's easy to get lost. And we are now ready to proceed to the Shrine."

"The Shrine of Boraster," A-Ram said.

"Yes, yes," she said. "Come, see…"

The Woman with the Gun stared at several papers. Her eyes roved over them, taking in every detail. She laid several out on a small table, creating an incomprehensible grid work of lines and intersecting circles. A-Ram looked over her shoulder and Alesta came in.

The papers were covered with circular charts, all carefully hand-drawn with a compass and caliper, all portioned off and filled in with names. Some were scratched out and re-written several times. All of them, however they were laid out, had a central theme. They all charted the doings of Lord Belmont, following the events of his life, his friends, his achievements, his loves and his various enemies. Many seemed drawn to Lord Belmont, both those who would love him and those who would see him destroyed. There were so many of each.

The Woman with the Gun selected one chart and tapped it with her fingers. "We are at an important crossroads. This task is done, and this one as well. Now here we are…"

She seemed perplexed. She stared at the chart and rubbed her chin.

"What is it?" A-Ram asked.

The Woman with the Gun considered her response. She pointed to the chart. It was a tangle of circles all nested together, forming a dizzying, complex symmetry. "Everything's changed since my last readings."

"Changed?"

"The Anatameter has caused the various universes in its vicinity to bunch up and overlap. In a normal situation, the universes all fit together in a neat order, nested one after the other, rather like rings in a tree trunk. Those rings are called *Circulums*, and they are orderly and predictable. The Anatameter has disrupted that."

"Did we know this might happen?" A-Ram asked.

"It was a possibility, however remote." She puzzled over the charts. "See on my chart how the lines of the circles intersect? They didn't do that before. These Lines of Intersection are points where two or more universes come together. There, the doings in one universe can affect the doings in another. Bad things can happen. Demons can gain entrance through these intersections—see here? And here? This is called a *Spiralata*. The universe is in flux, very difficult to predict and thus, very dangerous. If we are not careful, all of our previous work will be lost. This whole universe could be destroyed."

"What are we to do, then?" A-Ram asked.

The Woman with the Gun stared at the chart, her chin quivering a bit.

"My lady?"

She picked up a set of calipers and set them on the chart. "We must re-calibrate, and re-establish the correct path through this tangle to the Shrine. We must do this, we've worked so hard." She took several measurements, checked her work and started again. Her hands were slightly shaking.

Time passed; it seemed like forever. The Woman with the Gun labored over the chart, tracing circles, plotting points of intersection, wiping growing beads of perspiration from her brow. They had no notion of how long they watched her work. Time in Mons Eagle did not flow as they would have liked. Sometimes it sped up, sometimes it slowed to a crawl, to a stop, and sometimes it flowed in reverse. A-Ram and Alesta felt themselves awash in time, placing their safety completely in the hands of the Woman with the Gun.

A-Ram and Alesta fidgeted about. "Can we get you anything, my lady?" A-Ram asked after an indeterminate period of time.

"No, no, I'm fine, thank you. I'm sorry this is taking so long. I must solve this. I must."

"Take your time, we're in no hurry. Let's do this right," Alesta said.

As A-Ram and Alesta watched, they saw for the first time ever the cool and in-command demeanor of the Woman with the Gun, their host on this odd, arcane journey across the universes, falter, become unsure, become frustrated. Annoyance turned to confusion, which then turned to fear and finally despair. She stared at the chart, holding her calipers in shaking hands, understanding it less and less with each passing moment.

At last, she cast her calipers aside and sighed. "All of my previous charting is unusable. It's all in shambles. I cannot find a path. This is beyond my skill."

A-Ram pulled a small ochre disk from his coat. Seven names were arranged on the disk in a radial pattern. "Then, all of these names you gave us previously are no longer good? We've been using this disk as a guide. You gave it to us."

"I'm sorry," she said as she studied the chart. "They are no longer valid. I don't know the way ahead."

A-Ram checked the disk. Previously, it displayed seven names all laid out in a wheel-like pattern. He had memorized them:

Gwendolyn

Melazarr

Gwendolyn

Taara

Gwendolyn

Kat

Gwendolyn

?????????

All were people he knew:

Lt. Gwendolyn of Prentiss, a stern woman of Zenon society, a ship's captain, and most frequent lover at Bel's side. A *Merthig,* she was called in the universal scheme of things.

Melazarr of Caroline, a giant and outwardly off-putting Xaphan trollop concealing a very shy and insecure person within. In all their adventures to date, Melazarr of Caroline had always met with a terrible end. She was known as a *Merten,* an unwitting messenger carrying information within her very body. The universe seemed to want the *Merten's* blood, and it got it most every time.

Private Taara de la Anderson, the common girl from Bazz, a Marine and their friend from the *Seeker.*

Kat, who was Kat? He struggled to remember. Oh—the vile Black Hat who had nearly killed Lord Stenstrom with StT Shadow tech not long ago in the Ruins of Clovis.

Now, all the names were gone, replaced by a single one:

Bellathauser

"Who's Bellathauser?" he asked.

The Woman with the Gun didn't reply. She sat down at the chart-covered couch and put her hands to her face. Alesta came to her side to console her, as did A-Ram.

"What does this all mean?" Alesta asked.

The Woman with the Gun choked up and sought a reassuring embrace from them both. "Oh, my friends, it means I don't know what to do. We are finished! Bel is trapped in the Anatameter's power. He will fade away in time. The universe will turn its back on him. I will fade as well. I will never see my beloved husband again. The Shadow tech Goddess will no doubt soon come and wipe this universe clean. It's all my fault. I did this. I set this into motion."

"You have done this out of love," Alesta said.

"Then love has sounded the bell for this universe and all in it. The doings of love can be deadly too. Look what I've done!"

"Is there nothing we can do?" A-Ram asked. "Let's take a moment to clear our heads, start fresh and then try again."

The Woman with the Gun seemed deflated and diminished. "It is hopeless. Hopeless! I will be taken away and punished for this!"

"Who will punish you?" A-Ram asked.

As if in response to his question, there was a knock at the door. It startled A-Ram. Who could it be? There had been nobody else moving about in this time-locked world of Cammara that they had seen before. It was just the three of them.

The knock came again, harder this time.

2—The Shadow tech Goddess

"Should I answer that?" A-Ram asked.

The Woman with the Gun nodded with resigned despair. As Alesta consoled her, A-Ram got up and went to the door. He felt like he once had when he worked in Admiral Derlith's office at Fleet; there were always big, important-sounding knocks at the door he had to answer. The Admiral often made tiny A-Ram his first and last line of defense regarding the door and those important people waiting to pass through it and have at him. *"If it's Admiral Pax, I don't want to see him! Make up a story!"*

A-Ram opened the door a crack and peeked out.

Outside, an alluring woman in a shimmering black oilskin costume stood there, gloved hands placed on ample hips. She wore a silver helmet on her head that covered the upper part of her face, her ears and the back of her head, giving her head a bullet sort of shape. Built-in goggles with glowing, eye-obscuring lenses protruded from the helmet, staining the doorway in purplish light. She wore an aggressive set of spiky black heels and a light cape at her back that seemed to ripple in an unfelt breeze and radiate gal-

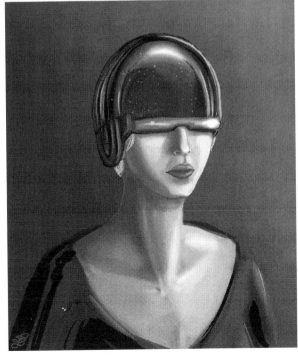

axies' worth of hidden starlight. A-Ram wondered who she was. She seemed quite young and also ancient in the extreme at the same time. Though she looked human, there was something decidedly 'in-human', or 'other-human' about her.

She pursed her lips. "Are you going to let me in?" she asked curtly.

A-Ram didn't know what to make of this. He felt on-the-spot and rather intimidated. He roasted in the purple light from her goggles. He used a technique he had learned at Admiral Derlith's office: when in the presence of an important and intimidating official, fixate on their teeth. Teeth, no matter who they belonged to, are never intimidating. Sharks' teeth are frightening, bear teeth and wolves' teeth as well, but not human teeth: white, pearly, well-cared for, sometimes bearing a bit of previously-eaten lunch, A-Ram had faced down many important sets of teeth in his day. He fixated on her teeth, which appeared to be perfect and unblemished. "May I ask who are you, my lady? Are you … expected?"

She pushed her way in, her heels clicking on the floor. "Me? I'm the idiot who sponsored this little disaster, that's who." She marched into the room and took control. "What is going on here? Why are we all sitting around, please? Somebody give me an update."

There was confused, awkward silence.

"Now …" she said in an unpleasant voice.

The Woman with the Gun wiped tears from her face and gestured at the chart. "We are at an impasse. *Spiralata*. We have no clear path forward. I have lost the way."

The newcomer was clearly angry. "You promised me you had this all worked out."

"I thought I had."

"Then what happened?"

"The universes have diverged. A demon has lent its influence."

The newcomer in black wasn't sympathetic. "Didn't I warn you that could happen?"

"I thought I would be ready for it."

The newcomer held out her slender hand encased in black. "Let me see! Give me the chart! Come on, give it to me!"

The Woman with the Gun sat there in Alesta's embrace. A-Ram selected the chart off the table and held it out. The woman snatched it away. She reviewed it, holding her free hand to her helmet as she surveyed the chart. "Look at this mess! Really? I could get sent to the Windage for this, you know." The intensity of her goggles increased. "For those of you here who might not know what the 'Windage' is, it's the hell of the gods, ok, and it's not a pretty place. So, guess what, if I go down, guess who I'm taking with me? Just guess."

Alesta found her voice and spoke up. "This woman is heartbroken. She has done all this out of love. Can you give her some peace?"

"No," was the tart answer.

A-Ram spoke up. "I don't believe we've had the pleasure," he said. "Who are you, Great Lady?"

The woman regarded A-Ram for a moment. She seemed rather annoyed, but then she smiled. "I'm the Shadow tech Goddess," she replied as she resumed surveying the chart.

He was taken aback. "You're the Shadow tech Goddess?"

"Yeah, why?"

"Well, I suppose I pictured the Shadow tech Goddess to be …"

She put the chart aside with a crinkle of vellum and stared A-Ram down. "To be what?"

"To be … more stern, more imposing, I suppose."

She put her hands on her hips. "What, do you want me to ugly up for you or something, is that it? Sorry to disappoint you, little guy. I guess I thought you'd be a little taller. So there."

A-Ram persisted. "But, if I may …"

The Shadow tech Goddess tapped him on the head with the chart. "Look, look, look, enough of the questions, ok? You're lucky I like you, otherwise I'd just have reduced you down to floating molecules or something by now. I destroy things, that's what I do, right?"

A-Ram didn't know what to say. Alesta jumped in. "I'd have thought a goddess to have more manners."

The Shadow tech Goddess huffed. "Oh, is that what you thought? Listen, I'm a little upset right now, 'kay? I sanctioned this little party, and if it goes bad, I'm the one who's going to get in trouble for it. Big trouble. So, cut me some slack!"

The Woman with the Gun was despondent. "Just take me then and be done with it. Do not hurt my friends, they are innocent in this matter. Let me send them home first, and then do with me what you will."

"It would be my right to do so, wouldn't it?" the Shadow tech Goddess stated. "I could just take you right now and start punishing you, couldn't I?"

A-Ram and Alesta doggedly stood by the Woman with the Gun's side. "But we're not going home," Alesta said. "We agreed to go on this quest to help our friend, and to help this woman who has lost her love. I know how I'd feel if I lost Rammy. I would cross any sea or any universe I could to get him back, and so would she. We are not yet ready to quit. There must be some way to correct this problem."

The Shadow tech Goddess thought about it and looked at the chart again. "Well, I suppose I'm a sap for puerile human romance. I suppose I can't just rip into her in front of you two, can I? It wouldn't be good form, would it?" She tapped her helmet for a bit. She held the chart out, noting the tangle of lines. "So, what we have here is …"

She stopped in mid-sentence. A-Ram had poked her in the shoulder with his finger, apparently to see if she had corporeal form or if she was composed of some sort of nether-world goddess material. The Shadow tech Goddess stared at him for a moment with indignation and then poked him back in the chest. "Never poke a goddess, okay?" She returned to the chart.

"Let's focus. So, what we have here is a *Spiralata*, and a really bad one at that. Look, look here. Sure enough, three universes have converged at this point and a demon has crossed through—a nasty one too, by the looks of it. It's dug itself in, deep. See, here and here, these are cataracts it created to purposely confound anyone trying to dislodge it."

She snapped her fingers at A-Ram. "What's the name you got on your disk there?"

A-Ram consulted the disk to refresh his memory. "Bellathauser."

She cursed inaudibly and adjusted her helmet. "It figures. All right, all right." She set the chart on the table and went to work, tracing lines, following intersections. "Our demon has set up two cataracts to protect itself. Here, and here. Very harsh work. Hmmm, what's this?" She turned her back to them and removed her helmet, revealing a dainty head of short, platinum-blonde hair. Odd diffuse light, possibly coming from her eyes, lit up the chart in a passing sublime wave of differing colors, giving it three dimensions and life. A-Ram was curious to see her face; he wanted to see it, he had to see it. He got up and walked around the table.

"Stop!" The Shadow tech Goddess held her hand up, not allowing him to see her face. "No peeking. I wouldn't want you to fall in love with me or something. Gods and mortals, it never works out. Go sit down. Sit."

A-Ram reluctantly resumed his seat.

She turned her attention back to the chart. "Yes, look here. The demon has dug in. It got past our boy, the *Kaidar Gemain* and killed his *Merthig*, knowing that would weaken any seeking to dislodge it."

Alesta thought about that. "What? The *Merthig*? In our past journeys across the universes, the *Merthig* is always Lady Gwendolyn of Prentiss. You mean Gwen is dead?"

"Is that her name?" the Shadow tech Goddess asked. "Yes. 'Gwen' is dead, and that will make sorting this out much tougher."

Lady Gwendolyn of Prentiss, the *Merthig*, the lady most often at Bel's side, was dead, killed by a demon. Even though they were speaking of an alternate-universe version of Gwen, even though the Gwendolyn they personally knew and called friend was back in their own universe safe and sound, the news of her murder in this alternate universe was crippling. They both grieved for her as the Shadow tech Goddess worked.

"Without the Merthig, everything falls apart," the Woman with the Gun whispered. *"The demon has won."*

"We must save Gwen!" A-Ram said.

"She's dead," the Shadow tech Goddess said.

"But can't we—"

The Shadow tech Goddess turned, covering her eyes with her hand. Purple light squirted out between her fingers. "There are no 'buts', ok? The demon has taken her out, and it's not by accident or coincidence; it did it on purpose, to create chaos, to strengthen its position. Let's get past it and try to get this worked out."

The Shadow tech Goddess turned away from them and placed her helmet back on her head, situating it, covering her blonde hair. She rolled up the chart into a tight curl and walked to the door. She stood there impatiently.

"Come on then, let's go. Somebody open the door for me, please."

A-Ram and Alesta stood, as did the Woman with the Gun. They were both in shock, grieving for Gwen.

Dead.

Killed by a demon.

"Where are we going?" A-Ram asked, dejected.

"To get somebody who can correct this mess. I'm a goddess, not a mapmaker. Where are your manners? Get the door. Let's go."

A-Ram opened the door. Tears streamed down his face. The Shadow tech Goddess stepped through. She regarded him and did not seem unsympathetic. "Thanks. Hey, you better perk up. Your friend is dead, it hurts, I get it. She is the *Merthig*, she exists in many other universes, safe and sound, totally unaware of what happened in this universe. Take solace in that. I think we might be able to fix this problem, but I'm going to need the two of you to do it, and I'm going to need your best effort. We've got a job to do, so let's buckle down. Dedicate it to the *Merthig*. Or dedicate it to your friend here with the gun, whose well-being depends upon this. Come on. Follow me."

They exited into the corridor, followed by Alesta and the Woman with the Gun. They moved back into the main area of the castle, time-locked into utter stillness as always.

Heels clicking with every energetic step, the Shadow tech Goddess led the way into the main viewing chamber where the frozen king and queen sat in their chairs, towering over them, their frozen gazes stern and implacable. As they entered the room, a festival of warm jewel-colored light stained the polished stone finery and the frozen forms of the king and queen. An archway at the far end of the room led to mysterious areas they had never seen before. The Shadow tech Goddess moved at a rapid pace, her cape shimmering. A-Ram and Alesta shambled behind, struggling to keep up. The Woman with the Gun did not enter the room with them. She held back.

"Are you coming?" Alesta asked.

She shook her head. "I can go no farther. Take each other's hands, hold tight and do not let go until you are told to do so. Promise me," she said with considerable concern. "Promise me you won't lose each other."

The Woman with the Gun's warning had a grim note to it. A-Ram took Alesta's hand, holding it as tight as he could. "We promise."

She embraced them one last time and kissed them both on the cheek.

Holding hands, they continued on, following the Shadow tech Goddess. Soon, the Woman with the Gun was left far behind.

"Come along!" The Shadow tech Goddess took them into a maze of chambers, twisting and turning, both A-Ram and Alesta hopelessly lost.

"Where are we?"A-Ram asked.

"Mons Eagle. Ages from where we started," she replied.

"What does that mean?"

She didn't reply. She glanced back, seeing they were holding hands. "Ah, good. Don't let go, no matter what."

"Why?" Alesta asked.

"You don't want to end up like your friend with the gun, do you?"

They certainly didn't. They gripped hands tighter, fingers interlaced.

They continued on, feeling uneasy, wondering where the Shadow tech Goddess was taking them and why it was so important they hold hands. A-Ram squeezed Alesta's hand as tight as he could, savoring the feel of her fingers and soft palm. Their hands were mutually sweating and going a bit numb, but they held on nonetheless. The sounds of the Shadow tech Goddess' footfalls were hypnotic, tolling deep.

Tock ... tock ... tock ...

A-Ram felt himself falling, lost in time and place, as if each step he took began in one age and ended in another. Alesta walked next to him, her footsteps making no sound. She seemed an eternity away and getting farther with every step. She seemed to transform before his eyes into an elemental state, into an infant, an alien creature, and a dying old woman many times. Her bearing and aspect also changed. He saw her in her familiar form as a Pilgrim of Merian, shoeless, wearing her homemade clothes; and also as a regal countess of Dare, an explorer, a raging demon, a harlot, and a sinister unprincipled woman, angry with life and uninterested in him. He clung to her hand, not wishing to lose her, as the Woman with the Gun had lost Bel.

He said her name, and it echoed across time.

Alesta

Alesta

Alesta

Alesta ...

At long last, they came to a door. The Shadow tech Goddess waited for them, impatient.

"Let her go. You're safe for the moment, but don't wander off, we've still a ways to travel." She threw the door open. Despite being told they could release their grip, they continued to hold hands, their touch mutually comforting.

Outside, the smooth gem-like city of Mons Eagle spread out before them in glittering lavender sunshine. They were familiar with the layout of the city, only this time it was filled with people dressed in elegant clothing of varied colors, walking, laughing, going on about their day; the city full of sounds and sophisticated life. They walked down the jeweled street, passing the nook where they had enjoyed their meal in solitude not long ago.

Ahead through the crowds was some sort of statue or artwork, awkwardly placed in the center of the boulevard. Many people stood around it, taking it in. As they approached, they could make out detail in the statue; it was of two people lying prone on the street, limbs intertwined, either wrestling ... or in the act of having sex.

Alesta's mouth dropped open and her face lost all color. "Holy Creation! Is that us? Rammy!"

A-Ram quickly moved Alesta past the time-locked forms of themselves having sex in the middle of the street. Though Alesta was mortified, A-Ram refused to be shamed or embarrassed. Dammit, he was proud; let them all look and take it in. Yet another bucket item could be removed: sex in full view of thousands.

Ahead, the great castle loomed. Standing before it was a familiar figure: the Woman with the Gun, only she was a towering giant, hundreds of feet tall, and she wasn't wearing her usual flight suit. She was wearing an armored breastplate, a metal tunic that went down to her knees, metal boots, and a giant-sized sword ten stories high. She stood solemnly at the entrance to the castle.

They approached. "Stand aside," the Shadow tech Goddess said, her voice reaching into the heights.

Wearily, the giant gazed down at them, her face partially obscured by the afternoon haze. "I was told not to admit you," she said in a massive, echoing voice. "And who are these with you?"

"Don't you know us?" A-Ram asked, his voice tiny.

The giant gazed at them solemnly. "No, and therefore you may not enter."

The Shadow tech Goddess became annoyed. "Step aside, before I decide to get angry. Shall we add a few millennia to your sentence, perhaps in less pleasant environs? I can think of several right off the top of my head." Her voice carried a hard edge of authority and power. The giant considered her words and then moved aside, the ground shaking as she did so, opening the way into the castle.

The Shadow tech Goddess marched in. As they passed across the threshold, Alesta craned her neck back and spoke to the giant. "Don't you know us? We're here for you."

The giant woman gazed down, considering her words. There were a great number of emotions hidden in her face: weariness, sadness, loneliness, resignation and unvarnished misery. It was as if, of all the inhabitants of this great city, she was the sole person in despair, a giant with giant-sized sadness. She said nothing in response.

A-Ram and Alesta puzzled over this—the Woman with the Gun, a giant who didn't know them at all. A-Ram could still feel the kiss she had given him on his cheek. He had always suspected that there was more to her than she let on; that perhaps she, like the Shadow tech Goddess, wasn't quite human. A-Ram was good at listening and piecing together little bits of disjointed information, by themselves all innocent and inconclusive, but, when organized and considered together, they formed a telling picture. The Woman with the Gun had said it herself in passing:

… the price I've paid …
… the ages of nameless servitude …
… the loneliness …

Their hearts ached for her but time was of the essence; the Shadow tech Goddess kept them moving at an impossible pace. Inside, the castle was clogged with people milling about the central corridor, the laughs, the smiles, the clinking glasses and poured spirits as if a great party were in progress; the misery of the lonely giant outside irrelevant. The Shadow tech Goddess pushed through the people, marching through the crowds as if they didn't exist. At the entrance to a grand ballroom clashing in noise and color, she stopped. "Follow me," she said. "We are nearly there, but we've ages to cross. Time is not linear here, I'm sure you've figured that out by now, and it is easy to get lost. As before, hold onto each other until we exit the chamber. Right? *Do not* become separated and *do not* lose me. I cannot help you once we enter. You must follow me. Are you ready?"

She didn't give A-Ram and Alesta time to respond. "Now, let's go."

The Shadow tech Goddess waded into the ballroom. Hands locked together, A-Ram and Alesta followed, doing their best to keep up. The floor was clogged with people. It was a cacophony of noises, smells and other sensations. Their senses were assaulted at every turn. Fine orchestral tunes piped out from the wings of the room, only to morph into brash, ugly roars of schizophrenic noise and then back again to pleasing notes. They smelled fine perfumes, sweet scents of powdered pastries, primal smells of pine forests and dirt, thick sanguine odors, smells of sex and rotting offal. People were everywhere; some dancing, some aimlessly milling about. Most paid them no mind, though some laid hands on Alesta's Merian garments, offering her drinks and food, trying to divert her attention, some trying to pull their hands apart. A-Ram held on tight, gripping Alesta with a sure hand. As they waded into the central section, people kept getting in the way, the slender black form of the Shadow tech Goddess momentarily vanishing in the crowd and then reemerging a bit farther away. It was like being a ship in an angry sea of bright fabrics, varnished hair and cloying perfumes, waves of strange faces and blank stares crusted with the din of mashed-up conversations with the black solidity of the Shadow tech Goddess moving into the distance, vanishing, reappearing, and vanishing again. A-Ram held onto Alesta with all his might and pulled her along.

"Rammy!" she called out in distress.

"Hold onto me!" he said.

He felt a gentle tap on the shoulder—it felt like being licked by a cat's tongue, the sensation of the touch quite shocking. Standing to his left was an attractive woman wearing a lacy blue suit of flattering contours. She wore a veiled hat, the veil covering the right side of her face. She stood there with an inviting smile.

"Hello," she said in a pleasant voice. "Are you Lord A-Ram?"

"I am."

She giggled and curtsied. "I was told to expect you. Please, this way. I will lead you."

A-Ram was hesitant. "The Shadow tech Goddess said to follow her."

She smiled and shook her head. "That woman is not the Shadow tech Goddess. Don't let her fool you with her lies. Come, follow me. I will take you to the proper place."

A-Ram didn't know what to think. The woman stood there in a pleasant fashion. "Who are we seeing?"

"Fiddler Crowe. He is the person you seek; the man who can help correct the matter troubling you. He is very wise, but difficult to find. Come. I am here to assist you." The woman had a marked air of authority about her.

The woman took A-Ram by the hand. She tugged on him.

"And who are you?" A-Ram asked, trying to keep his wits. He tried to pull his hand back but couldn't. Her grip was impossible.

"My name is Bellathauser," she said.

Bellathauser?

The demon?

"Come. He shouldn't be kept waiting."

A-Ram felt his grip on Alesta slipping, like she was a kite at the end of a long string slowly being pulled from his grasp by the relentless wind.

Alesta!

He noticed the people around him converging, closing in. He saw the same woman over and over again, staring at him, smiling, eyes wide, mouths open, hands grasping, leering. One of them pulled her veiled hat away, revealing a gruesome sight. The left half of her body was flesh; the right half, however, was a complex, well-made machine fused right down the middle to her left half with a rolled bead of flesh, as if it had been welded on. Servos flashed, lenses opened, refracting angry blue light. She opened her mouth. A tongue made of knitted chain mail rolled out over synthetic lips. With a horrid crunching of bone and sinew, she elongated in height until she towered over them.

All the women closed in on A-Ram and Alesta, hands raised, metal and natural claws bared. Cloth ripped. Bellathauser's robotic right arm was studded with knives, knobs, nails and serrated surfaces waiting to bite into his flesh, as if her machine half had been purposefully conceived to inspire fear and inflict pain. A line of tiny monitors splashed with her leering face were built in down the length of her arm, all mouthing synchronized dire words.

The glimpse of the image in the monitor screens froze A-Ram's heart.

One half of her face: Bellathauser. The other half was Gwen. Gwen's face, fused with hers. She mouthed the words: *"I called out for you, but you didn't come. Where were you, A-Ram? A-Ram! A-RAM!"*

"Come along," she rasped. *"I've things to show you ..."*

The women closed in, ready to take them.

Someone came in and pushed the horrid ghouls away, giving A-Ram and Alesta space. A-Ram pulled himself together and re-established his grip on Alesta's hand, reeling her in, holding her tight.

There was the Woman with the Gun, wearing her armor and knee-length tunic, shrunk down to normal size, keeping the demented crowd at bay with her sword.

"Toy soldier! Toy soldier! You can't stop us!" the mass of Bellathausers jeered. They moved around her sword to get at A-Ram and Alesta. The Woman with the Gun's tawny hair came to life, billowing in a sandy, cyclone-like cloud, rotating with fury around them, holding the masses back. Her power uncoiled and was on full display. Such strength she had, hidden from their view all this time, content to present herself as a mere human. The Bellathausers were no match for it. Those that tried to pass through the cyclone were scoured into nothingness, flesh eroded to skeleton, metal flaked away, linkages exposed, circuits sparking.

She gazed at A-Ram and Alesta with reverence and hope. "What are your names?" she asked.

"A-Ram, and my love, Alesta," he replied.

"Love?" she said.

"We don't know your name. You've never told us."

She permitted herself to smile. "My name is Lilly." Saying her name seemed to give her joy. "Ages have passed since I last uttered it. I have a love too." She pointed to the far end of the room. "Go. You said you were here to help me, so I place my faith in you. Help me."

A-Ram and Alesta scurried across the floor, the crowd of Bellathausers, all identical, cawing and reaching through the wall of sand, unable to breach it. Lilly's last words to them resonated.

Help me ...

They entered a corridor. The Shadow tech Goddess was waiting. "I told you to keep up. Look what almost happened."

"That woman, half robot. She tried to seize us."

"That's Bellathauser. That's who we're up against, trying to end this early. Come on, we're almost there."

3—The Library of Time

They moved down a long straight passageway marked with bluish stone blocks, the walls lined at regular intervals with recessed alcoves that at first seemed shallow, but were actually dark and nebulous, going back an apparent great distance.

"Where are we now?" Alesta asked, her hand still buried in A-Ram's. "This little adventure has been terrifying."

"You're in the Hall of Mirrors. You've been here before. This is the threshold between the universes."

"We've never seen it like this," Alesta said.

"It can look like anything." She pointed at an alcove ahead. A beam of yellow light snuck out across the floor and ran up the opposite wall. "Up here and we'll arrive."

A-Ram and Alesta trotted at her side. "Bellathauser told me something."

"Yeah? What did she tell you?"

"She said you're not the Shadow tech Goddess."

"Did she?" The Shadow tech Goddess laughed. "Who knows about anybody?"

They reached the alcove. "Isn't that right?" she asked as she led them inside.

A vast workshop awaited them; the walls lined with shelving and charts of immense complexity and impeccable organization. The shelves were stocked with a great number of round, rock-like devices, each of similar size and construction, but all varying slightly in color. A-Ram and Alesta recognized the devices, for they had seen a similar one many times: Anatameters, hundreds of them.

The Anatameter, innocuous yet unimaginably powerful, was the arcane device that had started this whole adventure across the plains, as they pursued it from one universe to the next.

A man sat at a workbench, his back turned to them. He was thin and elegant, working on yet another Anatameter, this one open; its complicated, bone-like innards exposed. He had long silvery hair that came to the small of his back over a delicate green silk shirt. He wore fitted grey leggings and a pair of knee-high boots constructed of a soft, woodsy material.

He set his tools down and turned to them; even the simple motion of turning his neck seemed fluid and graceful. He was beautiful, almost inhumanly so, his features delicate and perfect. A-Ram recognized him as the man sitting in the throne room frozen in time, always still and inscrutable.

And now here he was; living and whole.

He consulted his timepiece. "I knew you would be coming," he said in a thin voice. "You're late, actually."

The Shadow tech Goddess answered. "I try to be unpredictable. We have a problem. You must correct it." She held out the chart.

He glanced at it with disinterested violet eyes. "I am aware of your problem. I'm supposed to argue, to bemoan your presence in my workshop, to chastise you for allowing this situation to happen in the first place and to ask you to leave. I'll simply forgo those steps and take the chart, for there is no reasoning with you."

"Smart move," the Shadow tech Goddess said as he took the chart.

He glanced at it.

A-Ram and Alesta stood there feeling somewhat overlooked. A-Ram cleared his voice and spoke. "Good sir, we've not been properly introduced. I am—"

The man cut him off. "You are Josephus, 7th Lord of A-Ram hailing from St. Edmunds, Calvert, master helmsman of the MFV *Seeker*, Privateer Wing. With you is Lady Alesta of Dare, 10th Order." The man looked them over. "You realize, of course, that Lady Alesta is one hundred, forty-seven years your elder, as measured on your home world, and that she is a prostitute by trade."

"I certainly am not a prostitute!" Alesta piped, stunned—breathless, holding her green robe shut in a demure fashion.

The man regarded her a moment. "Hmmm, wrong timeline. My apologies."

A-Ram wasn't ready to allow the 'prostitute' remark to pass. He wanted to defend Alesta's honor and press this fellow as to why he called her a prostitute; however, the man had already admitted his mistake and apologized, so he let the matter drop.

The Shadow tech Goddess spoke. "This man is known by a number of unpronounceable names. Simply call him Fiddler Crowe, Lord of Mons Eagle, co-proprietor of the Library of Time and a craftsman of Anatameters. It'll save time, and that's important, right?"

A-Ram had a number of questions. "Did you make our Anatameter?"

"Of course he did," the Shadow tech Goddess said.

Fiddler Crowe wasted little time. "This chart details the life track of a *Kaidar Gemain*, specifically, a man named Stenstrom, Lord of Belmont-South Tyrol."

"Correct," the Shadow tech Goddess said.

He glanced at the chart again. "*Spiralata,*" he pronounced. "Very advanced. Very complex."

"No kidding, why do you think we're here?"

Crowe pushed the chart aside. "This particular plane of existence on your chart is bound for destruction. The role of the *Kaidar Gemain* is to protect the universe from deleterious beings that would do it harm. Sometimes they fail, as in this case, and the universe falls. Let it go, others will take its place. I suggest taking no action." He began working on the open Anatameter again.

"I can't let it go," the Shadow tech Goddess said. "The Celestial Arborium is watching this situation. If this universe goes, then I go with it. I need this *Spiralata* fixed."

Crowe sighed. "You are about to proffer a series of threats promising various punishments and tortures if I do not comply with your demands, none of which interest me in the slightest. Go to your fate. This matter does not concern me. You have no arguments to compel me to action one way or the other."

The Shadow tech Goddess was undeterred. "Sure I do. A demon is at work, taking advantage of the closed loop. It's a demon you know well."

That seemed to get Crowe's attention. He turned from his work. "Bellathauser? Bellathauser exists in this *Spiralata*?" He glanced at the chart a second time, this time with greater attention. "I hadn't anticipated that."

"Of course you didn't. You cannot track Bellathauser's movements. You have no idea where or when she's going to pop up. Well, here she is; in helping us, you help yourself, and your wife."

Fiddler Crowe stood; he was extremely tall to the point of being unnaturally elongated. "Then I will assist you, not only for my wife, as you mentioned, but to rid myself of your presence. Come, let us examine this situation." He cleared room at his worktable and went at the chart with an assortment of delicate silvery tools. He reached for a set of calipers and a lens, which he placed on his head and swung down over his eye.

He abruptly turned to A-Ram, his violet eye filling the lens. "No," he stated.

"Sorry?" A-Ram asked.

He resumed working. "You were about to ask if this woman here is the fabled Shadow tech Goddess. The answer is no."

She blushed slightly. "Well, that's awful presumptuous of you. Stick to the chart and let's make some progress here."

Crowe bent over the table and set to work. The Shadow tech Goddess moved close to A-Ram and Alesta.

"So, who are you, then?" Alesta asked.

The light from her goggles flickered a little. "Doesn't matter. You're here for love, for your friend. So am I. I have a loved one I'm trying to save too. What does matter is the challenge ahead of us, and it's a big one. The demon we're facing is Bellathauser. You saw her, out there in the ballroom.

She is what is known as a *V. Dogan.* A *V. Dogan* is a nasty type of demon. It's an entity that does not exist in the open face of the universe; they exist between the universes in the Hall of Mirrors. They exist nowhere, yet, as with the Hall of Mirrors, they have the potential to be anywhere at any time."

"What does that mean?" A-Ram asked.

"It means that, at some point in time, possibly the past, possibly the future, Bellathauser escaped into the Hall of Mirrors and has resided there ever since, hiding in the Nodes of Reality that lie within, and she was in there long enough to become a *V. Dogan* demon. The Hall of Mirrors functions as a threshold and safe passage from one universe to the next. You've been through it many times. The long corridor dotted with alcoves, that's it, remember? The Hall of Mirrors does not exist in any one universe, therefore the normal laws governing the universe do not apply there. It is technically nowhere, yet it can be anywhere, and so too can the *V. Dogan* lurking within."

A-Ram thought about it for a moment. "Well then, if this place is one where time is not linear, where it may be controlled to your liking, then why not go back in time and correct the matter?"

Fiddler Crowe jumped in, speaking in his droll manner. "There is an Impassability in Time when in the Hall of Mirrors. It does not matter when you were born, or how old or young you are, when you are in the Hall, you have *always* existed, from the beginning of time to the end. A *V. Dogan* entity is one that has managed to take up permanent residence in the Hall, coming out of the various Nodes of Reality at times of its choosing and creating havoc whenever it does. Naturally, they are extremely difficult to eradicate. Destroy one, and another may simply appear and begin the cycle anew elsewhere."

Crowe became engrossed in his work. As they waited, A-Ram and Alesta became a bit bored. They took the opportunity to browse the wonders in his workshop. Many Anatameters of various sizes and colors, all so innocuous, sat on the shelves. Elsewhere, there were ceramic bowls full of small silver cubes, each slightly smaller than a sugar cube. Alesta scooped several up and allowed them to clink about in her hand.

"*Sentrils,*" the woman who claimed to be the Shadow tech Goddess said. "Very versatile arcane items that can be custom-made to perform a specific effect. Name the effect desired and it can be done. Very powerful and quite rare, outside of this workshop anyway. Again, our host has the rare skill of creating them. Quality-made *Sentrils,* like those in your hand, are highly sought after by both the gods and by man. Those few you're holding in your hand, Lady Alesta, are worth a planet's bounty and more."

Startled by this revelation, Alesta put the *Sentrils* back in the bowl.

Another person entered the room from a side door. A-Ram and Alesta turned, as courtesy demanded, to greet the newcomer.

Standing at the door was a slender woman of indelible grace and exceptional height, similar to that of Crowe. She wore a complicated gown made of sumptuous fabrics and glinting jewels, cross-hatched with woven cords of gold. Her blonde hair was worked into an elaborate pinned and tucked style. Around her neck she wore a large, somewhat awkward golden locket sporting six compartments. Each compartment was filled with a vial of festive, brightly colored fluid that looked like liquid candy.

She stood there, her eyes somewhat insensate, her hands held at her midriff in a tentative fashion.

Alesta looked at the woman and gasped.

It was Bellathauser in the flesh standing there, returned to get them, although she was dressed differently than she had been before. A-Ram took Alesta by the shoulders, ready to lift heels and flee with her to safety. He expected some sort of reaction from either the Not Shadow tech Goddess or from Fiddler Crowe.

Crowe did react, but not in the way A-Ram had expected. He put his work with the chart aside, went to her and checked the locket at her neck. Tenderly taking her hands, he led her into the workshop, she following as if in a stupor. He stopped at a cupboard stocked full of vials of colored liquid like the shelves of a heavenly candy store, similar to the ones placed in her locket. He selected several depleted vials from her locket and swapped them out with fresh vials from the cupboard. He then kissed her on the cheek and returned to what he was doing.

The woman seemed invigorated by the changing of the vials. In a moment, gone were the blank expression and open mouth. Now she appeared thoughtful, intelligent and kind. She took notice of A-Ram and Alesta and went to them, gliding with new-found grace. "I'm sorry, I hope I didn't startle you. And who have we here today?"

This woman looked like Bellathauser, but didn't act much like her. A-Ram had a good eye for detail. He quickly gathered information, comparing the two.

Bellathauser, as he recalled, was flesh on the left and robotic on the right, split right down the center. Bellathauser had also been 'compressed down' a bit to disguise her considerable height. Yet this woman was the exact opposite: flesh on the right side and robotic on the left.

Bellathauser's robotic half was a nightmare of knives and ridges, chain mail and spikes all meant to inspire fear and create pain, which, as he had noted, was quite successful. This woman's robotic half was smooth and well-crafted, demure and doll-like in fine porcelain. In fact, it was difficult to tell she had a robotic half, so smooth and life-like was its construction.

She curtsied, her locket of colored vials glittering at her throat. "I am Wendilnight, ruler of this region, side-by-side with my husband, and co-proprietor of the Library of Time. You are most welcome here. I didn't mean to startle you." She noted their apprehension. "I take it from your reaction you've had some dealings with Bellathauser. Am I correct?"

Alesta nodded. "You are."

"She is quite horrid, so I'm told."

A-Ram and Alesta came forward to greet her and introduce themselves. Wendilnight seemed delighted with them. There was a pervasive feeling of benevolence radiating from her, unlike Bellathauser, who fumed with evil.

They made their introductions and Wendilnight curtsied a second time.

"Is she your sister, perhaps, Great Lady?" Alesta asked.

"She is me, my lady, or part of me at least, captured by the Ghrundids and made their queen."

A-Ram and Alesta looked at each other. "What are the Ghrundids?"

From the worktable, Fiddler Crowe answered. "We've no time for vapid explanations. Do not tire my queen."

"No, no," Wendilnight said. "Please. I'll show them. You continue, my love. Their question is fair. I'll show them."

Queen Wendilnight led A-Ram and Alesta out of the work area into a vaulted corridor of gold and lapis. As with the Woman with the Gun, Wendilnight towered over the both of them. A-Ram was becoming rather tired of always being the shortest in the room.

A long flight of grand polished marble steps awaited them. Along the way, they passed a magnificent library full of vast open spaces and inviting nooks lit up in towering golden window-light. A ghostly lady glided through the tables, her form delicate and translucent. She glanced at A-Ram as he passed and smiled. He wanted to stop and have a look, but Wendilnight kept them moving to the stairs. They went up to a small balcony overlooking a pleasant coastline. A telescope mounted on a delicate tripod stood near a rail. She looked through the telescope, training it on a distant point on the horizon.

"Here we are. Please have look."

A-Ram approached the telescope, but the view-finder was much too tall for him to see through. "Your pardon, would you have a stool for us to stand on?"

She blushed a bit. "I'm very sorry. Here, if I may?"

She gently placed her hands on A-Ram's waist and lifted him to the lens. She lifted him effortlessly, as if he were a small child.

A-Ram felt a bit undignified hanging there in midair. He looked through the lens. "What do you see, Rammy?" Alesta asked.

A-Ram squinted as he was held aloft in the gentle hands of Wendilnight.

"I see a bluff overlooking the sea. The water is quite unusual in coloration; it's a rather milky hue. Must be some sort of sediment giving it that color. I see waves breaking and sea foam."

Wendilnight put A-Ram down. "I'm sorry. That is not water you were seeing. Those are the Ghrundids, and Bellathauser is their queen."

A-Ram looked through the telescope a second time. "I don't understand."

"We are immortal here. All of us. A gift from the Elders of old, therefore time has no meaning. Every bit of us is immortal, down to the smallest molecule. The Ghrundids are not whole people. They are bits and pieces, dreaming with malevolence as to what they once were. We are Solfids here, we are whole; they are Ghrundids, they are not whole."

Wendilnight flushed up a bit. "I'm sorry, I am not whole. I am not a Solfid any longer." She stood there in silence, eyes distant.

"Pardon, Great Lady, you were saying?" Alesta asked, trying to stir her from her momentary trance.

Wendilnight smiled. "I'm sorry. The Ghrundids dreamed of a queen, and they stole me from Mons Eagle, splitting me down the middle, making me a Ghrundid too."

"That sounds truly terrible," Alesta said. "How did you escape?"

"I don't know. Obviously, I was not returned whole, but it was not just part of my body that was left behind, most of my soul was as well. My thoughts, my feelings, my knowledge, She has it all. It's only through sorcery that I function. My lockets provide the illusion and memory of what I once was. All of my thoughts and emotions roil in her body, clashing, mismatched, out of joint. She emerges from the Hall of Mirrors different every time. Sometimes she is mindless, other times she is benevolent and soft-spoken, and again sometimes she is cruel and conniving. In any case, her one over-riding goal is to join with me and take me back to the Ghrundids. The Queen of the Ghrundids cannot be in pieces, she must be whole. She is a relentless fiend."

Wendilnight became lost in thought as she sorted through the horrific events in her mind. The fluid levels in her locket bubbled and lowered a little. "Come, let us return. I believe my husband shall have important information for us. Please, come."

They returned to the workshop, down the stairs past the great inviting library, again seeing the ghostly lady gliding amid the books. "Who is that person?" A-Ram asked.

"That is Famela. She is a being we call a Reventor. A Reventor is similar to a Ghrundid, though it retains a consciousness of its own, generally of benign nature. It's an amalgamation of shed particulate matter come together and given form. I will introduce you later."

Along the way, Wendilnight faltered and became unsure of herself.

"Perhaps it's this way," she said tentatively, pointing in the wrong direction. She stumbled and then fell to the ground, her massive locket clattering on the stones.

4—Selecting a *Covus*

"Lady Wendilnight requires her medication immediately!" Alesta said as she and A-Ram assisted her into the workshop. Wendilnight was weak and trembling, her eyes lost in confusion.

Fiddler Crowe came to them and took Wendilnight. He consulted his timepiece. "Not time yet." He pulled out a chair and carefully seated her. Her eyes looked about the room, staring at nothing; her mouth lolled open.

"You see the life she lives," Crowe said, tending to her. "You see what they did to her? My queen is lost."

"Will she be all right?" Alesta asked.

Crowe returned to the work table. He didn't answer Alesta's question.

The Not Shadow tech Goddess came up. "Well, 'all right' is an iffy term. She most certainly is not 'all right'. It's well within Crowe's power to simulate the person Wendilnight used to be via sorcery, but that's all it is—sorcery. Without it, she'd be a mindless, angry Ghrundid rolling around out there in the Ghrundid Sea."

A-Ram stared at the chart, seeing the tangle of lines Fiddler Crowe had drawn. The lines made little if any sense to him; they were a scrawl.

"Have we made any progress?" he asked.

Fiddler Crowe returned to the chart. "Clearly. In this case the demon has not only murdered the *Merthig*, it has also acquired the Anatameter that I built specifically for Lord Belmont and absconded with it. With the Anatameter in her possession the demon is exceptionally powerful; hence the *Spiralata* it has created."

"But," the Not Shadow tech Goddess said, "taking the Anatameter will be the demon's undoing. Listen up; the demon is probably unaware that in stealing the Anatameter—which was made specifically for our *Kaidar Gemain*—she has screwed herself, because her *V. Dogan* Impassability in Time is rendered null in its presence. Bellathauser's Impassability in Time is her best weapon. She's been killed countless times by lots of different heroes, but she just keeps popping back up again—always there's that damn Impassability in Time. Now that she's got the Anatameter, if we can get at her, we can take her out for good."

Crowe continued. "The issue is, per our charting, that Bellathauser has created a parasitic sub-node of reality in which she sits as absolute ruler where, using the Anatameter, she is stealing matter from this universe and knitting it into a chaotic new reality. There is no entrance to this sub-node; the Hall of Mirrors will not go to it. As she consolidates her power, the node she has created will get larger and more destructive, eventually feeding on this universe until it is destroyed and, possibly, taking several others in the process. In order to correct this problem, we must reclaim the Anatameter. Once we have reclaimed it, the sub-node will vanish."

"If, as you say, this sub-node has no entrance, how do we get to it?" Alesta asked.

"We burrow, and we chart. We create a cataract and then we may gain entrance to Bellathauser's sub-node," Crowe said.

"What he's trying to say is we create a weak spot in the fabric of space and time where we can get into her realm," the Not Shadow tech Goddess said. "She punched a hole into this universe, now we're going to return the favor and punch a hole into hers. And then it's on. Then we take her out cold."

"And how do we do that?" A-Ram asked.

"How? With deeds, with monsters, little guy," the Not Shadow tech Goddess said. "With demons. We beat the demon with heroic deeds, and with other demons—fighting fire with fire, as they say."

"And is Bel going to have to face these demons?"

"Oh yes. He's a *Kaidar Gemain*. That's what he's supposed to do, like it or not."

"What demons?"

The Not Shadow tech Goddess adjusted her goggles. "That's what we're going to determine right now."

Fiddler Crowe pointed at the chart with a set of calipers. "We must install something truly horrific to create a suitable ripple in the fabric of space and time. Fortunately, per my calculations, Bellathauser's subnode is still new, just one deadly monster will be sufficient to gain entry. I have a whole cabinetry full of horrors to place." He pointed at an innocent-looking cabinet of cheerful yellow wood at the far end of the room. As A-Ram and Alesta studied it, the cabinet seemed to shudder slightly, to moan, to knock, to whisper. They could only wonder, and dread, at what was inside it.

"Keep 'em," the Not Shadow tech Goddess said. "I have just the thing." From nowhere, she produced a small enameled chest. She opened the lid. Inside was a tiny figurine of a dark, aquatic-looking creature sporting a set of crab-like claws which she placed on the chart marked by Crowe. A cloud of fog spewed from the figurine, soon obscuring it. Two tiny pin-pricks of light appeared in the fog, panning about like a pair of eyes. It made a mournful sound, along with a CLACK! CLACK! CLACK! noise, which was quite disquieting.

"This," she said, "is a tormented creature known as 'The Clacker'. He's the horror of choice for the Punts in their never-ending quest to locate me ... I mean the Shadow tech Goddess. Whenever they need a monster, they go for him. The Clacker will serve our purposes perfectly."

"I disagree," Fiddler Crowe said. "I can think of many more suitable candidates lurking in my cabinet."

"Can you?" she retorted. "It will be The Clacker, I insist." She pointed at it. "This is the reason I got involved in this venture in the first place, for this creature right here."

The little monster on the chart clacked and wallowed in the fog. Its white points of light for eyes blinked.

"What must be done with this entity?" A-Ram asked. "Kill it?"

The Not Shadow tech Goddess shook her head. "Oh, no, no, no, not so easy. It must be saved."

"Which is why it is not ideal for our needs," Fiddler Crowe said. "An easier challenge would simply be to kill."

The Not Shadow tech Goddess gazed at the patch of fog on the chart. "Regardless, I'm certain our boy, the *Kaidar Gemain*, will be up to it. So then, here we are, our piece is set, the path is clear. All we need do now is prevail. Your *Kaidar Gemain* will prevail, he must. I have everything staked on this."

Alesta stepped forward. "And, if I've properly understood all of this, our Lord Belmont, the *Kaidar Gemain*, our friend, must face the thing in the fog and then enter some sort of horror dimension and destroy a demon?"

"Correct," Fiddler Crowe said.

"But Gwen is dead. Bel is alone, probably despondent, in despair. He loved her so. How can we expect him to go off and do these things when his heart is broken?"

"He's going to have to get over it, isn't he?" the Not Shadow tech Goddess said. "He must do these things."

Fiddler Crowe listened to Alesta and thought a moment. He placed a fresh sheet of vellum on the table. "I agree with Lady Alesta. She is quite correct. We must make certain the *Kaidar Gemain* is fully ready to face the perils at hand. The *Merthig* is killed, the power he received from her gone. We shall locate a replacement for the *Merthig*. If the *Kaidar Gemain*'s heart is broken, we shall repair it, along with the universe itself. We cannot afford to fail. We shall find another to entrust his soul and ensure our success."

"And how do you propose we do that?" the Not Shadow tech Goddess asked. "The *Merthig*'s bond to his soul is complete."

Crowe scratched on the vellum at a furious pace, the page fast becoming dark with his writing. "*Covus*," he said. "We find him a *Covus* to compensate for the *Merthig*'s loss."

The Not Shadow tech Goddess shook her head. "A *Covus* is asking for trouble."

"What is a *Covus*?" A-Ram asked.

The Not Shadow tech Goddess answered. "A *Covus* is yet another Extra-Planar Entity. Think of it like this: suppose the *Kaidar Gemain* is a fast, souped-up ship, and the *Merthig* is a turbo super-charger, making the ship run much faster than it ordinarily would. Remove the *Merthig* and the *KG* no longer functions at peak capacity; in fact, the *KG* might not function at all without the *Merthig*. Eliminating the *Merthig*, Lady Gwendolyn, was a crushing blow and the demon knew it. But, in theory, the *Merthig* can be replaced by a person known as a *Covus*. A *Covus* is an anomaly, sort of a one-timer in the universal scheme of things. A *Covus* can restore the *KG* to full power, and beyond—*but*, and this is a big '*but*', you have to have the *right Covus*. A bad *Covus*, a wrong *Covus*, can ruin everything, can seal our *KG*'s fate—and ours too."

Crowe continued to write. "Then we must ensure we select the correct *Covus*."

"Select one?" Alesta asked. "You mean we here in this far away place are going to pick Bel's replacement mate for Gwendolyn?"

"Apparently so," the Not Shadow tech Goddess said.

"I don't like that idea. I don't like it one bit," Alesta said, shaking her head. "Where is free will? Where is choice?"

The Not Shadow tech Goddess pointed at the chart. "Uh, excuse me? When we took up this little quest a couple of universes ago, free will is one of the things that got thrown out the window, ok? The *Merthig* is gone—the demon did us on that one, so the *KG* doesn't get to pick. He's too busy moping around to pick. We pick for him. Crowe's right, we need a *Covus*, and, if you wish your friend to have a fighting chance in what is to come, we had better pick a damn good *Covus*."

A-Ram watched Fiddler Crowe scribble on the page. He wrote so much, the vellum spilled down to the floor in a bumpy curl, growing steadily as he added more, the whole thing black with writing.

"What is he writing?" A-Ram asked.

"Names, candidates. *Covus*. From this list, we will pick a name. And then, once we've picked one, we must take active steps to steer the two of them together. The *Kaidar Gemain* and the *Merthig* are drawn to each other naturally, but not a *Covus*. The *Covus* owe him nothing. We shall have to intervene on their behalf and throw them together. Sort of like a blind date. And the date had better go well."

"You mean Alesta and me are going to do this?" A-Ram asked.

"Would you rather I do it?"

"No. Absolutely not," Alesta said. "If Bel's life is going to be tampered with, then it shall be done by those who love him most."

"Sure. Fine," the Not Shadow tech Goddess replied. "Once Fiddler Crowe is done with the list, you two choose. Make it good—I can't stress that enough, you got me?"

"But how do we know a good candidate from a bad one?" Alesta asked.

As Fiddler Crowe continued his relentless scribbling, the Not Shadow tech Goddess shook her head. "Well, that's the whole trick, isn't it? There is no sure way to make that determination, which is why I hesitated when Crowe brought up the use of a *Covus*—you never quite know what you're going to end up with, do you? Crowe can determine who is a candidate to be a *Covus* for our *KG,* but whether the names on the list are good ones or bad, he has no clue."

A-Ram approached the Not Shadow tech Goddess. "Then, while we wait, tell us your name. If you are not the Shadow tech Goddess, what is your name?"

She considered her response, then: "Atha. My name is Atha."

"I don't know that name."

"You asked. I told you. Look it up if you want. I'm still a goddess, ok, just not the one you were expecting."

"What is your stake in all this, Lady Atha?" A-Ram asked.

Atha considered her answer. "Do you have parents, Lord A-Ram?"

"Yes."

"Do you love them?"

"Of course."

"Then you and I have much in common. That is my stake in this."

Eventually, Fiddler Crowe was done. He rolled up the vellum into an impressively large scroll and gave the list to A-Ram. "Choose. These are the *Covus.* Choose well. I cannot do it for you. Whether the *Covus* helps your friend the *Kaidar Gemain* or ensures his death and the end of this universe depends on your choice. I hope that is clear to you."

Both A-Ram and Alesta were appalled. "I don't think we're qualified to do this," he said, holding the scroll.

"You have as much insight as I do regarding the selection. I have no devices, formulas or glimpses into the future to aid me. You personally know the *Kaidar Gemain* and care for him as your friend. Perhaps that care will assist you in making a proper choice."

A-Ram unrolled the vellum scroll. There were thousands of names on it; the vellum was black with them. Alesta was overwhelmed.

"How are we to choose?"

Fiddler Crowe offered no further insight. He returned to his work with the Anatameter. Atha looked at A-Ram and Alesta and shrugged her shoulders. "Same goes with me. I could pick for you, but again, you know the man, you know his heart. Let that knowledge guide you."

Though hesitant at first, A-Ram was undaunted. "Come. I saw a reading room with tables and books, a very pleasant setting to perform our work.

Let us go there now and set to this." He turned to Crowe. "If food and drink could be brought to us, we would be grateful."

A-Ram and Alesta exited the workshop and went to the library room they had seen. It was a great open hall of towering dimensions and scrolled yellow woodwork lined on all four quarters by books. Shelves went upward hundreds of feet to the indistinct ceiling, all full of books; the spines creating orderly patterns of vibrant color, like dragon scales. They found a centrally-located table. A-Ram seated Alesta and placed the list on the table. Unrolled, the list was five feet long.

"This is hopeless," she said. "Better we shut our eyes, point our fingers and randomly choose."

A-Ram adjusted his lenses. "It's not hopeless. We shall go through every name and determine which is the correct one. They were right; if any must make this choice, it must be us. We will know when we see it." A-Ram took a fresh sheet and went down the list, name by name. He was thorough and meticulous, considering every name. Names he thought promising, he scribbled down on the fresh sheet.

Sometime later, a tray of food and drink came floating in.

"We are served by ghosts," Alesta said as the tray arrived.

"I am no ghost," came a lilting reply. Before their eyes appeared the drifting, somewhat abstract form of a robed woman, the same one A-Ram had seen before. From a distance, she appeared as a translucent, ghost-like figure of a slight pinkish hue, her rounded face, hair-line and robe vague and mixed together. Up close, she was made up of drifting particulate matter, like animated dust on an enchanted wind creating a partially human form alive with minute movement.

"Are you Lady Famela?" A-Ram asked, interested to speak to this entity.

The particles making up her face moved. She smiled. "I am. I am a condensation of many people, of many thoughts given proper order after ages of chaos and fragments of dreams. I have my sanity again, all the voices making up my being working together to provide me with consciousness, though I am, at a basic level, a collection of minute immortal particles. I was rescued from the Ghrundid Sea, and now I tend to the Library of Time and serve the needs of those studying here. This place is a paradise for me. I have brought you refreshments, as you requested."

"Thank you very much. We are pleased to have made your acquaintance."

"You're welcome. The whole of time, from beginning to end, can be researched here. Gods have sat in these very chairs trying to make sense of time itself. I served them, as I now serve you."

"The whole of time? Can we pre-read the outcome of all of this?" Alesta asked, a bit of hope in her voice.

"Of course. Please, before you ask, I can show you the outcome of your search for the *Covus*, but not their identity."

"Then, can we save our friend Gwen?" Alesta asked.

The dust forming Famela's airy form swirled a bit. The abstract form of her face frowned. "No. I'm sorry. The demon that took her life is Impassable in Time. You will try, but you will fail, always fail. I will get you a volume of interest. The future is always difficult to discern, even when it is plainly presented." She drifted away.

Alesta watched her depart. She was excited. "Rammy, I think we should try to save Gwen. If the past and the future are available to us here, then we should try. There must be a way."

"Fiddler Crowe and Atha and Lady Famela didn't seem to think that was possible. They are certainly more expert on the matter than we are. Tempting as it is, we should continue with the list, that was the direction we were given. Most of these names I don't know. But, mixed in here and there, are select names I do recognize. I think we should pick one of those."

"Why?"

"Just a feeling."

Alesta glanced at his list:

Alitrix, Lady of Zama
Tentha Semonea, attendant of Queen Ghome
Grand Dame Miranda of Rossel
Lessa, Lady of Walpole
Christiana of Z-Encarr, Planet Fall
Logan Tom, Charger, Super 6 Brandtball Team
Dorraline of Nalls, #40 of the Xandarr 44
Madame Kilos of Tusck
Trega the Naked
Christa Morgan, Masthead
Analine of Carlton
Mysti Parker of Kentucky, Songstress
Solbrooke of Codis Station
Vroc, Princess of Xandarr
Julia of Fountain-Lock

And on and on, A-Ram's list grew to an enormous length. He continued adding names to the list.

Jennamax of Waam
Annsafour of St Mary
Crewman Kaly of Onaris
Professor Hannah-Ben Shurlamp, Ev, University of Dee
Marie Celebrant of Alderveryl Convent

Allifar the Younger of Twill
Camilla, Baroness of Sorrander

Alesta took note of the last name. "Camilla of Sorrander? Isn't she a Xaphan lunatic who wanted to take over the planet Xandarr? Why in the Name of Creation did you select that one?"

"I don't know. I just thought it sounded intriguing." A-Ram crossed the name out.

Famela returned to their table carrying a great heavy book in her abstract hands. "If I may, Xandarr does not exist in this universe, my lady. The Black Hats wiped it out years ago and it is now a shunned place of darkness."

"Where we come from, Xandarr was saved from Shadow tech. I have a book on the subject," A-Ram said as he continued to add names.

"Not here, I'm afraid," Famela said.

Alesta took note of the book Famela had brought. "What is that?"

Famela set the book on the table. "The future, such as it is. Would you care to look? Though, I warn you, seeing the future is never pleasant."

The book was huge and heavy. Curious, Alesta opened it to a random, creaky page. "This can tell us the future? Can it help us save Gwen?"

"No. Never clearly understood is the future until it is the past, and then nostalgia clouds the issue."

Alesta looked through the book, scrolling through the pages, looking at the pictures. "Oh! I see Bel in the picture," she exclaimed. "He's wearing his HRN coat and is wearing his mask again. We saw that in the fountain on the city square."

"This is not the Lord Stenstrom you know," Famela said. "This image is of the Stenstrom existing in this universe, after the death of Lady Gwendolyn. He is a lost man. He takes solace in his mask, and prowls the city streets alone as a lunatic."

Alesta looked deeper at the picture. Lord Stenstrom was standing on the lofty rooftops of a city by the sea. He gazed out at the buildings around him.

"Oh, Bel," Alesta said, feeling sympathy for him. She turned the pages, skipping ahead in the book.

"Wait," Famela said, alarmed.

Alesta looked at the page she had flipped to. She saw another engraved drawing, this time of a bedraggled woman wearing cheap furs and torn stockings lurking in an alley. The woman appeared to be a prostitute of the most foul and desperate kind.

Alesta took in her features. Her mouth dropped open in horror.

"You are a prostitute," Fiddler Crowe had said.

The woman in the engraving was herself; foul with disease, haggard with the rigors of a hard, sorrowful life. The woman in the engraving didn't look much like Alesta, she just knew it was an image of her. No A-Ram, no wedding plans, no Pilgrims of Merian, no friends; just her, miserable and angry.

She just knew.

"In this reality, you never met Lord A-Ram or became a Pilgrim of Merian. Unfortunately, your life alone has been hard and unrelenting."

Alesta sucked in her breath in terror and shut the book.

Famela was right.

The future was horrifying. "I'm sorry. I'm certain that wasn't something you wished to see. I understand."

A-Ram consoled Alesta. "Are you all right, Bear-Bear?"

Eyes closed, she nodded. A-Ram considered the book. "Does this tome detail our search for the *Covus*?"

"It does, but again, it does not reveal the identity of the *Covus*."

Famela flipped through the pages. "Here, please attend."

A-Ram saw a full-page engraving scratched out across the vellum. In it, he and Alesta stood in a stormy field of grass and fallen masonry.

At their feet, a thin female form lay huddled on the ground in a curled-up position, the ridges of her backbone protruding sharply as if she was badly malnourished. A pile of filthy rags lay nearby, cast aside. Her back was wounded; a great puncture mark near her right shoulder blade dripped a steady stream of blood. Standing next to A-Ram was the sultry robed form of a Black Hat, her face covered with a featureless sash. Nearby, a basin of fire raged.

"That woeful figure, is that the *Covus*?" A-Ram asked.

"It is, yes."

A-Ram stared at the image. He was struck with inspiration. A-Ram got his disk out. Seven names were there, partially covered up by the newly scrawled name: BELLATHAUSER. Gwendolyn of Prentiss' name appeared four times, but she was dead.

The other names were:

Taara

Melazarr of Caroline

Kat

He checked the long list of names again, tracing along with his finger, making his way through the scrawl.

He stopped. He thumped the vellum with his finger.

"Rammy? What is it?" Alesta asked. "Did you find something?"

Nearly hidden amid the sea of names was a tiny, barely readable little scratching:

KAT

"This one! Kat! Her name is also on the disk!"

Alesta took exception. "Kat, who is Kat?"

A-Ram tapped the engraving. "Her! She is Kat, a Black Hat we encountered once near the ruins of Clovis. And here she is again in the picture."

Alesta thought back. "The Black Hat who captured you in Shadow tech. The one who almost killed you?"

"That's the one. Her name appears on my ochre disk as one of the original seven ladies Bel was to be paired up with." He tapped Fiddler Crowe's list. "Here's her name, right here: Kat. She is a viable *Covus*. I think we should select her."

Alesta was open-mouthed with astonishment. "W-why? Who's to say she won't try it again? Perhaps she'll try to kill Bel. If that's the case, we might as well select that horrid Camilla woman from Xaphan space."

"From the way Bel told me the story, I don't think she was trying to kill him. I think she was somehow fascinated with him, and she pulled him out of Clovis after the fiery explosion in the depths, remember that? We've heard Bel talk of Captain Davage's countess, Sygillis, how she was once a Black Hat and then became his loving wife. We've supped with her before—a very enchanting woman. And, though he didn't say anything, I think Bel was aroused by this Kat woman. He was intrigued by her, and he was very sad when she died later on in Caroline. Here she is, alive and well. I feel she is correct. She ... had spirit."

Alesta shook her head. "That list is moot. I'm not comfortable with the thought of Bel pairing up with a Black Hat. She could lead him to ruin."

"And she could save his soul, too. I think she is the correct choice," A-Ram persisted. "Bear-Bear, I'm certain of it!"

Alesta nodded and turned to Famela. "Great Lady, were we to select this Black Hat, how would we go about bringing her to Bel? Black Hats are very dangerous."

"Steps would have to be taken. Safeguards would have to be prepared."

Alesta looked up and down the list of names one more time. "Rammy, you're sure about this?"

"I am, Bear-Bear. Kat is the one."

Alesta put her arms around A-Ram, savoring his feel. "All right, then. I trust in your judgment. Kat it is."

Famela clapped with her ghost-like hands. "I will inform Master Crowe and Goddess Atha of your decision."

5—Buying a Black Hat

The small craft broke the line of angry clouds and wobbled through the rough air as it descended to the ground. It sweated curling streams of rainwater and soot from its recent re-entry; the water corkscrewing away from its aerodynamic shape. Down below, a sea of slate-colored water pounded the shoreline of a great continent, sending a steady stream of breakers and foam to the drenched rocky beach, one after the next.

The craft leveled out at a thousand feet and headed inland, passing over unbroken miles of olive, tumbled grassland and occasional ragged trees. The air was rough, but the craft flew straight and steady with a deft hand.

Down below appeared an area of leveled ground. The remains of a stone structure, possibly once tall and grand with fluted columns and carved balustrades peeked through the wild grasses, partially covered with weeds and flattened by the relentless march of time. The craft slowed over the level ground and banked, circling the ruins.

Standing in the ruins was a solitary figure wearing a shockingly bright scarlet robe, a black sash covering its face. The figure stood with practiced grace; arms crossed over its chest, hands nested in its sleeves. The ship landed a short distance from the figure. Hatches opened. Two people got out, immediately saturated by the rainwater.

The figure in scarlet didn't move as they approached. The rain came down in soaking streams but not a drop touched the figure; all the rain fell around it, changing course, leaving the figure perfectly dry. The figure spoke in a strong, clear voice easily heard over the rain and the fierce wind. "Welcome," it said in a staccato tone. "You have arrived exactly as you promised. We appreciate such punctuality."

The two stood before the figure and presented themselves; a man and a woman dressed in League clothing. They were both of slight stature; the man in a suit, the woman in a green brocade robe. The man carried a raincatcher, shielding the woman from the deluge. Her thick dark brown hair was pinned up, the loose ends catching life in the wind.

The size and shape of the figure in scarlet indicated there was a slender female under the sash and robe, though her voice was harsh and wiry, unidentifiable as belonging to a female.

"We understand you wish to buy the services of a Black Hat," the figure said.

"We do!" the woman in green answered, shouting to be heard over the rain.

"There are many Black Hats, scattered across the heavens. Their temples are no secret. Their doors are open to any who wish to pass. We entreat you to select one of those. This is a place of training ... and faith."

The man spoke. "We will not venture into the open door of a Black Hat's temple, for few ever come out again."

"And do you think death will not come for you here?" the figure asked. Tendrils of Shadow tech rose up out of the ground like headless snakes dangling on a string, surrounding the man and woman in a threatening fashion.

"Death comes for us all," the figure in scarlet added.

The man and woman showed no fear. "Indeed it does. However, here we are protected," the man replied. He reached into his coat and produced three silver cubes of fine workmanship. He placed the cubes on the ground around them in a triangular fashion. The Shadow tech snakes struck, hissing, seeking their flesh. They penetrated the perimeter of the silver cubes and instantly collapsed into wet cinders. All that entered were obliterated.

"You see, we are not helpless," the woman said. "We have the favor of the gods and access to their tools."

The figure in scarlet considered that and seemed impressed. With a wave of her hand, the Shadow tech creatures vanished. "Are those *Sentrils?*"

"They are, and of the finest quality. Worth enough to ransom this hellish place many times and again," the man said.

"How novel," the Black Hat said. "You must have mortgaged your paltry souls for such rare celestial help. Very well, what do you want?"

"We are looking for a Black Hat to trawl the ruins of our ancestral holdings in the Vithlands of Kana for us."

"Are you? It is not often we have visitors from the League looking to procure the services of a Black Hat. Such things are not forgiven by your beloved Sisters."

"We are looking for clues as to the location of our ancestral fortune. The Sisters have declared the area forbidden and offered us no recourse. We will have our fortune. We must take extraordinary action in this case. We must have results, and a Black Hat can surely get them for us."

The Black Hat appeared disappointed. "Such things do not interest us. Certainly some sailor or denizen from a lesser caste or League club could assist you. There are heroes in the League for hire, are there not?"

"And what of the Shadow tech Goddess? Does she not interest your mistress?" the man asked.

The Black Hat thought a moment and changed her tune. "The Shadow tech Goddess? What know you of this entity?"

"We know your mistress, the Black Abbess, lives in mortal terror of her."

The Black Hat disagreed. "Our mistress, the Black Abbess, is not capable of feeling fear, but please, go on."

"We have heard that information pertaining to the identity of the Shadow tech Goddess may be found deep in the darkness of our ruins."

"If such news is to be had, then we shall send a Black Hat of great power and repute to secure the information. Where is this information located?"

The man shook his head. "We require one from this facility to go, and the location is secret for now."

"There are naught but trainees here. Unfortunately, many shall not survive to graduate and strike out on their own. Such is the existence of a Black Hat. For every one that lives, hundreds die."

The figure awaited a reaction from the pair. "Does that distress you? Such nice League people … Such horrors you need never experience."

The man would not budge. "We know full well the brutality that takes place here, and should fortune smile, perhaps the League will come in force some day, free all those enslaved within and wipe this place clean. Until that happy day occurs, we want a Black Hat from here."

The figure in scarlet also would not budge. "And what is your reasoning, please? As I said, we have naught but trainees."

"Our reasoning? Shouldn't it be obvious?" the man said. "We will not be having some full-powered Black Hat tyrant running loose on our ancestral holdings, giving lease to all things unholy, releasing StTs and Creation knows what else, inviting discovery and reprisal from the Sisterhood of Light on our Household."

"We do not fear the Sisters."

"But we do and you ought to as well. We will take one of the wretched waifs cowering in the darkness here, else we shall take your advice and return to the League and hire some local hero to assist us. Your Black Abbess mistress will know nothing of what is found."

"Think you to leave here with such information?"

The Shadow tech demons came up from below in a smoky dance a second time, circling their protected perimeter, scraping, pecking, searching for a weak spot. The woman produced a silver rod from her robe and held it up. In an arcane vacuum, the Shadow tech demons were pulled into the rod, while others were destroyed.

The Black Hat was impressed by their display of the arcane and relented. "Very well, if you wish a trainee, we shall offer you four. Four shall ensure our mutual success."

"Four is fine. We wish to personally select these four."

The figure in scarlet bowed with a flourish. "First, our payment shall be weighty. First, we will have the information regarding the Shadow tech Goddess. Second, we demand those *Sentrils* you carry. Those are our demands, what say you?"

"You may have the information and do with it what you will," the man said. "As for the *Sentrils*, you may not have these as they are our protection. However, we can offer you others."

"Others? More *Sentrils*? The measure of your wealth is astounding. We accept the payment." The Black Hat vanished, leaving the man and woman alone on the stormy surface.

Soon, the figure in scarlet returned. With a wave of her tiny hand, a seven foot tall conveyor belt made of Shadow tech sprouted from the ground with machine-like precision and formed across the ruined platform. The conveyor came up from a passage leading down, went directly past the man and woman, and then went back down the passage, making a rather large circle. The conveyor sported an assembly of sharp hooks dangling from Shadow tech chains. It started moving, the hooks clinking together. Soon, smallish bodies clad in rags appeared from below and moved down the line in silent, efficient assembly-line fashion, swinging from the hooks like slabs of skewered meat.

"Here they are, fresh trainees on the hook, aren't they tasty? Please, we have many to choose from," the figure said.

As the hanging bodies passed by, they noticed the hooks were plunged into their writhing flesh, dripping blood. The woman put her hand to her mouth and said a few words to the man.

He addressed the figure in scarlet. "Must they be treated so?"

The figure delighted in their discomfort. "Yes, they must," it said in a giddy voice. "We will not trot them out before you like giggling school children. Pain and suffering is what we have here. They would understand nothing else."

The little bundles of dirty rags came and went. All of them were small females, some not much older than mere children. Some appeared to be dazed and out of their heads; some twitched in agony, breathlessly screaming. Others passively hung from the hooks, arms and legs dangling as if nothing was happening to them.

Ragged females passed by, one after the other, each filthy and half-starved. Each Shadowmarked. The man and woman inspected them carefully as they passed. So many. Hundreds went by.

"Will their wounds be treated?" the woman asked.

The figure shook her head. "No, League woman, they will not. Perhaps they will die. These are all crawler adepts, all threadbare and starving. Many shall not live to see the nightfall. All they know is pain and suffering with the unlikely prospect that they might one day be granted the power to inflict pain and suffering on others. I notice from your actions you seem to be searching for someone specific. Is that the case?"

"Yes," the man replied.

"A loved one perhaps, taken from your midst?"

"No."

"Then what are you seeking? Tell me."

"That is our business."

The figure in scarlet raised its hand and a great basin of fire formed at the end of the conveyor, the upcoming hanging bodies to be dumped into it and burned alive. "Well then, we shall simply do away with the rejects. If they are not good enough for the League, then they are not good enough for us. Nothing lost, we suppose. We shall replenish this school afresh."

The woman lost her composure and was terrified. She tugged on the man's sleeve. "Rammy!"

The first body neared the basin of fire, ready to be dumped in and roasted alive.

"Stop!" the man cried.

The line of bodies on the conveyor belt suddenly halted; the bodies knocked about on their hooks, their chains rattling. The fire basin remained unfed, demanding nourishment.

"See one you like?" the Black Hat asked, interested.

The man hurried down the line, inspecting each hanging body. Some murmured in pain as he passed. He said a prayer for them and continued. The woman moved along at his side.

"Is she here, do you see her?" she asked.

"Not yet. I simply didn't want the others to perish in flames. This is a place of unimaginable cruelty. I knew that would be the case, but to see it …" He shuddered.

They neared the end of the line. "What if she's not here?" the woman asked, frantically. "Rammy, what if she's not here?"

"I don't know, Bear-Bear. I don't know."

As they neared the end of the conveyor, the man stopped. High above him hung a bundle of filthy rags. A bare foot dangled out of the ends. Drops of blood came down in a steady cadence.

He moved the rags aside and studied the woman beneath them for a bit, then he pointed. "This one!"

"Rammy, are you certain?" the woman asked.

"I am. It's her, it's Kat!"

"This one?" the Black Hat asked. "Why this one? She's a wretch among wretches, not even worthy to present to Xaphan sailors as bait."

"This is the one. Bring her down at once."

"Very well."

The chain extended, roughly bringing the small body down to the ground. The man and woman sorted through the rags like opening a present to get to the naked body within. Uncovered, the female was tiny and emaciated, her starving bones protruding through her taut veil of dirty skin. She was coated with layers of dirt and soot. She stank, enough to make their eyes water. Even in the rainy outdoors her stench was choking. Her torn fingernails were black and clotted with blood.

Despite all that, the man and woman tended to her as best they could, laying their hands on her tiny body. As a result, hints of snowy skin and whitish blonde hair appeared through the layers of grime. Her Shadowmark stood out around her right eye. Streaks of hot blood from the hook pulsed down her back in steady ripples.

"May we please remove the hook?" the woman asked.

"Does it distress you that this girl is in pain?" the figure in scarlet said.

"Yes, it does."

The figure relented and the hook vanished, leaving a gushing hole. The man and woman tended to her. He removed his coat and pressed it against the wound. Her eyelids opened a little, revealing confused green eyes beneath. There was no hint of recognition or intelligence in her. Her mouth hung open in a flaccid 'O' shape.

The Black Hat burned with curiosity. "I ask again, why this one? She's smaller than most, and weak. She's a poor tender of our mistress' Shadow tech. My, doesn't she stink of all the pain we've inflicted upon her."

He double checked her Shadowmark. "This is the one," he said to the woman. He stood. "And I'll say again, our reasoning is our own. This is the one we want. We wish to take her with us this very day. She'll not endure your pits any longer."

"You may not have her. She belongs to us. She will leave when we believe her to be ready."

"Then we wish her healed and quickly sent to the place of our choosing."

"She shall need training first. She is a wretched crawler."

"Then train her."

"You have three more to select," the Black Hat said. "We insist upon four to ensure the information is timely gathered. Our mistress demands it."

"The next three down the line, they shall do," the man said.

The figure snapped her fingers and the three fell to the ground, each a writhing pile of rags, arms and legs. "We shall subject these four to an enhanced and rigorous training regimen." The Black Hat snickered. "They might die in the process, does that distress you?"

"This one cannot die," the man said, pointing to the girl at his feet.

"She might die," the Black Hat repeated flatly.

The woman whispered in his ear. "*What do we do? She can't die. All of our preparations ...*"

The man stood tall. "If she dies, you and your mistress will not have the information pertaining to the Shadow tech Goddess, and nor shall you have our *Sentrils*. Let your mistress quake with fear at that. Therefore, it would be in all our best interests if she lived."

The figure in scarlet didn't answer.

The man looked down at the girl's groggy face. He could smell her from where he stood. "She won't die. I know she'll be fine." He leaned down and spoke into her ear. *"Be strong. You have much to live for."*

She blinked. Her green eyes moved a little.

With that, demons in Shadow tech smoke came up as before. The girl was taken away, along with the other three they had selected. "Just remember," the man said. "We shall be watching."

The man and woman collected their *Sentrils*, returned to their ship and took their leave, both of them heartbroken at the terror of this place and fearing for the tiny girl they had saved from the fire.

You have much to live for, he had said to her.

6—Baked Chicken

Atha, the Shadow tech Goddess, whatever she chose to call herself, was furious. She loomed over A-Ram and Alesta, the purple light from her visor staining the pools of blood on the floor a dark black.

"This is the one you picked?" she spat, her voice shallow with anger. "*This?*"

A-Ram and Alesta leaned over Kat's twisted body, blood all around her. Another body lay nearby, throat ripped out, covered in dry blood. A-Ram and Alesta had seen it all from the fountain in Mons Eagle, and it had been horrifying. These two had fought to the death; Kat, their adopted daughter, and the one called Wheel.

Wheel dead.

Kat, mortally wounded, soon to follow.

Another body lay near the wall, a twisted up corpse draped in black feathers, the one Kat had named Bird. Horribly murdered.

They held Kat's hand; it was limp and clammy. They fretted over the terrible gaping wound Wheel had dealt her, her chest bubbling with Shadow tech poison. They tried to stem the bleeding, but there was no stopping it.

"She's bleeding out. I can feel her ribs through this hole," A-Ram said. "She needs help. Can you help her?"

Atha placed her hands on her hips. "You know, I had hopes that you two would steer right and make a good choice. I had hoped we'd all get out of this mess smelling like a rose. I thought you two were cute, you both impressed me with a good head on your shoulders—and that's hard to do, I tend to be a cynic. It's easy for the gods to be cynics. Now look where we are, standing in the bloody dark with Bellathauser laughing at us from the safety of her *Spiralata*, and I've got a twig-like Black Hat in front of me who smells like yesterday's dinner. You expected … *this* … to replace our *Kaidar Gemain*'s dead *Merthig*? What's she going to do, bore him to death?"

Alesta looked up scornfully at Atha. "She's going to die. Are you going to help her or not?"

Atha kicked Wheel's body over. Dead, nude, covered in blood, throat gone. "Why bother? Ha! At least this one's a got a little meat on her bones. Not a ratted-up string bag like the one you foolishly picked."

A-Ram struggled to pick up Kat's twisted body. "Bear-Bear, help me." Together, A-Ram and Alesta picked Kat off the floor.

"Where are you two headed?" Atha asked.

"We're taking her out of the dark," Alesta said. "We're going to help her if we can, since you will not. We need air and light."

They shambled away toward the shaft of light of the distant stairs. Atha watched them depart. "You know who you're talking to? You know what I could do to you both?"

They didn't answer. They began the long climb up the stairs to the day-light, carrying Kat's tiny body between them.

Atha called to them: "If she dies along the way, we're done, got me? Done! And you know what it means if that happens?"

They moved down the hillside, seeing the statues that the demon had defaced. Atha's words followed them as they hurried into the ruins, the both of them wondering with every step whether Kat would expire.

Somehow, she continued to breathe, continued to live. They brought Kat back to her 'home', the ruin she had selected. Here in the dusty rooms of hard stone, they saw the little pile of books she had collected but couldn't possibly know how to read; her clothes they had provided for her; the empty containers of food Alesta had made; the anti-Shadow tech *Sentrils* Fiddler Crowe had designed and, the centerpiece of it all, the photograph of Lord Belmont, decorated with carefully placed rocks and little trinkets of woven grasses. Much of the lavender soap Alesta had given her was molded into little pink figurines of people and animals, some crafted with remarkable skill—the one named Bird had made those.

All her keepsakes and sole possessions in the world were carefully cherished in this dusty room.

They laid her on the hard floor and removed her bloody clothing. She had gained a little bit of weight in both fat and muscle since she first arrived, eating the food Alesta had made for her, her body no longer the skinny pile of bones it once was. Her skin was relatively clean from washing in the cistern, rubbed smooth with rocks; despite not using the soap they had pro-vided for her, the vile, choking stench she once bore from the Shade Church was thankfully gone. Her hair was still a mess, a hopeless tangle of matted and snarled platinum-blonde locks. Her hands were clotted with blood—blood from Wheel whom she had killed. Alesta wept as she looked at her. Cruel Shadow tech claws sprouted from Kat's hands and an uncomfortable-looking framework of Shadow tech was fastened to her arms, torso and legs, forcing her into a contorted crouched position like a tiger. A long tail sprouted from the base of her spine.

"Look at all this," Alesta said, cradling her. "These claws, this Shadow tech bitten into her flesh. She sleeps on the naked stone like an animal, no pillow, no padding—they tore up the ones we gave them. Look at the pain she's endured. She's never known a day's worth of comfort or love."

"We loved her, Bear-Bear. We gave her hope."

The Shadow tech framework was horrifying to look at. A-Ram took the *Sentrils* and placed them around Kat's body. Instantly, the Shadow tech fell apart into cinders; claws gone, tail gone, framework gone, allowing them to lay her out flat. Alesta stroked her blonde hair, snarled and bedraggled, a hopeless mess. A-Ram checked the wound in her chest; it was terrible.

A folded piece of paper lay nearby. A-Ram glanced at it.

Dearest Kat

Soon our Lord Belmont is coming. It won't be long.

He has lost so much, right here in these very ruins. Every year he comes to stand here where his love and his spirit died. He is a shell of his former self. It is our hope that you will help him to re-discover himself, and in the process, discover yourself as well. We selected you, from a universe of candidates. There is so much potential in your heart just waiting to come out, we have seen it, such that we have entrusted the soul and well-being of our dear friend to you.

We love you.

"Why did you write her that letter, Bear-Bear?" A-Ram asked. "You know she can't read."

"I wanted to inspire her, to create some mystery, drive her on to learn what the letter said. I guessed the Shadow tech demon would have read it to her. I didn't know it would create such strife."

"So, is she dead?" came Atha's voice from across the room. Clacking on her black heels, she entered and moved toward them one deliberate step at a time, her starry cape fluttering lightly, the top of her face hidden under her helmet. "This little creature you staked everything on, is she dead?"

A-Ram took Kat's hand. "No, she lives, but barely."

Atha looked around the room, seeing nothing but dust and ruins. "Well then, I lost that bet, I suppose. Are you ready to admit the poor choice you made? Are you ready to begin your punishment for failure?"

Alesta hugged Kat round the neck and shoulders, protecting her. A-Ram stood, tiny but defiant, before a goddess. "We didn't make a mistake. We chose correctly, I'm more certain of it now than ever."

Atha scoffed, her helmet glinting in the dim light. "Yeah? You selected an unimpressive, filth-covered twig from the Black Hats' basement. I saw the list Fiddler Crowe gave you, I went over the names. There were warlords and Marists from the heights of Xaphan society. There were *real* Black Hats listed, a couple of Sisters mixed in too, some Fleet officers, Warbird captains, members of the Learned and the Chaste, of the Hospitalers and the Science Ministry—some pretty impressive names. There was even a fricken' Brandtball player on there! How cool would that have been?" She ground her teeth in a threatening manner. "So tell me, why this homely little … *nobody*, and your explanation better be good, otherwise I'm going to disincorporate the three of you right here and now and punch my own ticket to the Hell of the Gods. I'm probably going to be heading there anyways for all of this."

Tears dripped down Alesta's face. She gripped Kat tighter. A-Ram stood there, unafraid. He waited a moment, then walked across the floor, passing Atha along the way.

"Excuse me," he said as he passed. He located the pile of ceramic containers holding the food they had been sending her. He rummaged through the containers and selected one, bringing it to Atha. "Here," he said holding it out. "This is why we picked her."

Atha's lip curled in incredulous disgust. "*What's this?*" She looked into the container, seeing a few pieces of baked chicken in a simple peppery sauce.

"What's this?" A-Ram asked. "This is everything. This little girl, who seems like nothing to you, shines with rare light and these few pieces of food prove it. She saved this food for the one she called Wheel. She set it aside in the event Wheel would emerge from the depths hungry, in need of food; that same Wheel who tried to kill her and whose throat she was forced to tear out. The concept of sharing, of consideration, of sisterhood, and yes, of love, should be unknown to her, but she embraced them. She has endured more pain than anyone should ever be expected to, it's all she's ever known, and still she shines. Wheel behaved as Kat should have given her background: ruthless, selfish, obsessed with power, wanting nothing more than to inflict all the pain she'd felt in Shade Church on others, yet our Kat stayed in this place for love, for the promise of love. Love is something she has never known, it's yet another concept she barely understands, and yet she clung to it, keeping her sane through the darkness, allowing her to rise above the horrors of the Shade Church. And she managed to share her dreams with her companions, to enrich them, to save them from becoming mindless, hate-filled Black Hats with the prospect of a better life based on love. Though she was terrified, love drove her into the depths to try to save her companions, whom she loved. This innocent little girl did all that with no guidance."

Atha glanced at Kat's hands, clotted with blood. "Innocent, huh?"

"She did what she had to do, isn't that what's expected of us all? For all these things, this tiny soul is the person who can save our lord and make right this place, and if you can't see that, if you're fixated on ritzy names, on Marists and warlords and Brandtball players, then you're just as bad as

Wheel and the bloody demon."

Atha snickered. "Am I?" She turned to walk away.

"Don't you turn your back on her!" A-Ram shouted.

Atha stopped in her tracks. She turned back to them, lips pursed, eyes hidden behind her blaring purple visor. A-Ram wondered if this was it, if he had angered a goddess. "Alesta," he whispered. "Run, flee, save yourself. If there's killing here, I'll endure it. Go."

Alesta took his hand, not budging.

Atha saw all this and smiled. "You know, you never fail to amaze me. I threaten you with obliteration, and you respond to me with baked chicken. That takes some dash." She laughed, leaned down and looked at Kat's pale, skinny body with new appreciation. "I like the two of you. You're both full of surprises, which is good. Even a goddess likes to be surprised every so often. You give me a skinny little Black Hat trainee with an unsightly bird's nest of hair and a pair of bee stings for tits, and you sell her to me like a champ. Like a real pro." Atha threw up her hands. "Ok, you got me, I'm sold. You made a good choice, I'll admit it."

Alesta was full of hope. "Then you'll save her. Heal her wounds?"

"Sure, sure ..."

Kat gasped and convulsed a little. Alesta felt her hand move. Atha went to the window and looked out. "There, easy, wasn't it? You said she had no guidance. You're wrong—she had the two of you. If you can inspire me, you can inspire her too. Every day she lives to see the dawn, she has the pair of you to thank, not just for today, but for seeing her in the darkness of Shade Church. I suppose you're right, I wouldn't have noticed her, but fortunately you two did." Atha placed her hand on her chin and gave Kat another appraisal. "Would you like me to jazz her up a bit? Maybe a little padding in the rear end, some hip action, and maybe some semblance of a chest?"

Alesta lovingly looked Kat over. "Our lord requires none of those things. He will accept her as she is. I think she's beautiful."

"Then you're easily impressed, aren't you? Fine. Suit yourselves. Now, I'm going to blank her memory a bit, wash away all this unpleasantness. She'll remember the things she needs to know, but her companions and all this blood-letting today, she won't remember a thing. We don't want her wandering off—this is the place where she needs to be, right?"

"It is," A-Ram said. "Bel will be here shortly to mourn the anniversary of Gwen's death."

"Fine. Also, I notice there's a Black Hat missile sitting outside just waiting for the Sisters to come along and discover it. If they do that, they'll be crawling all over this place, and no *Sentrils* ever made will keep them from sniffing her out and butt-dragging her off to Valenhelm or Twilight 4 for a killing. I'm going to get rid of the missile for you, think nothing of it. So, when can we expect our boy, the *Kaidar Gemain*, to show up?"

"Two weeks."

"Good, good. So, our little blind date is in the offing. I hope our girl here makes a good showing."

Alesta doted on the unmoving Kat. "You're going to be amazed. Kat's going to be a true lady from day one. Our lord will be impressed by her grace and civility, and it won't be long before he cherishes her."

Atha shook her head. "Ok, let's get this show rolling. It's time for our girl here to get to saving the universe."

Part III

Kat

Stenstrom, Lord of Belmont-South Tyrol

1—Lord Belmont

There was something wrong at Clovis ...

For Stenstrom, the lord of the fabulous House of Belmont-South Tyrol, life had been a grand adventure, carefree and exciting. His father, Lord Stenstrom the Older, was a revered Warbird captain in the Stellar Fleet, his mother a socialite and top level sorceress wise in the hidden ways of Tyrolese black magic, an art she had taught to him and his stately twenty-nine sisters in the culverts under the city. Wealthy and with an abundance of spare time, he stood in the grand manor by the sea and dreamed of one day faring among the stars, like his father. His mother had once seen first-hand the desolation of the Planet Xandarr and developed a powerful fear of space faring. She insisted her only son, Stenstrom the Younger, keep his boots on the ground; in fact, she put him to a Blood Promise swearing he would never join the Stellar Fleet like his father. Under a pair of full moons and the flickering light of a flaming hot knife, drugged and carried out by the shoulders, she made him promise. Break the promise and he would die, his chest bursting open. The love of his overbearing mother often carried a heavy price.

But Stenstrom wouldn't let his dreams die. He figured out a loophole in the promise he had made. He had promised never to join the Fleet, but said nothing about faring the stars as a civilian. Tall and handsome, he pursued a profession generally populated by less athletic types: a paymaster; a clerk and behind-the-scenes bean-counter for lack of better terms. Bedecked with his NTH pistols and mystical MARZABLE daggers, Paymaster Stenstrom sailed the stars as a self-styled cavalier in his Vith hat and grand HRN coat; adventuring, fighting, putting his knowledge of Tyrol sorcery to the test and winning the respect of his Captain Davage. Years later, when the Davage's old ship, the venerable Warbird *Seeker* came up on the blocks, he used his wealth and 'bought' the captain's chair. Money talked in the Fleet; however, the Admiralty, hoping to cheat the 'clerk' out of his chair and make an example of him, half-scuttled the *Seeker*, leaving her in pieces in the hopes he would fail and forfeit his money.

Gwendolyn, Lady of Prentiss, commander of the scouting ship *Demophalon John,* had been sent by the Admiralty to stop him, clap him in irons or kill him if she had to. In the Deep Sea of space, as Lord Belmont struggled to get the scuttled *Seeker* to Bazz, they met as antagonists; the two of them pitted against each other by the schemes of the Fleet Admiralty, who were keen to see Stenstrom fail. But, despite their situation, they saw each other, feeling a kinship and bond, and then fell in love deep in the Kestrals' tank at Cronyn World. The first time he kissed her was on Bazz, dancing across a crowded ballroom floor at the Fleet Annex Teflegar Martin II, his mission won. He had kissed many women in his day, but politely kissing Gwen on that confetti-covered floor seemed a singular, seminal moment; a grand exhalation that had been a lifetime in the making.

There was nothing he couldn't accomplish with Gwen at his side. He was stronger, wittier, better ... a better man with Gwen.

But then Gwendolyn died, and all his zest for life, all his energy and restlessness died with her. His time with Gwen was relatively short, less than a year, yet he felt like he had known her the whole of his life, his spirit connected to hers across the Kanan landscape, waiting for the moment when they would come together at last. Mad with grief, he wasn't a quarter of the person he had been when beside her. He had wealth, he had his ship that he labored with Gwendolyn to acquire, but none of that mattered with her gone. He withdrew from society like a sorrowful spinster, drifting through his manor by the sea like a ghost. He neglected his ship and eventually lost it for his failure to meet his privateering quota. The Fleet took the *Seeker*, hauled her to Onaris by the nose and melted her down for scrap in the smoky boneyards of Inarri.

A fitting end for both the ship and the man.

His sister Lyra worried about him, seeing the light vanish from his eyes. Wearing his old mask, he took to wandering, leaving his manor for long periods of time, telling nobody where he went or when he would be back. Sometimes he was gone for weeks; his wandering the passing whim of a lost, heartbroken man in the hopes of filling yet another empty day turned to obsession.

Stenstrom often wandered out into the stately lands of Zenon and stared at Gwendolyn's family manor, old Prentiss Hall, rising up terraced and small-windowed behind ivy-covered walls. He imagined seeing her familiar sturdy face staring out at him through the windows. When the scouting ship she once commanded, the *Demophalon John*, made berth in Tyrol port, he always requested to board and walk the corridors, looking for some small trace of her passing. There was nothing in the ship commemorating her command; no portrait, no memorial plaque, nothing; not even dust accumulated in the corners. An Evidencer casing the ship for minute particles shed by Gwendolyn, a flake of skin or a tiny hair, would find not a trace. The ship had moved on, her tenure as its commander swept away and wiped clean, now just a forgotten footnote nobody but he cared to remember.

He had been to the Fleet annex on Bazz a few times since her death, standing on the fine wooden floor where they once danced, remembering the lace and confetti that fell, the cloying bubbles and spritz of uncorked champagne, the high hopes of a newly won command, savoring the return of her phantom lips against his. The music that had played still rattled like a dirge in his head.

There was another place associated with Gwen that he visited once a year, though he despised it: The Ruins of Clovis, the place where she died.

How he now wished he had turned the odd woman away, perhaps Gwen would still be alive. The woman had come aboard during the heady days of the *Seeker* hoping to procure his services. As a Privateer of the Fleet, he sometimes lent his sword out for hire. This woman, this Queen Wendilnight as she called herself, had an interesting story to tell, and he loved a good story. Per her instructions, all he had to do was transport a small device she called the 'Anatameter' to an underground area in the Ruins of Clovis and place it on a 'socket' that had been custom-built for it—and that would be all. She had money, several years of quota-worth just for this one small task. It sounded easy. Gwen was skeptical, thought it was a fool's errand unworthy of a Fleet Warbird, but he didn't listen. He accepted and took the tiny, uninteresting Anatameter to Clovis. He should have gone alone, he was the Sisters' man after all, glorious in the power they lent him, but Gwen insisted on coming. She could be so stubborn; the most stubborn person he knew.

The recriminations of that day were endless. He should have gone alone to Clovis. But there she was, tall Gwen, beautiful in her Fleet uniform, striding through the ruins at his side, locating the stairwell descending into the living earth where the old Clovis performed their arcane rituals. He struggled to keep his wits about him as they descended. Something wasn't right about the place. Hallucinations danced before his eyes. Stenstrom saw many versions of himself lurking about in the dark; some quite similar and others vastly different. He saw himself in innumerable guises, he even saw himself as a woman. And he saw many versions of Gwen swirling around him as well. She took the Anatameter and placed it atop a column of stone, a 'socket' where it seemed to want to go.

The visions were overwhelming.

He saw Gwen as his countess.

Gwen as a mariner. Gwen as a scholar.

He saw Gwen dead, as an angry ghost.

A short time later, she was dead.

The Anatameter gone.

Killed by a demon that had walked out of the walls in veils of blue light.

When the hallucinations ended and reality set in, there was barely anything left of her smoking, riddled body to return to Prentiss.

Clovis … where Gwen died.

And the anniversary of her death was coming soon.

2—A Persistent Professor

He had been beset by letters lately. Stenstrom never had much of a care for letters and League Society, and it was doubly so now after the death of Gwen. He left most of them unopened. His sisters still in attendance at the manor would handle anything pressing.

Gwen would have been on top of things ...

One gray afternoon, his closest sister, Lyra, came to him with a veritable sack of letters and dumped it out before him.

"What's this?" he asked.

"These are letters for you, Bel."

He glanced at the impressive stack. He was uninterested. "You attend to them, please. Or burn them, I don't care."

Lyra seated herself. "Burn them? I don't like this morass you're in, Bel. It's not healthy. I miss Gwen too, but you can't just sit here like nothing. Remember when Nylar's husband died, she acted as you are now, but we didn't allow her to fade away, did we? We took steps to get her living again."

Stenstrom didn't reply. He was in no state for a lecture; he barely heard her. He felt dead himself. This morass went beyond mere grief; it was as if his skeleton and his heart along with all his vitals had been pulled out of his body, leaving him completely empty.

Alive, but dead.

Undaunted, Lyra sorted through the letters, trying to spur him on, roust some life out of him. "These are all from the same person, some associate professor from the University of Dee. Odd. Do you know anybody from that school?" She held the letters in her hand, awaiting his response.

Stenstrom shrugged and shook his head.

Lyra tore one of the envelopes open, revealing a sharply folded letter of pink paper splashed with laser-straight lines of gorgeous handwriting. She read through the note.

"It's from an associate professor named Hannah-Ben Shurlamp, Ev. She says ..." Lyra continued reading the note to herself, her eyes moving down the lines.

After a time, Stenstrom stirred. "Well, Lyra, what's it say?"

Lyra closed the note and set it aside. "I'm sorry, this woman is clearly demented. I shouldn't have troubled you with these notes. I'll have them destroyed, burned as you suggested."

A bit of the old curiosity that once drove Stenstrom resurfaced for a moment. "No, it's all right. Leave them, perhaps they'll give me a good laugh."

Lyra stood. "Fine." She looked him over with a sisterly eye. "I haven't heard you laugh in awhile. Let me know if you need anything, Bel, promise?"

"Sure, sure." Stenstrom picked up the note and read it.

To: Lord Belmont
From: Dame Hannah-Ben Shurlamp, Ev, Associate Professor, University of Dee, Calvert
Good sir
I am an authority on a great many things, most of which are of no consequence regarding my correspondence to you. To the point, in performing research for my pending oR degree, I have discovered that a severe Spiralata *has developed, and that you are possibly responsible for it.*

In layman's terms, a Spiralata *is a weakening and/or possibly a break in the atomic fabric of the universe. This is, of course, a gross simplification of the matter for your benefit. I can provide you with a complete dissertation on the subject if you so choose. I believe this* Spiralata *has formed in the north-west region of Kana, possibly in Vithland, though I do not have a precise location at this time. I have reason to believe that you and your former fiancée were present during the creation of this* Spiralata, *and her death was due in whole or in part to it. Therefore, I require your presence in my office as soon as possible so that I may continue my investigation into this potentially dangerous situation. I must interview you at length, your presence is mandatory, and I'll thank you to be prompt with your reply.*

In summation, the universe we inhabit is in danger, and it might be your fault.
I await your response.
Dame Hannah-Ben Shurlamp, Ev

Stenstrom re-read the letter several times. This Hannah-Ben Shurlamp person didn't seem to be someone who took no for an answer—her letter had the tone of a command, as if he were hers to order about.

He wished he could simply dismiss her as a demented prankster, but she did seem to be onto something. *Something* happened at Clovis which led to the death of Gwen, and this professor from Dee somehow detected it. He read her subsequent letters, hoping to gather more information. They became increasingly technical and rather threatening in tone, demanding he respond, otherwise 'measures' would be taken. She spoke of multiple universes, the existence of which she attempted to prove via a bewildering set of equations. She spoke of thresholds between the universes and of Extra-Planar Entities, essentially beings that, in various ways, could break the bonds of space and time. She required data. Her **oR** degree could not be delayed on his account. He was bewildered. Perhaps he ought to speak with this Hannah-Ben Shurlamp after all, though he dreaded what she might have to tell him.

But, if Gwen's death was somehow his fault, he couldn't bear that, therefore, he decided to avoid the professor all together.

✷ ✷ ✷ ✷ ✷

Lyra was out of breath when she caught up to him on his private terrace facing the sea. "Bel, that crazy professor from Dee—she's here in the grand parlor and demands an audience. She says she's not leaving until you see her." Lyra wasn't finished. "And … I think she's got a few spies roaming the grounds, I saw them on the hill near the Merian hermitage. I don't like the looks of it!"

Stenstrom stood and put his coat on. "Who's in attendance today?" he asked, concerned about the well-being of those at the manor should matters with this professor turn ugly.

"Just us and the staff, I think. Father's out to sea as usual, all the sisters are away at their own homes."

"Good, the fewer in attendance the better. Let's have a look, shall we? And if there be ruffians about, we shall deal with them."

Lyra led him out to the trim western lawn, and up the steep hillside near where their mother was buried and where Stenstrom maintained a flower-strewn memorial stone for Gwendolyn. Lyra pointed at the old Merian ruins atop the hill; a huddle of small stone structures where they used to play as children. "There, see them?"

Skulking about the stone structures were several figures clad in dark cloaks, two men and a woman. One of them was peering through field glasses mounted on a tripod, another manned a portable terminal, and the third had a sniper rifle set up on the flat. The long barrel was pointing with a steady hand at the manor at the bottom of the hill.

Stenstrom and Lyra crested the hill and took in the situation. The view from the top was splendid. To the north, the city of Tyrol tucked against the seaside, sparkling with yellow and green evening lights. To the west was the dark gulf of the sea with its steady whisper of surf. The three intruders stood at their posts, going about their work in meticulous fashion.

"Hmmm, look at this fellow here," Stenstrom said, pointing at the man with the rifle. "From his position, he commands an unobstructed view of the parlor."

Lyra walked up and agreed, eyeing the man with disdain. "Looks like he's ready to ring you up cold had you made an appearance in the parlor, Bel. They appear to be using sophisticated ranging and windage equipment to assist with their aiming. It's a long shot from up here."

They milled amongst the intruders, casually taking it all in, impressed by the technology and professionalism arrayed against them. They were unseen and unheard, both of them masters at the skills their mother had taught them years before. Passing silent and invisible were just a few of the many arcane talents they had at their disposal. Apparently, the professor and her associates, though well-furnished with technology, had no idea what they were dealing with.

"Let's have this rifle here," Stenstrom said, yanking it from the surprised man's hand.

"What in the Name of Creation?" the man cried. The three went on alert, whirling about but seeing nothing. They drew weapons. "Are we detecting any Cloaks?" he asked.

"No, no Cloaks!" the woman said, somewhat frantic. She ran forward in the general direction of Stenstrom. Lyra stuck her foot out and tripped the woman, sending her tumbling down the steep hillside.

Stenstrom and Lyra both shook their hands, producing several Holystones. Lyra cast a red Holystone, sending the spies' terminal up in a tower of red flames. One of the men raised his weapon in Lyra's general direction. Stenstrom cast a green Holystone, wrapping the man in a tight ball of webbing. He gave the ball a healthy kick, also sending it tumbling down the hill.

Terrified, the final man fled down the hillside toward the city of Tyrol in confusion, where he tended to his mates, all of them gibbering in fear. Stenstrom and Lyra laughed, watching them depart up the Tyrol Road. "That should do the three of them," she said.

He checked the rifle. "It's loaded with powered darts, probably filled with tranquilizer."

Lyra picked up the abandoned pair of field glasses. "The professor appears to be tired of you holding up her **oR** appointment. I say we go down there and show her the door the hard way."

Stenstrom stood there holding the rifle. "Well, I must say I admire her pluck. It takes a healthy bit of bravado to plan a kidnapping right in one's own holdings. Right then. Let's have a word with our lady from Calvert. What could it hurt?"

Rifle in hand, Stenstrom and Lyra marched down the hillside toward the manor, their shoes becoming damp in the trim grass. They entered the parlor, Lyra continuing her fade into the shadows.

Professor Hannah-Ben Shurlamp sat on the couch with dignified sidesaddle grace, drinking a cup of tea. She was a handsome lady, tall and upright, wearing a pleasing gown of pink and black patterns constructed in the usual Calvert industrial style, a light traveling shawl and a pair of lace gloves. She was a swarthy lady, her skin a burnished olive in color. Her hair

was black, like Lyra's, styled long in the Calvert fashion with a tiny hat nestled on top. Though she was dressed like a typical Calvert lady of means, she had unmistakably Vith features; lean up-and-down build, high cheekbones, penetrating eyes. A small handbag sat on the table in front of her.

"Lord Belmont, at last ..." she said.

Stenstrom threw the rifle on the table. "Yes, well met. I had the pleasure of doing away with your hired help up the hillside just now."

The professor maintained her bearing and didn't bother denying her attempt to kidnap him. She took a sip of tea. "Yes, well, I don't appreciate being ignored, sir, especially with as much at stake as we have here. I thought drastic steps might be in order. You have the reputation of being a fighting man, a man of action; you prowl the rooftops of Tyrol wearing a mask like a raider. I thought you might appreciate such a droll display."

Indeed he did. The professor seemed to know a lot about him, and she appeared to have correctly anticipated his response, that his interest would be piqued. Impressed, he seated himself while Lyra, invisible, moved into the parlor and covered the professor, should she try something funny.

"A question," the professor asked. "Are they dead? My people on the hill."

Stenstrom shook his head. "No, merely terrified and routed from the premises."

"I see. Pity ... now I shall have to pay them a night's work."

He chuckled. "Right then. After all that, here I am. What's this all about?"

Hannah-Ben Shurlamp had come prepared. She opened her bag, set up a holo terminal and began a lecture on the mechanics of quantum physics as it pertained to the solidarity of universal matter—very heady material. The professor had a keen eye for when her dissertation threatened to go over Stenstrom's head, which was mere minutes into her lecture, and seamlessly switched to more simplistic generalizations.

"A 'universe' can be defined as a unified grouping of matter, space, and time. Additionally, per my research, all matter in a given universe vibrates at a common homogeneic frequency. Change the frequency of this core vibration and, technically, you are in a different universe, as illustrated by the Equation of Homogeneity. Note illustration 4A ..."

She pointed at a bewildering set of equations floating on-air in the parlor, Stenstrom barely following her.

She went on. "As this unifying frequency is of infinite range, there are therefore an infinite number of universes. The universes all fit together in an orderly pattern called a *Circulum,* one after the next, each independent of the other, rather like the rings in the cross-section of a tree trunk. Though these universes are independent, universes of similar frequency tend to be similar, as stated in the Theory of Commonality ...

"There are also alternate versions of you inhabiting *some* of these universes, repeated over and over again within a pre-defined Sphere of Influence. The Hospitalers have developed a flawed but, for our purposes, adequate algorithm known as the Equation of Opposites, which determines how many different versions of yourself there are, usually on the order of X to 24563rd power. Of course, the equation generates an extremely large number, but it's nevertheless quite small when compared with an infinitely large value. The Hospitalers call the sphere in which one exists in the universal scheme of things the 'Sphere of Mirrors'. In this sphere, the variation between you and your alternate versions becomes more pronounced from one end of the sphere to the other."

And then the professor went off the deep end.

"Extra-Planar Entities, or EPEs, which can be composed of matter, space or time, are either exempt from the laws of homogeneity or able to thwart certain aspects of them entirely. In some cases, EPEs are simply interesting statistical anomalies, not adding up to much of anything. Others occupy a unique place in the universal scheme of things and may safeguard the well-being of the universe, or, in a minor fashion, affect the doings in other universes. I refer to these as the 'helping EPEs'. Lastly, some of the more severe EPEs break the laws of homogeneity altogether, and are able to pass unhindered from one universe to the next. These 'hurtful EPEs' disrupt the orderly *Circulum* and cause two or more universes to vibrate at the same frequency in a localized area, or, in simpler terms, to '*touch*'. This is known as a *Spiralata*, and it is extremely dangerous as a severe *Spiralata* can cause an entire universe to vibrate at a new random frequency, thereby destroying it completely. I have detected the existence of a severe *Spiralata* that has formed on Kana and elsewhere. If this condition is not checked and/ or reversed, I believe all of us could simply cease to exist."

The professor paused, allowing Stenstrom to drink it all in.

Could she be referring to Clovis?

He saw many versions of himself at Clovis, many versions of Gwendolyn, as if they were different people from different places.

Lyra, standing near the professor, looked confused.

"And why do you believe this situation has anything to do with me?" he asked.

"Because you are an Extra-Planar Entity," she replied.

"I am?"

"Yes."

"And how do you know this?"

"Differential geometry, genealogy, cosmology and a few other quantitative disciplines I shall not tell here, along with standard mathematics. I have taken this entire topic from the rug-lined, incense-burning environs of Xaphan sage parlors and the small, random bits of Hospitaler learning and unified it into a proper learned field of study complete with mathematical data to prove all its claims. I simply require more data to fill in the remaining gaps."

Lyra appeared from the shadows, unable to contain her questions any further. "And you need my brother to add to your knowledge, to make you the founder of a new branch of science, is that it? You're certain of this?" Her sudden appearance, standing tall with her MARZABLE daggers in her hand, didn't unhinge the professor in the least.

"I am, and yes, you are correct. I need to study Lord Belmont in depth." She turned to Stenstrom. "Now then, the question you should be asking is what sort of EPE are you? Hmm? Are you a minor statistical aberration, are you a dangerous hurtful EPE that can spell the doom of an entire universe, or are you one of the select helping EPEs that guard the well-being of all things?" She paused, as if for effect. "You, sir, are what is known in old Xaphan texts as a *Kaidar Gemain*. I previously mentioned the Hospitalers' Equation of Opposites that determines how many universes one may appear in. I mentioned that the algorithm is flawed. It's flawed because it does not apply to you. You, sir, appear in all universes."

Stenstrom sat there, trying to use his sorcerous training to make sense or meaning of that. After a bit of confused reflection, it meant nothing to him. The professor went on.

"The good news is the *Kaidar Gemain* is a helping EPE. The *Kaidar Gemain* provides solidity and stability and performs an important 'cleaning' function, as various entities that could be harmful to the fabric of the universe tend to be drawn to you—rather like an antibody destroying harmful particles seeking to compromise the body." The professor took another lady-like sip of tea. "Being a *Kaidar Gemain* brings responsibility. You are a man of action; being a *Kaidar Gemain* demands such. I am hypothesizing that some sort of entity entered our universe and came to you, so beginning the *Spiralata*. Am I correct, sir?"

The demon in blue lights.

"I'm certain I don't know."

The professor made a quick note. "The fact that you just lied to me right now is telling. Now, your fiancée, the one who died, she was what is known as a *Merthig*."

"Wait a moment. A what? *Merthig*?"

"Your former fiancée, Lady Gwendolyn of Prentiss. Per my calculations, she appears at your side mathematically across the universes more so than anyone else, and that makes her a statistical EPE. The Extra-Planar term for that is *Merthig*, from the Cammarian word meaning 'soul', or soul mate. The *Merthig* acts rather like a fuel cell, providing you with enhanced power. My research into this matter has determined that your relationship with the *Merthig* is a symbiotic one; you both benefit and are more powerful together than you otherwise would be separately. That's why she died, isn't it? The public record doesn't detail how she died, only that she passed away. But we know how she died, don't we? The EPE that created the *Spiralata* killed your Lady Gwendolyn, didn't it?"

The thing in blue light that came out of the wall went directly for Gwen, ignoring him. It let him watch as it killed her.

Stenstrom sat there, the loss returning to him fully. He felt tired and empty. "I would like you to leave our home at once," he said.

Professor Shurlamp wasn't moving. "You, sir, are behaving like a heart-broken groom scrabbling for footing in a sea of sorrow. Now is the time for action, not oblivion. I have good news. I know of a way to remedy your problem, to transform you into a new man. A statistical EPE known as a *Covus* is a person who can replace your lost *Merthig* and rejuvenate you. A *Covus*, correctly identified, is a suitable substitute."

"A substitute? For Lady Gwendolyn? My brother is not a prize pony to be studded to prime breeding stock," Lyra said.

"I understand he is saddened by the loss of his *Merthig,* the pain he feels is debilitating and very real, but you must understand that much of his pain is because of his EPE connection to her. It's not simply lost love he feels, it's the loss of power she provided him. The *Covus* can erase that pain, can remove the sense of emptiness and restore him to his former self. Once that has been accomplished, he will be fit to seek out the EPE and destroy it."

"This situation you claim exists is not my brother's concern," Lyra said.

"Yes it is. The EPE was drawn to him, was given entrance by him, and must be dealt with by him, else this universe we inhabit shall no longer be."

Lyra pointed to the door. "I want you out of our presence at once. You may either walk out of our home of your own accord, or you may flee in terror like your associates. The choice is yours."

"Lyra," Stenstrom said, stirring. His voice was heavy with fatigue. "I can't go on like this. I'm alive, but I don't feel as such. I stumble from one day to the next, merely existing. I put my mask on and hide behind it, hoping the pain won't find me, yet it always does. Perhaps the professor is correct. What could it hurt to try?" He turned to her. "What must I do?"

Lyra backed away, the professor appeared pleased. "At last, some reason from you. You must present yourself in my office in Dee. There, I shall interview you at length, examine you, profile you, and then perform the required computations to determine a suitable *Covus*. It is exacting work and it must be precise. I have developed computations I am confident will allow us to locate a suitable candidate. Unlike the *Merthig* who is drawn to you by cosmic design, a *Covus* is not. You must therefore seek her, or he, out and create a connection. I assure you, once united, the *Covus* shall make you feel alive again. You shall forget your lost *Merthig*."

"I sincerely doubt that," he said.

"And what is in this for you?" Lyra asked, still holding her daggers. "Your reward for all of this is your pending EVoR appointment, is that correct?"

"That will be the natural outcome of our efforts, yes," the professor replied, putting her things back in her bag. "Your brother shall have his *Covus*, the universe shall be rid of its EPE demon, and I shall reap the rewards I justly deserve and take my place in the learned circles of the League."

Lyra turned to Stenstrom. "Bel, tell her to leave. Please ..."

Stenstrom thought about it. "All right, I'll agree—what more have I to lose? Give me time to sort a few things out."

"I would advise we begin immediately."

"I need a week, maybe two. I must make my peace with Gwen."

The professor finished her tea. "Fine then. I shall expect you in my office at your earliest convenience. I advise you not to tarry long, we've much work ahead of us and you shan't be disappointed. Do not commence any new relationships at this time, and I advise ending any that are currently in progress. We must have a clean, unentangled slate as we begin our search for the *Covus*. Do you understand?"

"I'm not seeing anybody," he said.

"I know that," she replied. "Ensure it stays that way."

3—Return to Clovis

August 40—anniversary of Gwen's death.

It was time to return to the place he dreaded most—Clovis, where Gwen died. He would go there, leave a flower at the site of her death, say a few words, and try to go on with his life. Clovis was a place he never wanted to see again. This would, with luck, be the final anniversary visit.

Stenstrom wasn't much of a pilot; his old friend, Lord A-Ram, used to fly him about before they lost touch after the *Seeker* was scrapped. He had lost touch with everybody; all his friends, most of his family gone. He rented an Automatic Ripcar, or 'Autocar' from a dealer in Tyrol for nine hundred sesterces, plus a one hundred sesterce deposit against unforeseen damage, the largest and most comfortable model available, a nice blue one. It had a hand-held control glyph that controlled all the craft's various functions along with a preprogrammed route for one passenger from Tyrol to Clovis and back. (Clovis was not a standard tourist or business destination, therefore its route there and back was extra). The glyph they gave him was easy to use and quite foolproof. He got in and allowed the Autocar to thrust up into the clouds and take him on the long, somber journey alone to Clovis, across the flat Esther marshlands, across the sea to the green lands of Hala and the eventual bare fist and knobby lands of Vithland, with its hardpan cage of mountains rising up like a towering cairn over Gwen's grave. Even from the air in the climate-controlled comfort of the Autocar, the mountains below gave him an eerie feeling of loathing and disquiet.

Lyra had demanded to come with him on this trip, but he refused. This time he was coming alone, as he should have before. He sat in the back of the Autocar, sinking in the splendor of his padded seat, lost with his thoughts as the ship flew itself, leaving civilization far behind. He would come to Clovis, do what he needed to do, then in a few days he would go south to Calvert and allow Professor Hannah-Ben Shurlamp to do whatever she would with him. If she could take away his lonely disquiet and grant him some measure of peace, he would be in her debt.

A pleasing automated voice came from the control glyph: *"Entering the environs of Clovis, 84, 15, north by west. Descending one thousand feet per minute to an elevation of 11,000 feet."*

Down the Autocar came, through the clouds into the thicker air, its blowers coming on to smooth out the descent, until a huddle of weathered brown buildings came into view, clinging to the base of several mountains like the disorganized wash of debris left behind after a flood.

Clovis, fabulous in its isolation.

The Autocar lazed about at treetop level, scanning for a nice flat patch of ground to land, finding a suitable spot several hundred yards south of the ruins.

"Primary landing site caged. If you would like an alternate location, another may be selected for a minimal surcharge of fifty sesterces. Would you like to cage an alternate location?"

"No," was his terse response.

The Autocar settled in: *"Vehicle set to idle. All systems nominal. Local temperature: 1.67 degrees C. Please watch your step. Enjoy your visit."*

He got out, feeling the harsh northern chill. He listened. Sudden, impenetrable silence all around, save but a breath of wind. He pulled out his HRN coat and slid his arms through the sleeves. As it always did, the coat blanked out the cold. His HRN had been with him for years, through space and all the amazing places he had visited. He felt nothing with it on, even his sadness was a bit less, but only a bit. He dropped the Autocar's control glyph into one of the HRN's many pockets, sashed his trusty NTH pistols, took a deep breath and trudged north across the broken pebbles and crushed shale into the ruins of Clovis—with luck, for the last time, for he wished to never come back to this wretched place ever again.

The isolation was staggering. There wasn't another city for hundreds of miles. His mentor, Captain Davage, lived about 400 mountain miles to the north. With such isolation, he felt like the sole person on Kana, with only the mountains to laugh at him. He looked back once, seeing the fancy blue Autocar sitting idle a surprising distance away—it was a hopeful little piece of newness amid all this desolation and decay.

The unsmiling buildings, the empty windows, the forlorn silence; it all came back to him. And as he walked north toward the site of Gwen's death, he felt that same confusion, that same feeling that 'many' versions of himself had stood here, had walked these grounds, along with many versions of Gwen and other people he did not know. If he shut his eyes, he caught quick images of the ruins occupied, full of life. People roaming about—Gwen still alive. Gwen a different person. A thousand different Gwens; all alive except for his.

The professor was right, many different universes 'touched' in this place, and he was subjected in a hypnotic dance to see them all.

Ahead, past a stand of statues of the old Clovis, up the hillside toward the roots of the mountain, were the stone doors fastened to the ground, the place where Gwen died. He stood there silently, feeling all the pain come right back to him again. The demon in blue light had done this, had taken everything from him; his love, his standing, his ship, his very will to live. All gone. Murdered.

Many emotions, many from other places packed into his chest, filling him up. Rage, fury, the desire for revenge—this was the most he had felt since Gwen died.

He could hear her voice on the wind, drifting from across time itself.
Bel! What's that, coming out the wall? Do you see it?

He could see her draw her trusty FEDULA, her family weapon. He saw her dying, over and over, the FEDULA clattering out of her hand.
Bel!

He stood there seething for his murdered fiancée ... The only woman he would ever love. No *Covus* could ever replace her, no matter what the professor said.

He marched up to the doors, they laughed at him.
You've returned...
Have you another sacrifice for us?

He knelt down and left a single pink rose that he had picked from her memorial stone on the hill near his home. He had nurtured it all the way from Tyrol, marring not a single petal. It was still fresh and vivid against the mottled browns of Clovis as he laid it down. "For you, Gwen," he said as he turned to leave.

He got the sudden feeling he wasn't alone. He sensed danger.

A gnarled voice spoke. "You came from the Temple of the Sun?"

There, sitting on the heads of the old Clovis statues on all fours was a tiny crouching woman. She looked to him like a bizarre Black Hat, though she was like none he had ever seen. Black Hats wore stunning scarlet robes and covered their faces in featureless black masks. This one wore a baggy tunic and leggings that appeared to have been a vibrant green at some point, but were clotted with dirt and streaks of food, staining them to a dull brownish color. Ragged strips of torn cloth were wrapped tightly around her wrists and ankles. He could sense the river of raw Shadow tech moving through her. Her head was also uncovered, revealing a mop-like tangle of whitish-blonde hair framing a small heart-shaped face and a pair of wide green eyes that sparkled with crazed light. Her Shadowmark wrapped around her right eye like a lover's embrace. Her face was marked up, the tell-tale signs of having been in a rough fight; blood matted her hair. She was contorted into a painful crouching position, like a cat. She sat there with firm, effortless purchase atop the statues, her hands and bare feet firmly rooted. She had a tail of sinuous Shadow tech that flicked and darted with easy, mesmerizing movements. Deadly Shadow tech claws danced about her fingers.

As he looked at her, she seemed odd, somehow deformed, as if she had too much flesh in the chest and in the rear-end, but it was difficult to tell as she was crouching.

Black Hats were evil and crazed; he wondered how she had managed to avoid detection by the Sisters, who protected Kana from their savagery.

"Do you live there, with the sun?" she asked. "What of the City of Love?"

She seemed somewhat familiar to him, though he was certain he had never seen her before. More flashes, more glimpses of other places. Across the universes, he had seen this person before.

Did you enjoy fighting me? came a voice whispered in a different universe.

"I did enjoy fighting you," he said, half in a dream.

"Say again?" she said, closing her eyes. "Speak, your voice is ... lovely."

"I didn't say anything. Where did you come from? Did you come from the vault down below?"

Her tail flicked. "I do not go below the living earth." Her accent was horrid and guttural, like an animal attempting to speak. To his ear, it sounded like: *"I donnn ghoo belooww daaa livvvvin' eartttttt ... "*

"Where have you come from?" he demanded.

"I have always been here."

"How is it the Sisters have not come to drop you off?"

She laughed. "I am greater than the Sisters. I laugh at them. I have been waiting for you ..."

"For me?"

She pointed at him with her sinister Shadow tech claws. "For you!" The Black Hat rose up a bit. As he suspected, she was inhumanly endowed in the chest and in the posterior area. Her breasts were so enormous, she could suckle a pair of elephants at once. She spied the rose he had left for Gwen.

"What is that? Pretty, how pretty ..." she said in a purring fashion. Her green eyes flashed. In a streak, she bounded down off the statues, galloped around him on all fours like a beast, and had the rose in her hand before he could blink.

She sniffed the flower. "Is this plant a gift for me? Is it from the Temple of the Sun or the City of Love?"

Seeing this filthy Black Hat holding Gwen's flower filled him with rage. "Absolutely not! Give me that back!" he roared.

He leapt up to get the flower and she sprang away with ease, her speed belying her massive girth. She sniffed the rose again. "Ohhhhh," she said, "you want this, do you? All men want something. You are a man, is this what you want? Why?"

They circled, like two wrestlers ready to lock up. "That is none of your concern. Give me that back!" he spat again. "I'm warning you! You're playing with fire, Black Hat!"

She clearly had no intention of giving it back. Her leg muscles were tensed up and bulging through her filthy clothes, ready to spring. She spoke in a growl. "I am not a Black Hat!"

He could hear the pent-up excitement in her voice, the glee, making her already challenging accent even more difficult to understand. He reached out to take the rose and she nimbly moved aside again, her speed incredible. "Come and get it," she snarled as she ran on all fours back into the central ruin proper; stirring up a cloud of dust as she ran, tail trailing in a series of limber ripples.

"Come and get it!" she taunted. She turned and waited for him to catch up, sitting up on all fours, tail flicking.

Following, he lashed out with TK. As it latched on, she sprang away with inhuman agility, again assuming a tensed-up position, ready to spring.

"Your garment," she said in an odd growl/whisper, noting his HRN coat. "The color of mercy ..."

"There shall be no mercy for you, Black Hat, if you fail to give me my rose back. Give it to me and I'll walk away and you can have this Elder-Down rat hole all to yourself."

She placed the rose behind her. She seemed troubled by her own giant-sized breasts. She had issues placing her arms, she was off-balance. The Black Hat was done with it. It seemed she had been wearing a harness that had mimicked her breasts and her rear-end, enlarging them to ridiculous proportions, but, its very size gave her trouble moving about. She cast the harness aside, revealing herself to be of thin, modest proportions. Free of the harness, she raised her clawed hand and beckoned him to come. "This is *our* place, provided by the gods. You have been promised to me, now let us abuse each other ... how I have waited."

What sort of demented Black Hat was this, he wondered? Black Hats didn't physically engage with an enemy; they preferred to hang in the shadows safe under a Painted Cloak and cast Shadow tech, and she had a lot of it flowing through her, raw and primal like an unbaked cake.

He launched himself into the air and landed in front of her in a hard breakage of rock and dirt. Like an uncoiling spring, she laced him with claws of micro-line Shadow tech, moving with uncanny speed, shredding his shirt and pants. Any normal man would have been gutted by such an attack. The Sisters, despite everything, still granted him their power. He warded off the attack.

He swung with a back fist and she ducked. She was so agile, like a panther. She was the fastest, most mobile person he had ever seen, and Black Hats weren't known for that. Quite the opposite; they normally stood in place and slung Shadow tech. While he was off balance, she bludgeoned him across the chest with her Shadow tech tail in a whistling hammering blow, sending him down hard.

She jumped on him, sitting on his neck. "You, your plant and your garment belong to me!" She cuffed him a good one, drawing a bit of blood from his mouth. "Say it!" she said with unbridled joy. "Say you are mine!" She made to hit him again, but this time he caught her slender wrist and sent her upside down and backwards into the stone, where she crumpled up for a moment in a daze.

He jumped up, ready to begin pummeling her. She reacted in a frenzy, clawing, biting and kicking. She barked out words, but he couldn't understand them. He got control of her arms just in time to take a punishing head-butt square in the forehead, followed up by another hammering blow from her tail. Stenstrom fell back.

Laughing, she threw herself onto him and they grappled in the grass. He managed to get some space and punched her in the cheek. She was stunned, her eyes grew foggy, and he hit her again, knocking her face-first into the grass. She quickly recovered. "Ahhhhhhh!" she cried, in apparent joy, wiping blood away. She was savoring this battle. He picked her up by the neck, arms and legs waving; she wrapped her tail around his arm and chest.

The rose!

Gwendolyn's rose! It was crushed, smashed up on the ground as a result of their pointless fight. It lay there in the cold dirt, flattened and sad, petals detached like little pink tears. Stenstrom put the Black Hat down, stared at it, and turned to walk away. He'd had enough; enough of this place, enough of this person.

He was done.

The Black Hat leapt over his head in a fluttering of cloth and landed in front of him, crouched down, claws displayed, ready to continue fighting.

"Get out of my way, please," he said quietly.

"This place is ours!" she said. "The gods are watching! Come, abuse me! That is what men and women do!"

He looked around, seeing the old desolation. He wanted to go home, desperately. "I'm done, goodbye. Pray the Sisters don't ever find you here." He moved past her. Growling, she quickly latched onto him from behind, her claws at his neck and her bare ankles crossed around his waist. "Do not turn your back on me!" she hissed. "Come to the habitation, I shall tend to your wounds."

He seized her by the back of the neck and roughly threw her off. She landed on her back and lay there in the sparse grass. Righting herself, she seemed puzzled, unsure what to do next. Stepping around her, he continued, making his slow way out of the ruins to his waiting Autocar in the distance.

He heard her claws clattering across stone. He felt her gaze on him. "Aww, what is the matter? Did I abuse you too much? Do you seek an embrace?" she called out in a chiding voice. She sounded like a child losing her playmate. "Embrace me! Listen to my heart beat!"

He paid her no mind. He shook his hand and the Autocar's control glyph appeared in his palm.

"The gods will not allow you to leave, Man in Garment the Color of Mercy. You are a gift to me."

"That a fact?" He looked to the sky: clear. To the east: light high altitude clouds heading out of Vithland. To the south: a bit of rolling fog moving across the ground, quickly dissipating.

"Seems the gods don't care one way or the other," he said.

"I have questions," the Black Hat leaping in front of him said with renewed vigor. "And you shall answer!"

Stenstrom ignored her. This little green ruffian seemed more a genuine nuisance than an actual threat. He raised his control glyph to power up the Autocar. It was simple; just press the button and the craft would power itself up, no hands-on needed, then he would step in and it would fly him back to his home in Tyrol.

Nothing happened. He pressed again, still nothing. Puzzled, he checked the glyph. It said: *"I'm sorry, Auto-Lock not found. Reconfiguring, please standby."*

He shook the glyph. "What in the Name of Creation?"

The Black Hat was back at his side, eyes wide, reeking of stale must. "You have an Autocon captured in your device?"

"What? No, this is an Autocar, not an Autocon, whatever that is. Do step away please, I'm launching out of here."

"What do you want?" she asked.

"I want to be away from this place and from you in particular."

The Black Hat wasn't giving up. "But why? You cannot leave. You are mine. Did you not enjoy abusing me? We may continue abusing each other, nude perhaps, or in the waters of the cistern. Perhaps you are tired. I order you to come with me into the habitation, there we will remove our clothes and sleep."

He laughed a bit. The thought of getting naked with a filthy Black Hat amused him. "Really? Slot Off."

The control glyph spoke again. *"I have no files pertaining to your destination. Please state destination."*

"Oh, for the Love of Creation. Tyrol. I wish to go to Tyrol."

"Configuring. Please wait."

The Black Hat continued pestering him. "I have clothing to display, and wondrous keepsakes." She pointed to a misshapen window at the top of one of the ruined buildings. A dreary, unsavory darkness covered with ages of dust peeked out of the empty frame. He glanced at the window and felt nothing but dread at what might lie within.

"Hear me. The moment this insipid craft gets itself together, you need never bother with me again. You may bask in this horrid place all by yourself; that is, until the Sisters come for you."

The Black Hat pulled at her tangle of hair, she seemed nervous and unsure of herself. She leapt up onto the hood of the Autocar. "Get off there!" he shouted.

The control glyph spoke again. *"Please specify weight to be carried."*

"Two hundred, twenty pounds."

"Configuring, 100 kilograms, plus or minus 15 kilograms for your convenience."

The glyph went green. *"I'm pleased to inform you, configuration is complete. Auto-Lock has been established for a direct approved route to Tyrol, 23,14 West, with a transit time of ten bells, sixteen beats, or four hours, fifty-seven minutes Kanan standard. Authorized payload: 115 kilograms. There shall be an additional fee of seventy-seven sesterces for the re-acquisition of destination. Do you agree to the additional fee?"*

"Yes, yes, I agree to the bloody fee. Let's go!"

"Thank you, beginning power up sequence." The Autocar's systems hissed. Lights came on.

The Black Hat was in a frustrated frenzy. "Tell me what you want!" she demanded. "Tell! Tell! Tell!"

"What do I want?" he said. "I wanted to come here and find peace with my departed love. Instead, what do I get? I get you, an insane Black Hat wearing a giant-sized 'breast harness' and an Autocar that doesn't seem to work right and is nickel and diming me into my grave. Now, all I want to do is leave."

"The harness was a gift for you," she said.

"For me? It was ridiculous."

The Black Hat rubbed her chin.

The Autocar's small lift engine vibrated to life. The Black Hat grabbed hold of the control glyph, trying to pull it out of his hand. "I shall take your Autocon and hide it!"

He lifted the glyph out of her reach and pushed her aside.

The Black Hat pawed at her head, trying to puzzle something out. "Ahhhhh!" she cried in jubilation, as if she had just solved some pressing mystery. She bounded away, fetched the sorry remains of Gwen's flower, and brought it back.

"You came here for your woman, yes?"

The Autocar seemed to be taking an eternity to ready itself. He waited impatiently. "Yes, I already told you that."

"And, and … your woman was killed, yes?"

"How do you know that?" he asked, somewhat astonished.

His Autocar was ready at last. *"I am pleased to inform you your craft is ready for launch. Please watch your step when boarding."* The door to the spacious cabin opened on its own, revealing the fine padded interior. He stepped in and seated himself.

"I saw her ghost!" she cried.

That was too much for Stenstrom. "What? Gwen? You saw Gwen?"

The Black Hat sprang inside the Autocar, bouncing on the opposite bench. The Autocar instantly reacted. *"Additional weight detected. 115 kilograms exceeded. There will be an added fee for the extra weight. Do you agree to the fee?"*

"What? No!" he cried.

"Please remove added weight. Standing by ... "

"Out!" he roared, pointing outside. "Get out, before I start pummeling you into the dirt!"

The Black Hat was undeterred. "Yes, I saw the ghost of your love."

"I don't believe you."

"She told me her name. It was GwendoltndePretniss."

What? Though the words were slurred, she seemed to have said Gwen's full name: Gwendolyn of Prentiss. She could not know that. She must be telling the truth. He felt all the heartbreak of her death return. If her ghost truly was still here, why did she not present herself to him? Why would she speak to a wretched Black Hat instead and not to him? Perhaps in death she wanted nothing to do with him. "What did she say? Did she tell you anything?"

"She said she was angry for being dead, and that she missed her handsome man."

The Autocar blinked. *"Please remove unauthorized weight ... "*

"Shut up!" Stenstrom roared into the glyph. "What else? What else did she say?"

The Black Hat jumped out of the Autocar, crouching in the cold gravel.

"Standby," the control glyph said. *"Weight limit authorized. Closing hatch."* The Autocar's door slowly swung shut. Stenstrom stuck his head out the window, awaiting more information. "What else!"

The Black Hat complied. "I know who did it!—I know who killed her! I saw the thing that did it! The creature in the atmosphere suit. In blue light!"

The demon clad in blue lights... part machine. Killing Gwen.

"The demon was drawn to you and you failed to destroy it," Hannah-Ben Shurlamp had said.

You failed Gwen ...

"And I know where it is!" the Black Hat said.

The Autocar was ready to go. *"Commencing launch."*

His mouth dropped open. "Wait. Delay launch," he spat into the glyph.

"Delay, damn you!"

"Launch delayed. Standing by." The Autocar's engines thrummed back down to idle.

There she was, smug, sitting in the gravel of Clovis holding the flower, her tail flicking with interest, green eyes nested within her tangle of hair and her Shadowmark. "Your love is dead, you failed to protect her, and the demon that killed her laughs at you in comfort and safety. And that is not all. I have more to tell. It wears her flesh."

Wears her flesh? Gwen's lovely body, defiled by a demon?

There was so little of her left to take back to Prentiss. His disgrace ...

She held up the smashed rose. "So, tell me what you want?"

He slammed the surface of the Autocar with his fist, making it shudder. "I WANT REVENGE! THAT'S WHAT I WANT!"

"Minor structural damage detected," the Control glyph said. *"Security deposit rescinded."*

He huffed and steadied himself. "If all I'm left to feel is rage and hate, then let it be so! If it costs me my family fortune, if it costs me my remaining standing with the Sisters and what is left of my reputation and finishes this universe off, so be it. So be it! I will have at this demon! I want revenge!"

She seemed pleased she had information that was important to him. She hunched up a little and giggled. "Well then, I know where the demon in blue light is. Your lady's ghost, she showed me." She tossed the rose aside. "If you wish revenge, then you must treat with me to have it."

Stenstrom got out of the Autocar and stood before her. "Tell me where the demon is."

"Aaaa ... heheh. Hhhheeeee ..." She slowly padded around him on all fours, close, violating his space, her Shadow tech tail hoisted over her head with excitement. "You want that I should tell you?" she said, her voice shaking a little.

"Tell me where it is," he repeated.

"Did you enjoy me abusing you?" she asked.

Her question triggered some dim memory from within. He remembered this same woman asking him a similar question, but it was a different version of this woman in a different place. She was wearing black trimmed with red, and a mask. She was taller and prouder, cleaner, more polished as a Black Hat, more dangerous.

Did you enjoy fighting me? another version of her had asked.

Yes, he had.

She lifted her hand, and with her long, black nails flicked him on the cheek. "Appears we have some bargaining to do first ..." Her voice was airy, breathy.

It was now his turn to ask the question: "What do you want?"

She continued orbiting him, clearly relishing this. "What are you going to do if you find this demon?"

"I'm going to destroy it."

"Ahhhh, ahhahahahaa …" She stopped dead in front of him and stood up straight for the first time, the linkages of her Shadow tech armature clicking and stretching out. She was head and shoulders shorter than he. "I shall tell you … I shall tell you …"

Stenstrom listened, awaiting the information. The Autocar's blower kicked on, as if impatient to depart.

"But, first … first …" She got very close and licked her lips. "I am hungry."

"I have no time for this, and I don't care if you've supped or not. Tell me where the demon is and then go dredge your foul dinner out the cistern."

"First, I am hungry. You shall feed me, then I shall disclose the information."

He lashed out and got her by the throat. She gagged and fell to her knees.

"Tell me or you die!"

"Abuse me all you want! I … am … hungry!" she stammered, choking but defiant.

He held his grip. Her stomach gave a loud gurgle as she struggled. He let her go.

She held her throat and stood. "Not … nice," she said, her eyes watering as she caught her breath. "I shall expect all the courtesy I have heard fine gentlemen offer their ladies."

"You are not my …"

She firmly placed two clawed fingers on his lips, stifling his rant. "Shhh … Shhh … You want to kill the murderer of your love—I have got it. And I shall not say a word until I have been properly fed, and been shown a little courtesy." Her fingernails were filed into needle-like points.

Stenstrom made to protest.

"Shhhhhhhh … shhhh," she said again. "Now, my handsome Man, shall we?"

4—An Unwelcome Dinner Guest

Feed a Black Hat? What was he supposed to do, take her to a street-side café in a city or town with many people coming and going and hand her a menu? She was no tourist, she was a Black Hat, and a fairly daffy one at that. If the Sisters caught wind of her presence they would execute her on the spot, and her information would die with her.

Die? He recalled seeing her die elsewhere. Her brains coming out of her ears. How sad that had made another version of himself feel.

Having little recourse, Stenstrom decided to take her home to his manor in Tyrol. It would take four hours by Autocar to get there, over the Vithland mountains, across the sea and through the Esther marshes.

"Get into my coach. Do not make any sudden or unexpected movements and do not assail me with questions along the way. Stay quiet, behave yourself, and you will be fed."

She glanced at the Autocar. "Leaving the mountains?"

"Yes, and thank Creation for it."

She seemed excited. "Are we headed to the Sun's Temple?"

"What? There is no such place. We're heading east. That way," he pointed.

She flexed her claws with delight. "Give me a moment!" She tore off at high speed, gasping, laughing, running along the ground like a fox, into the ruins, up the side of a wall, and into the window she had pointed at previously. Seconds later, she was back out the window, down the wall and galloping back to his position, this time carrying a dirty but rather quaint wicker basket by her tail. "Let us go!" she said.

Stenstrom stared at her grinning face and the basket she carried. "What? No, no, there's no need for you to fetch your things, you shan't be gone long. Once you've dined and disclosed the information, I shall be returning you here at once."

She paid him no mind. She scrabbled into the Autocar and situated herself, her feet on the seat, cradling the basket to her chest with both hands, her claws sticking out in an ominous fashion. She seemed puzzled by the cushions of her bench seat; she poked at them and pressed on the upholstery, bouncing up and down.

"Do not damage the seats, as I shall be held financially liable."

With dread, Stenstrom entered and seated himself opposite her. She smelled like stale meat. Best get this over with and be done with her as quickly as possible. After a painful session negotiating a three hundred sesterce surcharge for the Black Hat's added weight with the control glyph, the Autocar sealed itself, up-thrusted and gained safe altitude over the surrounding peaks. The Black Hat watched as the mountains surrounding Clovis dropped away, revealing a vast green, brown and white landscape of more, even larger snowy mountains in the distance for as far as could be easily seen. She gasped, seeing all these things revealed to her; the ruined buildings of Clovis becoming smaller by the moment as the Autocar rose. It seemed all she knew was the little huddle of forlorn ruins and the nearby mountains. She reached out to take Stenstrom's hand, but he didn't offer it. She pulled her hand back and clutched at her chest as the Autocar headed east over the mountains, Clovis falling away until it was gone. During the journey to the manor, she sat cross-legged on the seat, looking out the windows, fascinated by the passing landscape, taking it all in. One time, something down below caught her eye and she actually scrabbled out the window and was hanging over the side. Seizing her by the tail, he hauled her back in.

"What in the Name of Creation are you doing?" he asked, astonished.

"I saw the Temple of the Sun!" she proudly announced. "Down there!"

"There is no such place, I told you that. There is nothing in these mountains."

It was a long trip to Tyrol, the Black Hat antsy, obsessed with her padded seat, refusing to sit still, clutching her basket, her head thrust out the window. The Autocar kept dispensing spritzes of air fragrance to offset the Black Hat's dank mustiness. At last, the hellish journey neared its end and the Autocar came down from over the sea and settled into the flat familiar lanes and marshes of Esther, floating just over the cobbles, winding through the neck of the Eastern Continent north of Rustam, nearing Tyrol. The flat olive green Estherlands seemed to bore her. She turned her attention from the window to him, staring the whole time, studying his face, making him uncomfortable.

"It's quite rude to stare," he said.

"Garment," she replied, ignoring his remark.

"Pardon?"

"I have spent a great deal of time thinking about this. Your name shall be 'Man in Garment the Color of Mercy'. I am a giver of names. You are wearing a magnificent garment, and 'Garment', for short, shall be your name." She seemed rather proud of herself.

Stenstrom was astonished. "This 'garment' is my HRN coat, and I already have a name," he said perfunctorily.

She seemed puzzled, cocking her head to one side. "Like the sky, you are named already?"

"Yes," he said, having no idea what she was talking about. "Yes, that is correct."

"Who named you?"

"My bloody parents, that's who."

Silence. The Autocar moved steadily down the road, the skies turning wet and gray. He was sharing a ride with a filthy, smelly, tangled, barefoot Black Hat slathered in Shadow tech and stale food like a bum passed out behind a pub, but the rules of courtesy and standard decorum won out. He decided to offer his name, as was proper.

"I am Stenstrom, Lord of Belmont-South Tyrol, son of Stenstrom the Older, captain of the Fleet Warbird *Caroline,* and of Jubilee, 3rd Lady of Tyrol."

The Black Hat listened and wasn't impressed. "Garment is better," she proclaimed. "I have named many."

"Who have you named?" he asked.

She opened her mouth to answer, but then her eyes went lost, staring out in confusion, as if she couldn't remember those she had named.

More silence. Again, decorum won out. "And what is your name?" he finally asked.

"I am Kat."

"Kat? Just Kat?

"I am Kat. The gods named me Kat."

"I see. The gods again …"

The Autocar passed the tiny hamlets and sparse wetlands of Esther. As they neared his holdings, he produced several Holystones of various colors—magenta, lavender and olive green, and insisted she hold them in her hand. These Holystones would lessen or deaden the effects of her Shadow tech. She took them without undue fuss and dropped them into her basket.

"No, no, I want you to hold those stones until I tell you to release them." Remarkably, she fetched the Holystones from the basket and held them, her attention fixed on the window and the wonders passing outside.

The vast expanse of Belmont Manor appeared in the distance down the lane, partially obscured by low-hanging misty clouds threatening rain. The clouds matched Stenstrom's spirit.

Kat looked at the manor. "What is this place?"

"My home. Belmont Manor."

"A ruin?"

"No, hardly. And I shall warn you now, commit any treachery, perform any mayhem or attempt any harm and I shall put a quick end to you, regardless of the knowledge you claim to have. Do you understand?"

She gave him a quick glance, said nothing, and then resumed looking at the rapidly approaching manor, a wonderland of large windows and white, red and black bricks on a hill by the sea. She clutched her basket in anticipation.

A great many dishes were served at the grand dining table. This great table had been cherished by his late mother, where she held court with the family; all twenty-nine of Stenstrom's sisters. He still felt her spirit here, locked in the wood and carefully-chosen fabrics. Stenstrom sat with his eyes locked on Kat, the Black Hat. She appeared to be aptly named. She was at the end of the table, with her bare feet on the chair. She reached and grabbed like an unruly child, wolfing the food down. She didn't say much, simply looked at him and giggled every so often. Her chin and mouth were slick with sauces and hanging with bits of food. The western face of the dining room was open, with a grand view of the hilly gardens and Merian grounds beyond. Stenstrom had snuck her in that way, hoping to encounter nobody. He wanted as little interaction as possible—he didn't trust this Black Hat an inch and couldn't wait for her to be gone. As she noisily ate, he could see the red and white speckles of Gwendolyn's stone on the hillside, her memorial he kept tended with fresh flowers—one of the flowers was missing, destroyed back at Clovis. He felt the flower's loss, lamented taking it there.

The bizarre meal continued. This Black Hat, this 'Kat' person, seemed truly insane. She took great pride in unscrewing every jar of sauce, spice shaker and marmalade she could get her hands or tail on, proudly showing the unscrewed lid to Stenstrom. She then made a grand show of screwing the lids back on.

"I wish you to eat with me," she said, her chin glistening, unscrewing yet another jar and showing it to him.

"I am not hungry."

"Eat!" She grabbed a leg of chicken and threw it into his empty plate. "Eat, eat, eat, or I shall say nothing."

"I am becoming tired of this game," he said.

"But I am not," she said. "Think, Garment, how nice it shall be to kill that demonic machine in blue lights with your bare Man's hands."

"That is not my name."

"Yes, it is."

Frustration grew within him. Fine, he would eat—anything to appease and be done with this foul creature. He took his napkin and spread it on his lap. The Black Hat watched, mimicking his movements with her filthy fingers and sharpened nails on the fine cloth. He picked up his chicken leg and took a bite.

Kat tore across the tabletop, knocking dishes and steaming clumps of food to the floor, and took a bite out of the other side of the leg as he did so, the two of them biting from either end. Stenstrom dropped the leg and was open-mouthed in shock. Kat giggled and licked a bit of the savory juice off his lips. She then returned to her seat.

"Yummy ..." she purred.

One of the doors to the hall opened with a click—Stenstrom quickly turned. Damn! He thought he had locked them all. He didn't want anybody coming in here; it wasn't safe.

His sister Lyra appeared through the columns, wearing her usual silver Belmont gown and university pin; her thick black hair set in the Belmont style.

"Bel, what's going on in here? Why are the doors locked?"

He forgot Lyra could pick locks as easily as he could. Locking the doors would not keep her out.

"Lyra, I want you to turn around and go back out. Will you, please?"

"Why?"

She approached the table and saw Kat sitting there, making a mess. "Who is this?" she said with a hint of disgust.

"Lyra, please."

Lyra was incensed. "I care not who this person is, Bel, she shall not sit at our mother's table in such a fashion. Get your feet—your filthy bare feet— off the chair, sit up straight and do not eat with your hands."

Kat continued eating. "Who is this woman ...?" she said in a small but caustic voice.

"I am Lord Stenstrom's sister. I am a Lady of this Household. Now, kindly do as I asked."

"Or what?"

"Or I'll beat you within an inch of your life until you learn some manners."

The Black Hat showed Lyra her hand and created several ugly Shadow tech claws from the tips of her fingers. Lyra shook her hands and produced three MARZABLE daggers. The two of them stood off for a moment.

Kat giggled and slowly put her feet down. She grabbed a napkin and cleaned her face and hands. She then picked up her knife and fork, and, somewhat clumsily, began using them.

Stenstrom and Lyra watched her eat.

When she finished, she wiped her lips, belched mightily, and then scrambled on all fours across the tabletop in a blur like a wild raccoon, her basket curled up in her tail. Platters and silverware went to the floor in her wake. She jumped off at the far end, bounded through the door Lyra had unlocked, and was gone.

"Oh, good Creation!" Stenstrom roared.

They sprang from the table and went to the doors. "Was that a Black Hat?" Lyra asked, hiking up her gown and running at his side.

"Yes. Yes, I believe so."

They exited the dining room and looked around, seeing nothing. He ran toward the eastern corridor in a panic, Lyra following. "Why did you bring a Black Hat to our home?"

"Because she has information that I need! I thought I could handle her!"

"Yes! Well done, Bel. Well done!"

They moved through one corridor after another, seeing nothing. It was completely frustrating—she could be anywhere. He cursed himself for not having the Gift of Waft. His mentor Captain Davage had it, and he always felt rather envious.

The Sight might also be handy about now.

They heard a clatter coming from behind them. They both turned. Far off, at the distant end of the corridor, a tangled blonde head appeared from around the corner, low to the ground, then vanished.

"Come on!" Stenstrom yelled, feeling thoroughly enraged. They pursued the Black Hat in such a fashion throughout the manor, first led one way, and then the next, Kat content to lead them on a merry and highly frustrating chase. Her speed and agility were incredible.

Eventually, Lyra tired. "Bel, this is silly. I think she's baiting us. Clearly, she wants us to pursue her." She leaned against the wall and pulled her heeled Belmont shoes off, her feet aching. "I need to sit down."

The nearest room was the manor's main library, a massive open room several levels high full of the extensive Belmont collection. Lyra padded into the room and flopped into an overstuffed chair, rubbing her tired feet.

Stenstrom paced. "Who's present at the manor today? I want to make sure everyone's all right."

"Not too many. I think Deneba was here, but left this morning. Possibly Ione is roaming about. I think Virginia is planning to stop in this weekend with her children. Father's at sea as usual."

"How could I have been so stupid? I should never have brought her here. I thought I could control her."

Lyra sat in her chair and looked around. "I don't get the feeling she's a great threat, Bel. Call it intuition, but I mean, she's had ample opportunity to escape or start blowing things apart. Her behavior seems a bit odd. And I'll wager if we stay in here long enough, she'll come to us."

"What do you mean?"

"Watch—you'll see. I'm certain I'm right."

Sure enough, after several minutes had passed, the Black Hat appeared in the room with a clatter of wind, blowing books and papers aside, her basket still in tow.

Stenstrom was in a rage. "That was a deadly mistake, you manky ..."

She reached up with two fingers and closed his mouth. "Shhhhh ... shhhhh ..."

He batted her fingers away. "Do not presume to ..."

The Black Hat turned away from him. She looked about the vast room, taking in the multi-levels of shelving and books, her head swiveling this way and that. Scaling the walls effortlessly, she made her way up to the top, tail flicking.

"All right, Black Hat—I demand you keep your promise and tell me what you know regarding the murderer of my love!" he yelled, leaning back, looking up into the heights of the room. "You demanded to be fed, and you have been fed. You demanded courtesy, you have received it."

The Black Hat ignored him. "These are books, yes?" she called down.

He rolled his eyes. "Of course—a rather novel thought, as this is a library!"

"Not burned?" she said, moving gracefully along the railing. "Not crumbling?"

"Of course they're not burned."

She hopped around from shelf to shelf, eventually pulling out a large red-bound book. Holding it coiled up in her tail, she allowed herself to fall with airy grace to the floor. Quickly, she hopped up onto one of the tables.

She presented the book and laid it on the table top. "And these contain knowledge?"

"Yes—I have asked you a question," Stenstrom said. He was expecting backup and outrage from Lyra. Instead, she simply curled up in her overstuffed chair and watched. She had a slightly amused look on her face. She seemed to be enjoying this situation.

Still crouching on the tabletop, Kat looked at the book cover. "What does it say?"

"I have kept my end of the bargain!" he roared.

She impatiently tapped the cover of the book with her sharpened nail. "What ... does ... it ... say?" she repeated. She gave her basket a shake.

He leaned down. "It says *Practical Atlas of Kana, Onaris and Hoban.* It's an atlas—a set of maps."

She gasped. How easily he had read that. She opened the cover and turned to several maps, all highly detailed and hand-painted.

"Pretty," she said, staring at the map. "Is this a representation of where we are now?"

He looked again. "No—that is a map of the Gold Coast of southern Hoban. Again, I have asked you …"

"Show me. Show me where we are."

Stenstrom sighed and turned to the book. He flipped through the pages until he found a detailed map of the Estherlands of Kana. "There," he said, pointing to a blip on the eastern coast. "That is where we are."

She leaned down and looked. "Where does the sun live?"

"The sun does not live anywhere. It's a star. It's millions of stellar miles away."

Kat pointed at a word on the map. "What does that word say?"

"It says 'Tyrol'. That is where we are—in the Tyrol region of the Estherlands."

"And, and where were we, in the mountains?"

"Clovis."

"Show me."

Stenstrom flipped a few pages back and tapped a map detailing the mountainous Vithland region of Kana. "There. Clovis."

She stared at the page in wonder. Finally, she hopped off the table and stood up straight. "You shall teach me," she announced.

"Pardon?"

"You shall teach me to read."

"I shall do no such thing. I demand you disclose what you know, or I shall forget that I am in my home and thoroughly thrash you."

She crossed her arms and stood there defiant. "I have knowledge that you seek. Killing me shall seal my lips forever. You shall teach me to read, then I shall disclose what I know. I shall write it down."

Stenstrom stared at her, hard. She appeared to be steadfast. He whirled in frustration.

He turned to his sister. "Lyra?"

She sat there and shrugged her shoulders.

"Can you not simply tell me—then I shall swear to teach you after I have had my revenge? I give you my word as a Great Lord."

"No! Ha!"

"You are an insufferable sprite, you know that, yes?"

She smiled up at him. Her white-blonde hair was a mess. "Yes, I know that. First, you shall teach me to read, then I shall tell you what I know. No 'backsies', yes?"

5—A Dedicated Student

Time passed in Belmont Manor.

Stenstrom fully expected Kat to either tire of this daily game, or attempt some sort of treachery. But after a week had gone by, she showed no signs of doing either. Every morning at seven bells, she was up and ready to begin. She had been given a small room in an isolated section of the manor; a room loaded with monitoring equipment and Holystones should she try something funny.

Every morning, she rose, washed in her small bathroom and ate. She had significant issues with her bed. The mattress gave her fits. She swore it was painfully uncomfortable and terrifying to sleep in, preferring the floor. They eventually changed out her mattress with an extremely hard one, which she grew to grudgingly accept. Also, getting her to make use of bath soap as she washed was the most difficult part, as she disliked strong floral scents. Giving her fragrance-free soap solved that problem and the odd smell she once bore vanished. Her filthy green clothes had been cleaned, and they gave her several changes of gray workmen's clothes to supplement her wardrobe. She had mastered the art of using a knife and fork, but she still had a bad habit of sitting up on all fours, like a cat. Shoes had been made available to her, but she mostly shunned them.

Her lessons were from nine until fifteen bells. Things did not go completely smoothly. There were several drama-filled blow-ups in the library where he assumed the jig was up at last. She got frustrated several times as he tutored her, taking the book he was using as a teaching aid and blasting it into shreds with a burst of Shadow tech. They then came to grips, Stenstrom expecting her to fight to the death or to commence creating mayhem. But she centered her tantrums on him—the two of them sometimes bloodying each other like cage fighters. And, invariably, after a minute or two of punching, kicking and wrestling, she calmed and resumed her seat ready to continue.

If he was bleeding, she would always try to attend to his wounds first before continuing. If she was bleeding she would expect him to attend to hers.

"Why are you bothering with this?" he would ask, panting, dabbing her face with a cloth.

"Because I wish to read this book," she would reply, pointing at the red-covered atlas that sat on her desk.

In the evenings after dinner, he would continue her lessons. He was amazed how little Kat knew about anything; she was a virtual blank slate waiting to be filled, therefore her evening lesson was an attempt to furnish her with basic knowledge, consisting of:

Remedial arithmetic.
Teaching left hand vs right hand.
Remedial dining etiquette.
Remedial geography.
Remedial astronomy.
Remedial flora and fauna.

And Lyra had to assist with several more modest topics:

Basic feminine hygiene.
Proper use of one's bed sheets.
Proper wear of ladies' garments and accessories.
Best bathroom practices (after Kat created a near panic one evening on the patio).

The evening sessions often went late and often got quite lively. Despite everything, Stenstrom found he was enjoying himself teaching Kat to count and her left from her right, teaching her the names of the moons, the stars, everything. No topic, no matter how innocuous, was out of bounds.

Kat was given a strict set of boundaries in the manor she was not permitted to cross. She was allowed in the library, the mostly empty north wing where her room was located, the small guest dining quarters and the patio. She was not allowed anywhere else. Amazingly, Kat observed the restrictions placed upon her without fuss. She also had been given a job; helping out in the kitchens during midday, doing whatever was needed. She earned one sesterce a day.

Additionally, Stenstrom was being hounded by Professor Shurlamp. His week had come and gone. She was impatient for him to come to her in Calvert as he had promised. Yet he would not leave his home unattended until the Black Hat was gone. He wrote the professor back, making up an excuse, which did not please her in the slightest.

Time continued.

Fits of occasional temper aside, Kat was a remarkably determined student. After a week or so, she nearly had the alphabet mastered, the letters W, S and Z giving her the hardest trouble.

He came into the library one day after lunch, and she was prancing about, bouncing from table to table like a nimble sprite—he thought she had gone mad. She leapt in front of him and held out a piece of paper. "I have written my name!" she announced proudly.

He looked at the paper. Written in a rough, child-like script was: KAT. Close enough for now.

✶   ✶   ✶   ✶   ✶

Stenstrom and Lyra strolled down the walkway looking out on the green. Fall was just around the corner, such a pretty time in Tyrol, the trees waiting to burst into color. "So, where is she?" Lyra asked.

"I gave her a task to accomplish, and I'm fairly certain she's sitting in the library right now performing it."

He could see Gwendolyn's little stone surrounded by red and white roses on the hillside. The roses were looking poorly, with several bare spots. The roses needed tending. He had been neglecting them. Kat had been taking up most of his time.

"She is very committed. I don't think I'm really surprised though," Lyra said.

"Why?"

"Well, it was obvious from the start. She clearly craved your attention. Why go to all this trouble if she didn't?"

"She tried to kill me in Clovis."

"Did she? You're more of an expert on Black Hats than I am, but I'm told they don't simply come out and fight somebody. They hide, leave little StTs all over the place and let their Shadow tech do the fighting for them. If she willingly came to grips with you, maybe it's because she wanted to get your attention, or perhaps she just wanted to touch you or something."

"Touch me?"

"Yes, you handsome fellow, you." Lyra smiled. "Are you intentionally playing dumb, or are you simply making excuses?"

"What excuses?"

"You're trying to make excuses to deny yourself the fact that you like Kat, that you're becoming fond of her. I'll admit it. I like her a lot, she makes me laugh. I'm glad she's here."

He turned to gaze at Gwendolyn's distant stone.

"She loved you, Bel—Lady Gwendolyn. But she's gone. You're too young to become an old hermit. I certainly don't want that for my brother, and I don't think she would have wanted that for you either." She lit up. "You know what I think?"

"What?"

"I think Professor Shurlamp was right about the *Covus*, how it could help you. Maybe Kat is a *Covus*. Have you thought of that?"

"Of course not. What makes you say that?"

"Because you're not moping around like you were before. You're not depressing me anymore with your half-dead antics. I actually caught you laughing the other day during Kat's evening session—don't try to deny it. You like watching her reaction to new things as much as I do." She pinched his cheek. "And, mostly, because you seem like my brother again, not the soulless shell you'd become. I'm grateful to her for that."

They continued their walk.

* * * * *

Stenstrom walked into the library. He had several lessons he had prepared the previous evening for Kat to try. She was a compliant houseguest and an eager student, and, surprisingly, as time went by, he was becoming an eager teacher. He found himself creating little lessons for her to perform with gusto; he found himself thinking about the lessons while at dinner or prowling the grounds of his estate, and it was with a hint of pride that he was pleased with her progress. She knew her alphabet for the most part and was beginning to sound things out.

Odd—his shell of morbid emptiness inhabited only by himself, the demon and Gwendolyn's corpse, was largely gone. Days went by when he didn't think of her once.

Kat was filling things up.

The *Covus*, Professor Shurlamp had said. *The Covus will strengthen you.*

Kat.

Perhaps Lyra was right.

Perhaps?

Kat was not there that morning, her usual chair by the window was empty. "Kat?" he called, looking around.

Her tabletop was neat and well-organized. Her stack of blank pages sat squarely in the center, several of her favorite pens were lined up to the right side, and the prized red-bound atlas was sitting off to the left side. She was favoring her right hand to write with.

But no Kat.

He checked the guest dining room and she was not there either, though the staff said she had dined there for breakfast that morning as usual. Her apartment in the north wing was empty: bed made. There was her basket sitting in a corner.

He wondered what was in it. Though curious as to what might be kept within, he backed away, leaving the basket unopened. He would respect her privacy.

Stenstrom went down into the southern wing to get Lyra, so she could help him look. He heard laughter coming from her room.

Peering in through her partially open door, he saw Kat sitting at Lyra's

boudoir. Kat was well out of bounds—she was not allowed in the southern wing. Lyra was hard at work combing Kat's mess of white-blonde hair. What an amazing transformation. Some of it Lyra had sheared off, especially at the temples, leaving Kat with short whitish stubble over her ears and up the side of her head. But over the top and back of her head, Lyra had somehow gotten most of the tangles out and tamed it. Her hair was thick and lovely, pulled back out of her face and held with a felt clip. Lyra also had painted Kat's face and rosed her lips with powders.

The gray workman's clothes Kat had been wearing were not present. She sat there in one of Lyra's old dresses, a nice red one.

She saw him through the door and smiled. "Good morning, G." She called him 'G', short for 'Garment'. He had come to accept it.

He had to admit, Kat was very pretty. Coming from the wild in a significant state of dishevelment, he hadn't previously noticed Kat at all, his proper Belmont upbringing surely had biased his view of her; she certainly hadn't matched any of the aspects of beauty or grace he had been taught to appreciate. But now, cleaned and groomed, she seemed almost like a different person, one who demanded an immediate reassessment of her beauty. Her head had a lovely shape; long slender neck, nice cheekbones, well-proportioned facial features, handsome chin, an interesting demure nose, jade-like eyes and a fascinating, lattice-like Shadowmark of jet black that accented her eyes and skin tone. Her features weren't such that they grabbed one right away, they took time to appreciate. His sister Nathalie had been like that, never one to attract a gentleman at the beginning of a ball, but always had many to choose from by the end. And here was Kat, all cleaned up, a deceptive 'end of the ball' beauty.

Her accent was also changing. Her guttural, barking sort of speech was mostly gone. From listening to the cooks jabber in the kitchens in the evenings, she was developing a charming Tyrol drawl, similar to what his mother had once spoken with aplomb, mixed with a hint of that earthy wildness she had before. Her voice was becoming quite lovely to listen to. Her skin, cleaned and bathed, was snowy white and she was filling out, gaining several pounds of healthy weight.

He looked around. "What is going on here?"

"I'm sorry I'm late for my lesson. Please don't be angry with me," she said.

"You're a bit out of bounds, Kat," he said.

"It's my fault, Bel," Lyra said. "I invited her to my apartment. I wanted to get Kat something decent to wear for a change, and decided to have a go at her hair."

"Am I in trouble, G?" Kat asked.

He laughed. "No, no. I don't see why we can't expand your area of roam a bit. You've earned it. You've worked hard."

Kat gave him a large, toothy grin. Look at her teeth. They had been a crooked, discolored mess, but now they were straight and glittering white after two visits to the Hospitalers in Tyrol.

"See, Kat, I figured he'd see reason," Lyra said. "Now, Kat's hair was a challenge, it had probably never seen a comb the whole of her days. Some of it was impossible, I had to chop parts off, but most I salvaged. And then we started talking."

"Talking about what?"

Kat, basking in the chair, lazily spoke. "I saw one of the cooks doing something that confused me. I was asking Lyra about it."

Lyra patiently smoothed Kat's hair, continuing to free it from its remaining burs and snarls. It became thicker and lovelier with each pass of the comb. "Kat saw Elenor from the kitchens kissing one of the boys delivering groceries behind the larder the other day."

"Did she?"

"They were pressing their mouths together, 'kissing' as Lyra called it. What is kissing?" Kat asked.

"Go on, Bel, tell her," Lyra said, smiling.

He thought a moment. "Kissing is something people do to express affection for one another."

"Have you ever kissed anybody, G?"

Stenstrom blushed a bit. "Yes, Kat, I have."

"Does kissing hurt?" she asked, interested.

Stenstrom laughed. "It can, if not performed properly."

Lyra agreed as she pulled the comb through Kat's hair. "It certainly can. Remember that boy from Wiln I was seeing last summer? The boy was a biter. Terrible. The worst."

"What were you doing kissing the boy from Wiln?" he asked.

"What, are you Mother all of a sudden, Bel? I kiss lots of boys. Sorry to burst your bubble."

"Show me," Kat asked, shuffling in her seat. "It sounds interesting. The cook seemed to be enjoying herself the other day. I like you, G, come over here and get a kiss."

Stenstrom weighed his options. The thought of kissing Kat was intriguing, but now wasn't the right moment. "Perhaps another time," he said. Lyra just shook her head.

Kat attempted to press the matter with further questions, but then relented and moved on to another topic. "Lyra says you can do magic, G? She said you can make things appear from nowhere." She looked utterly content sitting there letting Lyra comb her hair.

"Yes, I can, so can she. We have the same training."

"Can you do something for me?"

He thought about it. "The morning is escaping us. Your lesson awaits."

"Don't be a party-pooper, Bel," Lyra said, struggling with a knot. "Show her something. My hands are full."

He thought about it a moment, then shook his hands. Several Holystones appeared between his fingers. Kat was impressed.

"How'd you do that?"

"Can't say. It's a skill we all have—of course, it's not Shadow tech."

"Can you teach me?"

"It's a family secret. You have to be in the family to know how it's done."

"Ah," she said, her eyes becoming a little dreamy. "I see."

Kat smiled and waved her hand. A bit of Shadow tech formed between her fingers and shaped itself into a flower. "Here, G—take it. It won't hurt you." The flower wasn't black, as Shadow tech normally was; instead, it was a brackish gray. Her Shadow tech was changing, just as Countess Sygillis of Blanchefort's Shadow tech had changed from black to silver. He had seen it with his own eyes during his days aboard the *New Faith*.

Carefully, Stenstrom reached out and took the flower. It twisted in his fingers, reached out and gave him a kiss on the cheek.

"I'm magic too," Kat said.

Kat's lessons progressed. She sat there staring at the simple phrases in front of her, leaning over her work, carefully sounding out the words, tracing her progress with her finger. Her black sharpened fingernails were gone, replaced with trimmed red ones—more of Lyra's handiwork. She struggled with one sentence, one with lots of Ws. Stenstrom stood over her, patiently adding his encouragement.

She eventually got through it; she had read her lesson for the day. She stood in triumph and they embraced. She looked up at him expectantly, caught up in the moment.

"G ..." she whispered. He felt her heart beating through his coat and shirt.

Kat was so pretty, he could feel the alluring tug of Shadow tech moving through her body. Captain Davage, married to a notable Shadow tech female, once told him in private: *"Kissing a Shadow tech female is like kissing a live power socket—the jolt it provides never ceases to amaze."*

He could kiss Kat, and probably more right now; whisk her to his bedroom and continue her 'education' under cover.

Look at her; eyes large, mouth parted. She was ready. Lyra had said it: *"...perhaps she wanted to touch you ..."*

He remembered the first time he had kissed Gwen, on the ballroom floor on Bazz. The moment struck him and he had kissed her.

But Gwen could take care of herself. Kat was ...

He couldn't—how dare he think such things? Kat was his student, a guest in his home, and she ought to be treated with the proper respect.

He pulled away. Without excusing himself, he left the room.

6—The IBBAANA Ball

The invitation sang out in bold 4-D holographics that would trigger only in the presence of an IBBAANA brotherhood member, which Stenstrom still was. He didn't bother to read it. It was an invitation to the grand IBBAANA (Interstellar Brotherhood of Barrs, Actuaries, Attorneys, Notaries and Accountants) ball at the top of the Mortimer Hotel in Bern—the same one where, two years ago, Gwendolyn had accepted his hand. Stenstrom had no intention of going.

"Why aren't you going?" Lyra asked, holding the unopened letter.

"I don't want to. Bad memories."

"Bad memories? Of Gwendolyn? How could her memory be bad? Go, Bel—mingle with your friends. Have some fun. Here's a novel thought—take Kat."

"Kat?"

"Certainly. She's proved she's not a threat. I think she's earned some time out for all her hard work. She would love to go."

Take Kat?

✳ ✳ ✳ ✳ ✳

He sat on the darkened rooftop overlooking the gray-walled cathedral near the sea. It was raining in a gentle mist collecting on the sturdy fabric of his HRN. Below the crags and buttresses of the heights, the burnt-umber city of Tyrol stretched out in front of him, hugging the coast in blacks and blinking garnets. He had his old mask on again from years ago, when it contained magics to protect his soul from the Sisters' power. With the stocks of his NTHs pressed against his ribs, he was all alone and lost with his thoughts. He wore his mask when he was troubled, clinging to its old magic like a favored security blanket.

Thoughts of Gwendolyn, his fallen love. Of the demon, her murderer; and of the Anatameter that beckoned to him, beyond his reach, but ever-present.

Of Kat, the newcomer he never saw coming.

After a bit, he smiled and turned. "Don't be shy," he said, sensing her presence. "Come on, there's room."

A lithe form in green bounded to his side from above, managing the heights with ease. Blonde hair pulled back, held in place with one of Lyra's clips. Her green Black Hat clothes cleaned and sorted.

"Been following me long?" he asked as the rain quickened, streaming off his hat in a gentle spray.

"For a while now," Kat said. "Why do you come here to the rooftops, G? Why do you run?"

"Just chasing dreams," he replied.

"I've dreams to chase, too. Let me run with you. I won't fall. I want to come."

She noted the mask on his face. "Why do you wear that?"

He laughed. "Not sure, really. I used to need its magics for arcane protection, but those days are past. It's just foolishness, I suppose."

Kat reached up and removed the mask. "You're too handsome to cover your face, G." She tossed the mask away. It lay on the rooftop, flat, collecting raindrops.

"You think I'm handsome?" he asked.

"Oh yeah," she said. "I've always thought that. I love looking at your face."

Stenstrom moved to the rooftop edge, his face uncovered. "Well, come on, then. See if you can keep up!" He tore across the skyway, leaping from building to building, TKing with joy. Kat effortlessly followed, bounding on all fours, their laughter unheard on the rainy streets far below.

✶　✶　✶　✶　✶

The IBBAANAs had reserved the entire penthouse ballroom and rooftop garden terrace of the stately Mortimer Hotel for the ball and spared no expense for a night of magic; the place glittering with bright lights and colorful party favors hanging from the ceiling and rolling across the ballroom floor. Expensive catered food lined the walls on streamer-covered tables. Punch and shaved ice in pinks, blues and oranges was ladled out to sparkling crystal glasses like a poured dream as the full orchestra devoured the silence with cultured full-beat dance music. Tonight was a night for the studious and rather introverted men and women of the IBBAANA to emerge from their windowless desk jobs and let their collective hair down. Many ladies in fine gowns of assorted colors roamed about the party, some in attendance with certain gentlemen, others alone, waiting to be offered a cigarette. Most of these ladies were members of a League social circle known as the 'Ballwigs'; beautiful ladies of high social standing who made it their practice to attend balls all over the League, report on the situation and create gossip. The IBBAANA ball wasn't necessarily a hot A-List event, but the Ballwigs loved to come every year just to see how many shrunken IBBAANA hearts they could break, how many rejected and humiliated IBBAANA pelts they could add to their collection. Most of the Ballwigs were clearly unimpressed with the little IBBAANA men, casting Stenstrom and a few of the other more desirable fellows occasional hopeful glances.

Wearing one of Lyra's finest teal gowns, her blonde hair pulled up and set, the sides of her head freshly shaved (a look she favored), Kat was ready to dance. Standing next to Stenstrom with a glass of punch, she watched people dancing on the floor, taking it all in, bobbing with the music, observing the steps. After several dances, she banged on Stenstrom's shoulder. "Come on, G, let's get out there. Let's hit it! Hell yeah!"

A bit of nostalgia took him: *He had formally asked Gwen for her hand on that floor.*

"No, Kat, I'm not a good dancer."

"Oh, come on!"

Some of the IBBAANAs came up, big-toothed, grinning, hands in pockets, asking for Kat's hand to dance.

She looked to Stenstrom. "Go on, Kat, have fun."

"Awwwww …"

Kat spilled out onto the floor and danced with the gentlemen, though she cast frequent glances back at Stenstrom, who lingered in the wings, content to watch. Kat danced, a little clumsy at first, but gaining in skill and polish with every set, the whip of her blonde Mohawk moving like a comet. Soon, she was dragging the IBBAANAs across the floor quite well—small wonder, considering how agile and rubbery her limbs were. She quickly became popular with the IBBAANAs, being whisked from one to another with many waiting their turn. Many of the Ballwig ladies, some who had wanted little to do with the IBBAANAs at the onset of the party, soon found themselves ignored in favor of the smiling, inviting, approachable Kat. They inserted themselves on the floor like colorful Ballwig marbles, hoping to regain the men's attention, give them hope and then crush their souls later. As they danced, the gentlemen spoke in Kat's ear. She responded by pointing at Stenstrom—apparently they were seeking to determine her status for the evening.

Some of the IBBAANAs approached Stenstrom, asking about Kat. They commented on her fascinating accent, they wondered where she was from, what House she belonged to. They appreciated her unique hairstyle and her decorated Shadowmark; they all thought it was a particularly handsome one. It had become the fashion in League society for ladies to paint a mark over their right eye similar to a Black Hat's Shadowmark; non-Black Hat ladies were generally feeling a bit left out as reformed Black Hats became more sought after. They countered by painting a mark over their right eye, to command the gentlemen's attention, and the fashion was spreading. Some, such as the Ballwigs, took the practice quite seriously, forming studious groups dedicated to researching and perfecting the art. Some went as far as to tattoo their chosen marks permanently.

Still, those were mere paint. The IBBAANA gentlemen had no idea

Kat's was a real Black Hat's mark.

All this attention directed at Kat affected Stenstrom. He was determined at the beginning of the evening to sulk and be nostalgic for Gwendolyn. She had danced on that very same ballroom floor, done up to perfection in her Fleet uniform; she had taken punch from the same crystal. As the night wore on and Kat was whisked from one eager gentleman to another amid the laughter and the approving glances, he became a little possessive; one might even say a little jealous. Kat was his student after all, why wouldn't he feel that way; protective, as a mentor might feel toward his charge? He determined that he was, at this point, quite attached to her—perhaps more. He wondered what it would be like to not have Kat there in the library every morning with her pens and paper awaiting her lessons. He concluded it would be horrible, to have nothing to look forward to again but Gwendolyn's shade. That was a lonely place he couldn't bear to go again.

He was now certain; Kat was indeed special. Whether or not she was some sort of Extra-Planar creature, a *Covus* as Professor Shurlamp called it, was irrelevant. With Kat around, the pain was forgotten. Life meant something again.

Stenstrom made up his mind to cast aside his dour attitude, to step out onto the floor and occupy a bit of her time. But before he could get started, he heard a cultured yet commanding voice from a nearby table. "I'd heard you'd taken up with an urchin from the wild, so I came to see for myself."

Sitting there with perfect, straight up and down posture was Professor Hannah-Ben Shurlamp in her familiar pink and black attire. A tea cup sat in front of her—punch and shaved ice appeared to be well beneath her. Though she was, by any measure, a beautiful woman, her formidable air and relentlessly unavailable presence seemed too much for the IBBAANA partygoers to overcome, and they left her in peace. She took a sip of tea. "It seems you've dressed her up for the occasion. She learns tricks well."

"Professor," he said. "I didn't know you were a member of IBBAANA."

She rolled her eyes. "Of course I'm not. I'm no notary or attorney or paid clerk, and I'm not a giggling, strutting Ballwig either, though they have begged me to join. There is no party on Kana or beyond that I cannot gain immediate entrance to, either via social or technological means."

Stenstrom seated himself across from her. The Professor seethed, but in a controlled, ladylike way. "It seems you have a short memory, sir. I recall asking you not to take up with anybody until we have finished collecting data and determined you a suitable *Covus*." She tapped her gloved fingers on the tabletop, awaiting an answer. "So then, who is this … person?"

The music was loud, the good cheer moving across the floor, the uncorking of bottles. Stenstrom had to speak up. "I haven't taken up with anybody. Kat is my student. I'm teaching her to read and write LC, and

I'm also teaching her to count, and then I'd like to teach her Esther if she's interested."

"'Kat', is it? How charming. There is no such official language as 'Esther'. It's, as they say, 'pidgin speech'. Might I suggest that there are any number of free shelters, vagrant asylums and convents across Kana that could fulfill such a role, and they are more than qualified to teach an illiterate woman to read, write and count." The professor's great brown eyes flashed. "Honestly, I had no idea you had such primitive caprices, sir." The professor locked him in her gaze. "Get rid of her at once. Send her off. Make her gone, immediately. We have work to accomplish."

"Thank you, Professor, no. I'm quite happy with Kat. I'm pleased at the progress she's making. And I'll proffer the thought; perhaps she is this *Covus* entity you enjoy mentioning."

The professor was unimpressed by that declaration. "What in the Name of Creation prompts you to say that?"

He shrugged. "I feel much better than before I invited her into my home. I feel alive again. I still miss Gwen, I probably always will, but her memory is now in the proper nostalgia. The emptiness, the physical pain I felt at her loss is gone. I'm ready to move forward."

The professor ground her teeth. "Impossible. You are not qualified to make that determination, sir. Perhaps your weakness for vagrants has temporarily clouded your judgment. Perhaps you are momentarily intoxicated with lust. *I* shall determine who your *Covus* is, and *I* can assure you she shan't be some identity-unknown illiterate, dyscalculia refugee from Creation knows where. Your *Covus* will be a person of high regard, from the finest of circles and from the heights of League Society."

Stenstrom looked about the floor. "So, you're saying my *Covus* will be an empty-headed Ballwig, then?"

"Possibly, but that is irrelevant, isn't it? Your dallying with this vulgar waif from the bush will taint our results, and, at a lesser level, sully your already precarious reputation. So, will you willingly do the correct thing and see her off ..." She took another drink of tea. "... or shall I do it for you?"

"I shan't. I am the master of my fate, not you, and not your bloody computations, which mean nothing. And, by the by, dyscalculia is a brain disorder preventing the sufferer from being able to count. Kat has no such issue, she simply was never taught."

The professor smiled. "I had the opportunity to scan your little Kat. According to my readings, that Shadowmark around her eye isn't merely paint, as is the droll fashion these days, is it? It's a real Shadowmark, making her a viable Black Hat. Shall I inform the Sisters of her presence? They don't take kindly to unregistered ex-Black Hats at roam in the League, do they? Seems to me, they'll simply take her off to Valenhelm or Twilight 4 where, in all likelihood, she will never be seen or heard from again."

Stenstrom shot back. "Yes, of course, assuming we hadn't already taken that step and registered her with the Sisters ahead of time." He stood up. "They have already acknowledged and approved of her presence. I believe this conversation is at an end. Good evening, Professor." Stenstrom walked away to locate Kat.

The music rose to a crescendo. Dancers clapped. The professor's steady voice cut through the noise clear and loud, barging into his ear. "You're going to force me to take action, are you? Very well. I wonder, as you look at all the happy faces in the crowd, sharing the merriment, if they are mere partygoers here for an evening of enjoyment with their peers, or if they're Ballwigs plying their chosen hobby … or if they are assassins, sent specifically to kill your little harlot. Never force my hand, sir. You've only yourself to blame for the consequences."

He turned to confront the professor. Her seat, occupied only moments before, was empty, her tea cup, partially drunk, sat unattended, her abandoned spoon clattered to the table.

He was certain the professor wasn't one to make idle threats. She was more than capable of having paid assassins here mingling in the crowd of IBBAANAs. Worried, he went out onto the floor, searching for Kat. He pushed through, some of the unattached Ballwig ladies getting in his way, smiling, drink in hand, seeking a dance.

"You want to offer me a cigarette, don't you?" one of them asked.

Assassins in the crowd …

"Thank you, ma'am, no." He pushed past the woman. There she was, at the far end of the floor with three IBBAANAs seeking her attention. He quickly made his way to her.

"G!" she cried, throwing her arms around him. "I thought you'd never get out here. I'm having such a good time! I love dancing! We're going to dance at home, right?"

"Kat, we need to leave. This very moment!"

"Awwww! So soon?"

The music pitched up. So many people.

"I'll explain later. Let's go!"

He put his arm around Kat's shoulders, leading her off the floor to the exits. When they arrived, the grand main doors leading to the hotel's lifts were locked; they rattled in their frame as he tried to open them. Through the glass panes was a long wall-papered corridor carpeted in tasteful finery leading a fair distance to the lifts. He saw a familiar figure standing alone at the end of the corridor.

Hannah-Ben Shurlamp. She smiled in a lady-like fashion as the lights in the ballroom went out.

Confusion. Sudden silence as the orchestra stopped playing. People milled about, wondering what happened to the lights.

Somebody dropped a glass. It shattered on the floor with a 'tink.'

Then: Pop! Pop!

Sounds of bottles uncorking, or the pop of a gun being fired. The crowd in the ballroom undulated in sudden panic. People crushed up against the doors, trying to get out. Stenstrom could pick the lock to the doors, but that would take some time, and there were too many people about—too many possible enemies in the employ of Professor Shurlamp. Thinking fast, he saw the doors across the ballroom leading to the rooftop terrace were still open. He moved Kat toward them.

A group of people bowled into them, separating Kat from his grasp and knocking Stenstrom to the floor.

"Kat, get to the rooftop! Go as fast as you can! Don't stop for anything!"

With a ripping of cloth, Kat formed her Shadow tech armature and crouched down. Galloping on all fours, she went up the side of the wall and tore out of the ballroom. As she departed, he saw pocks of pulverized plaster form in her wake: bullets hitting the wall. Somebody was shooting at her, finding her too fast to target.

Three men were on top of Stenstrom, grabbing at his sleeves, trying to hold him down. A woman came, a wadded-up cloth in her hand. Falling to her knees, she slapped the cloth over his nose and mouth. The cloth was saturated in some sort of knockout agent. The agent was fast, and he would be out in moments; no doubt awakening to find himself Professor Shurlamp's prisoner.

The woman was jerked away like a fish on the line, dropping the cloth, pulled out the terrace doors into the night. Summoning the Sisters' strength, Stenstrom pushed the three men off. He TKed into the darkened heights above the confusion on the floor and soared out the doors to the rooftop. Outside, on the hedged hotel rooftop, a grinning Kat stood over the fallen body of the woman who had tried to knock him out, her Shadow tech tail waving at her back. Lyra's gown was ruined.

"Come on, Kat!" he cried. She extended her tail, wrapping it around his waist. A moment later, she was in his arms as a crowd of people spilled out onto the rooftop after them. Stenstrom, with Kat, soared out past the edge of the rooftop, diving down several hundred feet. He leveled out and continued on over the dark waters of the Sea of Atalea, soaring fast. Far off, under a cloudy sky stained by city light, the peaceful skyline of Bern twinkled in the distant haze. When he had put a good deal of distance between themselves and the hotel, he slowed. What a debacle.

Kat was all smiles in his arms, her hair whipping in the night air.

"Hell, that was fun!" she cried.

7—Those who were Remembered

Soon after the IBBAANA party, all the restrictions Stenstrom had placed upon Kat were removed. She now had freedom to roam the Manor and its grounds, and Stenstrom was eager to take her on a guided tour. It was a beautifully clear fall day; the surrounding countryside festive in reds and golds. He had started off showing her the cliffs by the sea—always very pretty but quite dangerous, very steep, and studded with picturesque but deadly rocks with a precipitous hundred foot drop to the thin rocky beach far below. The beach itself was dangerous, just a tiny fingernail of land with the constantly churning gray surf replete with hidden rocks just beneath the surface and deadly undertows ready to sweep away the unwary. The harsh Tyrol coastline was certainly not for tourists.

Stenstrom was careful with Kat as she fearlessly leaned over the edge, the long fall just a step away, gently taking her about the waist, steadying her footing. Without missing a beat, Kat slid out of his grasp. Balancing on the edge, she girded the skirt of her blue dress to her knees and went over the side. He was amazed how she could nimbly traverse the sheer cliffs, bounding from outcropping to outcropping to the rocky beach. She stood there and waved, and then came back up again just as fast.

She was filthy and grinning, her shoes missing—not unusual with Kat.

Taking her arm, Stenstrom walked her around the sprawling grounds of Belmont Manor, allowing her to appreciate the great brick and mortar rectangle, five floors high, emblazoned with proud, white-paned windows and topped with a sloped, cranked-in rooftop decorated in fanciful stone loops and arches—he had to keep Kat from climbing it; there would be time enough for that later.

He led her down the hill from the manor to the Old Tyrol Road running south to the distant city of Conwell, and north into Tyrol where it ended in the city square. He had promised to take Kat to Tyrol, to show her all the old places his mother once loved; the shops, the squares, the city within a city few outsiders ever saw, a place full of mystery and wonder.

Stenstrom was eager to show it all to Kat.

On the other side of the road heading inland from the sea was a steep, cone-shaped hill covered in trim grass, all turning gold with the season. "This is Merian's Hill. It's the tallest hill for miles around. Though I despise mountains, I love hills; they feel more comfortable to me."

Kat trudged at his side. "Hey, G, can you give me a hand? It's a steep hill." She smiled and held out her small hand.

"So, you can go up and down the deadly seaside cliffs with no apparent difficulty, yet you need help with the pedestrian Merian's Hill?"

"Well, you know how it is, G."

He took her hand and she curled into him, holding his hand with both of hers.

He laughed. "Why don't you tell me how it is?"

She blew on his hand, possibly trying to kiss it but not knowing how to kiss. The spot on his hand where she blew was livid with coming and going striations of gooseflesh. Captain Davage had told him what it was like to love a Shadow tech female; his Countess Sygillis of Blanchefort: *"When she's heavy in Shadow tech, just holding Syg's hand is a wonderland of sensation. It's like going on holiday to a very electric place. When I pull my hand away, I see minute little strings of it have passed through her skin and latched onto mine. Imagine getting kicked in the teeth, and imagine further that the kicking feels ... marvelous."*

The Sisters' power within made him sensitive to Shadow tech. He could it smell inside her, moving around, like a metallic flower scented in dark perfume. Stenstrom concentrated and silently recited a litany his mother had taught him to ward off carnal delights.

About halfway up the hill were a stone column and a small semi-circular platform facing the manor below. "What's that?" Kat asked.

"That's my mother's gravesite."

"Why is it built into the side of the hill?"

"Mother was a stern matriarch. She ran our house with a tight fist. There were thirty of us to manage, but she did it with annoying precision. She taught us all everything she knew. The magic tricks I and Lyra can do are her legacy to us. We placed her gravesite there specifically on the hill because it commands the best view of the manor. Even in death, Mother would, no doubt, wish to watch over the manor she loved."

"Do you miss your mother?"

"Of course. She could be a demanding, rather difficult person, but I'd have her no other way."

"Wish I had a mother, one that I knew, anyway. Or a father. My angels, I've always thought of them as my mother and father."

Stenstrom embraced Kat. Though small, she felt good in his arms, so different from the much larger Gwen, but no less comforting. There was the Shadow tech again, fragrant, teasing. The powerful urge to give her a kiss returned, but he stuck to the litany and refrained.

Kat was still his student and his guest ...

At the top of the hill were a cluster of stone, hut-like structures arranged in a seemingly random pattern, mixed in with a series of tall poles stuck in the ground and a gallery of crude statues.

"What are these?" Kat asked, still holding his hand. "Are they ruins, like in Clovis?"

"Of a sort. These are what remains of an old Merian Hermitage. A thriving village of them once lived here atop the hill several hundred years ago. The Pilgrims of Merian are a sect of simple folk preaching an alternative view of the Elders and the history of the League. The ones who lived here moved on long ago. Merians tend to be wanderers. It's a shame they're gone; the Merians are good people."

Kat moved among the ruins, taking them in. She climbed up one of the huts and reclined on the cool stone, a sigh escaping her lips.

"You love lying on bare rock," Stenstrom said.

"Feels perfect to me, a lot better than that crazy bed you want me to sleep on. I could lie here all day." She beckoned. "Come up here, G. Try it. You'll love it."

"Thank you, Kat, but no. While we're here, I have a few unannounced tests for you to accomplish. I think you'll enjoy them. First test: somewhere amid these old structures is a fairly new and rather conspicuous bit of graffiti. I'd like you to locate it and read me what it says."

"Ok, but climb up here with me first. Come on, please ..."

He relented and climbed up the old structure, situating himself next to Kat. He used to climb these old huts as a child with Lyra; here with Kat in the afternoon sun he felt like a child again, everything fresh and new. Kat put her arm over his chest, toying with the fabric of his shirt. "Love this place, G. Feels like home. I could close my eyes and have a nice nap."

"I'm glad, I want you to feel at home. Go on, now. On with the first test."

Kat hopped off the hut. "Ok, ok, let's see." She wandered around and through the huts. "Not really sure I know what I'm looking for," she said.

"You'll know it when you see it."

She browsed through the huddle of huts and soon located, right at eye-level, a few words crudely cut into the stone. "Not this, is it?" she asked, pointing at the letters.

"That's the very one. Well spotted."

Kat placed her face near the stone wall of the hut and traced along with her finger. "Ummm, Luh, luh, luh, er, er, errrrr, rah," she said, sounding out the first word. "Luh ... er ... rah ..." Kat bounced up and down with excitement, pointing at the word. "Lyra! This word says 'Lyra'! Am I right?"

"You certainly are. Well done, Kat. Keep reading."

She moved on to the next word. "Luh, luh, ovvv ... sssss. Loves! The next word is 'loves'!" Kat stared at the word and touched it with her hands.

"Correct again."

Kat moved on to the third and final word. "Lyra loves ... Juh, juh, juh, ew, ew, ew, pp, pp, ee, tuh, tuh, tuh, er. Lyra loves Jewpeter!" Kat said proudly.

"Very close. It's Jupiter. 'Lyra loves Jupiter'."

"Awww, how sweet. Who's Jupiter?"

"A boy from Mercia she was keen on when we were children. She lived in terror of our mother discovering that inscription."

"Did Lyra kiss Jupiter?"

"I imagine she did. Apparently, she's kissed quite a few boys."

"What happened to him?"

"Don't know. He disappeared after a while. Lyra was rather fickle as a child. We can ask her at dinner this evening if you like."

Kat put her hand back on the word 'love'. "Still waiting for my first kiss, G."

He tingled to kiss her, but his litany against desire was working, allowing him to maintain an aloof air. "I could go get Lyra and have her give you one."

"You know what I mean."

He wished Kat would just attack him. If she made the first move, he would have an excuse to kiss her.

"I tell you what. If you can count how many Gaffer poles you see here, I'll give you a kiss as a reward. Counting the poles is your second test."

Kat gave him a large grin. "'Bout damn time! What are these poles for, anyway?"

"The Merians used to wrap canvas around the poles and paint them in bright colors when they were giving Service."

Kat returned to Stenstrom's side. "Count the poles, huh? I expect my kiss to be memorable." She counted the poles, pointing with her finger. "One, two, three ..." Stenstrom nodded as she counted, hoping she would get it right.

And then she slowed. "Four ... Five ... Seven ..."

"Try again."

Kat swiped the hair out of her face and cursed. "Goddammit ..."

"Kat, I must ask, who is teaching you speak this way?"

"What way?"

"The swearing. Is it the cooks?"

"Yeah."

"I'm going to have to have a talk with the cooks. Swearing is not lady-like, please remember that, and I really don't wish to have my kitchen staff cursing like sailors as they go about their day. You have a very impressionable ear right now, I don't want you picking up bad habits."

"It's fun to swear, G. It's like casting Shadow tech, only with your mouth."

"If at all possible, I'd like you to curb your swearing for the time being. Now, please count the Gaffer poles again. You were doing fine."

Kat jumped down off the Merian hut and went to the nearest Gaffer pole. "Well, hell, G, if you want me to stop swearing, you might have to give me a damn reward or something to make me stop."

"Like what?"

"I don't know. You might have to give me two kisses?" She banged on the nearest pole. "I've been waiting for you to kiss me like I saw the cook and the damn grocery boy doing. If I like kissing, you might have to kiss me all day to make me stop. One!"

He sat up, his back aching from the stone. He wanted to kiss her right now. She went to the next pole, and the next, and the next. "Two! Three! Four! That kiss better be damn good!"

The next set of poles was mingled among the old Merian statues. The statues were crude terracotta effigies depicting Merian worshippers and winged seraphs standing over them, once painted in the colorful greens and reds the Merians favored, now faded into a splotchy yellow color. Kat bounded up and banged on one of the poles. "Five!" She went to the next one and stared at it.

Six always gave her trouble. "Come on, Kat, recall your lessons. What comes after five? Relax and concentrate. Your kiss awaits."

Kat cried out in triumph and banged the pole with her fast. "Six! Goddamn six! Ha!" The next pole was situated among a group of seraph statues. Kat bounded over to it.

He awaited her response.

Kat stared at the seraphs, standing lock still which was unusual for her, she was normally quite fidgety. "Kat?" he asked. "What comes after six?"

She didn't respond.

He went over to her. She seemed fixated by the statues. "These are old statues carved by the Merians. My sister Virginia, who is very close to Lyra and me, used to be afraid of them. She thought they moved around at night and created Witchlights, which we sometimes see from our windows glowing in the moonlight."

No response.

"Virginia will be visiting soon with her husband, Lord Poole, and their children. I'm eager to introduce you. I'm certain you'll like her. She's a chef by trade, an amazing cook."

Kat was staring at the winged seraph, eyes transfixed, mouth hanging open, breath ragged.

"Are you all right?"

She slowly reached out and touched the stone wings of the seraph, birdlike with nested feathers carved in weathered relief.

"These wings ..." she whispered. "A winged person. I remember wings, not ... not stone ... but Shadow tech, feathery, black ... flapping, moving across the sky."

"What about wings, Kat? What are you remembering?"

Her eyes grew wide. She said something.

"What, Kat? I didn't understand."

"Not alone. Not alone! I wasn't alone at Clovis! There were others! There were others with me!"

"You were alone when I arrived. You said you inhabited Clovis alone."

Kat shook her head. "No. Not alone! There were others! I remember them now! Seeing these wings has jarred my memory. How could I have forgotten them? I loved them, G! They were my sisters! They should be here with us, enjoying all of this." Kat sounded desperate. "So lonely at Clovis! In the cold, forgotten ..."

She threw her arms around him, her counting lesson forgotten, the prospect of their first kiss forgotten. "Take me there, G! Take me to Clovis, please! I don't want them there alone!"

* * * * *

Stenstrom steeled himself. Here they were again ...

"Please watch your step ..."

The door to the Autocar slowly opened, revealing the reviled green and gold mountainous vault of remote Clovis, frigid in its isolation, haunted in its seclusion, fading to blue haze, the gallery of abandoned buildings scattered out in a grim tableau like a city of the dead. It offered the illusion of silence, of inactivity, but was in fact a vortex of partially heard cries, glimpses of hidden movement from other universes, clashes of steel, and the sounds of people dying replayed endlessly. He could hear it plainly, though he forced himself to dwell on other things: Kat, his sister Lyra, of quitting the area as quickly as possible.

Beyond the sad huddle of forgotten places and untrodden pathways once thriving with life was the innocent little path heading up into the mountains, ending abruptly by the reviled doors plunked side by side in the ground like a pair of tombstones, conspicuous as a knife in the chest.

The doors, the center of the vortex.

He wanted absolutely nothing to do with those doors. Nothing.

Best to get this over with.

Stenstrom got out and put on his HRN and hat. His NTH pistols jutted from his sash. Lyra followed him out, her long black hair alive in the mountain wind. She was improperly dressed in her Belmont gown with bare arms. She shivered and threw on a fur-lined traveling cloak to ward off the cold. "Gods, what a place," she said, her cheeks quickly turning rosy in the nippy air. "Vithland has always seemed a barren pocket to me. This doesn't even look like Kana."

"It's Kana sure enough. Do you need your gloves?" Stenstrom asked.

Lyra shook her head. "No, I want my hands free in case we're attacked."

Kat came out last, still in her blue dress, eyes wide, seeing Clovis with terror, hugging herself about the waist. She went to Stenstrom. He put his arms around her. She buried her face in his chest. "So, Kat, here we are. Do you need a cloak?"

"No ..."

"You say there are several other people here as well? Shadow tech females, like yourself?"

"Crawlers, from the Shade Church."

"Shade Church?" Lyra asked. "Mother taught us Shade Church is the scion of the Black Hats. Are these people Black Hats?"

"One of them is."

Lyra looked about the forlorn ruins. "The Sisters might have gotten them. I believe their stronghold of Westron isn't too far to the west. Surely they would detect the presence of multiple Shadow tech females here and investigate."

Kat shook her head. "Protection. We had protection. The gods gave them to me to protect us from the Sisters."

"What protection?" Stenstrom asked.

"*Sentrils,* from the gods."

Lyra looked somewhat astonished. "*Sentrils?* Bel, I didn't think *Sentrils* existed outside of a story book." She wiped her red nose.

Stenstrom held Kat tight. "I didn't think so either. Kat, these people, your sisters, might they have moved on? This place is inhospitable to say the least."

Kat seemed full of guilt. "They wanted to leave, but I convinced them to stay," she wept. "They're still here."

"Are you sure?"

She looked up at him, anguished. "*They're dead, G.* They're here in the ruins, dead. If I had let them go where they wanted, maybe they'd still be alive."

"Why did you want to stay in this desolate place?" he asked.

Tears fell down Kat's face. She said something, but he didn't understand. He wanted to press Kat further, but she seemed on the edge of delirium.

Lyra looked around. "Do you know where we should start, Kat? This is a lot of ground to cover."

Kat closed her eyes, trying to remember. "Everything's coming back to me, but in bits, in flashes. I remember! Water! The cistern!"

They moved into the ghostly passes of the ruins, the sound of their passage on the rocky path amplified. Lyra was on edge. She looked at the forgotten buildings and lost avenues. "I don't like this place, Bel. I feel like we're being watched. Who knows what sorts are hiding in these buildings, waiting to waylay us?" She shook her hand, producing three MARZABLE daggers from nowhere. She held them between her fingers like three claws ready to cast.

"There's nobody here but us," he said, though he felt the same disquiet. In the distance, he thought he heard the doors rattling in their frame. He glanced at his NTH pistols. The worn wooden grips jutted from his sash, their humble appearance belying their fearsome killing power. Nothing could stand before his NTHs.

The doors spoke to him. *Here again?*

The presence of his pistols comforted him.

Come to us ...

In the center of the ruins they came upon a fallen-in structure with bare metal beams still partially standing in rusty procession amid stony debris, like the ribs of a decayed animal. Down below was a pit filled with brackish water and fallen stones.

"Is this the cistern?" he asked.

Kat nodded. "We loved these waters. We played in them. We washed."

Lyra glanced down at the filthy, stagnant water littered with fallen debris. She wrinkled her nose at the prospect of 'bathing' in such a cesspool.

"And who is here?" Stenstrom asked.

Kat pulled away from his grasp and went to the edge of the pit. "Walker. My sister Walker is here!" She cast her shoes aside and dove in head first, disappearing under the dark water.

Lyra was worried. "Bel, this ruin isn't safe. She could get tangled and hung up on any number of hazards beneath the surface. This whole place is a death trap."

She seemed to have been under the water for some time. Stenstrom removed his hat. "All right, I'm going in after h-"

Kat exploded to the surface, gasping. With her was a headless, naked mannequin, much larger than herself. She clutched it around the torso, hanging onto it like a buoy.

No, it wasn't a mannequin—it was a headless dead body.

Using TK, Stenstrom lifted them both out of the water and onto the ground. Kat clutched at the body, hugging it, weeping uncontrollably. "W-Walker. My sister! My sister! I'm sorry! I'm sorry I left you here!"

The body was quite large for a Black Hat. It was meaty, long-legged, full-figured and perfectly preserved, probably from the Shadow tech within. No blood, no decay, and no smell either, save for the brackish scent of being immersed in dirty water. Had the body not been missing its head, it might merely have been asleep.

"What happened to her?" Lyra asked.

"Autocon killed her. Took her h-head. She was so beautiful …"

Stenstrom looked around; he didn't see a severed head about anywhere. Animals probably carried it off.

"And what happened to the Autocon?" he asked. "Those are Shadow tech demons, correct?"

Kat was inconsolable. "I killed it with *Sentrils*. Walker died defending me. She was the best of us, the strongest, the most beautiful. How could I have forgotten her, left her in the water? I should have died and she should have lived."

"You didn't die, Kat. You lived," he said. "Whatever overcame your sister didn't overcome you. You survived. You're stronger than you allow yourself credit for."

They wrapped the body of Walker in Lyra's cloak and carried her back to the Autocar. They opened the boot at the rear of the craft and placed Walker inside.

"How many more?" Stenstrom asked, closing the boot.

"Two more."

"Where?"

Kat pointed past the ruins, up the path to the doors built into the ground. Stenstrom was filled with dread.

The same place Gwendolyn died.

* * * * *

Stenstrom threw open the doors leading into the earth, saw the familiar uneven stairs going down to vile darkness. Lyra produced several yellow Holystones, shook them up and cast them down into the dark. They bounced down the stairs with an energetic rattle, revealing tired, light-starved stone, old mortar and the empty arch far below leading further into the ground. NTH pistols drawn, Stenstrom looked down, seeing the phantoms of his other selves coming and going from this horrid place in a never-ending stream, hearing their discordant cries. The visions and the noises were so strong here, so profound, he couldn't shut them out.

"You're certain they're down there?"

Kat nodded, hanging onto him with all her might.

Stenstrom was assaulted by the sights and sounds of other realms, like being forced to watch a thousand holos all at once. He spoke, his voice sounding muffled and distant. "There is something wrong with this place. I'm seeing glimpses of myself, other versions of me, coming and going, like a demented anthill where all the ants are me. Professor Shurlamp might be a mad woman, but perhaps she's correct about different planes of reality coming together here. Lyra, can you feel it?"

She nodded. "Yes, I do. I'm not seeing or hearing anything, but I can feel it, sure enough."

"Kat, are you ready?" he asked, sashing one of his pistols. She didn't answer, merely hugged him tighter, most of her small body buried deep within his HRN.

Protecting Kat, NTH pistol leveled, hammer cocked, Lyra with her MARZABLE daggers ready, they went down into the dark.

Voices assailed him with every step, glimpses into other universes danced before his eyes.

My wife ...
My father ...
Rescue her ...
SAVE HER!
And what of me? Is there no place for me?
WHAT OF ME?

He concentrated, shutting everything out as they passed the arch. Rolling several more Holystones in, the place emerged under dim yellow light. A vast man-made chamber lay before them. Rough hewn walls of stone covered in murals, aching with the remnants of ancient incense drifting about. Fallen debris, old dust, and a collision of universes rubbing together, spilling their sordid dioramas about the chamber in an incomprehensible jumble.

Nearby, a fluted column situated near the left-hand wall appeared in the light. "That column there, that's where we placed the Anatameter. It fit right on the top. Now it's gone."

"Over there," Kat said into his chest. They made their way to the column.

Stenstrom kicked something on the floor and it slid with a metallic rasp. Lyra picked up the object: it was a pair of protective goggles, dirty, scratched, dusted with grit. Kat took the goggles from her with shaking hands.

"These were a gift from the gods to protect our eyes, we were not used to the light. It was so bright. Bird wore them all the time, even after we didn't need them any longer. She loved them."

"And 'Bird' is one of your sisters?" he asked.

Kat nodded. "So gentle, so kind, so skilled with her hands. She couldn't wrestle, but she could make such things. I remember her so clearly now. She made me laugh and smile. How could I have forgotten?"

Past the column, two black masses lying on the floor emerged in the light of Lyra's Holystones. Dead bodies; both stuck to the floor like a pair of butchered carcasses. There was dried blood everywhere, splashed on the walls and carpeting the floor in a thick dark stain. One of the bodies was horribly mangled, a twisting of arms and legs; the other lay supine on its side in the illusion of peace. Stenstrom held Kat back while Lyra investigated.

Lyra knelt over one of the bodies, the twisted-up one. Moving her about, it was clear she was skinny and gangly. "It's a female, a small Shadowmark around her right eye. She's been stabbed, dozens of times."

Kat wept.

Lyra mouthed the words to Stenstrom: *"She really suffered, Bel."*

"Is that Bird?" Stenstrom asked. Kat wiped her tears and nodded. She held the goggles to her heart.

"Who did this to her?" Lyra asked, a questioning look on her face.

Kat pointed to the second body lying in a disaster of dried blood nearby. "Wheel. Wheel killed Bird." She trembled. "And then I killed Wheel."

Lyra moved down and inspected Wheel's body. Wheel appeared to be a small woman, like Kat, but fuller and more filled-out, like Walker. Her brown hair was a tangled mess, like Kat's had been. "Her throat's been ripped out. Did you do that, Kat?"

Kat pulled away from Stenstrom and approached Wheel's dead body, her tears wetting the blood. "Why, Wheel? We would have loved you, taught you, fed you ... Why couldn't you get the Black Hat out of your heart, out of your soul? Bird did it, Walker did it, I did it ... why not you too?"

Kat seized Wheel by her bare, dead shoulders, shaking her, demanding answers. "Why, Wheel? I loved you! All you talked about was becoming a Black Hat, inflicting pain. If you wanted to be a Black Hat, why didn't you get in the bloody missile and be a Black Hat elsewhere? You lied to me, when I didn't understand what lying was! Look what you've done! You lied to me, took my sisters from me!" Kat's anguish-filled voice echoed around the cavern. *"Why did you make me kill you?"*

Lyra inspected the pool of blood. She waved a yellow Holystone around. "I'm seeing a group of footprints in the blood."

"Gods," Kat wept. "The gods came for me in the dark."

"The gods? I'm seeing two sets of footprints: the impression of a man's shoe, a fairly small size, and a heeled shoe with a tapered front end—like a lady's boot. Looks like they came in, they knelt over Kat, and walked back out. These gods seem like flesh and blood people to me—wonder who they are?"

Universes clashed before his eyes. He saw them. Two people, a man and a woman; the man wearing a dark, modest suit and the woman wearing a shimmering green robe, like a Merian's robe. They went to Kat and held her hand. They wept over her fallen body, their love for her clear.

Creation, didn't they seem familiar to him.

And then a third person entered: tall, sinister, clad in black, eyes glowing with purplish light. The third person seemed angry. The man and woman then lifted Kat and carried her out. Whoever these 'gods' were, they were real. They guarded Kat's life. He was grateful to them.

Kat pulled him back from his vision. She rocked back and forth, asking the question over and over: "Why, Wheel, why?"

Wheel's dead body, missing its throat, gave no reply.

Stenstrom placed his hand on her shoulder. "Maybe she just didn't have it in her, Kat. Maybe whatever it was that happened to you and these other people far in the past in the Black Hats' pits left its mark, scarred her too much, damaged her beyond repair. Yet all those things that blackened her heart didn't blacken yours. You had the simple strength to overcome and move on. With your help, these two people did too."

As the gods had before, Stenstrom and Lyra helped Kat out of the darkness and back into the light of the surface.

✶ ✶ ✶ ✶ ✶

They placed Bird's body in the Autocar's boot next to Walker and covered them. Lyra and Stenstrom got in, ready for a horrid trip back home, sharing the vehicle with dead bodies. When Kat tentatively climbed back in, the Autocar reacted.

"Weight limit exceeded," the control glyph said. Hearing that seemed to push Kat over some internal cliff. She backed out of the Autocar in a demented fog. Eyes wide, full of hysteria, she bent over, clutching her waist.

"I don't want to be here all alone! All the death in this place." She looked at Stenstrom with pleading eyes. "Don't leave me here, G! Please don't leave me here!"

"Of course I'm not leaving you here, Kat. I'll pay the bloody Autocar to adjust its carry."

"Come on, Kat, get in. It's cold," Lyra said.

Kat looked about in panic, seeing nothing, hearing nothing. She staggered away.

"Kat!"

Weeping, she formed her Shadow tech armature, crouched down on all fours and tore off across the ruins, ripping the ground as fast as she could run.

Voices assailed her.

Come back ...

Murderer ...

Come back to the dark with us ... and never leave ...

The doors. The doors. She was heading toward the distant doors. No matter how they tried to get away, the doors were always out there pulling them back, never letting go.

She was caught from above, arms around her waist, and lifted into the air.

Stenstrom, at full TK, had her. She struggled and kicked.

"Where you going, Kat?"

"Let me go!"

He soared with her through the clouds and found a flat spot in the mountains far away from Clovis. Kat was trembling. "Let me go, G," she sobbed.

"Why did you run away, Kat?"

She held out her hands. "You saw what I did. I've killed with these hands. My sisters are dead. I was going to go below and beg the gods to bring back life to my sisters, and to take me instead."

Stenstrom took her hands. "Then I would wait in the dark with you. That's where I was before you came, in darkness, watching one day pass into the next, adding up to nothing. In Clovis, where universes touch and horrors have free lease to roam, you emerged, untainted by it all, given strength through innocence. Come, if you are to hide in the dark, then I will hide with you."

Kat looked desperate. "I don't want you in the dark, G! I don't want that for you! The gods told me you would come. That's why I waited in Clovis, because that's where they said you would come for me. I waited and waited, wondering what your voice would sound like, if you would be kind. To touch you, to wrestle with you, put my arms around you. I love you, G; even before I understood what the word meant, I loved you. And you'll not share my fate, I couldn't bear it."

"Your fate, Kat, is to come with me home to Tyrol, to climb Merian's Hill with me, read all the books in our library, to swear with the cooks in the kitchens and unscrew every lid you can get your hands on. Life has returned to Belmont Manor. Leaf and flower bloom, every new day is a gift to look forward to. You made that possible. Whatever forces conspired to bring us together, whoever these 'gods' are who guided you and provided for you and your sisters, I am in their debt. For the strength you had within to endure, I am in your debt."

He placed his hands on her face. "How I thought I'd never say the words 'I love you' again. Kat from nowhere, Kat from the ruins, waiting for me. Kat who had the strength to survive … I love you."

And they kissed for the first time, he parting her lips, taking her into his arms, trading the cold loneliness of the mountains for warmth and love.

✳   ✳   ✳   ✳   ✳

Weeks later, new monuments were placed atop Merian's Hill. One was placed at the northern end of the hill with a wonderful view of Tyrol village down the lane to the north. The inscription on the stone read:

MOUNTAIN WALKER

THE STRONGEST OF US

Nearby, another stone was placed. Several hollows were cut into the stone allowing room for birds to make nests. Already, a swallow had moved in, making a nest. The inscription on the stone read:

BIRD

THE GENTLEST OF US

And, nearby was a third new stone. The inscription read:

WHEEL

SHE HAS BEEN FORGIVEN

Part IV

Bellathauser

1—An Old Friend at the Dance

Not long after Clovis, Stenstrom wed Kat in a small ceremony in Tyrol, making her the first Countess of Belmont-South Tyrol. It wasn't a well-attended affair, as he had withdrawn from League society and Kat was a social unknown; just some of his family and many of the cooks from the kitchens whom she had befriended. The posts covering the event erred in reporting her name alternatively as Katherine, Katherwold, and Kattrine. They couldn't imagine that a brand new countess of a prominent Household would have a name as simple as Kat.

They did not consummate their marriage for nearly a month after the wedding. Kat, only newly introduced to kissing, knew little of the intricacies of sex, save what Walker had once shared with her. Stenstrom, always a gentleman, wanted to ensure Kat was fully briefed on what was going to happen between them before proceeding. Kat, sharing his bed, kissing him all night, was eager to try. Kat's rowdy friends, the cooks, had regaled her with all sorts of tawdry stories about their various sexual adventures, all of which she drank up with relish. As with many things, once they finally did get to explore the wonders of making love, Kat was a quick study, pulling him nude to the floor where she was most comfortable. Stenstrom had expected Kat to be shy and submissive, following his lead during their intimate encounters; however, such was not the case. She was aggressive and passionate.

One of the cooks had filled her ear with harrowing tales regarding her fondness for tying men up. Impressionable, Kat bound Stenstrom to the bed one night with Shadow tech and found she was enthralled with the experience. She bound Stenstrom to everything, to the columns facing the sea, to the marble busts in the empty western halls, to the dinner table, to the great urns in the gardens—whatever she could find. She especially enjoyed binding him to her sisters' monuments atop Merian's Hill by the dark of night so that she might share the experience with her sisters' spirits. By far her favorite sexual exploit was the 'Bouncing Egg'; essentially to surround the two of them in a sphere of Silver tech like a great egg (her Shadow tech turned silver shortly after their wedding), and, safe within, to go over the side of Stenstrom's grand balcony, bounce down the hedges over the cliffs and into the churning sea far below, all the while making love in the creamy, Silver tech-filled sphere, the two of them tossing about in unimaginable bliss for hours. Once sated and the egg dissolved, they would find themselves sometimes floating miles out to sea, where Stenstrom would have to discreetly

TK them back to shore and hope they weren't seen.

✶ ✶ ✶ ✶ ✶

Aside from her eccentric sexual practices, it didn't take Kat long to make a splash with the rest of the Belmont family in a big, schism-forming way. Years earlier, Stenstrom's mother, the late Lady Jubilee (Elders rest her soul, the usual toast at dinnertime), had designated that a silver gown accented with a sleeveless corset-like bodice of either black or silver should be the standard wear for ladies in the newly-minted House of Belmont-South Tyrol. All of Stenstrom's twenty-nine sisters, even the feisty Lyra, had observed their mother's design for years, even after her death, all of them laced up tight like silver dolls. Since the House was created after the marriage of Lady Jubilee to Stenstrom's father, Stenstrom the Older, League law dictated that she could not be the first countess of the House—that distinction would go to the first person married to a male heir, making Kat the first countess. That foible of law had infuriated Lady Jubilee the whole of her life, and she continually railed against it in Tyrol to anybody who would listen. As part of her estate, she left a lengthy, rambling, and somewhat threatening Vid to be viewed by the first countess in the event she was passed away. In the Vid, she implored that all the things she had created for the Household should be observed and made official by the first countess, especially the silver-corseted gown she had designed.

She demanded it.

Kat watched the Vid, saw the smoky, Pewterlocked image of Lady Jubilee, and listened to the thinly-veiled threats of curses, assassinations, visitations from the grave and other repercussions should her wishes not be observed. However, Kat loathed wearing a corset. Her body shape didn't favor a corset. Kat could handle a great deal of pain, could shrug off all manner of discomforts, but she had no tolerance for corsets—they reminded her of being buried alive in the Atmosphere Suit, a particularly reviled memory for her, and one she couldn't bear repeating. She preferred a less-restrictive garment that was more like a casual dress than a formal gown. She wanted sleeves to cover her scar, and she didn't favor silver much. Instead, she preferred wearing *Merian green.*

Julie, the bread-maker from the kitchens helped Kat create a simple green dress that she loved. This little dress, created in part by a commoner from the city, was Kat's choice to be the official wear of the House. Stenstrom predicted what was going to happen, and, indeed, much of what he thought would happen did happen.

Many of his sisters, most of whom were married into other Houses and no longer wore the old silver gowns, were nevertheless outraged by the change. Letters flew back and forth. Demands were issued. Threats were

made. His eldest sisters, Beryla, Wisteria, Antonia, Celesta
and Munnie, were so upset by
this development they came in
person to the manor, entourages
in tow, prayed at their mother's
gravesite for guidance, and demanded Kat wear a proper silver gown as designated by Lady
Jubilee. Beryla, the eldest and
most similar in temperament to
their mother, even resurrected an
old Tyrol custom: *Revenata*. She
appeared at the table in the full
image of their departed mother,
Lady Jubilee; her visage was the
same, her normally black hair
transformed into Pewterlock, cut
in her distinctive style, her voice
thrown to match their mother's.
She even had Mother's ubiqui-
tous cigarette smoldering in its stick. All this was intended to frighten and
intimidate Kat, as if Lady Jubilee herself had returned from the grave.

They also demanded Kat wash the Shadowmark 'paint' off her face and
wear her hair in the proper Belmont style, enough of the shaved temples and
lion-like mane, Mother would have none of that were she alive to protest.
All five of them swore they would not leave the manor until their demands
were satisfied.

Coming to Kat's defense were Lyra, Virginia, Embeth, Nathalie, Con-
stance, Xantrope, Deneba, Willia, Calami and Lucile—all of them arriv-
ing at the manor in force with their husbands and children to argue for the
countess. The two sides squared off as dinner was served. Lots of pounded
fists and pointed fingers at the grand dining table as the two sides argued—
all of them, except for Kat, done up in corseted silver like a set of angry
candlesticks, their various heads of black, Pewterlock and Half Pewterlock
like silver and black flames. It was the nearest thing to an in-family riot the
Household had ever seen.

During all of this ruckus, Stenstrom sat and stayed quiet—he could not
intervene on her behalf. If Kat failed to assert her authority over his sisters, especially the domineering *Revenataed* Beryla, if Kat gave into her
demands, then that would be it, there would be no getting rid of her. For
good or for ill, this was Kat's situation to deal with.

What could have been a boorish, contentious, and slightly supernatural situation didn't faze Kat in the least. After she had heard enough bickering, she tapped her knife against her glass several times, quieting the sisters. All eyes, both hostile and friendly, went to her.

"Well, I, for one, am loving having everybody here at the manor. All the people coming and going, all the noise and excitement, all the children playing on the hill. It's just so ... exciting."

Beryla, disguised as their dead mother in full *Revenata,* the eldest sister of all and Stenstrom's senior by seventy-five years, cast Kat a caustic glance. "This is a serious matter, 'Countess'. You, sitting here at *my* table, in a ridiculous green peasant's gown is unacceptable, and I shall return to my bloody death before I allow it to continue."

Lyra and Virginia shot up, ready to have a full go at Beryla regardless of what she looked like. Kat waved them into silence. This was Kat's moment to either assert her authority as the countess of the House, or to submissively yield to Stenstrom's fierce sisters.

Kat spoke, disguising her usual rustic drawl laced with profanity with a regal voice she had copied from the ladies in Tyrol. "I get your feelings on the matter. Your mother, the dearly departed Lady Jubilee, would be proud, and I wish I could have met her in the flesh."

"And what am I, Countess?" Beryla asked.

"You're ... Cloaked to look like the late Lady Jubilee. I'll have to ask my husband later what the point of that is. Regardless, I think I have a solution to this problem. It'll be fun."

"'Fun', Countess?" Beryla asked, fuming. "And what would that be, exactly?"

"G showed me the lovely Chalk House the other day. Down there near the lane. I'm told it's the official Belmont-South Tyrol ballroom. The inside is gorgeous. I loved the padded wallpaper, the chandeliers, and the open dance floor."

"I meticulously chose the materials and appointments for the Chalk House," Beryla said. "Everything was fretted over and well-thought out, including the choice of House gown."

Kat ignored that remark, returning the subject to the Chalk House. "A beautiful place, so much room to have a party." She giggled. "I'm told the Chalk House was destroyed once when a demon came to devour G."

Beryla's lip curled. "If you are referring to my *son*, Stenstrom the Younger, then yes, you are correct. The Sisterhood of Light sent a demon in the guise of a great fish to devour his soul, nearly destroying the Chalk House, the place where I was wed to my beloved husband, in the process. I restored it exactly as it was." Beryla still referred to herself as Lady Jubilee.

"Then it'll be perfect! I propose we have a dance competition—a dance-off in the Chalk House. We'll hire a couple of bands, get some great food in there and keep it going. She who can dance the longest without rest or exiting the floor may put an end to this argument, one way or the other."

Beryla was indignant. "A dance? What nonsense. We shall not settle this issue with a dance. Whoever heard of such a thing?"

Kat would not be deterred. "It occurs to me that I am the countess of this Household, Great Beryla, not you. I could simply demand that my re-designed gown be the official design, and that's the end of it, and you may return to your manor wearing your mother's face and rage through its halls until the ground shakes. But you are G's sisters, all of you are, and I love the lot of you. Let us enjoy each other's company, let us dance in the lovely Chalk House, and when it is over, we'll have an end to this matter."

∗   ∗   ∗   ∗   ∗

Kat's dance had been going on for five days in the Chalk House, the grand wooden floor crowded with people swaying to the music, the chandeliers glittering. Four orchestras had been hired, each taking over from the other after playing for hours; the music continuous. The rest of Stenstrom's twenty-nine sisters had arrived from all over the League, some against Kat and her green gown, some for her, mostly determined by age; the younger sisters were for Kat's re-design, the elders against it. After one day of dancing, the event officially became an 'endurocon', a ball that has no set end. Endurocons were always highly anticipated events in League Society, and it didn't take long for the dance to take on a life of its own. Word got out. People began showing up to attend in droves, many from Tyrol, many from all corners of Kana and beyond. The Ballwigs, wearing their distinctive Harrsprung pendants, arrived in force like a well-dressed, up-do'ed army.

Stenstrom was so proud of Kat as the dance went on, his heart full of love. This was truly her moment to shine in front of the whole family, to prove to his sisters that he had made a splendid choice. Kat's energy was boundless. She danced with him for hours until he could take no more and excused himself from the floor, then moved onto the children of his sisters, wearing them out and winning them over one at a time. As Kat could not leave the floor to eat (or to perform other unmentionables) Stenstrom fed her by lobbing bits of food from the buffet line that she would catch out of the air with her teeth, each toss and catch met with the approval of the many children milling about on the floor. Beryla, having to make do with occasional small, hand-held plates of food, most certainly did not approve.

Many of the sisters had already dropped out of the competition. Sabra, Ione, Lenta, Jonnia and Miranda only lasted for an hour or two before leaving the floor to mingle with the other attendees, disqualifying themselves. Stenstrom mused with humor that, perhaps, their laced-up, sucked-in corsets might have had something to do with their lack of endurance. Calami hated dancing and just watched. Nylar, Deserae, Elma, Celesta, Solona, and Io, who had begun the dance against Kat, found themselves changing their minds and siding with her by the third day.

✷　✷　✷　✷　✷

Beryla, still wearing the guise of their mother and fueling herself with various tinctures and potions, was Kat's lone opponent still in play. There were people everywhere enjoying the dance, most giving Kat their seal of approval. Strangers decked out in gowns of all makes and colors were scattered about the floor and dotting the walls. Ladies smoked from woodsy cigarettes offered by young gentlemen. Stenstrom was certain Professor Shurlamp hadn't given up; certainly she would try to send assassins into the Chalk House, dressed up in all their finery to have another go at Kat. Though they were wide open, no advanced security system, no cameras, no sensors dotting the grounds and an event like this would be fertile ground for an attack, Stenstrom wasn't worried. They had protection.

Older, sleepless things guarded Belmont Manor.

As he mingled with the crowd, he spied a familiar figure standing by the buffet line, holding a plate of food. It was a small man wearing a dark blue Calvert suit. He was hatless, had short blonde hair combed back away from his face, and wore an odd pair of lenses on his nose. The man gazed across the layers of smoke, out to the ballroom floor, staring at Kat who was slow dancing with one of Andromeda's sons. He looked at Kat from afar with obvious pride, like a father doting over his daughter.

Stenstrom approached the man. "A-Ram!"

The tiny A-Ram was all smiles as they embraced, Stenstrom towering over him. A-Ram had been his friend from the *Seeker* days, though they had grown apart following Gwen's death. He was one of the people Stenstrom had planned on reconnecting with once Kat was fully settled. It was good to see him.

"Where have you been, my old friend?" he asked.

A-Ram smiled. "I've been all over, actually. I'm engaged. I hope to be married soon."

"Excellent! Congratulations! Are you engaged to anybody I know?"

A-Ram thought a moment. "No."

"Well, I hope to be fortunate enough to receive an invitation to your wedding. I know we've grown apart, but I still consider you one of my finest friends. I swear I was going to seek you out."

"Of course you will." A-Ram flushed up a little. "Of course you will …"

Stenstrom looked about the floor. "Is she here? Your fiancée? I'd love to congratulate her in person."

"She's far away right now, but I know she's watching over us in her special way, even at this moment. She didn't want to create a stir."

"A stir?"

"That's not quite what I meant; she … didn't want to disrupt Kat's concentration."

Stenstrom wanted to get Kat's attention and introduce her to him, but A-Ram balked. "Hey, if you have a few minutes, I need to have a word with you. I'd like to share a few things, if I may?"

"Sure."

"In private, please."

A-Ram selected a few more things off the buffet line and they went out into the night air, the grounds and damp cobbles of the lane lit up in the soft glow of festive lamps. Faces, both familiar and unfamiliar, bobbed in the light as they came and went. Nighttime was always peaceful at Belmont Manor, just far enough away from the noise of bustle of Tyrol to be swallowed up by calm solitude framed by the distant, methodical stirrings of the sea. A treasure box of yellow and green stars spilled out in a gentle cascade of twinkling lights. The Belmont gardens stretched off for several maze-like acres—yet another creation of his mother's, every plant, every hedged turn, every bit of stone carefully planned by Lady Jubilee. For the longest time, the gardens had been deserted, tended daily by the gardeners but appreciated by nobody. Kat's dance had put a fresh breath of life into the Household, people milled about in the hedgerows, drinks in hand, seeing all the wonders his mother had intended for them to see, new couples looking for a romantic spot to be alone; perhaps in the years to come, they could look back to this evening with nostalgia and say this was the night they fell in love.

In the center of the garden were three giant-sized stone urns, again placed there by his mother, representing peace, love and unity. Under those giant urns, his mother had once plunged a knife into his chest, putting him to the Tyrol Blood Promise. Peace, love, unity … and a flaming hot knife wielded by a mother's hand.

Stenstrom and A-Ram came into the courtyard, A-Ram finding a bench to sit down with his plate of food. Stenstrom stood, looking back at the dim lights and white walls of the Chalk House, stained windows aflame with movement, seeing colorful minute shapes of people inside coming and going. He thought he saw Lyra heading out to Merian's Hill, her favorite spot for romance, with some fellow in tow.

"So, before I begin, Bel, I wanted to tell you how proud we are, of both of you. In this matter, you really showed your true colors."

"What matter? Are you referring to Kat?"

"I am. Many would not have been able to see the potential that lies within, what might be made of it. Many would have turned away from an unkempt person from the wild. We knew you would not. We told them."

Stenstrom was puzzled. How could A-Ram know such things? Kat was unknown to League Society, none of the stories of how they had met in Clovis had yet come out. Most of his own sisters didn't know except for Lyra and Virginia—that all might change now that Kat was a countess and a big hit with her dance. But, as of yet, Kat was simply another countess from a regular League House.

And another thing: who was '*them*'?

Before Stenstrom could press him for details, A-Ram continued. "I don't have much time, so I'll just cut right to it. Those footprints you saw in the Clovis underground, the footprints in blood—those were our footprints, mine and my betrothed."

Footprints in blood?

The gods?

Only one conclusion could be drawn: A-Ram and his betrothed were Kat's 'angels' she so often spoke of.

Stenstrom was speechless.

"Obviously, we have been a part of Kat's life for some time, long before she met up with you. We watched over her as she crawled in that terrible Black Hat dungeon, we wept as she suffered under their lash, but were continually uplifted by her simple strength and courage. The Black Hats were brutal, but Kat's will to endure was stronger, bolstered by a silent inner voice that would not yield. We argued Kat's merits before the gods themselves. We provided her with food, with clothing, with powerful magics, all in the hopes that you would discover her and see her for the person she is." A-Ram giggled. "I, I had to tamper with your Autocar a bit, to keep you at Clovis a little longer. I erased its memory."

Stenstrom thought back.

No configuration found ... the Autocar control glyph had said in its pleasing voice. That delay, with the time-consuming task of reconfiguring the control glyph, with having to re-enter and re-pay for everything, had given Kat time to pitch an argument to him, one that was ultimately successful.

What do you want?

I WANT REVENGE!

A-Ram and his lady, whoever she was, had made that possible.

Stenstrom wavered between shock, disbelief and a passing prickly feeling of anger, that his life had been somehow manipulated and pre-chosen for him. For a moment, he wondered what he should do: embrace A-Ram, or fly into a rage and chase him from the grounds.

A muffled cheer rose up in the distant glow of the Chalk House by the lane. He heard the dim sound of clapping coming from within.

Revenge? What of revenge? He hadn't thought of it in some time, had pushed it from his thoughts. All that unpleasantness, all that sadness … gone. Kat had taken all that from him. Kat was the medicine he had needed to continue with his life.

His beloved Kat was back there in the Chalk House, dancing for five days straight to appease his sisters when she didn't have to.

Kat, a girl from the Black Hats' dungeon. Kat, who somehow was watched over and guided to him by A-Ram, his old, distant friend.

A-Ram's footprints in the blood at Clovis, kneeling over the fallen Kat, guarding her life.

The anger quickly faded, replaced by curiosity and the warm thump of gratitude that this lovely evening with all his sisters present was due to A-Ram and his fiancée.

He burned with curiosity. Where to begin? What to ask? "Well, I'm listening," he said, presenting an even bearing, "go on, A-Ram. Continue."

A-Ram struggled a bit, deciding where to begin. "I don't have a lot of time tonight, Bel, there's so much to tell you. And … and if you're harboring any notion that we somehow predetermined your path, let me allay your concerns. We might have helped set the table, but you and Kat played it out on your own." He rubbed his forehead. "Now then, you of course recall a lady named Hannah-Ben Shurlamp, yes?"

"Professor Shurlamp? How could I forget? Do you know her?"

"Oh, I know her, that's for certain. Not directly, of course, but still, I've seen plenty of her. In all these places we've been, she is always the most unchanged, yet her role always varies the most, wildly so. Sometimes she helps, other times she's a pain in the rear. In any event, the Professor spoke with you about odd things, didn't she? About old gods and the infinite nature of the universe. Professor Shurlamp was correct about most things, about the nature of the universe and how there are many universes. She discussed with you the topic of Extra-Planar Entities, or EPEs as she called them—beings from other universes."

"She did, and I had little idea what to make of it."

"She was again correct. Extra-Planar Entities do exist, though she was spectacularly incorrect on several points." He looked down at his coat and brushed the fabric with his hand. "At this moment, I am an EPE, technically. I am Josephus, 7th Lord of A-Ram, I grew up in Calvert in the city of St. Edmunds, and I flew with you on the *Seeker*, but please believe me when I tell you, I'm *not* the A-Ram you know and served with. I serve with a different Lord Belmont. Where I come from, the *Seeker* still exists, it still soars the heavens, you are still its captain, and Lady Gwendolyn, alive and well, remains at your side. At this moment, I am a *Wulgrom,* a person from another universe, a different reality or plane of being—perhaps the Professor could explain it better. The A-Ram you know is probably back at the Fleet in Armenelos right now, in the mailroom or possibly the Admiral's office." A-Ram studied Stenstrom. "Do you believe me? Are you comfortable with this notion?"

"Do I believe you? Am I comfortable? Comfortable isn't really a good word for this situation. You seem to know things you couldn't possibly know, so what choice do I have? Besides, I've never known you to be dishonest, insane, or an imaginative story-teller."

A-Ram lit up and laughed. "That's true! It certainly is! That does seem to transcend the universes, doesn't it? When I become a father, Alesta will have to do the story-telling for our children, I'm not so good at it."

Stenstrom rubbed his chin. "Alesta? Is that your betrothed's name?"

"It is. She's a Pilgrim of Merian."

"It's a beautiful name, and she's a Merian as well? Perhaps that's why Kat favors the color green so much, Merian Green. You're doing fine. Please continue."

A-Ram finished his plate of food and set it aside. "So, not long ago, though it seems like it's been a lifetime, Alesta and I were approached to go on a bizarre adventure—pulled from our bed in the middle of the night, actually. We were told you needed our help, you needed guidance and we were to provide you with that guidance. We love you, Bel, we couldn't say no, so off we went. This adventure has taken us far away, to unseen places far from the League. When I think back on it, it all seems like a dream; standing in places no Leaguer has stood in thousands of years with Alesta at my side, seeing wonders I find difficult to describe. And we've not just traveled from one place to another; we have spanned the universes, like one might cross an ocean. I have, to date, had the honor of guiding five other versions of yourself, and as we venture farther away from our home universe, things get a little stranger every time. In one universe, you happened to be a woman, Bel, a tiny, comely woman. That was, uh, remarkable, to say the least. Alesta and I have put our marriage on hold until we finish this adventure."

Stenstrom was full of questions. "Well, I appreciate that. First off, who put you to this task and why?"

"I've been asked that question, by you, five different times already, and each time my answer is a little bit different as I learn more. We were put to this task by a woman claiming to be your wife. She isn't Gwendolyn, or Kat, or anybody else we recognize—she's a tall, elegant woman wearing a flight suit and a gun. Until recently, we had no name to call her—we simply referred to her as the 'Woman with the Gun'. Though it might sound odd, when in her presence, it really doesn't occur to you to ask her name—names seem pointless and unnecessary. She sometimes doesn't seem like an ordinary person, she seems more like a *presence*, if that makes any sense. She told us, in an alternate universe, that she is your wife and that she lost you across time and space, and that she needed us to help return you to her."

"And you believed this woman?"

"Again, you have to spend a little time with her to understand. She radiates goodness, truth, and a bit of sadness as well. Though her story was improbable at many turns, everything she told us turned out to be true. Alesta always suspected there was a bit more to her than she let on, that she might not be completely human, and that was proved recently."

"How so?"

A-Ram shrugged, struggling to adequately answer. "I saw her standing as an ageless giant in Cammara, her head breaking the clouds in a wondrous sky. In any event, the goal of our adventure was, and is, to guide eight versions of you through performing a series of tasks. When the tasks are complete, our work is done and we shall return to our universe and be married, and you shall be reunited with the Woman with the Gun. Not *you*—an alternate version of you will be reunited, if that makes sense. Your participation is required in order for the Woman with the Gun to be reunited with another version of you."

"I believe we're going to need a lengthier session to sort all of this out, possibly seated, with full bellies and a few stiff drinks in hand. What are these tasks I'm supposed to be doing?"

"They mostly center on a device called the Anatameter." A-Ram studied Stenstrom's face. "You remember the Anatameter, right?"

Anatameter …

Placed in Clovis.

Lost in Clovis.

Stolen … *by a demon.*

"The Anatameter—it doesn't look like much, but it's an incredibly potent arcane device, created by gods. Between every universe is a threshold known as the Hall of Mirrors. If you wish to traverse the plains, then you first have to cross through the Hall—Alesta and I have been through it many times. Anatameters act as a lock preventing most from passing, that's its usual function. But in some cases, Anatameters may be created for specific people. The one that was given to you by Queen Wendilnight was just such a case. The Woman with the Gun petitioned the Gods of Cammara, and they created one designed for you. What it does is it alters fate, or divine providence, something to that effect. When the knob is turned by seven different versions of you, then the situation will be ripe for the Woman with the Gun to be reunited with a new version of you. That's what we've been told."

"But I lost it. In Clovis. The vile creature that killed Gwen stole it."

More clapping from the Chalk House. People, gowned, colorful like jelly beans, filed out into the night air. A-Ram stood. "I know, and it's of critical importance that we retrieve it. I'm not exaggerating when I say that. We must retake control of it."

A tiny blonde-headed form in green wobbled out, greeted by more clapping. The figure made its way into the garden. It was Kat, a bit disheveled after five days of dancing, carrying her shoes. "G?" she called. "Where are you?"

A-Ram's eyes grew wide. "I don't want Kat seeing me tonight. She's been dancing for days—she's exhausted and she believes I am a god, or an angel, or whatever. Seeing me might be too much of a shock for her. Alesta and I will return in four days, at the top of Merian's Hill. We will reveal ourselves to her at that time when she's rested. Then, I hope you will be ready to hear our guidance and get the Anatameter back as soon as possible. Much rides on that, I hope you will heed me."

"I look forward to meeting this Lady Alesta."

"And she you. I must go!" He headed farther back into the hedges. "Four days, Bel."

Just then, Kat entered the courtyard. "G!" she exclaimed on seeing him. She came up fast and threw her arms around him. "I won, G! Beryla gave up, she even let her weird 'Dead Mother' disguise go. She's really pretty without the disguise. She embraced me, said I'd earned her respect and was headed straight to bed. She looked really tired."

"I'll bet."

"I've made so many friends. All your sisters are unbelievable. What are you doing out here in the dark?"

"Just talking to an old friend."

Kat looked around. "Oh? A friend? Where'd he go?"

A-Ram and his betrothed were Kat's 'angels'.

"We don't want to create a stir," A-Ram had said.

A-Ram was gone. Stenstrom saw a bit of fog rolling away to the north. "I'm sure he's around somewhere."

Kat leaned back and gave a prodigious, jaw-popping yawn. "Ohhhh, I'm so tired. Take me to bed, G, I could sleep for a week."

Arm in arm, they made their slow way out of the gardens toward the manor.

"So, how did you manage to go five days without visiting the bathroom?" he asked.

"Ladies' secret, G. You know, I danced with every one of Antonia's sons, I don't remember how many, and then you know what I did?"

"What, Kat?"

"I danced with her daughters, too. She has a lot of kids."

"She certainly does."

His heart full of love for Kat, Stenstrom took her to bed, she too tired to complain about the mattress.

He would worry about gods and demons and Anatameters later.

2—The Hall of Mirrors

Kat slept for two days after the dance, a deep cleansing sleep. She didn't even fuss about the bed, her body usually preferring the cold hard marble of the floor, which she found most comfortable. She didn't even want to tie him up and have sex. She was out fast. Many of his sisters took their leave as she slept, vowing to return soon to continue getting to know Kat, whom they now appreciated much more than before.

As she slept, A-Ram's words filled his head: *"We'll be back in four days. We'll meet you atop Merian's Hill."*

He teemed with questions, many of which he was impatient to have answered. He was certain of one thing, though: A-Ram and his love, Lady Alesta, had steered him and Kat together. A-Ram said he considered Kat his 'daughter'; they watched over Kat, fed her, clothed her, armed her. The topic Professor Shurlamp had proffered, the topic of *Covus*—a replacement for Gwen—danced across his thoughts. The Professor had wanted to perform research to scientifically locate him a suitable *Covus*, though she had assumed such a person would be a stately member of high society, not a filthy crawler from the Black Hats' Shade Church dungeon.

He lovingly gazed at his Kat as she slept, tiny in her nightgown, her blonde hair with freshly shaved temples mussed, her head sunk in a pillow's embrace. She snored a little.

He imagined A-Ram and Alesta somewhere far away, laboriously going about their task of picking Kat. Was it a big list they had to choose from, he wondered? Who gave them the list? Were there many names? Who were the other names, and how did they decide upon Kat, at first glance the most unlikely choice possible in a world of choices?

In any event, they had picked with their hearts, knowing him possibly better than he knew himself; out-performing anything Professor Shurlamp with all her data and statistics could have achieved.

All these things he would soon know.

✶　✶　✶　✶　✶

Once Kat was back on her feet following two days of deep sleep, Stenstrom wondered how best to tell her that her 'angels' were soon to visit, and that they weren't gods or anything of the sort; they were simply good people, friends, putting their own lives on hold in order to guide them.

"So, Kat," he said at the grand dining table. "We're soon to have visitors."

"More visitors? Who?"

"Some old friends of mine have promised to come and make your acquaintance."

"Oh, cool," Kat purred as she buttered her toast.

"You know them as well," Stenstrom blurted.

"I do?"

"They are Lord A-Ram and his betrothed, Lady Alesta."

"Doesn't sound familiar." Her knife scraped over the bread, spreading the butter.

"A-Ram was my helmsman aboard the *Seeker* some years back. He was at the dance."

"He was? I don't think I saw him. I don't remember that name."

"No. You were so tired from all the dancing, he didn't want to give you a start."

Kat giggled. "A start? Why would he have given me a start?" She took a bite of her toast.

Stenstrom decided to get it over with and simply tell her. "Because, Kat … A-Ram and Alesta were the ones who provided for you in Clovis."

Kat dropped her toast. "What?"

"A-Ram and Alesta were the angels who helped care for you. Alesta is a Pilgrim of Merian. They wear lovely green robes, just like the one you described seeing."

"I don't understand. How did …?"

Stenstrom threw up his hands. "I don't know. Darling, I don't have any details right now. A-Ram came to me at the dance. He knew all sorts of things, things he couldn't have known otherwise. That's why he didn't want you to see him; you were so tired the shock might have been too much for you. They're going to meet us atop the hill tomorrow, and they promised to answer any and all questions we might have."

Kat assailed him with questions, few of which he could answer. For the rest of the day, Kat was beside herself, pacing the halls of the manor, looking twice into every nook and alcove she came across, muttering to herself; clingy one moment, distant the next. She didn't want her lunch or her dinner, and she didn't even want to hang out with her friends, the cooks. She went out onto the terrace and stared at the sky for a long time, as if she expected to see A-Ram come flittering down from above. Despite what he had told her, Kat still considered A-Ram and Alesta to be gods, supernatural beings—though, technically, they *were* supernatural, *Wvulgroms* from another universe, that didn't make them gods. Yet she had operated under that notion for too long to cast it aside so quickly. The only way to convince her otherwise would be for her to stand in their presence, see them, and hear their words.

The next morning, Kat was eager and ready to go to the hill. She had removed her gown and instead was shoeless, wearing her old green outfit A-Ram and Alesta had given her. She even had her Shadow tech tail formed, though it had changed from black to a happy shade of silver. Also, she had her old battered basket.

Hand in hand, they went up the hill to the top where the old Merian ruins and the gravesites of her three sisters basked in the sun.

Hours passed. No A-Ram or Alesta. After a while of waiting, they got bored. Kat even opened the basket and showed him what was inside; the basket as well as many other things had been forgotten of late. She pulled out a few burned-out books she' had collected in Clovis, all written in what looked to be old Vith; some broken up bits of soap that appeared to have been sculpted into animal shapes (Bird had done that, she told him), and a dirty felt bag containing three silver cubes.

"*Sentrils*," she said, holding them up, the three objects nudging together in her palm like silver rocks.

Inspecting them, the *Sentrils* appeared like nothing more than small silver cubes etched with tiny markings. "What do these do?" he asked.

"Destroy Shadow tech, and hide me from the Sisters' gaze. They really work, too. Here …" Kat took the cubes and placed them in a triangular configuration around her body, one to her left, one to her right, and the final in front of her. He could feel the force the cubes created, the Holystones in his pockets shook with it, and after several moments, he couldn't see Kat any longer. She simply vanished, only to return a moment later as she picked them up off the ground.

"Well, those are remarkable," he said. "Even without instruments I could feel their potency. We'll look at them more closely later." Kat put them back in the bag and placed it in her pocket.

The final thing in the basket was a photograph Kat said was of him, though it was so dirty, moisture-stained and badly warped he couldn't make much out of it. Kat held the photo to her heart and carefully placed it back in the basket. "I fell in love with you over that picture, G."

"Awwww, how cute," came a voice from behind.

They both whirled around.

Standing over them was a bizarre woman in black. She was rather tall and undeniably curvy in a tight-fitting black oilskin suit. She wore black boots with precariously tall heels, gloves, and a light cape that shimmered in the afternoon sun. On her head she wore an odd metal helmet that obscured most of her face except for her pale nose, mouth and chin. A glowing purple visor covered her eyes.

Both Stenstrom and Kat reacted upon seeing her. The sight of her struck deep.

Stenstrom had seen this woman before, possibly in another universe. *You must want something,* another version of him had said.

I want you in my debt, the woman had replied.

"I know you," Kat stammered.

"'Course you do," she replied, her mouth movements very pronounced and expressive. The light from her purple visor grew in intensity. "You should know who saved your life. Yes, the last time you saw me, you were flat on your back, bleeding out after all that unpleasantness in Clovis. Our good friends, A-Ram and Alesta, convinced me you were worth saving, so I did it. I saved your life. I healed your wounds; I also knocked all those ugly memories from your head, though you seem to have recovered most of them. I suppose the next time I go knocking around in somebody's head I should do it a little harder."

"A-Ram and Alesta, where are they?" Stenstrom asked. "What have you done with them?"

The woman put her gloved hand to her heart. "I haven't done anything with them. They're indisposed, off assisting another version of you right now—the female version, I think. The various versions of you command much of their time, so I decided to come in their place." She smiled, showing her lovely teeth. "I'm nice like that."

Stenstrom didn't trust this woman. He put a protective arm around Kat. "And how is it you know A-Ram and Alesta?"

"I am … oh, how should I say it? I am A-Ram and Lady Alesta's 'boss', so to speak. Everything they've done, everything that's happened, has been by my leave and my sanction."

They were dumbfounded. Looking her over, she seemed to radiate a fierce other-worldly presence. Stenstrom spoke up. "So, what are you? Are you human?"

She giggled. "Do I look human?"

"Yes and no."

She seemed perplexed. "No? Hmmmm …" She puzzled for a moment. "So, in what way do I not seem human? Tell me, I'm curious."

Stenstrom and Kat looked at each other. "You have an off-putting, other-worldly presence that defies imagination," he said.

The woman put her hand to her chin and rubbed it. "Oh, I see. In any event, A-Ram was totally right about you. I'm thrilled everything worked out. I'm happy you two didn't fight each other to the death in Clovis, and that you're well on your way to learning to read, Kat. I could just give you the knowledge to read, you know, in any language you wanted, but look what the journey has brought you, both of you. Look what you two have created—I could just get all misty right here and now. But later … later. Right now, we have work to do."

"What work?"

"Important work. Work that needs doing. So, come with me, and let's make this happen."

A light came on in one of the Merian ruins. Cool musty air issued out of the open doorway. The woman went to the doorway and knelt down. Her light cape fluttered in the breeze. "You coming?" she asked.

"Of course we're not coming," Stenstrom said. "Whatever work you expect of us is none of our concern."

"Sure it is. Listen, I could force you to come with me right now. I could just put you in it and let you blunder around, but I don't want to do that. I want you to come with me on your own. You've always impressed me as being a good fellow, Lord Belmont. No matter what the universe, no matter what guise you take, you've never been afraid of responsibility, to place the lives of others before your own, so don't start now. You have all sorts of questions, about all sorts of things. I can answer them for you; all you have to do is come with me. Once this is done, you can look forward to a long life together however you'd like it to be, full of adventure or full of quiet familiarity. Don't come, and somebody else is going to have to do this for you, and that's not the sort of fellow you are. So, what's it going to be?"

Stenstrom gave Kat a kiss and straightened his HRN. "I'll come. A life with my Kat means everything to me. If there's work that needs doing, then let it be done. Kat, please return the manor and await my return."

Kat took his hand and bound it to hers with a twisting of Silver tech. "Like hell, G. You're not going anywhere without me to look after you. What are you thinking? So, let's go."

Bound together, they entered the Merian ruin with the woman in black.

✶ ✶ ✶ ✶ ✶

They found themselves in a long darkened corridor walled in tightly-fitted blue stone. The air around them felt humid and cold in comparison to the warm sunny breezes of Merian's Hill.

"Where are we?" Stenstrom asked.

The woman walked at their side, her boot heels noisy with each step. "You've had a quick primer on how the universe works, right, how there are an infinite number of universes? This is the fabled Hall of Mirrors; it acts as a threshold from one universe to the next. This is a null sort of place, it technically isn't anywhere in particular but it can be anywhere and it can look like anything. Realm-hopping really isn't good for the structure of the universe, and this place is supposed to prevent it. Regardless, some people spend a lot of time in here, they just never know it. And, that in itself is extremely dangerous. Bad things happen in the Hall of Mirrors. In case you're not aware, you've been in it quite a lot lately yourself."

"I have?"

"Yep."

Up ahead, they saw something. In the center of the corridor, a woman sat at a fancy cherry wood desk with dragonball feet. She was slender and quite attractive, raven-haired, sitting with perfect posture and grace, wearing a conservative Calvert ladies suit. Holographic screens racing with passing information floated in procession around her head as she conducted vast amounts of data with apparent ease.

Stenstrom instantly recognized her. "That's Professor Hannah-Ben Shurlamp, the one who tried to kill Kat."

"Kill me?" Kat asked.

"Over some nonsense, at the IBBAANA ball."

The woman walked up to Professor Shurlamp, who took no notice of her and continued working. "Don't worry, she can't hear or see us. There are many journeys into the Hall of Mirrors; each is separated by a thin but rather sturdy film of reality. The professor here has made it her life's work to understand the Hall and how it works and, ultimately, to control it at her whim, all without realizing she's often in it, working her computations."

Kat approached and looked the professor over. "She's pretty."

"She's a maniac," Stenstrom said.

"Why did she want to kill me?"

The woman answered. "Because in her experimentations she correctly determined that your husband, Lord Belmont here, is an Extra-Planar Entity, and that his losing Lady Gwendolyn created her an opportunity to further her knowledge."

"What opportunity?"

"To locate him a *Covus*, a replacement for Lady Gwendolyn. The broken heart of Lord Belmont could not have been repaired by just anybody, it needed a special person. That special person is a *Covus*. Essentially, the professor and A-Ram and Alesta were doing the same thing, both looking for a *Covus* to replace Lady Gwendolyn and heal his heart. But Professor Shurlamp's investigation was skewed by wealth, by social standing, pedigree and all those other things often given a high value in polite society. Her innate bias spoiled her findings. Her search for the *Covus* would have turned up nothing, would have been a disaster."

Kat was wide-eyed. "My angels ..."

"Yes. A-Ram and Alesta. They embarked on the same search Professor Shurlamp did, only they did not allow the foibles of society to taint their findings; they followed their hearts, ignoring names and titles, allowing their search to take them into the dark, meager places Professor Shurlamp wouldn't have thought twice about, looking for that perfect little bit of hidden light for their friend, Lord Belmont. And they were successful. They found you, Kat."

Kat closed her eyes and placed her hands over her heart. Tears came, running down her pale face. Stenstrom embraced her. The woman gently patted her on the shoulder. "Would you like to see?"

Kat nodded. "Yes, yes I would." She held onto Stenstrom. "This is a moment I've been waiting for, to see my angels, to look upon their faces."

The corridor around them, as well as the seated, laboring image of Professor Shurlamp, vanished. In its place, a sun-lit grand open space appeared; a vast library, appointed in blonde hardwoods carved into delicate, mystifying shapes. Razor-thin windows admitted powerful yellow light. Books of delicious colors, inset with jewels, lined towering shelves. Sitting at a long rectangular table were two people, a man and a woman, both of them leaning over a long vellum scroll that, unrolled, went off the tabletop all the way to the floor. The vellum was black with tight writing. Cups of half-drunk coffee steamed before them. The man, a smallish, blonde-headed fellow, wore a modest dark blue suit, his coat removed and draped over the back of his chair. His white sleeves were rolled up, lenses hanging down at the end of his nose, his face buried in the vellum. He was taking notes, a pen held tightly in his right hand. The woman sat next to him, her arm over the man's back. She was black or dark brown-haired, everything pinned up with a number of combs. She wore a sparkling green robe of jewel-like luster over a more modest white smock. A number of red and green necklaces clinked at her neck.

Kat took in the scene with tearful wonder.

So, here was A-Ram's betrothed, Lady Alesta. Stenstrom wondered—surely other versions of himself knew this woman, possibly called her a friend? He searched his memories, looking for a brief glimpse of her there, but got nothing. She was very pretty. Her face and blue eyes were haggard with their work, as if they had been at that table for ages, poring over the vellum, trying to make an impossible choice.

Kat looked at these people, at the green robe worn by the woman, awe on her face. "Are these …?"

Atha nodded. "Yes, this is Lord A-Ram and Lady Alesta sitting in the Library of Time on Cammara. On that vellum scroll are thousands upon thousands of names, as assembled by the Gods of Cammara. Each name on the list is a viable *Covus* for Lord Belmont—possibly Professor Shurlamp also came up with some of the same names. In searching for a *Covus* there is considerable danger, for if the wrong one is selected, disaster strikes, and there is no real method to tell the difference. This is the task A-Ram and Alesta were given; a grinding, methodical search—an impossible one—that eventually led to you, Kat. Then they protected you as best they could, provided for you, and guided you to where you are now."

Kat was breathless as she gazed at them, the color draining from her face, her eyes heavy with tears. "You all right?" Stenstrom asked.

She was transfixed, taking in their features. "I've been waiting for them, G, all this time. I wish … to hear their voices, to touch their faces. To fall to my knees before them."

"You'll see them in person soon enough," the woman said. "And there's no need to get on your knees; they will embrace you as their adopted daughter whom they love, whom they defended and argued before the gods to protect."

Kat reached out to them, to touch them, but the image of A-Ram and Alesta in the Library of Time faded, the dim stony corridor of the Hall of Mirrors returned. Kat's 'angels' were gone.

"Where did they go?" she asked.

"Come on," the woman said. "All in good time."

They continued on down the corridor, Kat reluctant to leave, taking Stenstrom's hand.

As they walked, Stenstrom was puzzled. "I don't understand why all this fuss over me. Why do things like this always seem to come about, with me at the center? First it's the Sisters and the power they insist I share, and then the Lady in Gray who haunted my childhood, and then Professor Shurlamp, and now I've witnessed my friend A-Ram and his love hard at work in some distant place, laboring to assist me. Why? Who am I? What is all this about?"

The woman wasted few words in response. "Ok, I'll tell you. You're a *Kaidar Gemain*. You've heard that term before. You—and others like you, for you're certainly not alone—are supposed to protect the universe from danger, from beings attempting to cross over. Like I said, crossing over from one universe to the next is bad news, and some beings can really do a lot of damage should they succeed—enough damage even to cause the destruction of various universes. The *Kaidar Gemain* is supposed to stop them, to protect the universe from harm, and for that, the universe rewards you handsomely with power, with accolades."

"I want none of that," Stenstrom said.

"Doesn't matter what you want, does it? The universe wants it. It's done. As such, all sorts of troubles find their way to you. They are drawn to you like moths to the proverbial flame."

They arrived at a crossroads. The corridor they were walking down dead-ended, while a new corridor running left and right went on in either direction for as far as they could see; the air dominated by a chattering, machine-like sort of silence where a multitude of unseen things bumped and banged about. To the left, if they squinted, they could see a pinprick of orange light far away in the distance, floating like a lonely star. To the right was a bastion of utter darkness. Something horrid stirred in it. Kat looked at the dark and shrank from it, wrapping her arms in with Stenstrom's.

"G, something's down there," she said, terrified of the dark.

Placed in the center of the crossroads between the two corridors was a fluted stone pedestal standing about waist high. A plain, bell-shaped device sat atop the pedestal. Before it, the shadowy, half-seen images of people, hundreds, possibly thousands, knelt in deep worship, going down face-first to the ground and coming back up in chaotic procession.

"Who are these people?" Kat asked.

The woman shrugged. "Punts. Don't worry about them for now. Right here is where all the action takes place, so to speak. This is the intersection of the Hall of Mirrors. The corridor we just came from is known as the Hall of Mundane. It goes back to where you started, back to sunny Merian's Hill in Tyrol, safe and sound in your own universe. The Hall of Mundane is the safe part. Most who attempt to cross over, like Professor Shurlamp and the Punts here, never make it out of the Hall of Mundane, and that's how it should be."

She pointed at the stone pedestal. "This is what stops them—the Anatameter."

Stenstrom's thoughts flared.

The Anatameter!

"Doesn't look like much, does it?" she said. "Don't be fooled, Anatameters wield incredible power. They are dug into the heartbeat of the universe. For each universe, there is an Anatameter sitting in the crossroads guarding it."

Stenstrom and Kat leaned in to have a closer look. The Anatameter was a smooth, bell-shaped device made from carved fine-grain stone. It was ochre in color, unadorned and remarkably unimpressive, though if they looked away from it, it seemed to carry a slight greenish glow. A single knob was placed in its center.

The Anatameter seethed with power.

"The guts of the Anatameter are complex in the extreme and can be crafted by only a select few. What does it do? It clouds the mind, it alters perception, alters fate, alters space and time, even reality itself. And here they sit, at the crossroads of the Hall of Mirrors. All those foolish people seeking to pass it fail, unless you have the authority to alter the Anatameter itself." She placed her hands on the Anatameter and turned the knob at its center one click.

Stenstrom looked at the Anatameter. So unadorned and plain. "I had a device like this."

What is this? he had once asked the tall woman in his office.

Anatameter, she replied.

Is it dangerous?

Very ...

"I know," the woman said. "And you lost it at Clovis. That Anatameter was made special, just for you. Turning its knob alters your fate, just a little bit, bending the entire fabric of the universe in the process. Turn the knob all eight times and quite a bit is changed. Only you can turn its knob but others can still claim it, take advantage of its power. You'll see in a second."

She walked past the Anatameter into the corridor beyond. Stenstrom and Kat followed. "Now, let's pay attention, right? This here is the second part of the Hall of Mirrors, the part very few ever see—the dangerous part, I must warn you. This is the Hall of Possibilities." She pointed down the corridor to the left, to the point of light in the distance. "See that light? That's the next universe. Go that way and you're there. The Hall of Mirrors links the two together." She pointed in the other direction to the right, to the hanging, clinging darkness filling it. "On the other hand, go that way and you'll run into the Hall's protector, the Shadow tech Goddess herself. Her throne is always to the right of the Anatameter at the end of the Hall of Possibilities. In a healthy universe, many times she's not there, her throne sits empty. But in less healthy cases she *is* there, sitting, miserable, not saying a word, waiting to come out, waiting to destroy. Those puttering around in the Hall of Possibilities invariably stir her up and they are never seen or heard from again; the Shadow tech Goddess gets them. Sometimes she'll continue on, past the Anatameter, down the Hall of Mundane and destroy everything, bringing the universe to an end in walls of Shadow tech. Just so you know, we have a pretty unhealthy case here, so it's most likely she's down there right now, sitting in her chair in the dark, waiting for us." The woman whispered. "We best not stir her up. See those Punts over there in the Hall of Mundane? They're worshippers of the Shadow tech Goddess, trying to curry her favor, to bring about her coming and put an end to the universe. They've been at it for centuries."

"Why?"

"Why do people do anything? Here they are, deep inside the Hall of Mundane, unwittingly oh so close to she whom they worship."

Stenstrom looked down the Hall of Possibilities into the darkness and cringed. He could feel the presence of the Shadow tech Goddess down there at the end of the corridor, like the jaws of death waiting to spring.

The Shadow tech Goddess. Memories flashed across his thoughts— memories belonging to other versions of himself.

Who are you?

I'm the Shadow tech Goddess.

"Aren't you the Shadow tech Goddess?" he asked the woman.

The woman thought a moment and tapped her chin with her gloved finger. "Ummmmmmm, no. I like to tell people I am sometimes; I've told you I am once or twice, but I'm not." She glanced at the Punts. "Here, watch."

She went past the Anatameter back into the Hall of Mundane and waded into the group of Punts, touching their indistinct heads, tickling their ash-like chins.

The Punts reacted, standing, dancing, shouting with apparent joy as they faded away.

"See, I gave them a little glimpse of me. It made their day; now they can go off to wherever and think the universe is about to end."

"Then who are you?" Kat asked. "You have shown us much, revealed my angels to me for which I'm grateful. You must be a goddess too."

The woman thought a moment. "Sure I am. I'm Atha, I'm my father's daughter. Don't puzzle over it for now. Come, let's walk this way." She led them down the corridor to the left, mercifully away from the dankness of the other end and the destroyer that might be waiting there. Along the wall were a series of notched alcoves set at regular intervals down the corridor, one after the next. The alcoves were mere recesses in the wall, like a place one might put a painting or a fine bust. The woman stopped them at a notch and pointed at it.

"These notches here are known as the Nodes of Reality. The Nodes do a number of things. They allow shortcuts across the universe, allow access into hidden places, and even passage if you wish. They're intended to be a sort of back door allowing certain beings to pass through. Your loved ones have passed through these Nodes; your deceased *Merthig*, Lady Gwendolyn, once passed through a Node such as these."

Kat looked at one of the Nodes, felt it with her hand. "What about me? Did I pass through, too?"

"Of course not. You're a *Covus*; the universe won't steer you to Lord Belmont, that's why A-Ram and Alesta had to do it. Now, listen up. Not only do your loves pass through these Nodes, your *enemies* pass through as well. It's the universe's way of directing them to you. Think of the universe as a great labyrinth, with a monster in the center of it. The enemies of the universe are like mice set loose in the labyrinth. The Nodes are meant to open and shut, to direct the mice into the center, where they may be dealt with before they can create mischief. And you, sir, and those like you, are the monsters in the center."

Down the corridor, a trickle of light spilled out of one of the notches, dim at first, but quickly strengthening to a bright blue shaft that ran across the floor and snaked up the opposite wall. "Oh, look. A Node has opened. Someone's coming through. Wonder who it could be?"

A figure emerged from the notch, stepping out with lurid grace, dappled with circles of whitish-blue light. Stenstrom saw the figure and drew his pistols. "Demon!" he cried.

It was the same creature that had killed Gwendolyn in Clovis; a nightmare of flesh and metal writhing together, shrouded in blue light. It turned to them, its gaze like ice. "Wendilnight!" it screeched as it surged in Kat's direction.

Stenstrom fired two shots; green pulsing globes burst from his NTH pistols, seared through the air and hit the demon in the chest. Without delay, it fell to the floor, quite dead.

"Good shot," Atha said.

Stenstrom ran up and kicked the demon over so he could look at it, Kat at his side. The dead creature on the floor was a mashed-up horror of flesh and circuitry, bonded right down the center, female flesh on one side, metal linkages and sinister construction on the other. Lights adorning its metal half flickered and went out in succession as the monstrosity shut down into death. Sprouting out of a compartment on its left arm was a cruel-looking saw, the blades spinning down into inactivity. He had expected the flesh half of her body to bear the visage of Gwendolyn, Kat had said the demon stole her flesh and wore it, but, her flesh half bore no resemblance to Gwen.

"That is Bellathauser," Atha said. "The metal half of her is the worst of Cammarian technology. The flesh part is one half of a Cammarian queen, Queen Wendilnight."

That name ...

I am Queen Wendilnight.

He took her hand and kissed it. Her head nearly touched the ceiling of his office, eleven feet off the floor.

"I know that name," he said. "And this is what killed Gwen and stole the Anatameter?"

"Yes."

Kat looked down at the body. "This is what tried to kill me in Clovis. Gwendolyn's ghost warned me of it."

Stenstrom stood over the fallen demon and gave the body a kick. "Then it's over. It's dead. Is this the work you brought us to perform?"

"Not quite," Atha said. "Bellathauser is one half of Queen Wendilnight. What you have to understand is that the people of Cammara, your ancient ancestors, are immortal. You and your people also have a bit of immortality to you, but the Sisters keep it suppressed. Immortality isn't really a very good thing, and Cammara is troubled with it to this day. Every bit of them is immortal, down to their molecules. Lose an arm, the arm still lives, and, what's more, the arm dreams of what it once was—whole. It becomes bitter, spiteful. There are two types of people on Cammara; the Solfids who are whole, and the Ghrundids who are just body parts but still living. The Ghrundids love to turn the Solfids into Ghrundids—to make them join the club, so to speak. They captured Queen Wendilnight and split her right down the middle, turning her into a Ghrundid. A great hero rescued part of her, the right half, while the left half remained with the Ghrundids and became their queen, Bellathauser. Bellathauser has most of Wendilnight's intellect and her soul, but it's all jumbled up, malfunctioning, lost in psychosis, while the right half of her is mostly empty and has to be kept alive via sorcery. Bellathauser is quite insane, and in her madness, is obsessed with rejoining to her other half. She drifts about from one woman to the next, thinking all of them are her missing other half, joining with them only to discard the flesh and join again when the opportunity strikes."

"She's dead. It's done," Stenstrom said.

"Ah, no it's not."

From the right hand corridor came a terrifying cry. Dappled in lights, a half metal, half flesh demon emerged from the dark, hands raised, speeding toward Kat. "WENDILNIGHT!" it roared. Kat crouched and darted aside, eluding the creature's grasp. Kat counter-attacked, striking fast with her Silver tech claws. They bit through flesh, bone and metal alike. Sparks! Smoke! Flashing lights! Before another moment had passed, the demon lay in sparking, bleeding pieces at her feet. Blood spurted and smoked.

"Eeeeugh!" Atha said. "That was also Bellathauser. Do you see our problem now? Here's what happened: Bellathauser managed to escape the Gods of Cammara who pursued her, and fled into the Hall of Mirrors long ago, and she has been in here ever since. She managed to thwart the Anatameter because she is, technically, Queen Wendilnight of Mons Eagle, the wife of the man who created it, and none of the Anatameter's tricks work on her. She became a demon haunting the Hall of Mirrors, known as a *V. Dogan. V. Dogans* can emerge out of the Nodes of Reality anywhere. Destroy one, another pops up just as fast, and to make matters worse, the rules of time and place have no meaning in the Hall of Mirrors, therefore Bellathauser can show up at any *time* as well, from the beginning of time to the end. Makes her pretty tough to deal with.

"The one that attacked you in Clovis was a bit slyer than the usual mindless ones who come out. It attacked and took out Lady Gwendolyn, your *Merthig,* leaving you in a funk, too out-of-sorts to pursue her, and she took your Anatameter. With it, she has created a pocket node of reality with no entrance or exit. Her pocket node is parasitic, feasting off the energy of this particular universe. Eventually, it will destroy this universe and everything in it; you and Kat will simply cease to exist. And that's where we come in. We are going to confront Bellathauser, destroy her and reclaim the Anatameter. What's better, she has made herself vulnerable to attack. If we take her out while she's holding the Anatameter, then all the other instances of herself will also be destroyed. She'll be gone for good. No more *V. Dogan.*"

"And we are to do this?" Stenstrom asked. "To slay the specific instance of Bellathauser, the one that killed Gwen and wears her flesh?"

"That's right. And the Anatameter too. Don't forget."

"And she has taken up residence in some sort of pocket dimension that has no entrance or exit?"

"Right again."

"So then, how are we to gain entrance and face this demon?"

Atha smiled. "Good question. If you wish to get to the center of a mountain, how do you do it? You make a tunnel, right? You burrow into the mountain. That's what we have to do; burrow, make a tunnel."

"How do we do that?" Kat asked.

"How? By manipulating fate, by altering little destinies here and there, that's how. You start small, work a little magic and get progressively bigger. Once that's done, we'll have made a hole right into Bellathauser's little playground, then we can destroy it."

Stenstrom sashed his pistols and put his arm around Kat. "So then, whose fate are we about to alter?"

"I've got the perfect thing to start with—you'll love it!" Atha said. "This way, let's go!" Nearby, a Node of Reality lit up in flickering greenish light.

"Here we are. So, our friends, A-Ram and Alesta, they make a fine couple, don't they? Tell me, Lord Belmont, you didn't recognize Lady Alesta, did you?"

Kat looked up into his face as he considered his answer. "No, I'm afraid I've never had the pleasure. A-Ram told me he was engaged, and apparently his betrothed is a beautiful Merian woman. They seemed like a fitting couple. I was happy for them."

"Yes, they do, don't they?" Atha said. "So good for each other, it really does warm my heart. It might surprise you that, in another universe, you know Lady Alesta very well. She flies at your side aboard the *Seeker*. She appears humble in her homemade Merian clothes, but she's a powerful priestess of her star and she had the guts to deal you some tough love a few universes back. But here, in this particular universe, A-Ram and Alesta never met, and you never got to know her. The circumstances that brought them together in other universes never happened in this one—how profound lost moments can be. So, starting small, here's our initial task; just as A-Ram and Alesta from a different universe brought the two of you together, you are now going to return the favor and bring them together here."

"We're going to assist my angels?" Kat asked, hopeful.

"Yep, isn't that fun? Once we get that done, we move onto some bigger fish."

Kat looked down at her clothes, at her old green jumpsuit she wore in Clovis braced by her armature of Silver tech with claws. "I would like that very much. I owe them, I can never possibly pay them back, but I need to change first."

"You're fine, just put your claws away, I'll take care of the rest." She glanced at Kat's unshod feet. "I'll even shoot you a nice pair of shoes. I love shoes, the taller the better." She motioned them to the node, lit up with swirling greens and wispy arms of white like a hypnotic fountain turned on its side.

Kat had a question. "All this seems pretty convoluted. Can't you just send us to Bellathauser? Not that I don't wish to help my angels, but are you certain this is all necessary?"

"Sure it is," Atha said. She offered Kat a toothy smile. "Trust me, I'm a goddess. I wouldn't send you on a wild goose chase just because I'm fond of these people, would I? Now, just go on in and remember—this is for A-Ram and Alesta. I will send them to you. It's time we gave back to them a little bit."

Stenstrom took Kat's hand. "Ready, love?"

She nodded.

Together they went into the node and vanished.

3— The Thing in the Bathroom

SNAP!

The cool dankness of the Hall of Mirrors was suddenly swept away by bright sunshine and a throng of people.

Stenstrom and Kat were standing on a busy street side. The sun high overhead was warm and cheery, tempered by a lovely salt breeze. The buildings around them were a tightly-packed mixture of wood and stone facades framed with modest windows and colorful doors, with hanging signs swinging overhead heralding businesses of all sorts. Most of the signs were carved from weathered planks of wood, others were made of metal and the fanciest had lettering splashed in 4-D ultra-neon heralding eateries, notaries, Barr, barristers and other assorted well-to-do establishments. Narrow alleyways deprived of fresh air and sunlight twisted away from the street to places unknown. Across the street was a noisy cannery churning out fumes and canned fish by the pallet. The sea, a nice tropical aquamarine, went off into the horizon in a long line. Seabirds cawed. A long Barbary dock populated by small fishing boats, larger windjammers and several star-faring vessels went on for a long way. A bustle of people came and went down the street in a steady stream; mustachioed men with oiled coifs and women in hats, coats, buttoned-up corsets and long dresses dyed a multitude of colors. Nobody seemed to have taken notice of their sudden appearance.

Kat looked around. "Where are we, G?" Her jumpsuit was gone. She was wearing a green gown laced with a false corset, and long black gloves. She winced and lifted her skirt: ladies boots with a heel were buttoned up on her feet, much more confining than she was used to. A lacy hat sat on her head, covering her blonde hair and her Shadowmark with a crumpled veil.

Stenstrom took everything in. "Well, it looks like Calvert to me. The fashions, the industry, the seaside, the buildings all mashed together; I'm certain it's Calvert. A-Ram's from Calvert, so it makes sense we're here."

Kat scanned up and down the street. "Where could my angels be? They could be anywhere."

"Atha said she would bring them to us. Let's keep a sharp eye out."

They waited out the afternoon, looking up and down the busy street, searching for the tiny A-Ram out of a throng of people and not finding him.

"I'm going to get a better view, G," Kat said, looking up the side of the building; four floors high. Easy. She lifted her skirt, staring down in disgust at her boots. After a quick moment, Kat, despite her boots, was standing on the roof, her blonde hair shining in the sun under her hat, Silver tech hooks fading into her gloved fingers. With Stenstrom at street level and Kat four floors up, they watched the area, looking for A-Ram or Alesta.

After several minutes of searching, Kat excitedly called down. "G! I think I see him!" She pointed up the street, past the cannery. "Over there."

Sure enough, far down the street, scuttling from one storefront to another was Lord A-Ram, appearing small and uncomfortable amid the people. He was carrying a satchel of unbound papers, which he pulled out, fussed with and continually sorted. He slouched as he walked, his lenses big and ugly on his face, his tiny form nearly obliterated by the passing crowds.

Kat came down fast, kicking up dust. "What do I do, G? What do I say? I now know he's not a god, but it doesn't matter. I've longed for this moment, to stand in his presence, to hear his voice, to try and convey to him what he means to me."

"Just let me do the talking, Kat. When you feel composed, please jump in. Just remember, according to Atha, this is a different A-Ram than the one who assisted you. We both must remember that."

"Ok!"

They quickly crossed the street, waded through the crowds, and intercepted him.

"A-Ram!" Stenstrom said warmly. A-Ram, somewhat startled, clutching his satchel and loose papers to his chest, turned to him.

He didn't seem to recognize Stenstrom at first, then: "Oh! Lord Belmont! Goodness is that you?"

"It certainly is. You remember me, right? From the *Seeker*?"

"Oh, oh yes! How could I have forgotten?" He blushed a little. "I guess we made a mess of things. I was sorry to see the *Seeker* go."

"It's just a ship. There are many more. Are you still flying?"

"No, Creation no. I'm back in the mailroom at Fleet. I got demoted out of the Admiral's office for flying with you. It's just as well—I shouldn't have gone off like that. The mailroom's where I belong."

Kat was invading A-Ram's space, staring at him with big eyes. A-Ram was clearly uncomfortable.

"Lord A-Ram, this is Kat, the countess of Belmont-South Tyrol. My wife."

"Oh, well hello! Very charming … lady." Kat, enthralled, continued to crowd him. "Umm, ma'am, would you mind so much? I say, could I ask that you …" A-Ram was so put-off he nearly dropped his papers.

Stenstrom pulled Kat back a little. "What are you carrying there?"

"Just some musings. Nonsense really."

"I see. We're here in …"

"St. Edmunds," A-Ram said, jumping in.

"Yes, in St. Edmunds seeing the sights. Kat has never been to Calvert.

It's amazing we met up today, but most fortuitous. Are you hungry? Perhaps we could press you to lunch."

A-Ram looked on-the-spot and unsure. He fumbled with his satchel, stuffing his papers into it. "Well, I, umm, I was heading home to put my papers away. And … and I have already lunched at the Tin Brewery. I always … always dine there. I …"

Kat took A-Ram's satchel and papers from his hands. "Let me carry your papers. I will take care of them. Please, allow us buy you some refreshment."

A-Ram looked to be in a general panic. "Well, I, I thank you. I don't wish to be an old boot, but I think I'll take a pass on this occasion, my lady. Perhaps next time. May I please have my papers back?"

Stenstrom put his arm around A-Ram's tiny shoulders. "A-Ram, I really would like to thank you for what you did on the *Seeker*. I consider you a good friend."

"You think of … me … as your friend, Lord Belmont?"

"Of course. I'm very happy we located you. I have regaled my countess with any number of tales about you, and she has been most eager to make your acquaintance. So, please, let us sit down, have a laugh or two and indulge in a bit of nostalgia. It would make me and my countess very happy. You'll be glad you did."

A-Ram thought about it and gave a bashful smile. "Well, then, I … I suppose I have a little time to spare."

"Any time you can give us will be most appreciated."

"Thank you, Lord Belmont."

"It's Bel, remember? My friends call me Bel."

"Ah, yes. Yes. Thank you … Bel."

"And I am Kat," she said. "Please call me Kat."

"Thank you, my lady."

They moved down the street, A-Ram shuffling along as if he had been kidnapped, continually looking over his shoulder and down side streets, searching for a route of escape. Kat was very handsy with him, her arms around his shoulders, pinching his cheeks, even kissing him on occasion. Her attention did seem to grow on A-Ram and soon she had coaxed several smiles out of him, even a genuine laugh or two.

"What are these papers?" she asked him again.

"Oh, hoho! Just stories I penned. Silliness."

"I'd love for you to read them to me," she replied.

"You would?" he said, shocked. "Nobody's ever asked to hear my stories before, and certainly not a countess."

"Well, today's the day!" she said, giving him another kiss on the cheek.

Several blocks down toward the heart of St. Edmunds was an imposing

structure of turreted red brick rising well above the flat-topped buildings around it, casting long shadows. The building took up a whole city block and seemed like it had been pulled out of a different age and place. There was nothing seaside or Barbary about it—it seemed like a besieged fortress plunked out of the frozen north to squat on the streets of St. Edmunds like a brazen conqueror. Like a city unto itself, it was curtained with walls, towers of varying heights, turrets and battlements defending against an invisible enemy, all capped with steeply arched eaves sheathed in surreal patina green. A terragrin sign mounted high above the street in flawless county green announced the building was the Empire Hotel.

Stenstrom was drawn to the ornate baroqueness of the place as they fell under its shadow. "This establishment seems like a fine place to sit and chat," he said.

A-Ram looked genuinely frightened. "Oh, oh, I've never dined at the Empire Hotel, it's very expensive."

"Let me worry about the expense, A-Ram. Today is on me."

"Oh well, well then, I suppose ..."

They entered the cavernous interior of the hotel, marveling at the grand lobby sheathed in fine red paneling, naked marble columns, stained glass, potted ferns in towering dream-like green, and other fabulous appointments all spun right out of luxury's beating heart. It was like being on a different planet--the people in the lobby dressed in fabulous clothing in a noir style Stenstrom had never seen before on Kana: revealing dresses, strenuously elegant footwear and netted stockings, feathered accessories, massive, impractical hats over ruby-red lips, flawless white shirts under stiff, uncomfortable jackets equipped with glittering watch fobs; the list went on and on. Finding their way, gathering their bearings, they saw several restaurants inside the hotel to choose from; each garish and costly. A-Ram clearly felt out-of-place among the beautiful people there, often looking down at his scuffed, buckled shoes; shoes commoners wore. The people in this hotel seemed to be mostly wealthy tourists, come to Calvert to enjoy the climate, dress up and revel in this posh, exclusive atmosphere, and gawk at the quaint locals—like A-Ram.

"Can you recommend any we should try?" Kat asked, whispering in his ear. "Remember, cost is no object. You are our guest."

"Well, my countess ..."

"Kat, I'm Kat to you."

"Thank you. My uncle once worked as a chef in the restaurant yonder. It's very good, I'm told. Lots of light. Very good food. I've never dined there myself."

Stenstrom smiled. "Then let's correct that." Ahead was a restaurant done up in rich woods, polished marble, glittering glass and succulent ferns all filling up a rich open space of light and color. Stenstrom approached the Maître d'. He searched his ledger, asked Stenstrom to sign it, and bade them follow. Into the restaurant they went, each aisle, booth and table a carefully executed study in finery. They passed displays of caged birds and bandstands of precise live music until they reached their table in the round, backed in comfortable velvet, quietly perched in a central part of the restaurant.

They were seated and received their leather-backed menus. As Kat went over the menu with A-Ram, Stenstrom looked around at all the seated faces. Everybody was proper and well-groomed, heads of hair parted and oiled, mustaches waxed, ladies painted up under grand hats and accented in pearls—and he wondered. This situation was to unite A-Ram with Lady Alesta. Alesta was a Pilgrim of Merian, penniless, often shoeless, preaching alternative news of the Elders. Merians were often scorned and laughed at. Merians did not sit in luxury in a fine, expensive restaurant. Atha had told him she would deliver Alesta to them. He comforted himself with that thought. Perhaps they would dine, gain A-Ram's trust and then locate Alesta outside the hotel once they had finished. Perhaps she would be standing at a corner with her Merian fellows passing out leaflets and other forms of literature to disinterested crowds. He imagined them approaching their group, maybe Alesta would offer A-Ram a leaflet, holding it out for him to take with her tiny hand, and then that would be it. Love would happen between two strangers.

That must be how it would go.

A-Ram was clearly feeling more at ease, going through the menu with Kat, who would be struggling to read the fancy, long-worded dishes. He chatted about the dishes, offering his advice as to what to order, drawing on knowledge his uncle, the chef, had given him.

As Stenstrom turned to his menu, he thought he heard something. The soft noise around him was the usual for an upper-scale eatery: quiet bits of nearby conversation, the clatter of silverware against fine china, the occasional pluck of stringed instruments and the passing of shod feet on the marble floor.

And—something else. He heard a pained moan, soft, buried under other sounds, but still audible and heartbreaking in its maudlin torment.

"Did you all hear that?" he asked.

Kat and A-Ram's eyes came up from their menus. "Sir," A-Ram asked. "Hear what?"

Stenstrom set his menu aside and stood. "Nothing. Give me a moment."

"What should we get you, G?" Kat asked.

"Whatever the waiter recommends. I'll be back shortly."

Stenstrom left the table, moving down the aisles, listening for that sound, which had been so horrid he really didn't wish to hear it again, but could not forget or allow to continue. Whatever had made that sound needed help, and he was going to investigate, offer help if he could. It didn't surprise him that nobody else in the restaurant appeared to have heard the sound; with the Sisters' power, he often heard things only the Sisters could hear. Their hearing was amazing. He moved into the darker, danker sections of the restaurant near the kitchens, where everything wasn't quite so nice and polished up. Dirty dishes were piled on carts waiting to be cleaned, rags soaked in filthy water, soiled linens lay in hampers. A dark corridor went off adjacent to the kitchen, going all the way to the back of the restaurant. People came and went from restrooms, double doors to the kitchens opened and closed, accompanied by a momentary bit of light.

And he heard it again, a pained, sorrowful moan coming from down the corridor. He entered, determined to learn what it was.

The noise came from a door situated at the end of the corridor. The door was paneled in red, scuffed from use, with a heavy-duty hinge pulling it closed; a shiny brass placard at eye-level read: PRIVATE. Stenstrom stood before it, pushed it open slightly and peered in—inside was a white, tiled room; looked like a bathroom. From within came a harsh smell, like bile or the primal sweaty smell of sex. "Is someone in here?" he asked.

"It's taken!" came a tinny voice from a stall.

Bound by his manners, Stenstrom backed out into the hallway. "Your pardon," he said as the door swung shut.

More sounds from behind the door: sounds of pain and animal-like fury along with the slamming of wood against wood and the occasional slapping of skin against skin.

And then there was silence.

The door opened and a man wearing a dark blue Calvert suit came out, straightening his oiled hair. He had a sheepish, rather satisfied look on his face. He adjusted himself, reached into his pocket and cast several coins into the bathroom, where they rolled about on the floor near the drain. He looked at Stenstrom. "I'd give her a few minutes to dry up," he said with a sneer as he walked away.

Alarmed, Stenstrom knocked on the door. "Is anybody in there? Are you all right?" He peered in.

There, emerging from a stall in a black lacy dress, torn and somewhat dirty, was a small skinny woman wearing the ratty fur of some dead alien animal slung across her shoulders. She appeared to be in agony. Blood and other secretions dripped down her leg. She held the small of her back as she leaned down to pick up the coins the man had tossed in.

Stenstrom's mouth dropped open in shock. "Alesta …" he managed to say. "Lady Alesta?"

Standing before him, reeking of sex and dead animals, was a demented version of Lady Alesta whom he had seen in the Hall of Mirrors. The lady he had seen was a beautiful, simple Pilgrim of Merian sitting with her love, A-Ram. This woman before him had crawled out of some hideous nightmare, her doll-like face was smeared with cheap make-up and she had been surgically altered in the manner Xaphan prostitutes used. Her right eyelash was two, maybe three times longer than what would be considered normal. The garish tattoo of a demoness holding a rose was splashed on her left shoulder. On the right side of her neck, she bore a brand in the form of some Xaphan chaos symbol, covered up in splotchy powder.

She looked at him, notes of misery and pain scarred around her haggard eyes. "Yeah, I'm Alesta … you here to see me?"

She licked her lips. Her tongue had been enhanced; it was very long, long enough to easily reach the tip of her nose or the base of her chin. A demon's tongue.

"I heard you cry out. I thought to see if you needed help."

"Help? The last guy likes it rough with lots of noise. I'm getting too old for this, I think." She composed herself, hiding the pain she was feeling. Her blue eyes came up to meet his. "I can be quiet if you want me to be quiet. I won't make a sound." She took his hand. "Come on, I won't bite you, unless you want me to." Her demon's tongue wandered out of her mouth.

Stenstrom stopped her. "I was hoping to treat you to a meal. Have you dined?"

Alesta seemed genuinely astonished. "Have I dined? That's a new one,

I'll admit. Listen, I'm a busy lady, do you want to have sex or not?"

"No, ma'am, I …"

Alesta reached into her bag and pulled out a jagged Xaphan dagger, her fingers fitting around the contoured handle. "Then piss off. I wouldn't want to have to hurt you with this, right?" The pain returned to her face, along with notes of unbridled misery and loneliness. "Go on, leave me alone." She motioned with her knife for him to go.

Stenstrom looked at her. Though she was disfigured and dripping with Xaphan paint, she still had a small hint of the characteristic innocence he had seen from Lady Alesta in the Hall of Mirrors. Staring at her dagger, he changed his tactics.

"Put that away. You are a practiced businesswoman in this trade, am I right?"

"Yeah, that's right. You know how many girls would like to work this restaurant?"

"Many, I assume." Stenstrom waved his hands, producing several Belmont sesterces from nowhere. Alesta lowered her dagger, she seemed impressed. She smiled slightly.

"And what is this?" he asked her.

"Money," she replied. "A lot of money."

"Do you want it?"

"Yeah, I want it," she said, her words stumbling over her enlarged tongue.

"Then I insist you dine with me, and you can have it all."

"Do I get alcohol?"

"If you like."

She put her dagger back into her bag. She processed this odd situation for a moment. "Sure, ok. Let's eat. I wasn't expecting a sick scenario like this when I started today. Do you want me to do something nice for you under the table while we're … 'eating'?"

"No, I don't. Come and eat, drink your fill. Nothing more is required of you."

"Give me the money right now."

Stenstrom handed her the coins. Her fingers were not quite straight as she took them, clearly once broken and not properly set. "Ok, whatever you want. I'll be your friend if you want me to," she whispered putting the coins into her bag. "I'll be your friend all day long." She opened the door to the bathroom. "Give me a minute to clean up, will ya?"

The door closed and Stenstrom waited outside. He wondered how this encounter was going to turn out. This version of Lady Alesta was a hideous ghoul in comparison to the enchanting vision he had seen in the Hall of Mirrors, and how would the much less worldly version of A-Ram, a man clearly struggling with his poise and confidence, react to her? Would they want anything to do with each other? He was reminded of the words he spoke to Kat in Clovis about her evil sister, Wheel:

... perhaps she was scarred too much ...

The door opened and out came Alesta, all the filth cleaned off her legs, a few notes of freshly applied perfume dancing about her head. She pulled the PRIVATE placard off the door and stuffed it into her bag, replacing it with a similar placard reading: LADIES. "Ok, let's do this," she said. "I'm your friend for the day."

He took her hand and led her out of the corridor. "I'll be your friend forever," he replied.

"Great," she said, walking with him. "That's great."

They moved through the restaurant, leaving the darker kitchen area for the brighter, more genteel areas toward the front. Alesta's mask of indifferent confidence wavered a little, as if the dark, seedy environs of the kitchen area were her established domain and natural habitat while the brighter, lacy regions of the front of the restaurant were a jazz-gilded fairyland forbidden and unknown to her. She gripped his hand a little harder, looking for comfort.

Their table was just ahead, situated in a semicircular ferny nook. Drinks had been served; the stemware sweated on the tablecloth. Kat had fully cracked A-Ram's bashful shell—they sat side-by-side, laughing warmly, sipping from their glasses together as he regaled her with witty stories of his lowly job at the Fleet and of flying on the *Seeker*, which clearly had been the most adventurous situation of his life to date. Satchel open, he shared his papers with her, reading from them. A-Ram (the other A-Ram) had told Stenstrom in the Belmont gardens that he wasn't much of a story-teller, but this version of A-Ram seemed adept at it, once he was at-ease enough to be himself. Kat was clearly relishing his stories, like a daughter listening to a beloved father speak. They saw Stenstrom and Alesta approach and stood.

Kat saw Alesta, and despite her augmentations, her eyelash, her tattoos, the serpent-like tongue lurking in her mouth, was elated. "Hi!" she cried, open-mouthed with joy.

Alesta's reaction, in turn, was far from gracious. "What is this?" she hissed, seeing A-Ram and Kat. She glanced up at Stenstrom. "You are some kind of kinky bastard, aren't you? I actually thought for a moment you really did just want to have dinner with me, but this? A four-way, right out in the open where everybody's eating? They'll kick me out of here."

"As I told you, dinner and nothing else is all I'm expecting," Stenstrom said.

She was skeptical. "All right, you need me to hold a chair down for you, fine. Let's get some good stuff over here and keep it coming."

Stenstrom began the introductions. "Kat, Lord A-Ram, may I introduce Lady Alesta of … I'm sorry, where are you from?" he asked, genuinely not knowing.

"From Hell," she replied, seating herself. "So, who have we here?" She looked at Kat and spoke with a lurid voice. "Listen, babe, this is my area, ok. I pay the proprietor to have this place all to myself. So take your shit and blow."

Kat was too stunned to answer. She had been expecting one of the angels of her dreams, and got something quite the opposite.

Stenstrom jumped in. "Kat is my countess, you needn't fear."

Alesta turned to A-Ram. She looked him up and down. "Who's this guy?"

A-Ram spoke in a hesitant voice. "I'm Lord A-Ram, seventh of my line. I, I come from this city."

Alesta sneered. "Yeah? This city stinks." She pointed at his thick lenses. "Oh, you got something on your face. Just there."

A-Ram blushed and removed his lenses. All of the progress Kat had made bringing him out of his shell was lost. He slumped in his seat, stuffed his papers back into his satchel and hid behind his menu.

"That wasn't very nice," Kat said.

"I'm not a very nice person." Alesta pointed at A-Ram's satchel. "What are those?"

"Nothing," he whispered.

"What was that?" she demanded.

"None of your business," Kat said, jumping in.

The waiter came and they ordered. Alesta appeared to have a large appetite and ordered several entrees and drank spirits in shocking quantities. A-Ram, eyes downcast, quietly ordered something light.

As the meal progressed, Alesta was harsh and rather cruel, seeming to enjoy prodding and insulting A-Ram. Kat recovered from her initial shock and disappointment. She was very protective of him, trading barbs with Alesta, the two of them nearly coming to blows. Alesta produced her ugly jagged dagger. Kat raised her hands, ready to form her Silver tech claws.

Stenstrom stood. "Kat, a word please."

Kat pushed her chair out. "Be right back," she said to A-Ram, kissing him on the cheek. The two of them walked away from the table into a mirrored smoking alcove nearby.

"I don't like her," Kat said. "Where's the angel I love? Where's the color of mercy?"

"Seems life has been hard on her," Stenstrom said.

"I won't stand for Lord A-Ram to be belittled by that creature. I don't think this is going to work."

"Sure it will," came Atha's voice.

Suddenly, Stenstrom and Kat were back in the dank mustiness of the Hall of Mirrors, Atha standing nearby, purple visor glowing. Kat was back in her green jumpsuit, blessedly free of her boots. In the Node, they could see the interior of the restaurant, A-Ram and Alesta uncomfortably sitting at the table opposite each other. A-Ram was looking around for Kat, for the security she had offered him. Alone, he had nothing to shield him from Alesta's caustic wrath.

"Why are we back here again?" Kat asked, a bit of distress in her voice. "I need to get back there. I need to protect him."

"From what?" Atha asked.

"From her! She's a beast."

"A beast? That is Lady Alesta. All the potential the one who helped you had, she also has. I was watching; you were babying him too much. Lord A-Ram needs to stand on his own, as any man would."

Stenstrom also was concerned. "I need to get back there as well. A-Ram doesn't have enough to pay for the meal. I told him it was on me, and I don't want to see him end up in legal trouble over this. I hope you're not going to make a liar out of me."

"You gave Alesta plenty of money, more than enough to pay."

"But I don't see her spending it in this case. Why would she? Please, let me go back there to at least give him some money."

Atha shook her head. "Can't. We're trying to scratch a hole into Bellathauser's horror realm. This is how we do it. I also don't think the two of you are giving Alesta enough credit. You're judging her entirely on what you see on the surface. Look a little deeper and have a bit of faith—A-Ram and Alesta taught me that."

Kat stared into the node, wringing her hands, seeing the aggressive Alesta and the shy A-Ram sitting at the table. They talked. A-Ram put his protective menu down. He seemed to tire of Alesta's insults and fired back.

They were arguing. Alesta stood, snatching up his satchel and dumping the papers within to the floor. She threw her linen napkin at him and marched from the table.

"Oh, his stories! What a soulless woman! I'm glad she's leaving. She doesn't deserve him," Kat said.

They could see Alesta as she walked away. She moved into the alcove where they themselves had stood. She was looking right into the node.

"Can she see us?" Stenstrom asked.

"No," Atha replied. "All she sees is a mirror." Alesta stared into the mirror, unaware they were watching her. She looked at herself, at her tired painted face, at the elongated eyelash. Her tongue seemed big and uncomfortable in her mouth. She hid nothing. She seemed dismal and miserable, ashamed of her existence, and so very tired. One of A-Ram's papers that she had scattered had drifted near her feet. She picked it up and glanced at the writing.

Eyes moving across the page, she read further. A small smile crossed her lips as she read. She looked back at the table, seeing A-Ram scuttle around trying to recover his papers, and seemed to come to some sort of internal decision. Alesta opened her bag and took out the dagger. She regarded it in her hand; the jagged blade, the holes in the grip where she could insert her fingers and punch with it; a very ugly dagger matching her very ugly life in one hand, a paper containing whimsical tales of love and adventure written by a romantic little man in the other.

She put the dagger aside, hiding it within the branches of a nearby potted plant and left it there.

Paper in hand, she turned and went back to the table. She said a few words to A-Ram. He listened, looking up at her. From her gestures and body language, Alesta seemed to be apologetic, offering him some measure of conciliation. She knelt down and helped him collect the papers. When he had them all, he stood, pulled out a chair and seated her. Stenstrom and Kat watched with growing interest as the pair continued their meal, engaged in conversation, Alesta frequently covering her mouth so A-Ram wouldn't see the demon's tongue. Bits of the jolly fellow full of wit and charm that Kat had coaxed out of him and Alesta had brutally beat back in returned. He told her stories. As Kat had enjoyed his stories, so too did Alesta. She laughed, and apparently shared a few of her own. Stenstrom and Kat watched them eat, daytime fading into early evening, Alesta now drinking coffee instead of spirits. When the meal was over, the waiter came with the bill. A-Ram squirmed in his seat. When he turned his empty pockets out, Alesta reached into her bag and paid with the money Stenstrom had given her. The meal over, they stood and walked away from the table.

The node faded to dark.

Red in the face, Kat put her arms around Stenstrom. "I really liked him, G," she sobbed. "After I got him talking, he was everything I hoped he'd be. He feels like a father to me. I want him to be happy. You think we can have them over at the manor sometime? I want to hear more of his stories. I want to make sure he's all right."

"Without question, love."

Atha seemed rather touched by all this. "Awww, well I think they're both going to be happy. Look what we witnessed; the small beginnings of two people falling in love. A-Ram was struggling to discover and assert himself, and Alesta's heart was buried under a whole lot of ugliness, but it was still there just waiting for the right person to uncover it. I think they're going to be fine. I think tomorrow for them is going to be a better day."

Kat wiped away a tear and nodded. She took Stenstrom's hand and kissed it.

"Ok, we're off to a great start. Now, things get just a little bit tougher. Let's go," Atha said.

4—Ottoman John and Melazarr of Caroline

Atha led them down the corridor, passing several darkened nodes. "So that was a good warm up; we all feel good about that, right? Now we're playing for higher stakes."

"And so, where next?" Stenstrom asked.

"Vain," Atha replied.

"Vain? In Xaphan space?"

"That's right. The League tends to consider its old enemies, the Xaphans, to be rootless lunatics. Whether that's a fair assessment or not is up for debate, but there's no question if there's a crazy part of Xaphan space, Vain is right in the center of it."

A node lit up in somber grayish light. Atha stopped. A dark cityscape appeared in the node under a colorful, nebula-fueled sky like a great never-drying watercolor. "Vain. Founded by the House of Conwell several thousand years ago after they fled the League. What else do you know about the city?"

Kat's knowledge of Xaphan space, other than Shade Church, was virtually nil. She shook her head. Stenstrom spoke. "I used to hear about Vain. It's the chief city on the Xaphan world Wundland, or, as they call it in the Fleet, 'Wunderland'. Vain is a safe haven for every quack, Cabalist, questionable sage and austere science imaginable; so I heard in my brief days as captain of the *Seeker*."

"For the most part, that's right," Atha said.

"I've also heard it's not a safe place for proper people."

"Well …"

Stenstrom was concerned. "What is our objective in Vain?"

"Training," Atha said succinctly. "Kat's knowledge of Shadow tech is infantile at best, I think you'd agree."

Kat was stung. "I've been practicing. I can form my claws and my tail at a moment's notice. And G's arranged for me to take lessons next month from Countess Sygillis of Blanchefort to further my use of it."

"I know," Atha said, nodding. "But I'm willing to bet the place you two are soon to be headed won't be pleasant. You'll need your Shadow tech, fully powered, to get through. Your Shadow tech, now changed to silver, can turn the balance and we don't have time for you to take lessons from Sygillis of Blanchefort. You need that knowledge now. You know, Sygillis of Blanchefort killed nearly one hundred thousand Kestral warriors in the Temple of the Exploding Head all by herself, and she used Silver tech to do it. That is power we need. The problem with Shadow tech is that it defies the gods. I can give you knowledge, of language, of history, of all sorts of pursuits, but not of Shadow tech. That knowledge can only come from you, from learning and hard-won experience. In Vain, though, through the power of man not the gods, we might be able to give you this knowledge all at once. It could be possible and it's worth seeking out."

"How?" Stenstrom asked.

"Vain is known as an 'information' center of sorts, where thoughts, talents and skills are bought and sold every day. Hear me out—imagine you are a woodcutter by trade. You've been cutting wood for years, you know all the ins and outs and are an authority of your trade. You have a lifetime of experience. And then, you wander into the wrong bar, talk to the wrong sorts, and some fool in Vain up and steals your knowledge and experience right out of your head, and furthermore, has the raw, unmitigated nuts to rent you your own skills back for a premium price. That's what happens in Vain. Everyday people lose their heads to the Trades--the MVs, the Mind-Vendors of Vain. It's been going on for so long people don't seem to think it's a big deal or odd occurrence; in fact, the people of Vain aid and abet this culture, buying and selling their skills regularly. Few if any have actually earned the knowledge in their heads through experience and hard work—they rented it, upgraded it and sold it back. They also prey on the unwary, selling their minds to the highest bidder: Vuggers, they're called.

"And so, our objective. Years ago, when the Black Hats grew in influence and spread unchecked through Xaphan space, a Black Hat Hammer named Paige du Long of Moane went to Vain and tried to establish a temple there. Usually, Black Hats have their own way wherever they choose to go, but Vain got the better of Paige du Long. She got Vugged and lost her head to the Trades, a sect of MVs known as 'The Rus', or 'the Yellows' as they're also called. Though Paige du Long is long since dead, her knowledge lives on in the Rus' database. I believe they've tried to sell it in the past to prospective clients but it didn't work; you have to have the genetic ability to use Shadow tech after all; simply getting the knowledge of how to wield it won't do. Our goal is to get at that knowledge and put it in Kat's head. She is a Shadow tech female, I think that might give her the ability to use Shadow tech much better."

Kat reacted. "I want nothing to do with Black Hats!"

"You need that knowledge."

"I don't want it!"

"Then do what the Vainers do—rent it for a while. Use it against Bellathauser and then, once the rental period is done, it'll drop out of your head like it was never there. Then you can go see Countess Sygillis and begin your advanced training. Sound good?"

Kat was conflicted and a bit panicked. She turned to Stenstrom. "What should I do, G? I despise the Black Hats. I-I-I don't want that filth in my head."

Stenstrom understood. Of all things, Kat hated the Black Hats most of all. "If you don't want it, then we'll get by without it."

The light from Atha's visor intensified. "Have you two not been listening? We're not going to be facing A-Ram and Alesta in a restaurant again; you're going to be facing Bellathauser in her kingdom of horrors. I repeat, you need those skills."

Kat flashed her Silver tech claws and showed them to Atha. "And I repeat, I don't want it!"

Atha sighed. "Look, I could just dump you two out there in Vain right now and settle this argument, but you both would probably end up getting Vugged and wandering the streets mindless ..." She pointed at Stenstrom. "Work this out with her, ok?"

Stenstrom pulled Kat aside. She gritted her teeth and rubbed her forehead. "I don't like the idea of having Black Hat thoughts in my head, G. I don't want to be a Black Hat."

"Knowledge of manipulating Shadow and Silver tech doesn't make you a Black Hat. Sygillis of Blanchefort isn't a Black Hat anymore. And Lady Poe of Blanchefort, the sister of my mentor, Captain Davage, is a Shadow tech female and she was never a Black Hat. The Black Hats believe these substances belong to them; it does not. It belongs to you, and what you do with it is of your making. I think Atha has a point; mastering its use will further liberate you from the Black Hats' legacy."

Kat was rank as she grappled with the thought of taking a Black Hat's knowledge into her head. She pulled at her blonde hair and bit her lip. "I mean, I hate the Black Hats!"

"I know, I know."

"You won't throw me out or anything, will you, G?"

"'Course not. Why would you ask me that?"

Kat relented. "All right! All right, we can do this for temporary. But then I want it gone and I want to have my lessons with Countess Sygillis as you promised."

"Agreed. You're very brave, Kat." He knelt down and kissed her on the forehead.

Atha raised her arms, ecstatic. "Well done! You won't be sorry. Now, I'm sending to you Vain, near the Street of Knowledge, the bleeding heart of Vain's mind trade. Remember, we're looking for a sect of MVs known as the Rus; they're also known as the 'Yellows' for the yellow robes they wear. We want to buy the knowledge of Paige du Long of Moane from them."

"How am I paying for this knowledge?" he asked.

"They'll take anything in Vain. Your Belmont sesterces will do fine. Remember, get the data and I'll bring you back. Do not tarry with the locals. You do not want to get Vugged. Oh! If you see a guy named Ottoman John and a lady named Melazarr, you should be able to trust them—they might be able to help you out, but nobody else. Got me?"

"All right. Ottoman John and Melazarr, we'll remember," Kat said.

Light from the node grew brighter.

"Ready?" Atha asked.

Stenstrom and Kat clasped hands.

Suddenly, both Stenstrom and Kat were standing in a murky, dirty alley. Kat's jumpsuit was gone again; this time she was dressed in a dark, rather artless dress that seemed to put off an air of dreariness. A dark hat sat on her head. Stenstrom was still in his HRN, but his Vith triangle hat was missing. His NTHs were tucked in their sash, and his kit was safely stashed in the interior of his coat. Kat was having trouble adjusting her hat. "G, can you help me with this?"

He helped adjust her hat, situating it to properly cover her Shadowmark. Her blonde hair was a shocking blast of color against her dark wardrobe. "I think I liked the Calvert clothes better," she said.

They heard the sounds of people passing nearby and went in that direction, coming upon a broad street busy with storefronts and crowds of traffic. Here was the Street of Knowledge, long and wide, a ribbon of dark stones in a gray cityscape. From what they could see, the city of Vain was a hilly sort, built in the center of a bumpy, rounded mountain range complete with bluffs, low valleys and abrupt shelves of higher ground littered with buildings at various elevations, dappled with cold lights and cross-cut with a zig-zag of streets. The Street of Knowledge itself was fairly flat, rising at a slow, steady rate to the north. There was a persistent fall of ash or soot in the air, coupled with the assertive smell of sulfur. They soon saw the cause of the soot—a cone-shaped volcano in the distance, smoking in a steady, ominous fashion. Soot was everywhere, like a black, unmelting snowfall galloping across the cobbles like herds of legless animals, gathering in the gutters. All the buildings were covered, giving them a lifeless gray color despite whatever color they might have been originally. The locals rolling about the street all wore relentlessly drab clothing. It was like a festival of cinders all competing to see which could be the grayest. Despite her hat, Kat already had soot in her hair and on her dress. Stenstrom brushed it out of his face.

While the city and the people were drab, the sky above was a wonderland of color. Vibrant streaks of red, yellow, blue and green painted a great abstract picture superimposed behind a fast-moving layer of black negative-image clouds from the volcano.

"What's going on with the sky?" Kat asked, holding onto her hat to admire it.

"I think that's the Great Xaphan Nebula, it takes up a healthy portion of Xaphan space. This planet must be really close for it to be seen so plainly in broad daylight."

They spilled out onto the street, joining the somber crowds.

"Where we going, G?"

"I suppose we're looking for this Rus sect, the 'Yellows' as Atha called them. She deposited us here, they can't be far."

"I don't see any yellow around here, or any other colors for that matter."

"Let's just keep moving. Something will present itself shortly."

They continued up the street for several blocks, Kat continuously brushing the accumulating soot out of her hair. At a busy intersection, a storefront window caught Stenstrom's attention.

"Kat, look!"

"What?"

Across the street, competing for space with the other adjacent shops was a modest gray storefront framed by a hopeful, cave-like door. Concise writing in several languages and alphabets efficiently covered the windows. Mixed in, written in League Common was:

OTTOMAN JOHN, ESQ. AND ASSOCIATE

Stenstrom read the name off to her.

"Is that the guy Atha was talking about?" Kat asked.

"Let's find out."

They went across the street, brushed the soot from their clothes, and entered, ringing a cheery little bell as they did so. Inside was a tiny office, drab, with mostly unadorned walls, two desks, a small sitting table and a back office area. A long, thin board hung on the near wall, composed of several rows of red lights. The lights lit up with great speed, forming gibberish words scrolling from left to right. A frayed, twisted cable hung down from the board, the ends naked metal, attached to nothing; the board should be non-functional, yet it scrolled with letters and odd symbols at a constant, dizzying pace. Stenstrom looked at the screen, seeing the words change from gibberish to a cryptic message.

Erat... KaidarGeMAIN...

aaB ... CLaimthE ... MErten ...

A fawn-haired woman wearing a tan cap equipped with a set of complicated goggles nested into the fabric sat at one of the desks, manipulating a holo terminal. A clay flower pot hosting an odd alien flower bursting with tropical color was a welcome bit of cheer in the room. She saw them and offered a big-toothed smile.

"*Vegae,*" she said, speaking in some odd language.

Stenstrom approached her desk. "Your pardon. We were told to see Sir Ottoman John, Esq. upon our arrival. Is he here? Can you understand me?"

The woman, hearing Stenstrom speak, switched to perfect League Common. "Leaguers!" she said. "We don't see too many Leaguers here in crappy Vain. Where you guys from?"

"Kana, Tyrol region."

"What was that language you were speaking just now?" Kat asked.

"Vertus, the Conwells' old language. This is a place founded by the Conwells so it's the usual tongue. Used to be if you didn't know Vertus you couldn't get into the Trades; the hotter robes, the AlbertCo, the Rus, the Nightrobes, wouldn't have you. I'm curious, the League's a long ways off; who sent you to us?"

"A friend."

"Gotcha. I'm Melazarr. I come from Caroline. I miss it a lot sometimes—my little flower here's from home." She looked at Stenstrom and squinted, studying his face. "Have we ever met before, sir? You look sort of familiar to me."

He saw the board flash.

Mmerem ... the MertEN is YouRS ...

Aaat ... Claim Her ... ewk

Though this Melazarr woman was a total stranger, her appearance and her name were familiar to him as well, at a primal, unspoken level. He was used to this by now, these odd Extra-Planar doings. This Melazarr of Caroline was an Extra-Planar Entity just like he was, she had to be. He knew other versions of him had seen this woman before, had known her, possibly bedded her.

Bits of information filtered into his thoughts.

Tall.

She is a giant. Melazarr of Caroline is a giant.

And the word flashed across the board struck a chord with him:

Merten ...

"No, madam, we haven't." He held out his hand to shake. Melazarr straightened her clothing and stood. As he expected, she was incredibly tall, nearly as tall as Stenstrom at 6'7".

"I guess you got one of those faces that just looks familiar," she said, shaking his hand. "Ooooo, strong grip, haha. I like that. In case you're wondering why I'm so tall—Carolines are tall. Some sort of flaw in our genes or something. I don't know."

"I'm Stenstrom, Lord of Belmont-South Tyrol. Here with me is Kat, my countess."

Melazarr acknowledged Kat with a nod. "Hi. Whoah, is that Shadowmark real?"

"Yep," Kat said.

"I've never met a countess Black Hat before."

"I'm not a Black Hat."

"Ok, fine with me."

The board on the wall scrolled and bleeped, constantly moving and changing.

"What's with the sign?" Kat asked.

"Oh that! I don't know." Melazarr grabbed the frayed end of the board's cable and shook it. "This place used to be a sandwich shop, I think. The sign displayed the specials of the day, people's orders, that sort of thing. I don't know. It's got a mind of its own, I guess. It just flashes a whole lot of nonsense. Whatever—it's just something to break up the monotony."

Stenstrom glanced at the board. It wasn't flashing nonsense at the moment:

... Sil ... oftheRus ... hasDATa ...

Erat... gum. Sil of the Rus ...

Neither Kat nor Melazarr seemed to be seeing the message, only him. More Extra-Planar activity, it must be.

"Anyway, glad to know you. You two are pretty far from home. My boss, Ottoman John, is a Leaguer too, also from Kana, I think. Leaguers are always welcome here. What can we do for you?"

"We really don't know," Kat said, jumping in. "What services do you offer?"

"Oh, we're a one-stop shop here on the Saarlands, the outlying blocks of the Street of Knowledge. We make it our business to assist Udders and Stinkos."

"Udders and Stinkos?" Stenstrom asked.

"Tourists, newbies to Vain, that's what we call them. And Stinkos are poor souls what had their heads totally emptied—really sucks. The most important piece of knowledge you can have is that the Street of Knowledge, heading up the street toward Pentagulle, is the Happy Hunting Grounds of Vain. Everybody out there is a potential winner, or a potential victim. You gotta know, it's open season, buying and selling memories, thoughts and skills is a rough business. Lots of the Trades up the street, the MVers, Vuggers and whatnot, can be proper dishonest folk, and if you're not careful, they'll steal all your Slate right out of your head before you can say 'lickety split'. We're advocates for the little guy, for the tourists and uninitiated. We can validate any data you buy, lots of sham squash and crap Slate floating around out there. We can Radar up any lost moments and, best of all, we can also make a complete Slate of what's in your head, as it currently exists. Should you manage to 'lose something' out there, if you get your Slate charmed out of your head, we can upload it right back in. If you can walk away from the Street of Knowledge with everything you came in with, then you're a winner. We offer all sorts of packages to help protect you during your visit. For the uninitiated, which you guys clearly are, I recommend our Premium Package. You get a complete imaging of your heads, which we'll back-up in our archives, we Radar you up to Max, we shoot you some swipe-scanners to help validate any data you buy, and we load in some Floaters in case you get Vugged down to Stinko in a Verti-Hovi park."

"Pardon?" Stenstrom asked.

"Stinko, it means you've had your head emptied. If you're a Stinko and all you can do is breathe and stand up then you've been Verti-Hovied—the Trades don't like having to pick Stinkos up off the ground. A Floater is a little instruction that will help guide you, even if you're Slated out. The Floater will remain."

Stenstrom and Kat discussed it amongst themselves. "Well, I didn't quite fully understand everything you said, but we were told we can trust you, and you seem like a goodly lady, so we'll take your Premium Package, for two please," Stenstrom said.

Melazarr clapped her hands together. "Great! Come on back and let's get started."

The door to the office opened. A thin man in a black suit wearing a Vain top hat came in, dusting himself off as he entered, revealing a sandy crop of short hair. He carried a bag of fragrant savory lunch fare.

"Hey, Johnny! We've got some customers!" Melazarr said to him.

He set the bag down and greeted them. "Ah, Leaguers—your coat, sir, is a dead giveaway. I'm a great fan of the brief but interesting exploits of the Hoban Royal Navy. I haven't seen one of their coats in a long time."

"Are you Ottoman John, esquire?" Stenstrom asked.

"I am. Sorry I was absent, I was out getting our lunch. I'm sure Melazarr here has served you well in my absence."

"She has."

Melazarr led them to the sitting table, offering them seats. As they situated themselves, Ottoman John fetched a fruity purple candle from a cupboard and shoved the blunt end into a metal base. Lights came on, displays printed out data. He input adjustments and then set the candle on the table-top.

"So, what is going to happen here?" Stenstrom asked. "We're feeling a little nervous."

"Understandable. We're going to make a complete image of your heads, and we're going to upload a Floater to assist you in case you get Verti-Hovied. We're going to use Smoque to make the image. Smoque is the fastest method of doing it, and it's also the most complete."

"What's 'Smoque'?" Kat asked.

Ottoman John showed them the candle. "This. We light the candle and we get Smoque. Smoque is nano-tech. You breathe it in, it gets in your lungs and quickly saturates your brain."

Stenstrom and Kat looked at each other. "I'm not certain we're comfortable," he said.

"I get that. We can get the image via ceril, or we can Dot-Dot it, but those are much slower and not as reliable. Listen, if we had wanted, we could have Verti-Hovied you two into Stinkos a thousand times by now. That's not who we are, that's not what we do, we're on your side. You're the clients, just tell us how you want to proceed."

"It's ok, G, Atha said we can trust them," Kat said, getting comfortable in her seat.

Stenstrom thought about it. "All right. Do what you need to do."

"That's what I want to hear!" Melazarr struck a match with her teeth. She lit the candle wick and a bluish undulating fire blossomed. The candle quickly made a thick, slightly sweet-smelling smoke that filled the air like temple incense. Melazarr returned to her desk and began working her holo-terminal.

Ottoman John watched with casual interest. "Just relax and allow Melazarr to perform her work. One thing you need to know about Vain, things are never what they seem at face value."

Stenstrom coughed. "And you're certain this Smoque is safe?"

"Perfectly. We image people all the time, because people lose their heads all the time. The image we make right now, before the Trades up the street in Pentagulle get at you, is like pure gold. The Trades hate the images we make because it takes money out of their robes. Instead of having to buy your thoughts back from them for top brass, you just upload it yourself for free. The Trades are always trying to put us out of business for good. They've even sent the ECSP after us."

"The what?"

"The ECSP—the cops. It stands for: Engineering Commando Squad Pentagulle. The Trades go crying to them whenever they want somebody out of business or dead. We're pretty good at shaking them, though. If you know all their tricks and can keep your head, they really don't know how to deal with you, and we can move our office at a moment's notice."

"Yep," Melazarr agreed from her desk. "Remember that one guy last week, Johnny? We squashed him up four times because he kept getting Dong-Dinged hard."

"Yeah, the poor bastard."

Data poured in. Melazarr processed·it. "Here it comes. We'll do the lady first."

Kat closed her eyes, falling into a trance as Melazarr worked.

Ottoman John spoke, his voice soft and hypnotic. "So, for your Floater, what sort of instructions would you like us to upload?"

"We're here for a specific order of business," Stenstrom said, feeling he could trust them. "We seek to purchase information."

"We call that the 'Slate'," Ottoman John said. "You've heard us tossing that term around. A Slate is information taken from people's heads. What Slate are you looking for?"

Before Stenstrom could answer, Melazarr spoke, punching up data as it formed in front of her. "Hey, Johnny, the lady here's Slating up like a Black Hat. She's got all of the markers."

Ottoman John raised a brow. "I see her Shadowmark, but I thought it was just paint. Is your countess a Black Hat?"

"Kat is a Shadow tech female, but she's no Black Hat."

He laughed. "Oh, you Leaguers do the daftest things, don't you? I'd heard it's fashion now in the League to court Black Hats. We don't think too much of them in Vain—nasty, fire-breathing ladies most of them, but your Kat seems charming enough. If I were a betting man, which I am, I would bet that you're looking for the Slate of Paige du Long of Moane. Am I right?"

"You are."

Ottoman John laughed again. "That's a nice, hard, cooked Slate for certain. The Rus have it in their central database up on the hillside in Pentagulle, right in the center of the Street of Knowledge. The Rus created quite a stir when they took it from her, thought they were going to score big brass in ransom and rental payments from the Black Hats for it. But, seems the Black Hats don't care much about such things and the Rus never got their payout, though Paige du Long losing her whole Slate seems to have put the Black Hats off conquering Vain for the time being, which, I suppose, is a good thing. You're going to want to see Sil of the Rus; he's their head guy. He's got access to it—I'll add his name to your Floater. Paige du Long's Slate is going to be expensive. You got the brass for it?"

Sil of the Rus

"The what?"

"Money. Paige du Long's Slate is going to be expensive. The Rus will sell you a copy on ceril disk. Bring it back here and we'll convert it into squash for you."

"Pardon?"

"Squash, or squashdat as it's known. It's a method of encoding data into a capsule about so big." He held his thumb and forefinger about an inch apart. "To upload the data, all you have to do is smash the capsule against your forehead and you've got it, right into your skin and skull, direct into your brain. Very nice and quick method of upload, but it tends to not be permanent."

"That sounds fine," Stenstrom said, feeling suddenly tired and dizzy. He struggled to maintain consciousness. The red scrolling letters on the board mesmerized him as they passed.

... *AArErat* ...

... *GonreetK* ...

DEmonAWaiTs ...

He stared at the board.

GOingtODIE ...

The next thing he knew, Melazarr was leaning over him, cap and goggles, all smiles. "Did you dream?" she asked. Stenstrom looked around. The candle was burned down to a nub. Ottoman John and Melazarr's lunches were eaten, the bag flattened and thrown in the trash. The board was back to random, nonsensical letters and symbols moving by.

"I don't recall dreaming," he said.

"Eh, some people do, some don't. We're all done," she said happily. "We have both your images Slated up and safe in our archives."

Kat stirred. He took her hand and rubbed it. Melazarr placed two small bags on the table. "Here you go. In each of these bags are twenty squash capsules. The white ones are for you, sir, the green are for the countess."

"We figure you two are going to get Vugged a lot," Ottoman John said. "You might even get Verti-Hovied. If you're out there and you lose something, if you find you're forgetting something you ought to know, just take a capsule and squash it right back into your head. That'll piss the Trades off right proper."

"This is the good stuff," Melazarr said. "Got right shiny nano in it. Squash this up and it's permanent—since it's an image of your own head you won't have to worry about it dropping out after a few hours. Don't let the Trades catch you with it, they'll drag you off to the ECSP."

Stenstrom took the bags. "Much obliged. How much do we owe you? I have Belmont sesterces to pay with."

"Seven sesterces will be fine."

Stenstrom produced his money bag and paid.

"Remember," Ottoman John said, taking the money. "You guys are going up the hill to get Paige du Long's Slate. You're going to be in it with the Trades deep, and you can get Vugged in a fast bloody moment. Watch smoke, because it's probably not smoke, it's Smoque. Watch chairs too— don't sit in strange chairs. Don't look into blinking lights, don't eat anything given to you on the streets and don't let anybody touch you or Dong-Ding you either. Watch out for the bloody Snake Heads."

"Yeah, the Snake Heads suck," Melazarr agreed.

"So, what you're saying is: don't breathe, don't sit, don't eat, don't shake hands with strangers, and watch out for snakes," Kat said.

"Essentially, yes."

"Are there any defenses you can sell us, for protection from all this?" Stenstrom asked.

"Well sure. We can sell you masks to filter out Smoque, and lenses to protect your eyes from cerils. But—if you two go walking up the street all armored up, and you don't have a 4D tattoo floating around your head that says 'P-Force' you're going to be asking for trouble. They're going to come at you in force, and there's no single defense against everything. Your best bet is to lie low, look like you know what you're doing, and not attract attention."

Stenstrom and Ottoman John shook hands. Kat gave him a hug. "We'll be careful, and we'll be back soon with our data."

Ottoman John handed Kat a coin-sized silver device. "Take this. It's a swipe-scanner. I've got it junked to look for Paige du Long's Slate. When the Rus give you the disk, swipe this across it. If the right data's there it'll light up green. If it's not, it'll turn red. Remember, trust nobody. When the soot stops falling you're there in Pentagulle with the Trades. Be careful."

Kat took the disk and dropped it into her bag. "Got it, thanks!"

Melazarr looked conflicted. "Hey, Johnny, these two are real Udders and they've got all sorts of dat the Trades won't be able to resist. Maybe we should go with them, you know, keep 'em from getting into trouble and help out with the Rus."

Stenstrom looked at the odd message board continually flashing messages but connected to nothing. Thoughts assailed him.

Melazarr of Caroline is a Merten, herald of the universe's news.

Mertens always die.

Melazarr always dies ...

He didn't want her to die. "No! No, thank you, my lady. Most kind of you, but we'll be fine."

"You sure?"

"Yes, please, you've done more than enough, and thank you."

Melazarr motioned for them to stay a moment. "One sec. I'll be right back." She disappeared into the back office, emerging a few minutes later carrying a jar full of dark blue capsules. She opened the jar and gave one to both of them. "Go ahead, just smash 'em into your forehead. It's fun."

"What are these?" Kat asked.

"Vertus. Squash these up and you'll be speaking perfect Vertus for a couple of hours. That'll throw the wolves off you a little."

"Good idea, Mel," Ottoman John said.

They hesitated a moment, then Stenstrom smashed the capsule against his forehead, feeling it crack open and spill out a cold, runny interior against his skin. Kat did the same. Ottoman John offered Kat a cloth. She accepted it and wiped her brow.

"Should we be feeling anything?" Stenstrom asked.

Melazarr laughed. "Nope. Only that you're now speaking awesome, accent-free Vertus."

"We are?"

"You are. Neat, huh?"

Stenstrom bowed to Melazarr. "Thank you, how long will this last?"

"Several hours."

"And how much do we owe you?"

"Nothing, it's on us."

Ottoman John took Kat's hand and kissed it. "All right, then, we'll expect you back shortly to convert your Paige du Long data into Squash. Remember what we've told you and use the swipe-scanner. Speed well and safe dreams."

Placing their sacks of squash into their pockets, they went out into the sooty afternoon, thankful for the acquaintances they had made.

5—The Street of Knowledge

They moved down the street, leaving Ottoman John's little office far behind, keeping a close lookout for anything suspicious. The center of Vain featured a distinctive triumvirate of three impressively steep mountains of hard, smooth rock situated in a rough triangle. They loomed over the Street of Knowledge which meandered between them, each dominating a section of it. This, according to Ottoman John, was the heart of the street and, possibly, the most dangerous area. As they neared the three peaks, the street became a noisy confusion of color, bright lights and odd smells. The first thing they noticed was that the soot from the volcano was absent, the overhead sky free of it and of black clouds, allowing the splendor of the Great Xaphan Nebula to reign unhindered. Some sort of force shield seemed to be diverting the soot down the street. Under fluttering banners of light blue, dogwood red and canary yellow tents and stalls were set up, lined with inviting cushions and modest reading tables with vendors sitting or standing, smoking woodsy menthols as they dealt with passersby.

"Well, look at this," Kat said. "I see all sorts of stuff, and there's a bunch of yellow banners. Yellow's what we want, right?"

Stenstrom looked around. Yellow, red and blue were liberally mixed together, all vying for the passing crowd's attention. As he looked further, each of the three mountains was exclusively adorned in one of the three colors. The mountain decorated in yellow loomed off to their left. Side streets went up the mountain in a bumpy climb, the buildings getting taller, flat-topped, made of clean, glittering glass and metal, more and more aggressively technological the higher up they were.

"I suppose we head off to that one and make inquires."

They took the long walk down the twisting street, assailed on all sides by pillowed Sage Sanctums and smoky Dens of Knowledge. Men and women on the street garbed in colorful robes sought to lure them into various establishments, promising answers to all their questions and to buy whatever wares they were selling. Ladies who appeared to be prostitutes harassed Kat, trying to sell her knowledge in exotic whoring techniques and to recruit her into their ranks. They became increasingly aggressive. One of them, smoking from a mounted cigarette and wearing a headdress of writhing mechanical snakes, blew a cloud of smoke in Kat's face. Kat coughed and the mechanical snakes all came up to meet her gaze, moving hypnotically, their eyes flashing.

Watch out for the Snake Heads … Ottoman John had said.

The color drained from Kat's face, her eyes became distant and cloudy. Laughing, the woman sank back into the crowds.

Stenstrom pulled Kat aside. There was no recognition, her movements all stilted as if pre-programmed.

"Kat?"

No response. In only a few moments, Kat's head had been emptied.

A pair of people wearing blue robes approached. "Having trouble?" one of them asked.

Stenstrom glanced at them and pushed them away. "We're fine. Be off."

The blue robes shook their heads. "Your lady doesn't look fine to me. She's a Standing 10x, all she knows how to do right now is breathe and go Verti-Hovi if she falls down."

One of the robes held out a light blue card flashing with circuitry. Kat's smiling face appeared in a corner. "Come see the Night Robes. Our prices are reasonable, we'll get you on a bargain plan and you'll have your lady back in no time. Or, if you want her better than what she was, we can go Premium, squash her up however you want. You want a goodly lady, we can deliver. You want a death-dealing whore we can do that too."

"We can turn her into a real freak in the sack. You'll wonder what you ever did without us," the other blue robe said.

Stenstrom waved them off and led Kat up the street, looking for a semi-private place to attend to her. The two blue robes followed, staying close. Stenstrom dragged Kat through the crowds, the robes pursuing. Moving Kat was difficult, she moved her legs only in a pedestrian, back and forth fashion, not generating any speed, so unlike the lithe, panther-like Kat he loved.

Unable to evade their pursuers, Stenstrom stopped, pulled her into his chest and Faded into the Shadows.

The robes soon arrived. "Voinks!" one of the robes said, "he's gone all Vaudevilly."

"Hoi, Udder!" the other one shouted. "You make us come chase you, her plan's going to get real brassy right quick!"

Stenstrom, invisible, moved several blocks down the street until he felt safe. Unable to see Kat, he unfaded from the Shadows and looked to her. She was drooling, her expression witless. As he watched, her hand came up on its own in a robotic fashion, felt about her pockets, and slowly pulled out her bag of green squash capsules.

What had Ottoman John told them?

"We uploaded a Floater, just a simple set of instructions to assist you if you get Vugged..."

Kat must be acting on the 'Floater' Ottoman and Melazarr implanted into her brain. Methodically, she opened the bag, selecting a squash capsule where it shone in the sun with a transparent emerald luster. She slowly brought it to her forehead. She pressed it against her head, but the squash didn't break. Stenstrom brushed her hair back as she tried again. This time the capsule broke and the contents spilled out against her head. He wiped away the excess. As he touched the green fluid, he had a momentary hallucination, seeing flashes of Kat's life pass through his mind like acts in a play, and then drop out.

Almost immediately, Kat blinked. "What happened?" she asked.

Relieved, he embraced her. "You got Vugged, by the lady with the snake headdress."

Kat looked confused. She gazed up at him. "What did you say, G?"

"I said you got Vugged, darling. Ottoman and Melazarr's squash worked just as they promised, their Floater instructions worked as well. We owe them much for their help."

Terror dawned on Kat's face. "I can't understand you, G, you're speaking some weird language."

"I am?"

Stenstrom thought back. Melazarr gave them the Vertus squash *after* they had their images made. Reloading Kat's head must have nulled out the Vertus. Stenstrom had no conscious idea he was speaking a language other than League Common. He could understand Kat but apparently all he could reply in at the moment was Vertus. They could no longer communicate until the Vertus squash wore off or they reloaded his head, too. It was important he keep hold of the Vertus. He tried using hand gestures to calm Kat down.

"Guess you're speaking that weird Vertus stuff, huh?" she said, somewhat dejected.

He nodded in reply just as a pair of hands roughly pulled them apart.

It was the blue robes again. "Hoi, no! Where'd you get that Dirty Squash from, criminals?" one asked. "It's confiscato time, hand it over!"

"Yeah, that'll cost ya some time in the P-Force's dungeon, I'm thinkin', or maybe out in the Verti-Hovi park with the other Stinkos."

One grabbed Kat by the hair. "Don't fuck with the Night Robes! We're makin' us a Robe arrest, an' don't think you're gettin' out of paying us. We'll knock that crap squash right out your head and make you brass-up double for our bloody inconvenience. Yaa!"

Kat formed her claws and rammed them into the guts of the nearest robe.

"Yerk!" he cried, doubling over. The other robe pulled a capsule from his pockets. Stenstrom skinned his NTH pistol and shot him in the chest, dropping him and his robe to the ground. Quickly, they hauled the two dead robes into an alley, took Kat's card, and moved on as fast as they could.

Kat chattered about the experience as they quit the area. "Ok, I guess they probably gave you something to speak the local lingo, right? I mean,

I don't remember a thing about that. Thank Creation for Ottoman John and Melazarr's image of my head they made, otherwise..."

"Otherwise, we'd be renting your head back from the Night Robes."

"I have no idea what you just said. You know, it's sort of cool listening to you speak a foreign language. I like the sound of it. I'll just stay quiet and let you do the talking for the time being."

They continued up the street, keeping all the vendors and prostitutes at arm's length, averting their eyes from lights and avoiding patches of Smoque as best they could. Mixed into the crowds were soldiers dressed in green, wearing armor complete with helmets, eye-covering lenses and oxygen. They carried weapons. Patches on their shoulders announced the word P-FORCE in gold threads emblazoned with some sort of pouncing animal. 4-D tattoos of flapping wings, glittering horns, flexing claws and other animal accessories floated about their bodies.

"Are those the cops, the ECSP Ottoman John called them?" she asked.

Stenstrom nodded.

"Maybe they're out looking for us."

Stenstrom agreed again.

Continuing on, he became somewhat accustomed to the characters populating the street. There were various seedy vendors in their vests, girded loins and sweaty turbans selling all manner of product from local fruits to sinister technology. The wealthier vendors, sporting nicer clothes and more sophisticated set-ups, appeared to be sponsored by one of the three Trades; the reds, yellows or blues. There were prostitutes, hanging in the wings, blowing Smoque and seeing everything, on the lookout for customers and new recruits. As with the vendors, various sects of prostitutes were affiliated with different Trades. The Snake Heads, the ones wearing the mechanical snake headdresses and little else, the ones who bagged Kat, seemed to be the most aggressive with the backing of the blue robes, assaulting people as they passed by, all in full view of the armored ECSP. In fact, the only time the 'P-Force' took action was when a victim resisted getting Vugged; then they would assist the Vugger. The blue robes, the 'Night Robes' seemed to be taking up much of their time, pulling them aside with great frequency.

And then there were local civilians, people of various lineages mixed in, buying and selling with greater and lesser levels of success. Finally, there were foreigners, visitors and tourists who somehow found themselves in Vain on the Street of Knowledge where danger lurked everywhere. Stenstrom watched a mother and her three children moving up the street wearing clothing from Holly, which he recognized by the broad-brimmed hat the mother had on. The mother seemed to realize she and her children were in a fair measure of danger as her young ones became mesmerized by the wonders in a yellow vendor's tent.

He watched them lured into the depths of the tent by the vendor. After waiting a minute, the mother went in to get them.

Stenstrom never saw them come out. "Kat, wait here," he said.

"What, G?" she replied, rubbing her booted foot.

He gave her a hand signal to wait. He went across the street into the smoky tent, its shelves lined with blinking gadgets and wondrous toys— things no child could resist. He held his breath and kept his eyes downcast. He saw no sign of the mother and her children. There was a back exit leading to an alley. He poked his head out; all he found was her hat lying on the floor near a back exit.

The mother and her children were gone. Vain had gotten them. Despondent, feeling he had failed them, he went back out and got Kat, holding her hand tightly.

Moving on, they eventually reached the entrance to the yellow mountain where the road wound up its face at a steep angle.

They rested a moment. Kat was suffering in her traveling boots and longed to remove them. "I hate these shoes. These Xaphan women must have hooves for feet," she said, rubbing her foot.

Stenstrom sighed. Not being able to talk to Kat was a hindrance.

Kat looked around, seeing all the people coming and going. Occasionally, they saw floating, open-bed vehicles moving up the street. The vehicle beds were crammed full of people of all sexes and ages, being tended to by people in red, blue or yellow robes. By their posture and their blank, empty stares, Stenstrom knew they were Vugged people, their minds stolen, their insensate bodies being taken who knows where. Stenstrom looked at the people in the flat bed, searching for the mother and her children, ready to draw his pistols and free them. He found no sign of them.

"This place gives me the chills," Kat said. "The sooner we're gone and back with Ottoman and Melazarr, the happier I'll be."

He nodded.

Evening fell, the night sky awash with glowing colors from the great nebula, imparting a permanent carnival-like atmosphere over the city. Soft glows from tents lining the street created long veins of ruddy light; the main drag of the Street of Knowledge being the most ruddy and throbbing vein of all. The crowds showed no sign of thinning as night fell; the party continued.

Stenstrom took Kat's hand and they headed up the yellow mountain, the street pitching up dramatically in elevation, revealing a hive of tightly-packed buildings, tents, stalls and other establishments all decorated in yellow.

"So where do we go? Can we go to any of these places and get what we need?" Kat asked.

He shook his head. "We're looking for somebody named Sil."

"I have no idea what you said. Lead the way, G."

They stopped at a stall fluttering with yellow banners selling all manner of blinking, whirling trinkets. Stenstrom inquired where 'Sil' might be found. The merchant directed them farther up the hill to a large tent. They walked there, feeling less easy with every step.

A large tent, bigger than a small house, staked and permanently poled into the ground, surrounded by greenery and a host of veiled dancers, presented itself. Next to the tent was a vast fenced-in area. Roaming about within the fence was a herd of people, aimlessly moving around. They were in various states of squalor, some wore clean clothes, others filthy rags, and some wore nothing at all. As Stenstrom noted, they all had that same look Kat had after she got Vugged, that maudlin, mindless stare offering no hint of intelligence or emotion. A flatbed floated by, offloading a number of people, guiding them into the fenced-in area to roam around with the others like cattle.

"More Stinkos have arrived!" somebody cheered.

 Stenstrom looked about, searching for his mother and children. They weren't there. As he watched, passersby paid a yellow-robed attendant to be let into the fence. They wandered about as if in a petting zoo, tormenting the Vugged people, pushing them down and laughing as they mechanically stood back up. Some stabbed them and watched them bleed, some painted their faces and posed for garish photos with them. Some purchased squash from a line of vending machines, went in and smashed the squash against the Vugged people's faces, causing a variety of effects. Some capered about like dogs on all fours, or danced with ballerina-like precision. One man paid a sizable sum and lit one of the wretched Vugged people on fire, the doomed man blazing like a tree until he toppled.

Infuriated, Stenstrom and Kat could watch no more. This was a place of utter cruelty and it turned his stomach. If he could, he would burn this entire city to the ground. Kat wandered over to the line of vending machines, putting her hands on them, looking at the goods sold. She returned to his side, smiling. "I screwed those machines over, G! I gummed them all up with Silver tech. Good luck fixing that, losers! Maybe those poor people out there will get a little bit of peace tonight!"

He kissed her on the forehead. "Well done, love!"

They went to the tent. It was a vast comfortable place, deep with soft rugs and colorful hangings. Pleasant incense drifted out of brass burners and droning music played on easy Xaphan instruments. Soft orange lamps dimly lit the interior. It was sparsely populated with locals dressed in canary yellow robes, some seated on benches performing 'research', others flopped on the rugs staring at the canvas ceiling, lost in a Kooked Up haze.

The place seemed to Stenstrom to be a den of vice rather than a place of knowledge. A skinny, unhealthy-looking man sat in a corner surrounded by insensate males and females in yellow veils, all swaying to the discordant rhythms of the street. He seemed to be the leader. He pulled from a brass pipe connected to a menthol-loaded decanter via a woven hose. He watched Stenstrom and Kat enter, and smiled.

"Welcome," he said, smoke drifting out of his mouth in measured puffs. "Strangers, I see. What may the Rus do for you?"

"Are you Sil?" Stenstrom asked.

"I am."

Wary of the smoke, they hung out of the tent just beyond the entrance so they could get fresh air, though it was tainted with the smell of burning flesh. Stenstrom noted, with some satisfaction, a commotion going on at the non-functional vending machines. People fussed, beating on them, trying to get them to function. He was proud of Kat for destroying them.

"We seek a Slate," Stenstrom answered, putting his newly-learned street vocabulary to the test. "I'm told you can assist me."

"Ah, many come here for answers. You have chosen well. I shudder to think what might have become of you had you gone to the other Trades, the AlbertCo or the Nightrobes—despicable, the lot of them. The Rus treat their customers well. Might I ask where you are from, for clearly it's not here? You're tonguing solid, right-proper Vertus, but I'll wager you've had it squashed up into your head to simulate Vain locals. A very wise precaution; you never know what sorts you'll bump into out there. Am I right?"

"Never you mind. Understand that we are fully briefed on the antics perpetrated on the Street of Knowledge, and should action be called for we are ready to respond with deadly force." Stenstrom moved his coat aside, allowing the man to see the grips of his pistols. Sil puffed a few rings of smoke upon seeing them.

"I shouldn't think you'll be needing your weapons. Please come in and be comfortable." He turned to a grinning man nearby. "Fetch drinks! Fetch food!"

"We shan't enter," Stenstrom said. "Is that smoke you're smoking, or is it 'Smoque'?"

He smiled. "Just to add to your knowledge, 'Smoque' doesn't come from a water-based decanter—water fouls the nano-tech. This is merely a smoke engine filled with my favorite blend from Midas and a little water to cool it. But, if it will comfort you, I'll put it away and clear the domicile of smoke at once." He hung the tip of his smoker from a hook and opened a small box to his right. Instantly, a breezy column of air consolidated the smoke into a whitish-gray, tendril-like vortex dancing about near the tent ceiling. "There, the air is clear, both literally and figuratively."

Stenstrom and Kat cautiously entered, eyes darting, looking for any possible treachery. Fine wooden chairs were brought to them and placed on the rugs. Plates piled with food were offered by teetering servants in yellow.

"Care you to sit? Can I press you to an oiled date?" Sil asked.

"Thank you, no," Stenstrom said, eyeing the chairs with suspicion.

"Well then, seems you're aware of all our tricks. All of them harmless, I assure you. So, what sort of Slate do you seek? We have much to choose from. We have Slates from here to the moon."

"Paige du Long of Moane. We wish to purchase her Slate."

"Really? I must say I am disappointed a little. Paige du Long of Moane's Slate is a bit of bad juice squatting in our mainframe. There isn't much that can be done with it."

"Is it for sale, yes or no?" Stenstrom demanded.

"One moment, please," Sil said.

A Kooked Up man came stumbling out from the back of the tent, holding a tray with a bell sitting on it. Sil picked it up and rang it.

ding   …   Ding!   DING!!!!   DINGDINGDINGDINGDING-DING!!!!!!!!!!!!!!

Stenstrom and Kat both went limp. Several servants caught them before they could fall to the floor and manhandled them into the chairs.

Sil laughed. "Apparently, whoever briefed you on the sundry perils of the Street of Knowledge forgot to mention that sound is a wonderful method of rendering a head full of goodies nice and quiet. It's called 'Dong-Dinging' in street slang. I'm just dying to know what you've got in there, and how much it's worth, both to the market and to you to get it back. I'll bet there's some right proper Slate in there. Seems we are not selling today, are we? We're collecting."

Holo screens jumped up all around them. Data flashed. Lights streaked across the tent. "Now, let's see what we have here."

"Wait just a moment, Sil of the Rus!" came a shrill voice from outside the tent. A group of men and women wearing red robes came rushing up, most breathless from trudging up the hill.

"Madberrie Saddle of the AlbertCo!" Sil said, taken aback. "Get your robes off our hill and trundle off to your own pathetic hill, you Slags!"

The red-robed AlbertCo were going nowhere. "We got a hot tip you have a whole Udder-full of out-of-Vainer fresh milk you're hoping to churn to sweet butter." She saw Stenstrom and Kat flopped in the chairs and pointed at them. "Right there, they are. That butter is ours! We've had a marker out on these two all day, we think they 6-Feeted a pair of Night Robe Lurkers down the street after they Verti-Hovied the lady fair and square. Seems you can't do a good Vugging these days without people fighting back. You're going to give them to us so we can sell them to the Night Robes!"

"You out of your robe, Madberrie Saddle?" Sil squeaked. "You want us to pay you for Slate we Dong-Dinged, Slate we mined? You must have squashed-in a bad load today. Slot-off to your own hillside before I decide to 6-Feet you and your lot."

"Wait!" came another voice. A group of people wearing light blue robes, the hoods pulled over their heads, came up. "That Slate belongs to the Nightrobes!"

"Lymon Huffboy!" Sil cried. "You Nightrobes have no business here. We laugh at your robes."

"The Nightrobes are the most fearsome Trade on the three hills. You AlbertCo, your robes are red like my ass. You Rus, your robes are yellow like my favorite concubine's teeth. The Nightrobes have been keeping Vain Black Hat free for ages. We were dimed-up today with some hot skinny that a rabid Black Hat did 6-Feet a pair of our best Lurkers. Hear tell she's trying to set up shop in Vain and we claim her as God's own." He pointed at Kat. "And there she is, already Dong-Dinged prostrate for us. Now you hand her over and let me save us all from her evil."

"This woman was Dong-Dinged by the Rus. We haven't scanned her yet. Your robes are uncleaning this place of learning with your presence."

One of the Nightrobes handed Lymon Huffboy a scanner. "She's a Black Hat for certain, Lymon. Got a classic Evil-Bitch matrix up in there."

"Yeah!" Lymon cried. "We'll be taking her, and the Newbie-Brainy dude for our troubles."

"Tellie no!" Sil cried. "We're taking their Slate, then the girl's going to the Snake Head Whores and the dude is going Stinko to the Verti-Hovie range outside, where the Citi-Goodies can have at him."

Madberrie Saddle of the AlbertCo reacted. "The pair of them be ours! Touch either of their Udder heads and we'll be squashing-in a proper fighting Slate and handing you all your robes!"

The Nightrobes all revealed a pull-down pocket on their robes filled with dark capsules. "Then let us test out our latest squash. I call it: 'Kick the Asses of the Rus and the AlbertCo' squash."

Sil stood, furious. "That's it! We're vacating the lot of you from Rus Mountain." He wildly gestured at his yellow-robed associates. "Fanquil, David, Techma, Hansu, Sobe, all of you squash-into this fight and load up a No-Mercy squash!"

On all three sides, capsules of various colors emerged. There were an odd few moments while foreheads were slapped and all contestants were suitably squashed-up with the squash of their choice. Soon, the three sides of apparently untrained people were transformed into poised, deadly fighters, all jumping about with precision, flashing blades, raising hands against equally skilled opponents. The battle spilled into the tent in a chaotic wave, overturning chairs, knocking over boxes. Sil, not a participant, retreated out the back.

Stenstrom and Kat were knocked out of their chairs, both of them lying limp on the floor, both of them slowly trying to stand up. A Nightrobe deftly plunged his dagger into a defending Rus and had an open path, claiming them as his prize. He put his arms around them, trying to lead them away.

Kat stirred, barely aware of what was going on. She didn't know who she was, or where she was. There was a man next to her, who was he, and who was this man dragging both she and him across the floor?

Something replayed in her mind. Images of a man in a hat and a tall woman floated across her jumbled thoughts, images of a bag full of green capsules, and of breaking the capsules against her head. What did green look like? Tentatively feeling about her clothing, she found a bag; inside were a bunch of pretty capsules that looked good enough to eat. Green—that's what green looked like.

Smash it against your forehead ...

Moments later, Silver tech claws exploded into the Nightrobe's chest, spilling a torrent of blood to the rugged floor. He fell.

Kat scrabbled free of his dead grip, her claws dripping with the man's blood. Her thoughts restored, she saw Stenstrom lying face-first on the floor a few feet away, unmoving. She turned him over.

"G?"

Stenstrom had a blank thousand yard stare on his face. No intelligence. He needed his capsules, the white ones Ottoman John and Melazarr had given them. She fumbled with his heavy HRN coat, reaching in looking for the bag. All around her, people in yellow, red and blue robes battled in a complex harmony of destruction. Two red AlbertCo advanced on her, moving with skill and speed.

Where was his bag?

The two AlbertCo were on her. She commenced a fight for her life, battling against the two, they evading her claws and counter-attacking with startling skill. Only Kat's speed, darting, bouncing off the walls, saved her from being subdued instantly. The AlbertCo were too strong, too skilled, she needed room to move—room to fight. She saw she was in a tent. She lunged for the nearest wall and cut her way out into the night air, the Albert-Co fast on her heels. She saw a large fenced-in area populated by a number of still, zombie-like people, some of whom were undressed. She wasn't sure what was going on, but she had a fast idea. She darted from one person to the next, slamming her green-capsuled squash against their foreheads as the AlbertCo pursued.

Instantly, the six people she had squashed came to life. Moving like Kat, they jumped around in a chaotic bunch like an entire team of Kats, displaying her speed and agility, though their joints popped with the effort. With their combined might, they attacked the AlbertCo high and low, knocking them down, punching and kicking, quickly overwhelming them.

"G! G! Where's G?" they said in a chorus, jabbering amongst themselves. Male and female, young and adult, all of them believed they were Kat. She bounded back into the tent, along with the squashed people, to Stenstrom. He had managed to stand up like a statue. They went through the many pockets lining his HRN, looking for the bag of squash.

"G! G! G!" they all chattered in noisy unison.

Several Rus came into the tent, moving toward Kat. Frantic, she and several others pulled an assortment of items from his HRN, throwing them at the Rus, hoping to slow them down.

One of them had a green Holystone. She threw it. Webbing erupted, engulfing the Rus. Another one had some of his silver pans and tools. He threw them at the webbing. Continuing their search, they finally found the bag of squash. Kat pulled a capsule and applied it to his forehead. The Rus worked their way out of the webbing. Kat and four others attacked the Rus, quickly battering them to the ground.

Stenstrom, his forehead slick with squash, shook his head. "Where are we?" he asked, speaking normal League Common again.

All of the Kats answered.

"I don't know!"

"Somewhere on the street!"

"Vain! We're in Vain!"

The others pawed at him. "G! G! You all right, G?" they asked, all thinking they were Kat.

Three Rus attacked. Stenstrom shot and killed one with his pistols while Kat and three others engaged the other two, fighting in a deadly dance, her clothes shredding, her tail erupting from her back. She clubbed one over the head, sending her down as the last stabbed in, looking for a weak spot. The other Kats tried to create Shadow tech, seemed surprised when nothing happened.

Another shot from Stenstrom's NTHs.

The Rus was dead.

Stenstrom cocked his pistols. "Listen, you people, head down the street away from the mountains to the office of Ottoman John and Melazarr of Caroline. It's a couple of miles down the street. They'll help you."

"But why? But why? I want to stay with you, G!" they replied.

"Go! Hurry, don't stop for anything."

The group of Kats turned and bounded out of the tent, some of the robes pursuing them. Stenstrom grabbed Kat by the tail. "Not you! You stay."

The remaining robes saw the destruction in the tent and momentarily forgot their dispute, all of them coming for Stenstrom and Kat.

"Out the back, quickly!"

Stenstrom TKing and Kat running on all fours, they tore out the back of the tent. They quickly saw a small, bent person huffing and puffing up the hill at slow speed to safety.

"Is that Sil?" Kat asked.

"Don't know. He's wearing a yellow robe. Let's get him!"

The man momentarily turned, saw them pursuing, and squashed a capsule to his head. Suddenly, he was running like a professional athlete, all arms and legs, tripling his previous speed. It wasn't enough. Kat was on him, tackling him from behind in a tumble of yellow robes, revealing his pale skinny legs and ill-fitting underwear.

"Ah!" he cried, protecting his face with his hands. He babbled in Vertus.

"Paige du Long's Slate! Now!" Stenstrom roared.

He pleaded with them in Vertus. Kat put her bloody claws to his throat. "Paige du Long's Slate!"

He nodded and pointed at a building a short way up the hill. They dragged him there, entering a multi-leveled building festooned with yellow banners and bright lights. Inside was a group of officious-looking Rus sitting at various terminals, counting money. They all stopped what they were doing as the three entered.

Sil cried out in Vertus as they entered. "Banga! Banga! Banga! ... *Kill Them!*" he added in LC. The surprised Rus stood, drawing weapons.

Stenstrom gunned them down with his NTHs, the Rus falling without resistance. Kat moved a dead body aside and roughly seated Sil at a desk. "I'm guessing you can understand me. You can understand, right?" She shook him. He slavered in fear.

"Now—the Slate. Hurry up!" she roared in an uncharacteristically savage voice, her silver claws gleaming at his throat.

"This ... this is an unprotected terminal," Sil pleaded in LC.

"Do it!" Kat roared.

Shaking, Sil pecked at the keys, moving data around. Outside, the remaining Rus, AlbertCo and Nightrobes arrived. They banged at the door which Stenstrom blocked. He fired his NTHs at the door, the green globes passing through it harmlessly to the outside. He heard the startled cries through the door as the globes did their work. Bullets came whizzing in through the windows in response. Stenstrom returned fire. "Kat, mind the windows!"

Sil pulled a drive open and handed Kat a disk. "Here! Paige du Long of Moane's complete archive. Take it ... you ... bitch ... you ...!"

Kat wasn't convinced. "This is it? You sure?"

"It's there. It's all there! ...*Stupid ... whore ...*"

Kat pulled out the swipe scanner Ottoman John had given them to verify the data. She swiped it across the surface of the disk; a red light came on.

No data.

Kat reacted and partially sawed through Sil's left ear, drawing a huge amount of blood. He screamed.

"You sneaky bastard! Shall I slice off the rest of your ear and keep going till I get to your tongue and then your nuts? The data, now!"

Whimpering, he resumed pecking at the terminal. "All right … I'll get you the data. All right … where's the P-Force? Kill you. I'm … *going to … kill … you!*"

A Nightrobe dramatically came spinning through a window. Stenstrom fired but missed. He leapt around the room with Kat-like agility.

Sil stopped what he was doing and cheered. "Yeah, that's right, he's got a gorilla squash! Now what are you going to do, criminals? You're both going to die! Haha! Banga! Banga!"

As he neared Kat, blades poised to rain down on her, Stenstrom found the range and shot him in the face. He died, crashing through a desk with a dramatic death-flip.

"Whaaaat?" Sil gasped.

Kat pulled on Sil's lacerated ear, drawing a pained whimper. "Last chance! The data, or you're going to be down on the floor next to him."

Sil hyperventilated as he continued with the terminal, mumbling in fear. He clacked on the keys. "All right, where's the P-Force? Where's the P-Force? It's done. It's done! Please … *you stupid … cow!* Here's your data!" The drive opened. A fresh disk gleamed in the drive.

From outside, the wiry amplified voice of Madberrie Saddle came in. "Sil? Sil baby, you keep your robes on. We'll have these criminals taken care of in no time!"

Another voice barged in, this one harder, more authoritative. "Attention, criminals! This is the ECSP! We've got you surrounded! You cannot escape! Come on out, and get strung up like a man!"

"Hurry, Kat!" Stenstrom said.

"*The P-Force!*" Sil cried like a little girl. He trembled with excitement. "Hear that, criminals? That's the P-Force outside! You're dead! Whore! Bitch! Slut! You can't have that disk I just made! It belongs to the Rus … give it to me!"

Kat's tail wrapped around his throat and squeezed.

"Gah!" Sil squeaked.

Kat pulled the disk out. She scanned it.

Green this time.

"G, we've got it!"

Kat pushed Sil to the floor, he gasped for air. Stenstrom took her and fled up the stairs as a hoard of armored green police and various robes smashed through the door and came charging in.

"Aaahhhh, they've cut off my ear! They strangled me and they stole Slate! Get them, you Trades! P-Force, all praise the P-Force! Kill them! Get the data! Get the data! Bring me the woman! I'm going to Squash her into thinking she's a giant vagina!" Sil cried, blood from his ear bubbling through his fingers, the whole lot in torrid pursuit.

Climbing several floors, Stenstrom and Kat reached the roof, the night-time of Vain glittering before them. Holding Kat, Stenstrom TKed into flight, quickly leaving the deadly scene behind. The Street of Knowledge, blinking, lined with lights like a bed of gems, looked rather peaceful from the air.

*   *   *   *   *

Faded into the shadows, flying low to avoid detection, they soon arrived at Ottoman John's office. Melazarr was elated as she greeted them. "You're back! Looks like you two have seen some action."

"We have the data," Stenstrom said.

Melazarr took it. "Let me have a look."

"All three Trades were gunning for us."

"We did that," Ottoman John said, emerging from the back. "We thought you'd have a better chance if all three Trades were looking for you. We call it a 'Robe Wrangle'."

"It worked. Fighting amongst themselves saved us."

Sitting in the rear of the office were the six people Kat had squashed to think they were her. They had been cleaned up and fed, the remnants of their meal sitting on the table in front of them. The nude ones were covered in blankets. They were sitting in a thick cloud of Smoque.

Stenstrom and Kat were elated. "Oh, they made it! We were so worried about them," Kat said.

Ottoman John replied. "They arrived a little while ago, all of them carrying your Slate. We're sorting through the markers whoever Vugged them left behind. Once we know that, we can try to hack-in and get their heads back."

"They were being subjected to torture up the street."

Melazarr nodded. "Verti-Hovi parks are popular up in Pentagulle."

Ottoman approached and placed a shiny disk on both Stenstrom's and Kat's foreheads. Data uploaded into their brains, filling in the events of the day that they had lost since getting Vugged.

"We kept track of your movements. Those Radar Disks should fill in the blanks of what you lost—it's part of your Premium Package."

Stenstrom remembered the missing parts of the day. He was concerned.

"I saw a mother and her children get Vugged this afternoon," Stenstrom said. "I tried to help them, but they vanished. I hope they can be found and given their souls back."

Ottoman John smiled. "A woman and her children? Three children, perhaps?"

"Yes."

Ottoman pressed a few keys at his terminal. "These?"

A woman in a broad-brimmed hat and her three children emerged from the back office. Stenstrom was elated. "You've found them! Ma'am, I was so concerned for your welfare today!"

The woman said nothing.

"They're not real, Lord Belmont," Ottoman John said. "They're BUDs, or 'Blow-Up Dolls' as we call them. They are holograms; Fintrons, actually. I create several dozen of them every day and set them loose in Pentagulle, altering their appearance a little each time. I try to make them as innocent-looking and bewildered as possible so the Vuggers will go for them as an easy mark and maybe leave a few real visitors alone."

Stenstrom reached out and touched the lady's face. As he did so, she disappeared, leaving only her hat lying on the floor. He smiled. "Had me fooled." He pulled his moneybag out and left it on the table. "Here, for your trouble and kind assistance with these poor souls."

Melazarr checked the disk. "Data's good. It's Paige du Long of Moane's Slate all right, nice as you please. Let me get this squashed for you." She went into the back.

"I was hoping we could keep the disk. Might help us further our knowledge," Ottoman John said.

"Keep it. How long do you think it will be before you can restore these people?"

"A couple of days. Don't you worry, we'll have them all up nice and bright."

Soon, Melazarr returned with a bag full of red capsules. "Here you go, brand-spanking new Paige du Long of Moane squash. It's on a timer, about three or four hours a squash. If you need longer, it's going to take us a while to get it ripped."

Stenstrom took the bag. "It's fine as is. Thank you. I can't tell you how much your services have helped us, and for other souls too who otherwise would find no mercy or help out there. I hope our presence hasn't endangered you at all. They called the ECSP on us."

"Nah. The robes and the P-Force aren't as bright as they think," Melazarr said. "We're fine."

"You're certain?"

"100% max."

They said their goodbyes and went outside. They hadn't gone far when, down the street, a contingent of yellow and red robes flanked by green ECSP soldiers stopped and pointed at them. "There they are! Get them!"

"Halt, criminals!"

Stenstrom drew his NTHs and Kat her claws.

A moment later they were standing back in the Hall of Mirrors.

6—The Desolation of Xandarr

"You got it!" Atha said, standing there in her black costume. "Great work. You two make an awesome team." Kat's sooty gray dress was gone, she was back in her jumpsuit again.

Stenstrom was in a panic. "We couldn't have been successful without the help of Ottoman John and Melazarr. We need to get back there, they're about to be attacked for helping us."

"They can handle themselves."

"Melazarr is a *Merten*. And ... *Mertens* die. They always die—I don't know how I know that, but I do. I don't want her to die!"

"Well, you're right about that, *Mertens* do tend to die, and Melazarr of Caroline has died many times across the universes, often in your arms. I think this one's going to be fine. It's her proximity to you that gets her killed; once she's delivered the universe's message, that's it. But in this case I think she's all right. As a *Merten*, she's drawn to you, that's how your status as a *Kaidar Gemain* affects her, but she's far off in Vain with another man. That distance will protect her—just don't go back there anytime soon. I'll even check up on them if it'll make you feel better."

"You're certain they will be safe?"

"I'm pretty sure this isn't the first time they've come to grips with the Trades and the city police. They're good, I promise."

Atha shuffled them down the corridor. "Now then, it's time for our next challenge. If all goes well, we will know exactly where to attack the demon. Our journey is nearly at an end."

A node lit up in healthy, vivid green.

"Where are we going now?" Kat asked.

Atha climbed into the node. "Come on, I'll show you."

They followed Atha into the node. They seemed to be in a dense forest, surrounded by thick trees, the air full of the loamy smell of growing things. They were standing on a level cobbled path that carved a passage through the trees. Over their heads was a hanging canopy of green. Through the breaks in the branches, they could see a dark sky filled with twinkling stars. Despite the greenery, the air was cold, almost uncomfortably so.

"Any idea where we are?" Atha asked, leading them down the path.

"None."

They emerged from the trees. Before them was a clearing of trim, well-tended grass. Many paths, all paved with tight-fitting stones, went off in various directions. The air was crisp and clear, free from turbulence and humidity, allowing seldom-seen stars to sparkle bright. To the east they saw a massive range of snow-covered mountains that, for a moment, reminded Stenstrom of Clovis. To the west, rising above the treetops were many towers and castle spires, softly backlit and capped with slowly blinking red lights.

"Now I know where we are!" Stenstrom cried. "That is Castle Blanchefort to the west, and so we must be in the Telmus Grove."

"Correct!" Atha cheered.

"This is where Countess Sygillis lives?" Kat asked with interest.

"It is. There's a statue of her around here somewhere," he said.

Atha pointed to the south, in the direction of a looming hill topped with a jumble of craggy tombs and vaults. "It's over in that direction, but that's not where we're headed." They reached a crossroads where several paths came together. Atha turned to the north. The path they took soon plunged into a dark line of reaching beech trees.

"Neither one of you has asked me why or how I got involved with this quest. Why would a goddess involve herself in something like this, that's not something goddesses normally do, right? My sisters have never bothered much with the doings of the Younger Folk. Well, you're about to find out why."

They made their way through the beech trees, moving past the knobby, haunting limbs.

Dim light up ahead.

They entered a circular courtyard lined with a small wall tall enough for sitting. Jutting into the trees to the west was a large statue on a pedestal. It was lit from below on all sides by dim lights built into the ground, shining upwards. The statue was carved into the smooth likeness of a great animal of some kind. Kat was puzzled by the statue.

"What sort of creature is this?"

"It's a seal, an aquatic mammal common here in the north of Kana."

There was a large inscription carved into the pedestal. Kat came up to read it, placing her fingers on the carved letters.

"It says: cuh, cuh, cuh, ar, ar, ah, ah, ah, hil. Carahil. Who's Carahil?"

Stenstrom looked up at the statue. "Carahil is a mythical scion of the House of Blanchefort. He's their protector and guardian spirit."

"There's nothing mythical about him," Atha said. "Carahil was created in Silver tech by Lady Poe of Blanchefort in a fountain just over there in the trees. This is the place of his birth. She made him so well, in fact, he became a god and took his place in the Celestial Arborium. He is very kind and loving, full of life and good cheer. His statue is often said to move, to change positions, to vanish from its pedestal and hide in the trees. Carahil has a love of pranks. Children often come and leave little notes here, sharing

their hearts with him. He is hailed as a god and patron spirit of the Planet Xandarr, where there are many parks and temples dedicated in his honor."

"Xandarr?" Stenstrom asked, raising an eyebrow. He looked at the base of the statue. He saw no notes. There was no feeling of joy or wonder, no feeling of magic and innocent pranks—it seemed like nothing more than a statue of a seal fashioned from cold stone. "There are no temples or parks on Xandarr; the Black Hats destroyed it."

Atha snapped her fingers. "Ah, so that's it, isn't it? Where's the magic? Where's the wonder? Why does this particular statue of Carahil not move? Here, Xandarr is destroyed and cursed with Shadow tech, but in many other universes, Xandarr thrives as a place of commerce and tourism. It's even part of the League, having quit the Xaphans. Whereas here, Xandarr is dead, elsewhere, Xandarr is very much alive and it was Carahil who saved it. The gods are privy to the tide of coming events, and Carahil foresaw the destruction of Xandarr by the Black Hats. His heart is pure, he couldn't allow all that misery and death, so he took steps to save it, to enlist the aid of heroes like the Blancheforts, to save it for him, and it was done. The King of Xandarr was reborn as a good man, all thanks to the kind spirit Carahil, the god who cared.

"But in this universe, Carahil took no such action. Here, he did not save Xandarr. He saw what was going to happen, he listened to the gods and took their advice, and he did nothing. The Black Hats attacked. Xandarr died. After it was all over, he went to Xandarr and saw first-hand the destruction, the toppled stone, the wandering souls, the terrified screams locked into the ages forever. He realized that by doing nothing, all the death and destruction that had happened on Xandarr was his fault, and his alone.

"And he lost his soul. In his grief and guilt, Carahil went mad on Xandarr and became a demon, inhabiting the old Gods Temple by the river in the Valley of the Moons, turning it into the cursed Cathedral of Bone and Wire, lost in an eternal fog. He's been there ever since, a hideous vision of angry claws, often summoned by those who would turn his madness to their own ends—the Punts we saw earlier in the Hall of Mundane, they love using him as a tool and pet slave. His claws have destroyed and killed many, but always he has a claw around his own throat to remind him of his curse."

"What does this have to do with you, Lady Atha?" Stenstrom asked.

She stood there a moment, the purple light from her visor flickering. "I am Atha of the Quest. I am the youngest daughter of the nargal spirit Carahil and the windwalker Mabsornath, my mother. I was raised with my brothers and sisters atop the universe's Great Tree. I suppose my childhood was near perfect, I had my mother and father and my brothers and sisters, and we had the whole universe to play in. I often drew my parents' ire for being a bit of a hellion. My brothers and sisters were so good and compliant, they often lectured me on how I should be a more humble goddess and not trouble my parents so. True, I am a wanderer and I follow my wild heart, but, at the end of the day, I love my parents, and I was loved in return.

"In my wanderings, I and my brother Lannis, encountered the demon version of our father long ago in the Cathedral of Bone and Wire. We were just children. We pierced the fog and saw what lurked within. There he was, barely recognizable, but it was he, our father in a demented form. We fled in terror. Lannis wanted nothing further to do with him. 'Leave him,' he said. But I couldn't forget what I saw—the torment, the misery. This pitiful version of Carahil is not my father, is not he who raised and loved me, who taught me right from wrong, but he is still Carahil and I would not see any version of him consigned to such a fate. Alone of all my brothers and sisters, I determined to save him, to see him made right. Me, Atha the unruly, Atha the wild and untamable … Atha, she who is devoted to her father no matter what guise he might take; even the demon in the Cathedral of Bone and Wire. That's when I learned just how powerless the gods are, to act, to make change. We can do all these amazing things, we can see so much and go where we wish to go, yet we cannot directly alter fate. That is the purview of man, not the gods. Thus, my payment for sponsoring this quest is the saving of my father, undertaken of free will by a man and a woman, and it is time to do just that."

"You wish us to go to Xandarr and encounter this demon?" Stenstrom asked.

"Yes. Pierce the fog, make him remember who he is and where he comes from. Ease his tortured soul." Atha held out her hands. In one hand was a small clay pot, in the other, a tiny trowel and a clear glass jar.

"Take these. Use them on Xandarr. You will understand. Make my father remember that life is strong. Make him see that life endures."

Kat took the pot, the trowel and the jar. "I've never had a father. Sitting at the restaurant with A-Ram was the closest thing to a father I've ever had. But it felt good. It felt good, and I understand." She stood there holding the items. "Come on, G. Let's go."

The statue of Carahil took on a dark hue, radiating magic. "Touch his statue and you will be there," Atha said. "Once there, I'll do what I can to assist you, but I cannot go myself. Locate the River Torr and follow it west into the mountains 'til you come to the Valley of the Moons—it's a place where all seven Xandarrian moons can be seen at once. The cathedral is not far from there. Once you have saved my father, walk the Destroyers' Road—he will know the way—and you will be returned to me."

"We understand," Stenstrom said.

They stood a moment. Atha held out her arms. "You two could give me a hug or something. I'm a goddess, not a cactus."

They both embraced Atha. She hugged them back, her body slender and warm. "Remember, Bellathauser has probably been watching, and she'll be aware of the hole we're burrowing into her pocket dimension. I think she'll be waiting for you on Xandarr. Use the knowledge of Paige du Long of Moane and save my father and walk the Destroyers' Road. Then we will have calculated exactly where to pierce Bellathauser's realm. I know you can do it."

Taking a last look at Atha, they both touched the statue on the nose and were gone.

＊　＊　＊　＊　＊

Smothering black. The healthy, living space of the Telmus Grove was gone. Darkness prevailed. Stenstrom reached out, feeling Kat's mass standing next to him, though he couldn't see her. She cried out, the sound of her voice swallowed by the darkness.

It was Shadow tech, all around them in a dense, water-like cloud. Stenstrom could smell it, could taste it on his tongue, feel it entering his lungs. Shadow tech was deadly toxic, such amounts should be instantly fatal. He had the Sisters' power, he was immune to the toxic effects of Shadow tech, and Kat, as a Shadow tech female, was also immune. The overwhelming quantity of it was drinking up any available light and swallowing any sounds. It was even draining the warmth from their bodies. It was like standing at the bottom of the sea with a vault of black, crushing water all around them, only it wasn't water; it was dense, smoky Shadow tech.

He felt Kat's arms come around him. She screamed "G!" into his ear, though he barely heard her.

They could not survive this for long, they would be eaten up by the sheer volume of Shadow tech. With the Sisters' power, he could cast Shadow tech aside, render it inert, but there was far too much for him to deal with. He had to try, otherwise this was the end. Straining, he combated the waves of Shadow tech, pushing it away from them in a small, confined sphere. That was all he could manage.

Kat was there with him, barely seen. "Holy crap, G! What are we going to do? I never thought it possible so much Shadow tech could exist."

Stenstrom gritted his teeth, deep in concentration, keeping the Shadow tech back. "The ... squash, Kat. Use it. We need to ... get away from ... here."

"But what good will that do?"

"Hurry!"

Kat pulled out the bag of squashdat Melazarr of Caroline had given them, full of deep red capsules. She took one, staring at it in her palm in the dim light.

"I love you, G," she said as she smashed the capsule against her forehead. She stood there a moment, absently wiping the fluid from her head.

"Kat, anything?" he asked, feeling his control of the Shadow tech around them slipping. He fell to his knees, the effort too much.

Kat looked around. For a moment, her expression was alien, foreign, that of a different person Stenstrom had never seen before, but after a few moments the expression faded, and Kat was back. She knelt down and put her arms around him.

"I'm all right, G. I'm fine. I think we need to get above this Shadow tech."

"I can't hold it back much longer," he said.

"One sec."

Kat pulled a felt bag from her jumpsuit. She emptied three shiny silver pieces onto her palm.

Sentrils, given to her by A-Ram and Alesta.

"These nullify Shadow tech. Let me get them placed." She set the *Sen-*

trils on the ground in a triangular pattern around them. So tiny, how could these *Sentrils* hold back so much Shadow tech, he wondered? They couldn't possibly work. But to his shock, the *Sentrils* immediately created an impenetrable wall around them, creating a straight triangular column cutting upwards through the turbid layers of Shadow tech in a laser-straight line. Stenstrom thankfully ceased his concentrations and rested a moment, his head pounding from the effort.

"Great job, G, great job. I love you for how hard you worked. The *Sentrils* were gifts from the gods, they've never failed so far. Sorry I didn't think of using them sooner," Kat said. Stenstrom recovered his wits and assessed their situation. They were standing on a patch of barren, hard-packed earth. Beyond the barrier created by the *Sentrils*, dense folds of Shadow tech swirled in oily black-on-black patterns. From where the *Sentrils* had been placed, they had just enough room to stand side by side. Looking up, they saw a dim dot of light high above.

"Up there," she pointed. "That's where we need to go."

"This cloud of Shadow tech has to be thousands of feet high. I can TK us up there."

"But then we'll lose the *Sentrils*. We might need them again. I think I can whip up a Shadow tech craft to get us up there."

"You can do that?"

"Yeah, easy, I think. That Paige du Long lady had all sorts of things rolling around in her head. It's pretty cool actually, I never knew you could do so much with Shadow tech. So, here's what we'll do. I'm going to step out of the triangle and get it set up. When I'm ready, I'll step back in, we'll collect the *Sentrils,* and I'll lead you to it. Sound good?"

"You're certain you can manage being out there unprotected?"

"I should be fine for a short period of time."

He embraced her. "All right. Don't be a hero. Come back in for rest if you need it." He shook his hands, producing a small roll of twine. "Take this, and don't let go of it. It's pitch dark out there."

Kat giggled. "Why do you have a roll of string in your coat?"

"Comes in handy sometimes. Go on, take it."

She kissed him on the cheek and tied the string around her wrist. "Ok. Here I go."

Kat stepped out into the black torrent and vanished, the string paying out several feet before stopping. It bobbed a bit as she moved about in the dark. It seemed like she was out there for a long time. Stenstrom paced back and forth within the triangle, holding onto the string, worried for her. He called her name several times, but she didn't answer. Finally, the string slackened and she stepped back into the safe area.

"I needed the string, I would have gotten lost without it," she said. "I'm almost done. Can I have four of your yellow Holystones, G? Those are the ones that make light, right?"

"They are." He waved his hands and produced four yellow Holystones, giving them to her. Kat shook them up, creating four star-like balls of yellow light in her hand. She marched back out into the black, the string going taut. She returned several minutes later.

"Ok, it's ready. I've got the string tied to it. Let's pick up the *Sentrils* and I'll lead you to it."

"What sort of craft did you construct?"

"It's neat. You'll see."

Stenstrom scooped the *Sentrils* off the ground. Instantly, the wall of Shadow tech fell in upon them, immersing them in total darkness. Following the string, they wandered out several paces to some sort of vessel sitting on the ground. He couldn't see it, but he felt it, a smooth wall-like structure with a flat railing about three feet high. He climbed over the railing and came aboard. Kat gently placed a breathing mask over his face. Clean, cool air filtered into his mouth and nose.

"Ready, G?" came Kat's voice through the mask. Lights came on around them, four dim glows obscured by Shadow tech, but just bright enough to cut through the murk. He felt the craft around him shudder and move, pitching up, picking up speed. Holding on, he saw the yellow lights of his Holystones cutting through the haze, getting brighter and brighter. He saw moments of sunlight from above.

They broke the surface, suddenly engulfed by blinding, unobstructed daylight. They were floating atop a great black cloud of ground-hugging Shadow tech. The sky above was a thin purple color—he recalled Xandarr was once famous for such a sky—dappled with several silvery moons and a great curling haze that seemed to be more Shadow tech far away at a great altitude. Looking around, he saw what Kat had created: it was a canoe-like boat about twenty feet long, silver, constructed in an etched, alien style that must have come from Paige du Long's influence. It was flat-bottomed with a broad central area giving them plenty of room to walk around. The bow and stern of the boat were identical in appearance. In the center were four long oars that tapped at the Shadow tech surface, moving in unison, righting the boat. Mounted on poles were four lanterns bright with yellow light, his Holystones, glowing within. The boat floated easily atop the churning Shadow tech cloud as if it were water. The boat was level with several wispy banks of clouds, indicating they were quite high above the ground.

Kat beamed. "What do you think, G?"

"Very smart work, Kat. Very impressive."

"I just dreamed it up and out it came. It wasn't hard."

Under Kat's command, the oars moved on their own, dipping into the

Shadow tech, gently churning the boat forward. Stenstrom produced his Megaeye spyglass from his coat and had a good look around.

What he saw didn't look promising.

"It's like an ocean of Shadow tech. We are thousands of feet in the air, and it goes on for as far as I can see in all directions. I can find no hint of life. No birds, no insects, nothing. The Black Hats truly did obliterate this place."

"Well, Atha says her father's here somewhere, we just need to locate him. We're looking for a river, right?"

"The Torr. It's the largest river on Xandarr. Who knows if it's buried under all this Shadow tech?"

"Dunno."

"We need to send out scouts to give us information."

"Ok, cool," Kat said with excitement. "What sort of scouts should I send out?"

Stenstrom thought a moment. "Well, I know Countess Sygillis favors using StTs. They're small and versatile, and can be programmed by you to perform any number of tasks."

"Oh, yeah, yeah! Paige du Long of Moane loved StTs, she killed a lot of people with them. One sec ..."

Kat held out her hands, and droplets of Silver tech formed. The droplets changed shape into tiny, insect-like creatures crawling about on her hands like a swarm of silver ladybugs.

"Yeah, these are cool," Kat said. "These will be our eyes and ears—I can see and hear what they see and hear. Let's call them our 'Belmont Buzzers.' I'll send them out in all directions. Maybe we'll get lucky and find that river."

The StTs, like tiny silver beetles, opened their wings, taking flight, skittering away in all directions, Kat watching them go like a mother seeing her children off. "This is so cool! Now we just have to wait."

Hours passed. Kat's boat moved in a general northwestern direction, sculling through the Shadow tech smoothly, Stenstrom estimating they were moving about four knots. Moving, although aimlessly, was far better than just sitting. To the south was a storm Stenstrom observed through his Megaeye, the Shadow tech choppy and whipped into an amber frenzy. They avoided the storm and continued north.

"You seeing anything?" Kat asked.

"Nothing. I see the storm to the south, but not much else. What about your StTs? What are they finding?"

"Not StTs, they're Belmont Buzzers! Nothing so far. They are far away now. Just a lot of Shadow tech. Here, let me rig something up so you can see too." Revising her Silver tech, Kat created a bank of terminals slung under the bow railing, each displaying what the StTs were seeing. She also created a comfortable couch in the center of the boat for them to sit. Stenstrom glanced at the terminals. All the same. Nothing but Shadow tech. They seated themselves on the couch, lazing about, watching the monitors, waiting for something to appear.

One of the StTs had wandered into the storm they were avoiding. They saw the terminal following its progress go dark with Shadow tech haze. It shook with turbulence. Stenstrom stared at the monitor. "Kat, do you see something moving in the storm?"

Kat looked at the terminal. "I see a lot of scary stuff. That storm is one place we don't want to be."

Stenstrom pointed at the monitor. "Look there. I saw something huge moving about, something that blots out the screen."

"Another ship, maybe?"

"No, it was dark and fluid. It was Shadow tech, just colossally enormous, and much denser than the cloud."

Kat looked off to the south in the general direction of the storm, now too far away to be visible. "Whatever. Don't want any part of it regardless."

More time passed. More Shadow tech. More cutting through the surface like a dart. "Get some sleep, G," Kat said. "I'll keep a lookout. Not much to see so far." She fussed with his hair. "We'll find that river later. Love you."

"Love you too, sweetheart." He sat back and stared at the empty purple sky, feeling tired, allowing the first pleasant brushes of sweet sleep to pass over him.

He looked deep into the sky.

"Wait!" he said, standing up. "I thought I saw a glint of light high above. Just there!" He pulled his Megaeye and looked skyward. "I saw something for a brief moment, like a passing vessel. I don't see it now though."

"What do you think it was?" Kat asked.

"I don't know."

Kat pointed ahead past the prow. "G!"

Ahead, a shining point of light came down and hovered over the surface of the Shadow tech for a moment. Stenstrom focused in with his Megaeye. "I see it. It's metal, approximately the size of a small man. It seems to have some sort of fluid movement—it's rolling about in midair. I can't tell exactly what it is."

Without warning, the metal object shot toward their boat, moving at high speed just above the Shadow tech. Stenstrom drew his NTHs. "Halt and identify yourself!" he shouted, garnering no response from the object.

As it approached, he fired two shots, both globes hitting it square. The object immediately went out of control and careened into the Shadow tech, bouncing several times before abruptly disappearing.

Kat stared over the railing at the wake in the Shadow tech created by the object's passing. "What in the name of hell was that?"

"It looked like a metal construct, but I couldn't see it clearly."

Breaking the surface of the Shadow tech cloud, three angled objects appeared, two to the boat's starboard side, one to the port, each protruding like a shark's fin. They kept pace with the boat, maintaining a twenty-yard distance, slicing through the Shadow tech with ease. The objects seemed to be constructed of blue metal, ridged and perforated with white and red lights. Stenstrom locked in with the Megaeye.

"Creation, Kat! Those objects are metal arms sticking out of the Shadow tech. I can clearly see a clawed hand, a wrist and forearm, an elbow, bent, and a triceps. All of them are the right arm. Kat—it's Bellathauser!"

The three arms sticking out of the Shadow tech attacked in unison, one from the left, two from the right, moving in fast. They rose up out of the Shadow tech, revealing half a metal torso and a leg. Weapon ports opened on all three of them. "G! Get down!" Kat cried.

They both hit the deck as several shots of deadly fire peppered the boat, the sturdy Silver tech railing protecting them. Stenstrom cocked his NTHs, rose up, and returned fire.

Both misses.

THUNK!   THUNK! THUNK! The demons' metal hands latched on, pulling themselves over the side, revealing themselves clearly for the first time. They were robotic constructs built in human female form—head, neck, torso, arm, leg—but only the right half; the left half was missing, split right down the middle. The constructs were leering, with lamp-like glowing eyes, chainmail hair, and studded with pits, blades and claws, designed to snare and inflict pain. Small video monitors were built in unison down the length of the constructs' arm and leg. A horrid grinning face hovered in the monitors, showing her teeth.

The constructs locked in on Kat. "WHHENDILNIGHT!" they roared with half their mouths. Panels opened. Saws and whirling blades came out and spun up. Kat responded. Blobs of Silver tech formed on her hands while her tail came up like a great lariat and hammered two of them. One engaged Stenstrom. He fired his NTH's.

PFT! PFT!

Two shots hit the construct in the chest. Lights flickered and went out. The construct, no longer moving, no longer functioning, wobbled. He pushed it over the side into the Shadow tech, where it abruptly sank into the blackness.

He turned to assist Kat.

She had finished one of the constructs attacking her, cleaving it to pieces with a Silver tech axe, the blade buried in its head. The other spun about near the stern, covered with Kat's StTs, their tiny forms crawling all over its metal surface like an army of invading ants attacking a giant, armored crab, locating the weak spots, getting inside its metal armor. The robotic form thrashed about. It screamed, StTs bursting out of its mouth. The monitors running down its arm exploded. Stenstrom took aim to finish it off.

"Wait, G!" Kat yelled. "Just wait. Watch!"

The metal construct fell to the floor of the boat where it shuddered. After a moment, it stood up straight, its saws and blades folding up and returning to their ports. Stenstrom leveled his pistols, ready to fire.

"I got it. Look at that, G, I got it! The Belmont Buzzers strike again!"

The construct stood silent, its destroyed monitors smoking a bit. "Take a seat," Kat commanded, and the Bellathauser robot obeyed, seating itself on the couch, leaning over.

"Sit up straight," Kat said. The construct complied.

Kat was ecstatic. "Whamo! How about that, G? I infested it with Buzzers and took it over cold. This baby is working for us now."

Stenstrom cautiously approached the robot. It was hideous, constructed of cruel linkages, barbs, razors and other atrocities. The monitors lining its arms were dead, its lights flickered, its half-constructed metal face impassive.

"Atha warned us Bellathauser might be here waiting for us. Seems to be confirmed. How long will you have control over this construct?" he asked.

"For the duration, G! I figure we can use her as a body guard or something. She's armed to the freakin' teeth. I think we should call her 'Paige', for Paige du Long."

"Fine by me."

Stenstrom dumped the inert metal carcass of the first robot over the side, while Kat created a fresh swarm of StTs which crawled about the rails and flew in unison with the boat like a squadron of fighter craft. "These Buzzers are awesome! I love 'em! I can't wait until I can create these babies on my own and not depend on somebody else to do it for me. If we get attacked again, our Belmont Buzzers and Paige will take them right out."

They sailed through the evening and into the night, the two of them looking up at the inviting collage of stars. Paige went to the stern of the boat and stood quietly, lights blinking, metal hair blowing in the slight breeze. Kat found that the squashdat knowledge only lasted a few hours; as Paige du Long of Moane dropped out of her head, she gawked at the things she had created, having no idea how she had done it. The oars stopped responding, the lanterns flickered, the boat even threatened to sink. Ominously, the monitors adorning Paige's arm and leg began coming back to life, indicating Kat's control over her was waning. Kat took another capsule and soon the boat was cutting through the Shadow tech at full speed.

"Paige, head up top-side and orbit around. Let us know if you see anything," Kat said. Tiny rockets built into her metal body lit and Paige snaked into the air leaving a smoky trail, going so high she was soon just a blinking light high above trailing a thin line of smoke.

Seeing no further sign of Bellathauser, they sat back, enjoying the peaceful starry sky filled with unfamiliar moons and twinkling lights along with Paige's blinking form far above. Stenstrom pulled a small timepiece from his HRN and set it to alarm several hours ahead so Kat could refresh her squash; they didn't want to let the robot fall out of her control. They eventually allowed themselves to sleep, Kat curled up into Stenstrom's side, confident in the StTs milling about on the rails and poles and flying nearby to alert and protect them.

Morning came, the alarm went off. Kat squashed up another capsule. They estimated, given the rate they were going through the squash, they had three days' worth in the bag. Seeing the red squash reminded them of Ottoman John and Melazarr—they truly hoped they were all right. They also reminded them of cherries.

Kat chopped her teeth. "Really getting hungry, G."

"Me, too. I could do with a good Belmont breakfast. With any luck, we'll be done with this soon. Where's Paige?"

"Up there. Want me to bring her down?"

"No, she's fine where she is." Stenstrom rubbed his tired eyes and checked the row of monitors Kat had slung under the bow.

At the back end of the boat, Stenstrom noticed something that hadn't been there previously. "Kat, your basket's here."

Kat's wicker basket sat innocently near the stern of the boat. "Oh!" Kat cried. "Just like in the old days. Did my angels visit us during the night?"

"More like Atha did it, I would say."

They opened the basket; it was full of steaming hot breakfast items in ceramic jars: eggs, sausage, heaping crispy bacon, sliced oranges, toast with various jellies, a decanter of red wine and a large vessel full of coffee. A note sat innocently to the side. Stenstrom read it:

I thought you guys would be hungry. It's the least I can do.
--Atha

They tucked in, savoring the food, sharing several platefuls each. As they ate, they watched the monitors from Kat's now far-flung StTs.

Shadow tech.

Shadow tech everywhere, just like yesterday.

"Look there!" Kat cried, her mouth full of toast. "That's different. I see land. One of our Belmont Buzzers has come across land!"

In one of the monitors, they saw a coastline, a thin fingernail of dry land, arid and sandy, stretching off to the horizon.

"I see it too. Where is that one?"

"To the south, about three hundred, fifty leagues. See—I was paying attention during your geography sessions. Let's get there!"

Kat turned the boat, the oars biting deep into the Shadow tech. The prow rose as the boat dramatically picked up speed, leaving a wake to mark their passing. Paige came down, took hold of the stern and fired her rockets in a smoky fuss, propelling the boat ever faster.

"How fast do you think we're going?" Kat asked.

Stenstrom looked over the railing. "About twenty knots I'd say, give or take." Stenstrom cleaned up, placing everything yet to be eaten back in the basket. He took up watch on the prow, scanning the horizon.

* * * * *

Hours of hard rowing and rocketry later, they spotted the yellowy signs of land in the distance. It was a welcome sight. The Shadow tech sea was abating, giving way to dry land. It was lying over the ground like a vast oily gel. It had a definite boundary, like a steep black canyon that dropped off abruptly to the ground far below. The boat reached the edge and began traversing the steep sides, surfing and tacking one way then the next until they reached the ground.

Stenstrom hopped out, savoring the dust on his boots. "I suppose we're TKing from here." He raised his Megaeye. "I see a body of water to the south. It could be the remnants of the River Torr at last. Let's go."

Kat put her hands on the boat's rail. "Get back in, G! Let me show you something." Stenstrom got back into the boat. The oars powering the boat shipped themselves, the paddles pointing upwards. With a great cracking, they changed shape, bending at the center into long, knobby-jointed legs that came down and dug into the ground. The boat rose up about ten feet and was soon 'walking' in a spidery manner across the dry landscape, making fairly impressive time, Kat proud of her ingenuity. Paige got into the boat and stood silently at the prow. Looking back, the diminishing Shadow tech cloud was like a great black plateau slowly falling into the distance. They soon arrived at a shallow body of slow-moving water not more than a few inches deep, lazily winding its way westward in a mirror-like sheen. The boat stepped in, the paddles splashing and thunking against rocks nestled in the bed, hardly getting wet, following the water west. Stenstrom hopped out, the water barely coming up to his ankles.

"What are you doing, G?" Kat called down.

"Checking the water." He knelt down, scooping up a few handfuls, smelling it, tasting it. He puzzled for a moment, then TKed into the air, catching up to the boat and stepping aboard.

"Whatcha' find?" she asked.

"It's fresh water. Very hard, probably come up from an underground spring. It's clear, not stagnant at all. I'm pretty sure this is the Torr, Xandarr's great river that used to span nearly around the entire planet."

Kat gazed down, noting the feeble layer of water. "Doesn't look like a great river to me."

"I don't know. Maybe it's been eradicated to nothing like everything else here. I'm certain this is the Torr. Let's follow it."

Kat's boat walked on, Stenstrom and Kat seated on the couch like a pair of tourists riding a silver elephant while Paige stood forward like a masthead. After several miles, the water increased in depth in a slow but steady manner until the boat, with its shallow draft, could float; the oars straightening out and resuming their work.

Kat watched the arid landscape pass. "I love cruising on rivers. Remember when you took me on that cruise of the River Seven? So romantic. You know … I sorta feel like having sex, with Paige watching and everything."

But Stenstrom was troubled as he looked about. "I'm sorry, darling. I'm amazed that we're not seeing *any* signs that this was once a fully habited planet. The Black Hats laid waste to this place, so I would expect to see bodies lying about, floating in the water, skeletons perhaps, and what of ruins, wreckage, abandoned vehicles, twisted metal? If this body of water is in fact what remains of the Torr, then there should be all sorts of indications of the civilization that once flourished along its banks. This river, an oasis in an otherwise arid climate, would have been the life-blood of the planet. But there's nothing. Everything that was once here has simply gone."

Kat's enthusiasm to have sex faded. They looked about at the passing landscape: no sounds other than the wind and the occasional coin-like clinking of Paige's chainmail hair. No fish, no birds, no obvious sign of life. Stenstrom felt very isolated, rather like how he felt in Clovis. But whereas

Clovis was merely an uninhabited area rife with ruins in an otherwise thriving world, there was simply nothing here. He and Kat were all alone in this dead place. They clasped hands, drawing comfort from each other's touch.

7—Valley of the Moons

They followed the stream for a long time, watching it grow steadily larger and deeper as it flowed west.

Kat squashed up and sent out another swarm of StTs ahead of the boat to see what awaited them downstream. They got the basket out and dined on the leftovers. As they ate, they managed to stave off some of the eerie disquiet they felt, reveling in their mutual company.

"Hope this is our last meal on Xandarr," Kat said. "I'll be glad to go home."

"We can only hope."

Kat took another bite of bacon. "I think that we …" Her eyes grew wide. "G! The Buzzers down river, they're seeing something."

"What is it?"

She pondered for a moment, dumbstruck. "I have no idea. There's something! Whatever it is, it's huge!"

They put the basket away and scanned the horizon, waiting with dread for what was to come. Soon, they saw it, well off in the distance, great patch of black. At first they thought it a looming storm, but as they neared it revealed itself to be a hulking black shape that broke the clouds, at least several miles in height.

It was some sort of Shadow tech beast, colossal beyond imagination, swaying in the distance like a great mountain. It was composed of a black sphere that served as a rudimentary head, perched atop a waving mass of innumerable black tentacles. It seemed to have lighter colored areas on the sphere that served as eyes. As the boat approached, the beast seemed to get larger and larger until it was a dizzyingly tall, terrifyingly engulfing mass. It seemed to be scraping at the ground, stirring up a cloud of dust. Stenstrom went to the prow and trained his Megaeye at the thing.

"Could the Black Hats really have created such things?" Kat asked.

"Apparently so. Kat, I'm seeing the beast scooping up things from the ground and lifting them high into the air. I see a great mouth opening, a jagged maw taking up most of the available space on its head. I see it dropping bits of stone and other assorted items into its mouth." He lowered his Megaeye. "Creation, Kat—that's why there is nothing left on the surface—this creature has eaten it: everything, the people, the metal, the stonework, the animals and all."

A second beast came into view; this one crouching on the ground, its gigantic maw open, sucking in river water in titanic quantities, quite literally drinking the Torr out of existence.

"Kat, get us off the water! Now!"

Forming the oars back into legs, Kat had the boat exit the northern bank, walking inland at a fast, stilty pace.

"You think they spotted us, G?" she asked, staring at the two impossible creatures.

"We'll find out soon enough."

"Where should we go?"

"Let's track north, giving us plenty of space between us and them, and then push westward, parallel to the river."

Kat turned to the robot. "Paige, watch our backs." Paige blasted into the air, trailing a thin line of smoke from her rockets as she climbed skyward.

The landscape was a bleak and arid bowl surrounded on two sides by a dusty range of mountains. Behind them, as they trekked inland, they could hear the enormous beasts tearing up the ground and sucking down water. They couldn't be gone from them fast enough. The far away mountains to the west sported a dry reddish hue. Overhead, seven moons populated the sky, Paige connecting them with a line of smoke.

"Kat, look! Seven moons! I think this is the Valley of the Moons Atha mentioned. Carahil can't be far!"

"Maybe those things out there ate him, if he's here."

As the boat trekked westward and the mountains approached, the orange hard-pan rock and sand changed in color to a dark, flat green. Paige came down from high above. She pointed toward the mountains to the west. Stenstrom climbed the prow, his Megaeye to his face, looking ahead.

"Avast! Kat, I saw the hint of a spire through the peaks yonder just now. I think we're almost there to Gods Temple!"

Before Kat could reply, a terrible ground-shaking roar deafened them both, nearly rattling the boat to pieces.

Something shot down from the sky fast. Stenstrom reached out to protect Kat.

The oars cracked. Paige veered aside as the boat overturned, dumping them to the ground.

* * * * *

Sometime later, Stenstrom opened his eyes. He was lying face down on a bed of something prickly and uncomfortable. He sat up—everything hurt. He wasn't quite sure what had happened. He assumed they had been spotted by one of the Shadow tech beasts, and that it probably reached out from a great distance to swat them like a tiny bug, destroying Kat's boat.

That must have been what had happened. His NTH pistols had the supposed ability to slay anything they shot, no matter how arcane or how huge.

Looking around, his NTHs were gone, though he still had his trusty MARZ-ABLE daggers. He waved up three of them, just to know they were there.

He was in a vast low-hanging mist that filled the entire valley bowl with a clinging layer of white. He was also heavily tangled in some sort of ground-hugging growth hidden in the fog.

Kat! Where was Kat?

He freed himself from the tangle, stood and looked around. All around him was the wreckage of Kat's boat; oars, silver planks and other flotsam strewn about over a fairly wide area, the various bits of the boat peeking through the fog.

Smoke. He dug through the fog and found the smashed half-body of Paige lying on the ground. Lights dead, whatever had attacked had damaged her beyond repair. A little bit of Kat was inside her body turning a horrid demonic construct into a familiar, comforting presence, a friend even. He lamented her passing. He said goodbye to her and walked away.

A patch of blonde hair wallowing in the mist some distance away caught his attention.

"Kat!" He ran toward her, his shirt and pants tearing on prickly ground cover. As usual, his HRN coat withstood the thorns without damage.

To his relief, there was Kat, all crumpled up on the ground. He skittered to her side. She was alive, but quite stuck in thorns that had caught on her jumpsuit. He looked her over. Anything broken? She was a little scratched up about her face and hands, but otherwise seemed whole.

"Kat … Kat!"

She groaned and slowly opened her eyes and held her head. "G? What happened?"

"We were attacked by Shadow tech. It happened so fast I didn't see it, but what else could it have been?"

"Where's Paige?"

"Dead, over there."

"Dead?" Kat wailed.

He scanned the skies in all directions. His heart skipped.

He saw four Shadow tech beasts looming in the distance to the east and the south, reminding him of towering black silos, thousands of feet high. They lurked in the distance, their shiny eyes trained on him and Kat like giant cats waiting to snare a pair of lonely mice.

Stenstrom stood frozen over Kat.

Then one of the great beasts reached out with a colossal tentacle, spanning an impossible distance, moving in their direction as if in slow motion, darkening the sky.

"*Sentrils!*" Kat said, searching for the bag. "The *Sentrils* will protect us!"

It wasn't there. Like his NTHs, the *Sentrils* were gone.

The creature's tentacle stretched out like a great black gulf in the sky, rapidly nearing their position. But in spanning the miles over the valley, the tentacle quivered, lost cohesion and fell apart into a dark, soaking rain, leaving the beast with little but a stump. Stenstrom heard it moan in frustration as black rain fell all around, tamping down the fog a bit.

Something about the valley protected them, keeping the beasts at bay. He had no idea what it was that gave them that protection, but apparently safe for now, he turned his attention to Kat. "Are you hurt?"

"I don't think so."

She tried to sit up and check herself over, but had difficulty. "G, I'm stuck." Obscured in the fog, Kat was lying in a patch of dark green weedy plants studded with impressive thorns. It took some doing, but Stenstrom freed her. He carefully picked her out of the stickers and set her down. "Oww!" she cried, jumping into his arms. The stickers hurt her feet, which was somewhat odd as she could normally walk over pretty much anything and not be fazed.

"These damn things!" she cried with anger. "Let me fix the boat so we can get out of here." She raised her arm to begin the process, but nothing happened.

"G, something's wrong—my Silver tech, it's gone, drained somehow. I'm empty."

Something occurred to him as the black pieces of the tentacle came down around them. "Kat, I just had a thought—look at this valley, look at those Shadow tech beasts out there waiting for us, but staying at a distance, something disintegrating them as they try to enter. Look at these plants that grow here in abundance. Weren't we lamenting not long ago that there is no life on Xandarr—the Black Hats and their Shadow tech beasts killed everything, vegetation included? But look—this plant, just a pesky weed, but here it is, surviving—thriving even."

They watched the cinder-like Shadow tech come down, and as they watched, the plants seemed to grow and writhe before their eyes, becoming denser, sharper, bigger with each passing moment. He carefully picked a plant, wary of the thorns. It was just a fibrous, olive-green weed, studded with savage thorns with an ugly but functional yellow flower growing on a fibrous, nettle-laced stalk. Minute golden dust trickled out of the flower at a steady rate.

"This is what saved us. The Shadow tech beasts have scoured the world clean, but here, this little plant devours them, devours Shadow tech."

The beasts capered about in the distance, frustrated.

Stenstrom gazed at the plant with wonder. "Remarkable—this plant, a troublesome weed anywhere else, but here is nothing short of a miracle. See how life endures—Atha was right. And look, this flower. Why have a flower if not to attract a passing insect?" He reached down into the thorny mass and fished around—the troubling stickers having no effect on his HRN.

"Ah!" Stenstrom cried. He cupped something in his hands and returned to Kat's side. "Look! Look at this!" He opened his hands; resting in his palm was a gray bug, tiny and fragile. Kat inspected at it. "It's also highly resistant to Shadow tech." She placed the bug on a Silver tech plank from the boat. Like a grasshopper eating a stem, they watched it nibble away at the Silver tech, infusing it with light and color.

"Yes," he said. "Life returns. Shadow tech is abundant, and therefore the new life feeds upon it. What a thing to see. Give it time and this planet will burst with life afresh. These plants and this bug are the progenitors of all things to come."

Stenstrom conjured up the items Atha had given them; a small clay pot, a trowel and a jar. He used the trowel and collected a few plants in the pot. He placed several bugs into the jar and covered it with a cloth and then made them all vanish. They listened to one of the distant Shadow tech beasts moan in frustration.

"Grumble all you want!" Kat said, mocking it. "You can't get us! Ha!"

They searched through the wreckage of the boat for their things, the low-hanging fog making progress difficult. Kat's basket was gone, Stenstrom's NTH pistols were also gone. Paige was gone as well, her body missing from where it had been, Stenstrom figuring she had been devoured by the plants and bugs.

Kat frantically searched the wreckage, turning over everything.

"G, the bag of squash is gone! Gone! I had it sitting out on the couch when the boat overturned. I can't find it anywhere!" She clutched at her hair in growing panic. "Once this current load runs out, I'm done. What are we going to do?"

"We'll proceed as best we can. My NTHs are gone, the *Sentrils* are gone, and the squash is gone, but we've a job that needs doing." He pointed to the west. "I saw a spire that way. That's the way we go."

Kat, eyes half-closed, wobbled a little and leaned over.

"Kat, what's wrong?"

"I feel sick ..."

Stenstrom helped her stand. She leaned on him for support. "Silver tech's gone. Feel dizzy. I can't stay here for much longer. But if we leave the protection of the plants, the Shadow tech beasts will get us. They're just waiting for us out there."

"Here's what we'll do. I'll put the HRN around you and I'll fade into the shadows. The beasts shouldn't be able to see us. We TK west, to the mountains and beyond."

Weak, Kat put her arms around him, falling deep into the warmth of his HRN.

"Ready?" he asked.

She nodded and up they went, several feet off the ground. The Shadow tech beasts grunted in dismay and shook the ground as he faded into the shadows, no longer able to see him. Up he rose, twenty, thirty, forty feet; their shipwreck site now a small bit of chaos on the ground. The tallish purple mountains looked not too far off in the clear air; he headed for them as quickly as he could.

The distance he soon discovered was deceptive. The mountains that looked fairly close were apparently very far away, the valley floor beneath giving way to bare orange ground again.

Shadow tech beasts were everywhere, milling about, looking for more things to devour. As he had hoped, his fade into the shadows seemed to be protecting them, their passage unnoticed.

Eventually, after hours, he was exhausted. They had reached the foothills. Still carrying Kat, he made his way up the gentle hills, occasionally spying the silver spire glinting through the spaces in the mountain tops. Soon, the footing became too treacherous and he had no choice but to lift off with TK and soar. He weaved soundless through the empty valleys and canyons, Kat's hair blowing in his face.

She stirred after a bit. "G? Where are we?"

"In the mountains. The beasts are far behind."

"G, stop. Set me down."

The strain of the TK was killing. He landed in a rocky pass. Kat came out, seemingly much better rested. He sat down to catch his breath and let the pain pass. Kat wrapped around him and ran her fingers through his hair. She kissed his forehead, the green cloth of her sleeves soaked up and radiated the afternoon sun.

"Feel better?" she asked.

"A little, thanks, Kat. Do you have any squash knowledge left?"

She shook her head. "No, it's gone. I remember creating all those things but I have no idea how I did it. How could I have lost the squash?"

"It's done. Can't stay here. We need to keep moving." The distant roar of a Shadow tech beast drove the point home. Propping each other up, they continued down the hill and around a bend of mountains to the south-west.

And there it was.

Rising up alone on the sandy flat was a tarnished silver structure surrounded by a flat pan of white fog. It looked like a great pile of horns or tusks stacked up and arranged in a semi-cohesive, somewhat bony-looking mass. It was arranged rather cathedral-style with a noticeable cruciform pattern. There was a long nave facing north and south, with a smaller east-west transept and two much taller tusks placed at the southern end, giving them the appearance of two bell towers. The whole thing looked like the carcass of some prehistoric creature.

Kat didn't like the look of it. "This is where Atha's father Carahil lives?"

"Apparently so. Captain Davage spoke of him often. He is a creature of good."

Kat was dubious. Look at this hideous structure—what good can come out of that?

They came down the path and waded into the fog, which was quickly smothering. Unable to see, Kat stood on Stenstrom's shoulders, guiding him toward the forlorn structure.

Something came down from the sky with a crash. One of the Shadow tech creatures had arrived, searching for them. It swished the fog about with its tentacles, trying to fan it away so it could more easily locate and devour them.

"G! What are we going to do? Are we invisible right now?"

"No, I'm exhausted from TKing. Can't concentrate."

They shambled to the north, trying to stay away from the beast as best they could, but being so huge, it was difficult. Several times, a sun-blocking tentacle came whistling just over their heads, obliterating the fog.

Stenstrom and Kat came to an abutment, the mountains rising up steeply. They had nowhere to go—should the beast see them, it would snuff them out like a thousand-foot high building falling on a pair of ants. Kat put her arms around Stenstrom, trying to protect him.

The beast took notice of the cathedral: Gods Temple. It moved toward it, giant mouth opening, ready to feast on the stone, on the rusted finished metals. Once it was done with that, it would dessert on Stenstrom and Kat. Like an octopus ready to engulf a much smaller crab, the beast put its tentacles on the stone.

Instantly, something inside the cathedral grabbed hold of it. The beast reacted and fought back, trying to free itself, locking its tentacles down, shaking the ground, pulling hard. As Stenstrom and Kat watched with trepidation, the great beast steadily lost ground, its spherical head rapidly pulled down toward the cathedral arch. The moment its head was near the arch, something CRUNCHED onto it. The beast wailed in misery, its tentacles giving way, flapping high into the air, some collapsing into cinders raining black down on the land for miles around. Inch by agonized inch, the beast's head was pulled into the cathedral, snapping and crunching, its cries of helpless agony so mournful and unbearable to hear that they both felt sorry for it as it suffered. When the last of its head disappeared into the cathedral, the quivering rest quickly followed. Soon, all of the towering Shadow tech vanished through the arch and was gone.

The mountain spur was suddenly quiet, the moans hushed into forever silence, with only the sublime thuds of cinders falling.

They looked at each other, stunned. "Um, G, did Carahil do that?"

"I suppose so."

"So … if he can do that to a giant Shadow tech beast … what's he going to do to us?"

Stenstrom stood. "Let's find out. He just dealt with a giant, we'll see how he deals with two tiny souls under his feet."

Steeling themselves, they pressed on, wading into the fog. Up close, the cathedral's structure was made up of a number of great bony horns lashed together with what looked like rusty wire; the great arch at its center, a hundred feet tall, a rotten open mouth. It was the ugliest structure they had ever laid eyes on, making the Clovis ruins seem like a cheery paradise.

In silence, they approached and entered via the open southern archway, feeling the ghost of the Shadow tech beast and its suffering walk with them.

The interior was foggy and still. A dripping sound came from the rear of the cathedral, breaking the silence with a steady beat. From what they could see of it, it was bony and clean. The nave was open and lofty all the way down, like the throat of a great animal. They brushed themselves off as they entered. The dust and grains of sand they shed seemed to flee and exit out the door in a bouncing fashion.

Kat listened. "What's that dripping? He's way back in there, do you hear him? How are we going to do this?"

"Matching him power for power is pointless. If I had my NTHs I could kill him, I suppose, but his death is not our mission. Atha told us Carahil, in his grief, lost his soul, forgot who he was. I think the best way to go about this is to vigorously remind him who he is."

Stenstrom put his hand to his mouth and called out as loud as he could.

"Carahil! Carahil! We have come on behalf of your daughter, Atha of the Quest, for she is concerned for you, as are we! Carahil, come out and remember!"

Kat whirled around. "Oh, G, what have you done?"

There was a moment of silence marked by several drips, then a strained, haggard voice answered: "Who is there? Do I hear something that lives?"

"Carahil, it's it I, Lord Stenstrom of Belmont-South Tyrol. I am a friend of Captain Davage, Lord of Blanchefort, and of his sister, Lady Poe—your creator. Carahil, we have come to assist you, and bring you good news!"

Bump … Bump … Bump came from the back of the cathedral. A pair of white spotlight eyes appeared in the fog, hovering high overhead. "Good news?" came the voice. "How can there be good news?"

From the western arm of the transept, a large mass emerged; a great darkness obscured by fog. Two points of bright white light from deep within the cloud peered down at them.

Malice radiated from it.

"Carahil?" Stenstrom asked. "We beg your counsel! We beg you to hear us!"

A pained voice replied. "You should not have come here …"

"Carahil, show yourself and come with us to your daughter who loves you!"

The great mass of fog hesitated. "Very well." The fog dissipated and a gigantic gray form emerged. It appeared to be the face of Carahil, as they remembered it from the statue in the Telmus Grove, silver, seal-like; only in this case his face was rather large and at least eighty feet off the ground. Most of his body was obscured from their view by the eastern nave. The only thing they could see of him at the moment was his muzzled face and glowing eyes—he stared off to the east, and the rest of him was still hidden around the corner.

Drip … Drip … Drip …

Large slimy tears dripped from his face to the floor.

"I do not know you," he said. "What are you doing here?" His voice was booming, and tinged with a forlorn sadness.

"We have been sent here by your daughter. She is worried for you."

Carahil, still staring off to the east, considered his words.

"Daughter? I have no daughter …"

He turned to look at them for the first time. The light from the huge eyes went out, leaving a dull red—the eyes of a demon.

Bump, Bump, Bump.

He came fully around the corner of the transept. His body was scarred and blackened with grief. Growing out of his silvery back were four immense claw-like hooks on sinewy arms. He ran the hooks along the ground, moving him forward, creating the "Bump, Bump" sound on the bony walls and floor of the temple.

The demon looked at Kat, seeing her Shadowmark. "A Black Hat? Come to appreciate your handiwork, have you?"

"I am not a Black Hat," Kat said, defiantly.

"Ah …"

One of the claws was clamped firmly around his own neck, squeezing— his eyes sticking out, his tongue lolling.

"I am your destroyer, Black Hat," he said in a booming, half-choked monotone. "You have come to me with your lies."

"I am not a Black Hat!" Kat screamed.

He raised his claws over his head and attacked in a lope, the claws opening and closing in a scissor-like movement. "MORE LIES!"

Kat sprang out of the way as a claw came crashing down, biting into stone. Carahil reared back and, open-mouthed, came at Stenstrom—his phlegmy mouth filled with rows of triangular teeth, like a shark.

Stenstrom girded himself and caught his jaws, holding them open with the Sisters' power.

"Carahil—What has become of you? Remember who you are!"

"I am Death, I remember that. What has become of me?" the demon that once was Carahil said. "Nothing has become of me. I am as I have been!"

He righted himself, seized Stenstrom by the waist with one of his hooks and slammed him into the ground.

Kat sprang to his aid. She had regenerated just enough Silver tech to form her claws. The hook suddenly fell apart into several pieces, Kat slashing it to bits.

Carahil lurched toward her, sprouting more hooks from his back, sending them all in her direction in a gristly crunch. She slashed with her claws, shredding several of the hooks.

More came and she was seized, the hooks crushing down on her ribs. She screamed as he lifted her off the ground. Another claw clamped on, ready to tear Kat in two.

"Carahil!" Stenstrom roared. "Let her go!"

"The Black Hat is going to die!" Carahil growled. "And, afterwards, so are you!"

In agony, Kat spat through gritted teeth. "I am NOT a BLACK HAT! I am here as a free woman, side by side with the man I love. I hate the Black Hats as much as you do, for what they did to me and my sisters! I have chosen to come here … for you!"

The demon hesitated. "For me?"

There was no way to deal with this demon other than with reason. Kat had found a small crack in his demented armor, now Stenstrom had to get through to him. "Why are you doing this, Carahil?"

"Why?" he wept as he held the struggling Kat like a doll. "Look around you—what do you see? Miles of nothing, empty whispers and old dreams replayed with none to hear. This planet is dead—everything is dead, and IT'S ALL MY FAULT! It's all my fault! I saw what was to come and I chose to do nothing but sit back and try to pretend that everything was going to be fine. Does this place look fine to you? Does it? You came looking for the Destroyer, I am the Destroyer! Me! Through my inaction, I killed this place!"

He clamped down tighter on Kat. She screamed again in misery. "And now, I'm going to kill you too—for bringing me all this pain right back afresh! For lying to me about a daughter that does not exist."

"Carahil, wait!" he cried. "Let me show you something we've discovered! We promised you good news, and we have it! If this doesn't inspire you, then ... you may kill both of us and be inconvenienced no longer!"

Carahil turned to him and loosened the pressure on Kat—she struggled fitfully. "You wish to show me something? Fine, let me see it, and then become the latest to die in this cursed place ..." He scissored his claws.

Stenstrom waved his hand, producing the flower pot. Carahil looked at it. "What is this?" he said.

"This ... it's just a weed, a thistle—an 'Ouch-hand' I think the gardeners on Kana call it, because its stickers go right through their gloves. This is probably the most worthless plant one could ever find—but look, look where it grows. Out there, in the arid wastes it grows; a whole valley of it."

Carahil looked at the tiny flower again, with a bit of further interest. "This plant ... grows here?"

Stenstrom waved his hand again. He held the jar with the bug within. He released it. The bug took wing and buzzed around—Carahil watching it fly with wonder. "But the Shadow tech? The beasts?"

"This plant and this bug feed on Shadow tech. The beasts outside fear these tiny things, are powerless against them. Yes! Look! That is our good news, that life is more persistent than you have given it credit for, and all the Shadow tech in the universe cannot prevent its coming. Life returns to this place, and perhaps one day birds will fly and fish will swim. Life is waiting to re-take Xandarr. Carahil, you've been hiding here, wallowing in your guilt for far too long. Take a first step toward redemption, and save a life. Please let Kat go."

Carahil considered his words. "I can't. I can't let go." He squeezed. Kat screamed.

"G!"

"Carahil, remember who you are! Remember where you came from! I do not know you personally to any great degree, but I do know one thing, given all the good people who have vouched for you—and that is that you have a heart, and it is that same heart that has condemned you to this place of bone and wire, driven you mad and given you no peace. Look at the daughter who loves you—not in this place, but in others, where you saved Xandarr, where children come to you for comfort, look to you for inspiration. All true! Stop punishing yourself, Carahil, and please let Kat go."

After a moment, the claws opened and Kat fell out. She scrambled to Stenstrom's side.

"Now, let yourself go too."

Slowly, Carahil opened the claw that had been choking his throat.

Carahil diminished in size, the claws dried up and fell off. The scarred, blackened hide dropped off, revealing shiny smooth skin. Two red covers fell off his eyes and vanished, leaving bright silvery eyes shining in the light.

He stood there on his flippers. "I'm sorry," Carahil said, still looking at the potted flower. "I'm so sorry."

Stenstrom approached and embraced him around the neck. Kat hung back, still wary, holding her ribs. "I have been given to know of a place where none of this happened. You saved Xandarr. You inspired the people to take action, and they did so, granting you your arms. You performed a miracle, sweeping the Shadow tech from the skies and from the ruins below. A King emerged, a good King, and Xandarr was reborn. It even joined the League and is a thriving place. There, you are memorialized, not as a god but as a defender, as a dear friend. This has been made known to us."

"I did?" he said. "I helped save Xandarr?"

"You did."

His silvery seal's face lit up.

"Just a moment," he said and he took the rim of the pot into his teeth and bounded away, disappearing around the corner of the transept.

"G—we should get out of here," Kat said.

"No, he's fine. He isn't going to hurt us."

"Tell that to my aching ribs."

He tousled her hair and gave her a kiss as Carahil returned. He was carrying something in his mouth.

"Ah, such love—it warms my old heart. What is it about Shadow tech females, I wonder? Just irresistible, aren't they?"

"They are, indeed."

Carahil grew a tad in size and placed the items in his mouth on the floor. "I destroyed your boat and took these items from you. I thought you were the Punts, coming to force me into servitude again. I'm sorry."

On the floor were several of the missing items from their boat. There were Stenstrom's NTHs, Kat's basket, as well as the tiny bag of red squash capsules. Kat was elated, taking the bag up and marveling at it.

"What about the *Sentrils*, Mr. Carahil?" Kat asked. "Do you have those too?"

"I'm sorry, just what's here. I know of *Sentrils* of old, very powerful, things even the gods covet. I didn't see any as I destroyed your boat, I would certainly remember if I had."

Something entered the cathedral, casting a long shadow, staggering, creating a metal-on-stone grating with every pained step.

Kat squinted to see. "Holy crap! It's Paige!" she cried.

It was Paige, alive and functioning, but as she neared, she seemed odd. There were two fully-formed halves of her, a robotic right side as before and a new mottled silvery/green left side. They went to her, took her by the hands, her metal hand and new greenish-silvery hand, and assisted her into the cathedral. Her liquid green eyes were wide, full of wonder as they led her. Carahil loped away, returning a few moments later carrying a gilded chair of hammered gold in his teeth.

He set the chair down. "Here, allow her to sit. This was the old throne of Xandarr Keep. I took it from the wreckage in the aftermath of the attack, along with other odds and ends."

They seated Paige in the vast bucket of the chair. She looked about, her eyes lost in confusion. Stenstrom examined her new silvery half.

"Somehow, Paige, while lying on the ground in the weeds, has generated a partially-vegetable, partially-Silver tech body." He gently squeezed her hand. "Her hand feels like flesh. It's warm. I feel bones or some sort of rigid structure beneath the flesh." He leaned down and sniffed her. "She smells like loam."

Carahil leaned in. "She's in a rapid state of flux. I sense her system changing before our eyes. Look, see the little streaks of gold forming in her skin? See there? She's absorbing the gold from the chair she's sitting in and taking it into herself. Amazing!"

Kat watched with wonder. Streaks of gold raced around her body, filling her eyes with golden light. "But, how is she doing this?"

Stenstrom shook his head. "I don't know. The conditions in the valley must have been right, perhaps some sort of accidental combination of elements that allowed this process to happen." He checked her robotic hand.

"Look! Look at her hand!" In her metallic palm, welded into the metal, were three articulated cubes etched with arcane writing. "*Sentrils*. Here they are. She must have been trying to fetch them for us after Carahil inadvertently attacked and sank the boat. They must have reacted with her body, triggering this process."

✳   ✳   ✳   ✳   ✳

They stayed with Paige for several days, watching her grow before their eyes. Kat found an apple from the bottom of the basket and gave it to her, watching her delicately eat. Before long, an entire tree bursting with fat apples grew from her body like a leafy parasol over her head. With joy, Carahil took the tree and planted it in the courtyard behind the cathedral at the base of the mountain. The life he had so longed for was now taking hold full-on. As the days passed, the metal part of her right side was slowly being shed, like bits of falling armor, giving way to an organic silvery-green body. The metal from her right hand fell away, the *Sentrils* buried deep in her flesh, fueling her transformation. The courtyard behind the cathedral soon was stocked full of the wonders pulled directly from Paige's body. Kat fed her the remnants of a piece of chicken from the basket, and soon, a long vine sprouted from her body with large chicken-like eggs growing from the vine like watermelons. Soon, a small brood of green and gold chicken-like

birds were scratching around the cathedral. The vine was joined by a tree sprouting white tissue-like leaves after Stenstrom had taught Paige to wipe her mouth with a napkin. Kat gave Paige a sip of wine from a decanter and soon a dark, fragrant tree with purple leaves smelling of delicious wine was planted in the courtyard. A big drink of cold water from the basket begot a tree that literally 'rained' cold, clear water from its bluish leaves. That tree Carahil planted with great care; soon a small lake formed.

"And I had thought this girl was a Punt. I dashed her into the ground," Carahil said, surrounded by birds and other new life sprung from Paige's flesh. "Remarkable, the life that is taking hold here, and I didn't even notice what lived in the valley; so content in my grief I didn't see the very life I longed for. Please, tell me about my daughter. I wish to hear of her."

And they told him of Atha, how she was mysterious and smoky, yet full of hidden light, just like her father, Carahil closing his eyes and nodding as he listened. "I will remain here and protect the life that grows. When life stands and lifts its eyes to the heavens, I will be there to greet it. Then, I will seek out my daughter, embrace her and thank her for thinking of me."

And then they told Carahil of Bellathauser, the demon and her pocket realm. They told him of the Destroyers' Road.

"I know the place. It is befouled with Shadow tech, but I will take you there. Come on—hop up!" He increased in size until he was large enough for them to both ride. Stenstrom sashed his NTHs and climbed up on his back. Kat, holding her bag of squash, tarried behind.

"Oh, come on," Carahil said to her, regaining a bit of his humor. "I don't bite … not anymore, anyway."

Paige stood there, draped in fabrics Carahil had stashed in the cathedral, green, streaked with gold, most of her metal body shed.

"What about Paige?" Kat asked.

"She will stay with me and be the progenitor of all life on a reborn Xandarr. I shall protect her, as a father does his daughter."

Paige approached Carahil, trying to climb up on his back and join them.

"No, no, Paige. You stay here and be safe," Kat said. Silent, golden eyes confused, she took a step back. Kat embraced her. "I won't say goodbye. We will return to check on you. I had my angels, and we will be yours. Be well, Paige, make a good world of this place."

Stenstrom came and embraced her also. She looked up at him, eyes pleading for them to stay. "You will be safe here with Carahil, and, as Kat said, we shall return someday."

They climbed up Carahil's back, Kat seating herself in front of Stenstrom. Taking a last look at Paige, Carahil bounded out into the purple sun, the light glinting off his silver body. "Are you sure you want to go that way?"

"Positive," Stenstrom said.

He gently lifted into the air and drifted west. "The way to the Destroyers' Road is chock full of Shadow tech beasts, but they tend to give me a wide berth … at least they used to."

Carahil lifted up about a thousand feet and picked up speed. Far off on the horizon was a small but dense patch of black, rapidly approaching. Soon, the distant patch was a growing, rolling storm with ugly clouds of Shadow tech boiling into the heights. Great beasts flew in it.

Kat looked back, her hair flying. "G, we're going to be overwhelmed!"

"Do you have your Silver tech back?"

"Yes, I think so."

"Then squash up. We're going to need it."

Kat took a capsule and mashed it against her forehead. Stenstrom took the bag with the remaining capsules and made it vanish for safekeeping.

"Here we go!" Carahil shouted.

They plunged into the storm. Shadow tech rain pelted them, trying to latch on. Stenstrom pushed it away and Kat lashed at it with deadly micro-point beams.

In the distance, sorting itself out from the surrounding darkness was a hanging rope of swirling night—a Shadow tech funnel, roaring and death-bringing.

Carahil swerved away from it but, like a living thing, it moved to follow, to overwhelm and annihilate.

Faceless beasts and triggered traps came skyward; some chopped into tiny pieces by Kat, others blown into smoky nothingness by Stenstrom's NTHs.

Many Shadow tech beasts came up, flying at a distance.

"I see lights coming from the beasts' heads!" Stenstrom said. He conjured up his Megaeye and had look.

His mouth dropped open. "I see dozens and dozens of Bellathauser's mechanical half attached to the beasts' heads, the hand of each plunged into the Shadow tech. I see bolts of energy coming from each one, linking them together. I think they are controlling the beasts, enslaving them."

Several of the beasts swerved in to attack, the multitudes of Bellathausers attached to its head giving the impression of a stubbly layer of hair.

Kat wound up and loosed a great lance of Silver tech. It reached out across the distance and hit the beast square in the head, destroying many Bellathausers in a long scrape. As if it was being eaten away by acid, the scrape expanded into an open wound, which became a vast, ever-expanding canyon. Soon, the beast fell away, its head half eaten, spiraling into the ground far below.

"Silver tech melts Shadow tech!" Kat cried.

Several more came in, Carahil swerving across the sky to avoid them. "Nearly there!"

They suddenly broke through into daylight, the towering wall of black in close pursuit. Carahil descended to the ground. Ahead was what appeared to be a forgotten dirt road leading into a fast approaching stand of hills.

From above, fingers of Shadow tech reached. Stenstrom fired his NTHs, Kat released as much Silver tech as she could, but she was becoming exhausted as she split and bisected incoming threads of Shadow tech—Stenstrom held onto her as she began to slump.

Ahead, at the end of the path was a gleam of light. "There it is! Go! I will stand against the Shadow tech. Hurry!" Carahil cried.

"Take care of Paige!" Kat said.

The gleam ahead expanded into a pulsing film of glowing material. As the wave of Shadow tech threatened to engulf them, Stenstrom and Kat plunged in.

8—Gelt

Suddenly, they were on a rain-drenched world of heavy gray cloud and pelting rain, their boots and feet sinking into the oozing, water-logged ground. They were instantly soaked to the bone.

"Where are we?" Stenstrom asked, shouting to be heard. Kat stood there in the rain, looking like a water-logged mouse.

Purple lights. A figure approached.

It was Atha, standing there in the rain, though she was completely dry and untouched by mud; the rain seemed to fall around her. "Oh, Creation, Creation, Creation!" she said, all smiles. "Look what you did for my father! I saw it all! I shed tears, real tears! You two have my eternal favor, and I mean it!"

Atha whirled about in the rain that was not touching her body, dancing in the mud that did not dirty her boots. "Hey, I'm sorry about the rain and the mud. Let me take care of it." She raised her arms and the blanket of rain was diverted, cast aside like a swarm of bees crashing into the ground. "You guys did great, did I already tell you that?"

"You did," Stenstrom said. Both he and Kat stood there like drenched rabbits, steaming slightly.

"Well, it bears repeating." Atha looked around. "Some place, huh? This is Gelt, a rather rural world in the remote backwater of the League. Thanks to our friend Fiddler Crowe at Mons Eagle, we know exactly where to enter Bellathauser's horror realm." She held her arms out. "Right here it is. Fabulous spot for it, suitably depressing and uncomfortable as one might expect."

Stenstrom looked around, seeing nothing but sheets of falling rain machine-gunning the ground and a flat expanse of mud and limp grass. "Here?"

Atha pointed to the ground. "Down there, about fifty feet." They looked at the ground, seeing an ocean of mud.

"You know the story of this place?" Atha asked. "There used to be seven earthen hills here—the locals called them the 'Seven Wives' after the Sisterhood of Light." Atha looked around at the flat landscape. "No more hills, are there? The hills were razed to the ground about thirty years ago by Sygillis of Metatron. Ring any bells?"

Stenstrom knew the story—he knew the tale. Atha told it, saying things he already knew.

Atha continued. "The *Triumph* was a brand new warship for the Stellar Fleet, huge and grand. In her jealousy, the Xaphan criminal and socialite Princess Marilith of Xandarr stole the ship with her followers and tried to murder Captain Davage and his betrothed, Sygillis of Metatron. After a heated battle in space, Sygillis managed to steal aboard the *Triumph* and confront the princess personally. This place is where the *Triumph* fell out of the sky and plowed into the ground like a meteorite as Sygillis, single-handed, fought Princess Marilith and her Fanatics of Nalls, putting to death every soul on that ship, impaling them on spikes like a forest of the dead. Like my father, Sygillis, injured and alone, facing the horrors of what she had done on the *Triumph*, went mad. She leveled the Seven Wives in the hope of covering the *Triumph* and everything else to hide what she had done. This is where Captain Davage came and saved her a second time. And here the *Triumph* has remained, buried after only one flight, a shipwreck on dry land, too horrible to be dug up and refurbished."

Atha kicked at the mud. "The interior of the *Triumph* is the entrance to Bellathauser's realm—Fiddler Crowe's calculations prove it. We dug a hole to get to it, and now here it is, fifty feet down."

Stenstrom and Kat stared at the mud. Kat hugged herself, placing her head into Stenstrom's chest. "I don't like small buried spaces."

"It'll be all right, love, I promise."

"So, Bellathauser's down there. So too is your Anatameter and your revenge, if you still want it," Atha said. "I could scour away all this mud, but I prefer you two to do it. The universe likes it that way."

"Then I guess we dig," Kat said. Stenstrom handed her a squash capsule and she broke it against her head. "We dig hard," she said again, in a more forceful voice. "Stand back."

Stenstrom and Atha stepped back. Kat first created a roof, larger than the area of no rain Atha had made. From the roof she created a powerful drill head out of Silver tech and began digging. A geyser of debris shot into the air as the drill head did its work, quickly biting into the drenched ground. Atha funneled the debris away.

It wasn't long before Kat hit metal. She retracted the drill head, setting it aside in the mud, allowing the rain to stream off its impressive teeth. They peered down into the hole, seeing nothing but a dark tube going into the ground. Kat swirled her hands about, creating a shining, egg-shaped ball of Silver tech. "I'm creating a few Belmont Buzzers. I'll have them scout out ahead and see what's about down there. Can I borrow a few more of your yellow Holystones?" The Silver tech formed into the wiggling shape of several large cockroaches—a standard StT shape, small and versatile. "Gods, I love these little guys. They totally rock!"

Stenstrom waved up four yellow Holystones, shaking them into a yellow glow. The StTs took the Holystones in their front legs and flew down into the hole Kat had cut, the light from the Holystones panning about like a group of miners descending into the dark.

Down below, buried about fifty feet, the StTs hit metal. Glinting in the yellow light was a hint of the cursed ship *Triumph*. It was soiled and dingy, like a dug-up fossil. Stenstrom was apprehensive—after all he had heard about this ship, all the horrific things that had happened within, seeing it in person was a bit ghastly. He knew *Triumph*-class ships fairly well, having been assigned to one for several years, but he couldn't get a bearing on what he was looking at; at what portion of the ship.

"I think that's the aft ventral quarter, lower decks," Atha said, looking into the hole. "She's nose-down at a fairly acute angle."

Kat lined the wall of the hole with a smooth layer of Silver tech. She added a winding set of stairs, and slowly they made their way down.

"Wait!" Atha said. "I think this is the end. If all goes well, you probably won't see me again. The gods tend to lose themselves in time. The next time I'm on Kana might be centuries from now. Just know how I love you, and should we meet again, you might not know me, but I'll know you." Atha wiped a tear from her face.

Both Stenstrom and Kat felt a warm kiss on their cheek. "Go on, good luck," Atha said, fading away. "*I love you guys,*" her voice echoed.

They continued down. The exposed bit of the ship loomed large, like a rising coffin uncovered from its grave. They reached the bottom; the metal of the ship was stained a putrid reddish-brown color in the StTs' light. They could find no access points to enter. Kat, using Silver tech, cut a deep hole through the thick metal plating. Blackness and foul air came rushing out. It was very dark within. Very little of the interior of the ship could be seen. The StTs crawled in, illuminating a small area of corridor inside.

Before he could take a step, Kat nimbly crawled in and vanished. Stenstrom knelt down and peered in. "Kat! Kat!" He didn't see her anywhere inside.

He folded himself up and climbed in after her.

The air inside the ship was thick and hard to breathe, laced with unpleasant scents. He had to grab onto the nearest wall—the ship was steeply pitched downward with no working gravity; it was difficult to maintain his footing. Yellow lights from the StTs bobbed about, creating a nightmarish amber effect before him.

"Kat! Where are you?" It was morbidly quiet. "Kat!"

In the distance, Kat emerged, sitting on all fours near a side wall. She was peering down a long corridor that trailed off into the dark. She bounded back to his side, finding purchase on the walls and ceiling; her agility, even in this compromised footing, was unmatched. "This place has a bad feel to it, G," she said.

"I agree."

They made their way down the corridor, Stenstrom having to hang onto whatever he could on the walls with every step.

Kat bounded ahead. "Come on, G, use your TK and let's go." She leapt ahead, the light-carrying StTs following.

He tried lifting off with TK and gliding down, but nothing happened. *Nothing happened! Where was the Sisters' power?*

With no TK, he had to make his careful way down, hanging onto the insulated plumbing pipes. Eventually, he caught up to Kat.

Stenstrom slid down to a four-way intersection and held there a moment. Murky darkness waited beyond. The light-bearing StTs lingered there in the open space, hesitant to go forward.

"Where are we, G?" Kat asked.

"Somewhere in the aft of the ship, I'm guessing Deck 3 or 4. We're going to have to traverse up before long into the high decks, 20 and upward. Can we send the Buzzers forward to scout?"

Kat called the StTs to her. They bobbled before her face, lighting it up. "I need you guys to go forward, ok? Let me see what you see. Go on."

The StTs wandered ahead through the intersection.

"Why did you ask them to move forward? Why not just command them to go?"

"These Buzzers are like our children, and it never hurts to be polite."

They waited in the dark a few minutes.

"See anything?" he asked.

Kat gazed off into the darkness. "Nothing so far, just a sad, empty ship. Wait! Wait, I see something up ahead lining the walls. I can't quite make it out. The StTs are approaching." She was quizzical, questioning. "What is that?"

"What, darling?"

Kat sucked in her breath. She recoiled. "G! They're bodies!"

"Bodies?"

"Yes! Many of them, down the passageway about a hundred feet. There's a lot of them. They are oddly preserved—they appear ruddy and fresh, as if they have been newly killed. The bodies are stuck up on the walls on Shadow tech spikes like flippin' scarecrows."

Stenstrom shuddered. "I've heard stories of the battle that took place on this ship—the Countess of Blanchefort alone against Princess Marilith of Xandarr and her Fanatics of Nalls. Those bodies must be the corpses of the Fanatics."

"The lady I'm going to be taking lessons from did all of this?" Kat asked.

"She did, in a moment of pain and insanity."

"Wow! It's pretty scary down there, G," Kat said. "Creation, I want to go home."

She bounded a few paces into the dark, Stenstrom following as best he could in the unsteady footing. Kat was fastened against the wall, having no trouble with the footing. Seeing him struggle, she offered him her Silver tech tail to use as a handle to hold onto, which he gratefully accepted.

The dark quickly swallowed them up as they made their way down the corridor. Up ahead, they could see a distant flickering of yellow light: the StTs oddly festive and alive in this horrendous charnel house of death. Kat scrabbled along the wall, using her claws to stick her on like a gecko, Stenstrom holding onto her tail for support.

Aside from the dank atmosphere, sour with old decay and mold, there was a terrible heaviness in the air—a dark taint that got worse with every step; it made them both shudder. Every so often, Kat looked back at him to make sure he was still there.

"You all right?" he asked her, tightly gripping her tail.

"I'm fine."

"Anything more from the Buzzers?"

"Just more bodies. Lots of them."

Soon, they passed into a solid forest of robed bodies, protruding branches of limbs with the floating will-o-the-wisps of the StTs lighting them up. The bodies were tacked up on the sides of the corridor like horrid pieces of pre formed art. Some were upside down, some were positioned parallel to the floor, and others were stuck up on the ceiling—all nailed in place with curved Shadow tech spikes just as shiny and sharp as the day they were formed. The material of the robes they wore reeked of must and old material. And, as Kat had mentioned, their pained, contorted bodies appeared quite fresh, the horror etched on their faces seemed newly formed, their mouths locked open in dead screams. In order to avoid the bodies, Kat leapt down onto the floor, her Silver tech claws digging in, and continued.

Every so often there was an empty spot amid the mosaic of hanging corpses, as if there had been a body there at one time, but which now was gone.

Stenstrom stopped to puzzle over this. "Why is there no body here? Where did it go?"

Kat craned her neck up. "It seems like a body should be there. Perhaps it fell down at some point and tumbled away." She scrabbled up the side of the wall, moving quickly, silently, over the hummocky terrain of bodies and Shadow tech spikes, and inspected the empty space.

"Look here," she said, investigating a particular spot, her tail flicking. "There's a hole in the wall where something had been jammed through."

"A Shadow tech spike?"

"Looks like it."

"So where did it go?"

"I don't know."

Stenstrom didn't like this one little bit.

She leapt down. "G, one of the Buzzers is seeing something different now. It's reached a platform of some sort—there's a lot of wreckage all around, as if the interior has been hollowed out somehow."

"Hollowed out?"

"Looks to be. The Buzzer is climbing down to have a better look. There's a pit heading down at an acute angle; let me see."

Kat's eyes grew wide. She reacted. "G! The bottom of the pit is full of body parts!"

"Body parts?"

"Yes, like they've been tossed in there: arms, legs, torsos, heads. They look to be … armored somehow. These parts aren't dressed in robes like the bodies here in the corridor."

Kat grabbed Stenstrom's lapels. "The Buzzer is hearing all sorts of things! There's something alive in that pit!"

"Can you move the Buzzer around to get a better look?"

"I'm trying, but—something just attacked the Buzzer! I got a glimpse of something moving at speed for it, and then it dropped the Holystone! The Buzzer is terminated—it exploded—taking whatever attacked it as well, if luck is with us. Oh, Creation, G!"

"Kat, those body parts—I think that's what Atha was talking about. Our immortal ancestors from Cammara. This is Bellathauser's realm, filled with pieces and parts; the Ghrundids, she called them." He closed his eyes. "And there's one more thing I need to tell you."

Kat anticipated his response. "The Sisters' power—is it gone?"

He looked around and took a deep breath. "Yes. It comes from starlight. Here in the depths, it cannot reach. I have no enhanced strength, no invulnerability and I have no TK."

"I was wondering why you weren't TKing. Then you stay here, G. I'll go on."

"You're not going on alone. I'm not helpless. I still have Tyrol sorcery. I still have my NTHs. That coupled with your Silver tech should be enough."

"What are we about to face here, G—creatures that cannot die? How are we going to do this?"

"As best we can. For everything we know, for the home we wish to have and life we wish to forge, we must be swift and we must successful."

They held each other for a few more moments. "Oh, how I love you," she said. "Just hold onto my tail and don't let go, ok?"

They moved deeper into the ship, getting their bearings. "Looks to be we're in one of the cargo holds. I'm not sure which one—there are four on a *Triumph*-class vessel." Stenstrom shook up another yellow Holystone and held it cupped in his hand, directing the light like a torch. Scattered around the room were broken and tumbled cargo containers. Windows looked out on compacted earth. They appeared to be alone in the room—no dead bodies, no Ghrundids—and he boldly presented the Holystone.

"Let's make a point to remember this location. If we need to make a fast exit, we can exit through the windows and burrow upward." Kat agreed. He produced a MARZABLE dagger and plunged it into a container. "Now, with the dagger planted here, I'll be able to zero in on it without fail. That's a trick I've used in the past."

Ahead was the closed door exiting to the main corridor. They approached cautiously.

"Do you have any Buzzers left—I recall you creating three in total?"

"There's one left, I think—but the Holystone's gone out—it's in the dark somewhere in the ship. I don't know where. My poor Buzzer. I want to get it and us out of here."

They cracked the door open and Kat sent a tentative streamer of Silver tech out to investigate the hallway. "I don't think there's anything out there, G. I can't see much, but I'm not feeling anything. I think it's clear." She retracted her stream.

Stenstrom drew his NTHs and checked the cinnabar strikers. "I'm wondering what the effect of my NTHs will be, as these Ghrundids are supposedly immortal and, apparently, unkillable."

"I guess we're going to find out."

Covering the Holystone, they opened the door and spilled out into the corridor. It was dark and silent. Following the acute slant down, they went as quietly as they could, Kat helping him with the terrible footing. Soon, they came upon another four-way intersection. Stenstrom stumbled with the angle, and Kat helped right him with her tail.

There was a guide plate. Stenstrom approached it and carefully shone his light on it.

"Ok, ok—this is junction L27. So, as we thought, we're in the lower section of the ship toward the aft end. If we move on an intersection or two, we should come to a lift and we can head upwards."

They continued past the intersection.

Green light appeared. There was movement in the distance and a sound. They hid themselves as best they could against the left hand wall and readied.

A synthesized sound echoed out from the dark, creating a humming sort of speech: *"Beth-or?"*

Something that appeared to be a disembodied arm emerged from the darkness, carrying its own green light like a space-faring vessel. It was moving like a snake, easily gliding along the ground. It was a left arm, the fingers of the hand lightly tapping along the floor. It was wearing tight-fitting articulated armor that went all the way up to the shoulder joint, where it ended in an elaborate, gear-like knob. Strong green lights ran up the length of the arm. The fingernails on the hand were replaced by sharp-looking metal claws. The arm appeared utterly hostile and belligerent.

As they hid in the shadows, the crawling arm went past, casting them in a green pall. *"Beth-or,"* came a synthesized sound from it as it continued on.

The hand froze, seemed puzzled. A tiny panel in its armor lifted and a fat panning beam of blue light issued forth, bathing the corridor in a sweeping arc this way and that. Before they could react, the beam caught them and held.

The arm whirled around. *"Solfids!"* came a sound. The arm tensed, as if ready to spring. Kat quickly pinned it to the ground with a surge of Silver tech. The arm struggled, looking like a fish caught in a deadly net.

Stenstrom cocked his hammers and leveled his NTHs. "Kat—drop the Silver tech, let it go! If I shoot your Silver tech, it could kill you too."

"Are you ready?" she cried.

He took aim. "Ready!"

Kat released the Silver tech, and with incredible speed, the arm surged out and came at Kat. She sprang away and the hand's metal claws dug into the corridor wall, missing her by mere moments.

Stenstrom fired his NTHs, hitting the arm square with both shots.

Nothing happened. The arm continued after Kat. A panel opened on its armored sleeve. It fired a rapidly pulsing red energy beam at Kat, who just had time to leap away.

Stenstrom took aim and fired again, hitting the weapon, and it went dead. Unlike the hand, the armor's robotic systems appeared to be fully subject to the NTHs' killing power.

More panels opened in the armor. Four curved blades emerged and began spinning. The hand sprang at Kat again.

THUMP! One MARZABLE buried itself in the arm's wrist, pinning it in mid-flight to the wall.

THUMP! A second MARZABLE.

THUMP! And a third. The arm was solidly pinned to the wall, the deadly daggers having cleanly penetrated the armor.

He went to get Kat. "You all right?"

"Yes, yes."

Producing more MARZABLEs and holding them at the ready, Stenstrom knelt down and inspected the impaled arm. Its hand clenched and unclenched. It strained to free itself. Its claws furrowed into the metal wall.

"Beth-or! Beth-or!" came the sounds over and over again.

"G—this is terrifying. Can this thing be real?"

"It must. And it's immune to my NTHs."

"What is 'Beth-or'?" she asked.

"Nothing good, I'm certain."

He inspected it with his Holystone. Its armor was a soft, foamy green and was delicately jointed together. The arm furiously worked, trying to free itself.

One of the MARZABLEs came loose.

With a swipe of her hand, Kat quartered the arm with a micro-beam of Silver tech from her fingers. Another swipe and she cubed it into a steaming pile of metal and sundered flesh.

The sundry bits of diced flesh continued to move. In their minds, they heard it wail in anguish. They covered their ears, but there was no drowning it out. It was the most pitiful sound they had ever heard.

Stenstrom shook his hand, producing several red Holystones.

"What are you going to do?" Kat asked.

"I'm going to burn it—put it out of its misery. Fire consumes all."

Stenstrom threw the Holystones and the pieces caught fire, burning in an oily smoke that sank to the floor in a greasy film and lingered there.

"That was very kind of you," came an accented, elfin voice from behind.

They both whirled around, ready to be attacked by a host of fresh horrors.

A steady ticking came from the dark reaches of the corridor—like the regular beat of a metronome.

tick ... tick ... tick ... tick ...

The voice came again between the beats. "You gave the nasty, death-dealing Ghrundid peace."

Moving with refined grace that defied the steeply pitched corridor, a cloaked figure emerged from the dark. It was a slender man, dainty and somewhat feminine in appearance, wearing a silvery pair of leggings, light boots and a heavy cloak. The steady ticking came from the man, from an odd geared device hanging at his throat

"Identify yourself!" Stenstrom said, holding two MARZABLEs and his NTH.

The man put his hood down, revealing a pretty face and thin, yellowish hair. "My name is rather long and difficult for a tongue under one hundred thousand years of age to pronounce. My traveling name is Fiddler Crowe. I favor that name. I know your ways. I am an occasional visitor here."

He pointed at Stenstrom. "You are Stenstrom, Lord of Belmont-South Tyrol." He turned to Kat. "And you, you are Taara de la Anderson, yes?"

"No," she replied. "Who?"

"Are you Lady Gwendolyn of Prentiss?"

"No!"

"Then you must be Lady Miranda of Rossel, or perhaps …"

Kat was becoming angry. "I am none of those people! I am Kat, first Countess of Belmont-South Tyrol!"

The man appeared surprised. He ticked in contemplation. "Hmmm, oh, yes. I see you're a *Covus*. Always elusive, the *Covus*. Ah well, such is the complexity of things."

She fumed, feeling a bit left out.

"How do you know who I am?" Stenstrom demanded.

"I'll spare you the details, as you have no time. You told me yourself who you are, though it was a different version of you, in a different timeline. I am here repaying a debt that I owe … *you* … and am performing my part of a bargain that was struck between the two of us."

"Me? More Extra-Planar nonsense?"

"If you like. You, sir, saved my wife, Queen Wendilnight. For that I am in your debt. You and that lovely woman you were with—Melazarr of Caroline."

"Oh, Melazarr!" Kat said happily. "We know her."

"I will honestly say, she was much more attractive and clearly more capable than this small person you have here in this reality."

Kat turned red with anger, but she held her tongue.

The smoke from the burning arm clung in the hallway and made them cough. Crowe waved his arm and spoke to the smoke. "Go on, you're free, drift about, make friends with the universe, you certainly don't deserve it."

"Who are you talking to?" Stenstrom asked.

"The Ghrundid. Oh, it's not dead, is that what you thought? You set it free, changed it into a Revantor."

"A what? Are you implying that burning doesn't kill?"

"Of course burning does not kill. Burning releases it into trace elements and free molecules—just as immortal as ever. In a few hundred years, it'll learn how to manipulate itself in such a state, turn itself into a sort of ghost of cinders. My assistant Famela in the Library of Time is just such an amalgamation of such creatures. It can even enter your body and take you over. Fortunately, these Ghrundids aren't overly intelligent, and fear burning and the freedom it offers."

He looked down the corridor. "Come, we've no time."

tick … tick … tick …

Dubiously, they followed him down the gloomy corridor. Stenstrom instantly noticed something.

"How are we walking so easy? This vessel is pitched forward at a steep angle; I've been struggling with it since we entered, yet now we are walking as if perfectly level."

"Gravity is not my king," Crowe said. "Walk easy in my presence."

"Could have used you earlier," Kat said.

"Of course."

That was somewhat of a relief. Stenstrom had many questions but saved them; the results were enough for now.

"Why are you ticking?" Kat demanded as they walked.

"It reminds me that time for you moves at an insanely rapid pace. Time means nothing to me. My wife and I have momentary conversations that, for you, would seem to last decades. This errand I am performing for you has forced me to enter into a ridiculously rapid time pacing. I am eager to conclude matters here and resume my usual routine."

"And you are immortal?"

"I am. Do not look to the uncouth Ghrundids as an example. Immortality, when properly measured and disciplined, is a marvelous gift. I am hundreds of thousands of years old."

He turned and lightly stepped down a side hallway. "You realize I created the Anatameter you lost?"

"You?" Kat said. "You're responsible for this mess?"

"I created the device to the specifications the goddess Atha gave me. What happens to it after that is not my concern."

Stenstrom had questions. "I recall the goddess Atha mentioning your name. For what purpose was this device built?"

"To create a new, separate version of you, the All-in-One, that your Nargal friend could claim as her own."

"Nargal friend?"

Crowe pointed down the hallway. "The Nargal spirit who calls herself by several names: 'The Woman with the Gun' is one; 'Lillian of Gamboa' is another."

"I was once betrothed to Lillian of Gamboa. She was a mundane my mother favored. Very talented, but not arcane in the least. We drifted apart after I went off to the university. I haven't spoken to her in years" Stenstrom said.

"In this reality perhaps. She is a Nargal spirit made of sand; she is completely and totally arcane, pretending to be a mundane woman. As such, the universe has branded her an outcast, unfit to love a *Kaidar Gemain*. The Anatameter I created would subvert the will of the universe, creating a new superior version of you just for her."

Stenstrom puzzled over this. "But …"

Crowe seemed to tire of the subject. "Your pardon. We are going to go up several floors, and then enter the main area of the Ghrundid clans—that is the heart of Bellathauser's realm. The decks have caved in, creating a vast open gallery. Nearby, in a Hall of Many Faces is the Anatameter and the demon Bellathauser herself. Kill the demon and turn the knob of the Anatameter and it shall be done. This horror realm will collapse, the *Spiralata* shall heal, and your universe shall be safe. My debt repaid."

They arrived at a lift door, which was partially open. Crowe reached into his cloak, pulling out a small device. He pressed a few buttons. Soon, a car arrived and they got in.

"Please allow me to brief you before we arrive in the Ghrundids' lair. There are four Ghrundid clans at work here in this horror realm. They come here for solace and to feast on the ample foodstuffs that are here for the taking. They are immortal, yet they still feel, above all things, the desire to eat. Cammara is a savage place. The clans are at war, not only with myself and those like me, but with each other as well—it seems a Ghrundid feels most alive when it's fighting and tearing, and that is basically all they do. I shall not burden you with the clans' actual names—you have already proven unable to move your mouth in the proper fashion, therefore I shall identify them by the appellations given to them by the lovely Lady Melazarr."

"Her again," Kat spat. "I mean, I loved her in Vain and all, but this alternate version of Mel is pissing me off."

"There are the Greens, and Reds, the Yellows and the Blue clans, she named them."

"What?" Kat cried in disgust. "No, no, I'm the giver of names, not this messed-up version of Melazarr. Right, G?"

"She chose the names of the color their armor most closely matches," Crowe said.

"Ah, ok. Now I will give them proper names—forget what Mel said. The Greens will be the 'Avocados', the Reds—'Tomatoes', Yellow—the 'Custards', and the Blues …" Kat thought a moment. "Blues, blues … what food is blue?"

"Are you feeling hungry, darling?" Stenstrom asked.

"I am yeah, hell yeah. Blue, blue? Ah! Blue will be the 'Mint' clan, after the peppermint jelly I love so much."

"Those are the names you wish to call them?" Fiddler Crowe asked.

"Yes," Kat replied, quite happy with herself.

"So," Stenstrom said, "I take it the arm we previously found was an Avocado then."

Crowe agreed. "Yes. Now then, I have some accessories here with me that you might find useful." He reached into a pocket in his cloak and drew out two sets of goggles. "These will assist you to see properly in the dark."

Kat took her set and popped them on, as did Stenstrom. "Reminds me of Clovis, and of Bird. She loved goggles."

The corridor lit up in the goggles.

"And take these as well. The Ghrundids are immune to your standard shot. These strikers, of my own design, will suffice."

Crowe handed Stenstrom several strikers made of a purplish material. He unscrewed his cinnabar strikers and replaced them with Crowe's. "These will kill the Ghrundids?"

"No," Crowe replied. "They simply put them to sleep for several hundred years. For your purposes, the net result is the same."

"Fine. What is our plan?" Stenstrom asked. "Since we are novices regarding this odd enemy, we shall have to rely upon your expertise."

"That is wise. In my final service to you, we are going to parley with the Avocados, as we have no way to pass into the main area without first passing through areas under their control. Please, allow me to do the talking. Do not be alarmed by what you hear—follow my lead and do not react."

The lift stopped. They slowly exited. Stenstrom held his NTHs cocked and ready and Kat formed two quick killer StTs, which scurried after her.

Crowe held no obvious weapons. He lightly walked, his ticking ever steady.

"We are nearly there," Crowe said. "Gravity has now righted itself without my assistance."

Stenstrom recognized the area as part of the botanical lab. A high angled ceiling stood in the dark, covered by wreckage. Outside, through the windows, they no longer saw compacted earth—here they saw undulating bands of color; reds, blues, and greens all twisting together in a torrid fashion over a background of racing stars. Through the windows was pure, seething chaos. They were no longer on Gelt—now they were standing in the horror realm of Bellathauser.

There was movement all around. Arms dropped down, all clad in tight-fitting green armor. There were legs flopping around, armored torsos, and a few heads mounted on green spinning platforms. The heads were horrible: eyes wide open and fixed in an insane stare, mouths opening and closing, tongues elongated and prehensile, like a ruddy tail.

Stenstrom and Kat got back to back, ready to fight.

Crowe appeared unimpressed.

The various parts began jumping around, consolidating themselves into cohesive assemblages.

Four armored torsos levitated into the air, floating on small bluish jets. Three legs and three arms, creating a sort of tripod effect, attached themselves to geared ball and socket joints built into each armored torso. Additionally, six heads, in various stages of completeness, levitated on blue jets and ratcheted into housings at various points on both sides of the torsos. No head went to the top of the torso, where a head might normally be expected to go. Four of these armored green, tripod-like assemblages stood before them in the crawling dark.

They spoke in a synthesized fashion.

"Brona ..."

"Tharquil ..."

"Bethor ..."

"Annimus ..."

The Bethor assemblage was missing its right arm—they had slain it in the corridor. Several free-floating arms jostled about and violently had a go at each other, competing for the open spot. After a bloody moment, one came up and took its place, fingers flexing in triumph.

The two sides stood there, Stenstrom and Kat in near terror, wondering what was about to happen.

One of the assemblages, Tharquil, took a shambling step forward. One of the six heads migrated from its place on its upper-right torso and went to the shoulders. It spoke in a partially mechanical voice:

"Ahhhh, we have the crafty Fiddler Crowe in our midst at last. And what have we here, two more Solfids who appear rather whole and toothsome. Such treasure. This is a wondrous surprise."

"Tharquil, you are a nefarious creature indeed," Crowe replied. "These Solfids are a gift I was planning on sharing with your unholy grouping."

"Ah, we see, we see ... and what is the price for these rare treasures? Certainly they are not free?"

"Of course not—safe passage to the Hall of Many Faces and counsel with your queen Bellathauser is my price, as usual."

Another head migrated to the top of Tharquil's shoulders, replacing the previous one. "I do not trust this accursed Solfid Fiddler Crowe. We should take him and sunder his flesh and increase our wealth. The others are but appetizers. Crowe has been our desired main course for centuries."

"Yes, but of course, Tharquil, you will not have me, as per normal. Would I have simply walked into your wretched presence without a second and third option available to me awaiting easy invocation? How soft do you think I have become?"

A third head came to the top. "You cannot hold out against us forever, Fiddler Crowe, and we have forever, do we not? We will add your bounty to our wealth, it is all a matter of time and how much destruction it will take to see it done."

Crowe wagged his finger. "Yes, time that is wasting. These Solfids are but a portion of the treasure I have brought."

"Give us the rest immediately! Give it to us!"

"Alas, I have already given those gifts to your hideous peers out in the great area. They are feasting hearty even as we speak."

The four green assemblages began an agitated stirring.

"All that wealth to be distributed to the likes of the Aryshindebezzel-morths and the Kaityrustalumnutas? It is an outrage!"

The Avocados shambled about. "We will go and take this wealth for ourselves and make our enemies suffer! Bethor—you remain here with this lot and see that they do not escape. We shall return soon, heaping with fresh treasure."

With that, Tharquil, Brona and Annimus shambled away on their green tripod legs, flanked by a neat squadron of flying armors arms, the various heads attached to their bodies shouting war songs as they departed.

Bethor, now alone in the corridor with them, appeared quite agitated. One of its six heads came to the top. "Where did you get these Solfids, Fiddler Crowe?"

"Does it matter?

"And you are simply going to hand them over?"

Crowe smiled. "Bethor, you have a touch of intelligence about you, yes? You know I'm not planning on handing them over at all."

Bethor gave a roar and sprang like an uncoiling doll.

There was a great confusion of sound.

Stenstrom produced several MARZABLEs and sent them flying. Kat jumped up and slashed with micro-point Silver tech.

"What are you two doing?" Crowe asked in a haughty, annoyed fashion.

Stenstrom noticed something. "Kat, wait. Wait!" He took a step forward. "What's this?"

His MARZABLEs were stuck in mid-air; all four heading for various parts of Bethor's assembled body. Its left arm and its left leg were in the early stages of being cleanly sliced into small strips by Kat's micro-point Shadow tech. Delicate slices of flesh and globes of splattering blood issued forth from the wounds.

Kat inspected the frozen MARZABLE hanging solidly in mid-air. "Are they TKed?"

Crowe joined them. "No, Bethor is in the early stages of being savagely stabbed and sliced by your remarkable Silver tech. Quite an adaptation—I shall devote several hundred years of contemplation toward it at a later time. You have been time-socked. I have sped up time a bit—which is incredibly fast, even by your standards. I have included you into my circle—again, part of the debt I owe. We are now moving at a rate beyond the Ghrundids and their petty, mindless ways. Now, follow me quickly."

Crowe lightly stepped through the lab toward the forward hatch.

Stenstrom and Kat followed. "If you had this ability, why bother with these theatrics? Why didn't you simply move more quickly in time before?"

"Because I am not your slave, and the debt you hold only goes so far. Also—adding yourselves to the time-sock might disrupt things a bit in ways

I cannot fathom. It all makes for fine intrigue."

They went into the corridor. There, stacked everywhere like a grim charnel house, Ghrundids lay about—body parts occupying side rooms, alcoves, maintenance hatches and so on.

"These are the lesser Ghrundids—the ones awaiting their turn to couple with a greater clan. These are the ones you really have to worry about—utterly mindless, except for creating mayhem and chaos, in which case they are quite clever. Once they merge into a clan, they can enjoy some of the sensory experiences they once did—they feast and they may also think a bit in a more cognitive fashion. You see, your weapons and Silver tech might have been effective in the initial stages of a complicated battle, however, given the volume of lesser Ghrundids here, you would have been overwhelmed in short order."

They pressed on and entered a lift passage. Crowe again pulled the small device from his cloak and summoned a car. When it arrived, inside were more Ghrundids—smaller, in more pieces: fingers, eyes, ears, entrails and other unidentifiable parts.

"How can these sad-sacks live like this?" Kat asked in disgust.

"What choice do they have?"

"Burn them, G," she said. "Burn them, please. I feel for their cursed souls. Crowe, you said burning offers them change into a more satisfying form. Then burn them, please."

Stenstrom produced several red Holystones and burned the pieces, watching the fire take root as a colorful, glass-like ornament, frozen in movement.

"Oh, they're burning, all right, in their time," Crowe said. He seemed impressed. "You are most compassionate, Countess. The lovely Melazarr didn't give these creatures any regard."

"I am not that woman. I can hear their cries in my mind and I want them silenced."

The lift stopped and they stepped out. They were in the upper tier of the ship. At least seven decks had been hollowed out and swept aside, creating a gorge-like cavern of empty space lined with twisted metal.

A battle raged all around them—transfixed in time.

Ghrundids were locked in a seemingly formless conflagration. There were the Green ones, the Avocados they had seen earlier, along with a host of disembodied parts in green armor soaring into the open space on bluish jets, like fighter planes surrounding a much larger mother ship.

They were fighting a host of other Ghrundids. There were ones in red armor—the Tomatoes. As with the Avocados, there were greater and lesser assemblages of parts, some individual pieces, and some coming to savage grips with other pieces. The Greater Tomatoes were put together in more of a quadrupedal fashion, having four armored legs mounted on a supporting torso. Mounted parallel to the lower torso was a second torso, sporting two arms and two shoulder-mounted heads, like a demented centaur. The Tomatoes' red armor was also put together with a slightly more gothic flair.

Mixed into this horrific mess were the Custards, in slightly watery-looking yellow armor. The Greater Custards were assembled in a cart, or truck-like fashion, with four torsos knitted together creating a rather flat, roughly rectangular surface. Surrounding the perimeter of the 'cart' were ten legs arranged caterpillar style. The interior of the cart was studded with reaching arms, at least twenty of them. Some were carrying weapons, others were holding wide-eyed, leering heads.

Crowe seemed proud of himself. "Ah, yes, you see the chaos my ruse has created."

Stenstrom and Kat held each other for a moment, lost in the horror. He shook off the rush of nausea and began trying to sort out the situation. Stenstrom found a good spot and looked about. High above the carnage of the battling clans, near the forward sections of the ship, was a cone of strong, white/blue light.

Stenstrom knew the light, so too did Kat.

Blue light.

The demon.

"Up there, G! Do you see it? Blue light."

"I see it."

"And there is the demon, the stolen personage of my wife. You have the advantage of the time-sock; Bellathauser will, as with the Ghrundids here, appear immobile to you. Be advised; the moment you lay hands on the Anatameter, the time-sock will be released. As with all things, use your time wisely."

Crowe turned to walk away.

"Where are you going?" Stenstrom asked.

"I am finished here. The demon is part of my wife—I cannot face her, that is for you to do. Be somewhat comforted—these Ghrundids are fully absorbed in each other at present, that should also be of some assistance."

He walked away.

"Mr. Crowe?" Kat asked.

Crowe spoke without turning. "You are a well-selected *Covus*. My debt is paid."

With that, he vanished down the corridor.

Alone in the center of a grotesque time-frozen battle, they assessed their situation.

"At least everything feels level now," Kat said.

"All right, we know these horrors won't come back to life until we touch the Anatameter; that gives us time to prepare, at least."

Kat made two fists. Silver tech bubbled, coating her hands. "We can do more than that." Kat formed StTs, her Belmont Buzzers, their tiny bug-like bodies falling from her hands in droves, scurrying about on the floor. They took wing, swirling around Kat. She gave them their orders, orders they would follow to their deaths. "Avocados," she said, and a mass of StTs flew off, landing on the various Green clan-members.

"Tomatoes," she said. "Custards." The StTs, like locusts, swarmed about the open area, landing on their assigned clans until they vanished into the stillness.

"I've given these Buzzers orders to explode on my command, good and hot. I hate to see them go, but, when I say the word, this place is going to go up like a bonfire on Saluting Day. If they're going up, they're going up hard."

Stenstrom was puzzled. "Saluting Day? I don't think I've ever mentioned Saluting Day to you, Kat."

"The cooks talk about it all the time, say they love getting drunk on Saluting Day."

"I see, well, great thinking. So now, let's make our way up to the top."

Kat had no problems bounding about from one Ghrundid to the next, rising up on precarious perches. Stenstrom though, denied his TK, could not follow. Kat went all the way to the top near the blue light. She looked about a moment, then bounded back down.

"The coast is clear," she said. She extended her tail. "Come on, G, let me help you."

Using her tail as a rail, he managed to climb up, seeing the leering faces, odd technology and disembodied time-locked parts of the clans up close. As he neared, Kat would leap up a little higher to the next level, grabbing onto Ghrundids and bits of metal; anything she could hold onto, and then assist Stenstrom with her tail and so on, until they reached the top. They moved across the open span of wreckage. The place below was a frozen diorama of the grotesque and the bizarre.

"The Custards are pretty rotten," Kat said, trying to make light of the situation. "I'd rather the Tomatoes. They sort of remind me of horses. I like horses."

"They're all fairly horrific to me," he replied, grunting, pulling himself up on her tail.

Once at the top, they saw their objective: a corridor heading forward awash in strong blue light. They entered the corridor. Stenstrom drew his NTHs and Kat created a fresh swarm of StTs, this group orbiting around them in slow menacing circles.

"It's like having the Belmont cavalry here with us," she said. "It's going to suck when I forget how to make these little guys."

"Countess Sygillis will teach you."

"You know, I was all set to get rid of that Paige du Long squash, but I don't know, I might be tempted to keep it around. Maybe put the bag in a safe or something where I can't get to it for casual stuff, but we'll have it in case of an emergency. What do you think?"

"If you like."

They made their way down the long corridor, which Stenstrom recognized as leading to the central engineering bay. At the end of the corridor was the thermoplant room; one of three that powered the large *Triumph*-class ships. It was three hundred feet square and went up several decks. The thermoplant normally took up most of the space—however, it was not present. The floor in the room was mostly gone, fallen in, though a little remained around the walls, creating a precarious ledge. Kat's StTs moved with them, ready to deal with anything.

The light coming up from the missing floor was bright. They removed their goggles.

In the center of the room, spanning the section of fallen-in flooring, was a vast web. It was difficult for them to take it all in at once. The web was composed of interlinked, disembodied arms, all wearing etched blue armor, hands clasped with hands, blinking lights caught frozen in time. Smeared on the web at various points were clusters of heads staring goggle-eyed at nothing. A flock of disembodied hands swarmed about, blue tail-fires trailing them. All around the web, supported by disembodied arms bolted to the walls, were row after row of heads, all staring wide-eyed to the center.

Here, in the former thermoplant room, was the Hall of Many Faces.

And there was the demon; clinging to the web in a great metal construct that looked generally like a giant spider. From their perspective, the spider was upside down, clinging to the underside of the web. From where they were standing at the edge of the room, they couldn't see the top of it, only its undersides. Peering out, they saw under the web a great emptiness awash in bright, fruity light, an abyss stretching out into the vastness of chaos, colored in streaks of sanity lost, going nowhere for eternity.

The spider construct was huge; possibly thirty feet tall with a leg span of a hundred. It had only four jointed legs, and a plump machined abdomen composed of acid-etched ridges and dapples of blue light. At the other end, its head was a great glass sphere fifteen feet across. The sphere was flawless except that it sported a dark ring of circuitry spanning its central axis. Inside the sphere was a flowing, bluish fluid, cloudy in its viscosity, jostling like a science experiment in a beaker. A dark form floated in the fluid like an infernal giant-sized embryo.

Surrounding the spider, both above and below the web, was a swarm of armored hands and arms, flying about like angry blue hornets, all frozen in a moment by Crowe's time-sock. As they had Kat's StT's protecting them, Bellathauser also had the airborne Ghrundids protecting her.

Stenstrom took in this horror with trained objectivity; he wasn't here to be horrified, he was here to kill the beast, to perform his revenge and reclaim the Anatameter. He could be terrified later in his nightmares.

"Where's the Anatameter?" he asked, barely hearing his own voice.

Kat, standing next to him, was surprisingly stoic. She sent her StTs forward in a cloud, moving all around the infernal thing hanging beneath the web. "I don't know. Maybe it's someplace we can't see from here." On all fours, Kat left the safety of the corridor and waded out onto the web of flesh and metal, balancing on the narrow runs, completely unafraid of the terrifying eternal drop into perdition beneath her, her tail steadying her like a rudder.

"Come on, G!" she said, offering her tail, stretching it out, wrapping it around his waist. He took hold of it, careful of the footing.

Kat went out far, never putting a foot wrong, until they reached the center of the web. She attached a Silver tech strand to the web and spun it out, allowing both she and Stenstrom to drop down below the web. Stenstrom didn't look at the churning, yellowy abyss beneath him. He concentrated on the spider. From their new perspective beneath the web, they inspected it from front to back.

They saw a fleshy umbilical cord attached to the spider at a point just behind its head. The cord trailed off a distance to a mountain of flesh and blood that seemed to be pulsating, though they saw no real movement in it.

Stenstrom stared at it. That fleshy cord? Was that the tap Bellathauser was using to drain their universe of energy? Could that be the case? He noticed that at the point where the cord connected to the spider's head a dim glow of green light radiated in a circle.

"There, Kat! I think that's the Anatameter, right there, mounted to the spider's head and connected to the very life-blood of our universe."

"Let me move us in a little closer."

There it was. As they got closer, the green glow got brighter, such that Stenstrom could see its circular structure. In Clovis it had appeared as an uninteresting round rock so vapid that it failed to capture Lady Gwendolyn's attention; not so here. Though covered by the cord of flesh, it shone like a green star, vivid and terrible, pulsing, a great engine taking the energy from their suffering universe, processing it through this insane machination and pumping out turbid, pre-processed reality, expelling it from a symmetrical line of exhaust ports jutting out the dorsal section of the spider's abdomen. The top of the spider's head all around the Anatameter was protected with an interwoven carpet of bare, interlocked arms, sentinels just waiting to rend apart anyone trying to get at the device.

From their up-close position, they could also see what was floating in the glass sphere at the head of the spider. It was a naked woman, cupped up in the fetal position awash with blue fluid.

Bellathauser herself on the left side, the sundered body of Lady Gwendolyn on the right.

The demon wears the flesh of Gwendolyn of Prentiss.

Stenstrom took in the horrific sight without flinching: he would allow himself to suffer this sight another time.

When they'd had their fill taking it in, Kat pulled them back up to the web, and then back to safety at the edge of the corridor were they could stand.

"Well, that's a hell of a thing, isn't it, G? That's Lady Gwendolyn in there, isn't it?"

He nodded.

"You ok?"

"I'm fine." He wasn't fine. He concentrated on the task at hand. "And the moment I touch the Anatameter, the time-sock ends and we engage in battle."

Kat rubbed her chin. "Ok, ok, let's think about this. The floor is missing and I don't like the look of that big empty space out there one bit. I wouldn't want to fall down in there, would you? Why don't I build a floor underneath it, a nice sturdy Silver tech floor? That way, we could stand out there in safety and collectively beat the demon to death with nothing to worry about."

"Sounds fine to me."

She hit herself up with a fresh squash and went to work, slinging Silver tech around, creating, in short order, a silver interwoven floor beneath the web. The bright light from the abyss went out as the floor was completed, requiring them to put their goggles back on to see. Soon, Stenstrom was standing directly beneath the spider; the floor Kat had just made firm and solid under him.

He inspected the situation. "I think I see some holes in this cord where I can place my hands and get at the Anatameter. We're going to have to cut this cord away to dislodge it."

Kat was nearby, busy creating dozens and dozens of StTs. She sent them all over the spider, crawling into its inner workings as only they could.

"Maybe I can take this thing over with my Buzzers, like I did with Paige on Xandarr?"

"Possibly, but I doubt it."

"It's worth a try. In any event, I'm rigging this bitch to blow, Buzzers galore. If I can't take it over, I'll blow it to bits. There won't be anything left of it when I'm done. Bellathauser's not going to know what the hell happened. I'm hitting all her goons up too, Buzzer-style. I might have to rest up a bit, I'm getting a little low."

Kat seated herself next to Stenstrom. She looked up into the glass sphere. She saw the black, mass of Bellathauser floating in the blue liquid. "Looks sort of peaceful, like she's asleep in there or something."

"I suppose."

After a short rest, Kat was ready. Stenstrom helped her up. "Remember, we can't effect any damage to this machine while it's time-socked—Crowe told us so. We have to first synch time. Once we get this going, we hold nothing back. This demon must be utterly destroyed. Unfortunately, civility and mercy do not apply here."

Kat thought a little bit more. "Ok then, now that I've powered up a little, let's get more back-up on our side." She formed three great blobs of Silver tech and cast them to the floor. The blobs twisted and reformed into the life-sized likenesses of three silver females; one bore a pair of wings, the second carried a great axe, and the final one had on a belt carrying a number of dinner plate-sized hollow rings.

"It's Bird and Walker, isn't that awesome? I thought it would be a nice touch having them here fighting with us," she said.

The final female with the rings stepped forward and curtsied to Stenstrom in a lady-like fashion.

"Is this a likeness of your final sister, Wheel?"

"It is. She needs to be here too. So, here's what we'll do—you get the Anatameter, which will end the time-sock. Crowe said we'd have a few moments as time synchs back up; while that's going on, me and my sisters here will handle all the Ghrundids flying around. You get away from the spider as quick as you can, then I'll either take it over cold, or I'll Buzzer bomb it to bits. We'll just pick the Anatameter out of the wreckage once it's all done and get the hell out of here. Sound good?"

"Not particularly, but I can't think of a better plan at the moment. Let's proceed."

With Kat and her three Silver tech automatons at the ready, Stenstrom approached the cord of flesh, placing his hands on it. It felt rigid, like smooth stone against his palms. He could see the green glow of the Anatameter within. Several holes dotted the cord; he stuck his hands in, searching for the stony surface of the Anatameter.

"You got it, G?" Kat asked.

"Nearly." He shoved his hands in farther, going up to his elbows. "Be ready."

The tips of his fingers brushed against the Anatameter. A surge of heat and pain ran up his arm.

FWWWWEEEEEEEEEEEEE!

The world around him seemed to compress; noise, cries, wailings, all assaulted his ears at once. The spider shuddered in surprise, the cord throbbing, its abdomen pulsing back and forth, belching out chaos. The interlocked arms around the Anatameter came to life, waving about, their hands clenching and unclenching, seeking flesh to tear apart.

Banging!

The naked form in the glass sphere was banging on the sides with her hand.

Bellathauser, wearing Gwendolyn's right side, was enraged.

He drew his NTH from its sash and aimed, ready to shoot the demon dead.

From below, something rocked the silver floor he was standing on, knocking him off his feet. As he tried to right himself, he became aware of a foulness filling the air, destroying his lungs, every breath like swallowing a ball of uncoiling barbed wire.

 The walls of the chamber, the heads! The heads were belching a foul exhalation of noxious fumes straight from the depths of hell, the air becoming more impossible to breathe by the second. He couldn't see what was happening to Kat, he could only imagine. This attack against Bellathauser and her Ghrundid horde, mere seconds old, was quickly turning to a shambles.

The interlocked arms on the spider's head pulled themselves free, dropping down on him like oversized maggots. Gasping for breath, he turned his NTH and pumped shots into them, seeing the arms go limp. He had to locate Kat and get her out of here as quickly as possible.

Another tremor rocked the floor. As he watched, a great sinuous arm clad in etched blue armor came slicing up through the Silver tech floor like a butcher's knife slicing through a burlap bag. With great effort, the arm sawed through the floor, admitting the bright yellow light from the abyss below. A second arm appeared, ripping away chunks of the floor. A towering robotic suit of armor, possibly twenty feet tall, pulled itself through the hole in the floor. It moved with articulated grace, like an octopus, its arms and legs rolling with tentacle-like fluidity. Atop its broad shoulders where its head should be was a vast ovoid hole.

Bellathauser pointed at Stenstrom. The great robot snapped out its fist and picked him up like a doll. Before he knew what was happening, it whisked him through the hole it had made and into the vast, dreaded emptiness of the abyss below. Rockets at its back smoked as it maneuvered through space. It seemed to consider for a moment what to do with him— fling him into the nothingness, or pull him apart like a fly.

Panels opened and saws came out, whirling.

Or—saw him into quarters, that was an option as well.

He aimed his NTH and fired. The glowing NTH shot, tinged purple by Crowe's striker, hit the robot in the chest. It instantly seized up. Lights went out, smoke poured from vents, its smooth dance through the openness now an out-of-control, lifeless tumble.

Stenstrom worked himself from its grasp, the two of them falling side-by-side into eternity.

A glint of silver from above. Before he knew it, he was in the arms of Kat's Silver tech reconstruction of her sister, Bird, silver wings flapping, her hair alive with movement. She placed some sort of breathing mask against his mouth and nose, providing him with clean air. That was something, Kat was sure to be still alive up there. Effortlessly, Bird reversed course and flew him back up toward the opening.

A gaggle of blue armored body parts headed down toward them fast, like a school of piranha fish on the attack. It was a host of Ghrundids spoiling for their blood. He drew his second NTH as Bird flew into the crowd.

Arms, legs, and heads slammed into them, some moving with sinister life, others charred and burning like a match head, beginning their long eternal fall. Stenstrom unleashed a torrent of NTH shot, shooting at anything that got near to him, hitting many. Ghrundids fell away in vast numbers like an immortal rain as Bird worked her way upwards.

She shuddered and screamed. Many clawed hands had latched onto her, ripping away pieces of her silver flesh, digging into her throat. He tried to shoot them with his pistols but couldn't get a clear shot—if he accidentally hit Bird, she would be destroyed and he would resume his fall into the abyss.

Shot after shot, Ghrundids falling away, more attacking in vicious waves, Bird screaming as they took their toll on her. Though she was just a Silver tech creation, Kat had made her, poured her love into her. It was like the real Bird was dying all over again. A swarm of Ghrundids attacked, seeking their flesh, more than he could manage with his NTHs.

As he watched, Ghrundids were sliced in twain, sometimes into quarters, one after the next was picked off on the wing, others exploded in a grisly cloud. From above, scores of expertly thrown Silver tech disks wrought destruction and misery on the Ghrundids, taking them down with precision. With the rain of disks, with Kat's exploding StTs, the Ghrundid hoard was thinned out enough for him to manage with his NTHs as Bird worked to return him to the platform.

Nearly there. Explosions, fire, body parts falling away as Kat's StTs did their deadly work. Bird staggered through the hole in the floor and released Stenstrom. She was hopelessly snared by the grasping hands, pulling on her head, digging into her throat, her silver hair, her shoulders, tearing away chunks of silvery material, her wings flapping helplessly. Stenstrom tried to help her, to pry the Ghrundids from her body, but he was under attack too, so many living parts of bodies swarming about he couldn't shoot them fast enough. Wheel stood a short distance away, her Silver tech disks, thrown precariously close to his head and neck, zipped past, dispatching the Ghrundids with deadly speed. But, for Bird, there was no helping her, the Ghrundids were dug-in, ripping away silver flesh. Clawed fingers came around, putting her eyes out. Spinning around in torment, Bird and the Ghrundids fastened to her fell through the hole and were gone.

Enraged, he increased his rate of fire; he wanted revenge for Bird. More Ghrundids met their end. Wheel leapt to his side, casting a continuous torrent of disks as he blasted away with his duel pistols. She was fighting hard, courageously, with skill and grace, so unlike the evil, selfish Black Hat-tainted Wheel that Kat had described to him.

"G!" came Kat's voice.

Wheel took his arm and led him away from the hole toward the corridor. Kat was there, wearing a similar gas mask to the one he wore. Nearby was the Silver tech construct of Walker, swinging her great axe, cleaving Ghrundids from knuckle to bone. The walls of the chamber were wreathed in flames, many of the heads that had been spewing noxious gasses were either missing, on fire, or cloven in two. The spider with the Anatameter and Bellathauser was caught in a strong Silver tech net, being hauled in by Kat, away from the hole in the floor. It struggled and thrashed about.

"G, get over here!" she cried.

He fought his way to her side. Wheel took up a defensive position, sending out Silver tech disks in a blur. This clearly was the Wheel Kat wished she had been, not the selfish creature she actually was.

"She's been trying to escape, but I got her! I was kind of able to take the construct over, but it didn't fully work. Now that you're back and she's far enough away from the hole that we won't lose the Anatameter, I'm gonna blow it!"

From the hole, a second headless robot appeared, knifing its way into the chamber. It saw the snared Bellathauser and went to her aid, trying to cut the Silver tech net and free her.

Fiery explosions like a string of fireworks went off along the spider's body, blowing off legs and large bits of metal--Kat's Belmont Buzzers had done their work with horrendous results. The robot was thrown back, its metal body smashed and on fire. In a cascade of flames, the spider went down. The glass sphere containing Bellathauser detached and rolled away from the inferno like a marble.

The burning robot still functioned. It rose and went back into action, moving with amazing speed. It seized the glass sphere and placed it on the open spot between its shoulders, seating it with a twist, the sphere now acting as its head.

The giant, with its new glass bubble, turned to Stenstrom and Kat, and quickly acted. Before either one of them could move, it lifted its arm and sprayed them with a fast-acting mist. In an instant, they were stuck in place, like flies on sticky paper. Panels in the armor opened. Weapons appeared. Rapid energy pulses shot out. Walker dove in front of them, absorbing the shots. She buried her great axe in the robot's midsection, creating a gout of sparks and smoke. Undaunted, Bellathauser's robot pressed the attack, using its long arms like deadly swords, slicing Walker in two. Walker attacked one last time, making a small chip in the glass sphere with her axe. She then dropped it and went dead.

Bellathauser cast Walker aside, surveyed the burning chamber, and went for Kat with an armful of spinning blades.

She spoke in a demented voice; *"I killed your woman once, I shall do it again..."*

Wheel attacked, peppering the robot with a hail of disks.

Kat managed to work herself free and leapt aside, while Stenstrom remained stuck. She righted herself and took aim, slashing with micro-point Silver tech. The robot's right arm fell apart and smoked. Shocked, the giant robot came at Kat missing an arm.

Slash! Wheel sliced its other arm off. Kat took out both of Bellathauser's legs with a single swipe. The robot fell, face first, sparking and wrecked. Kat picked up Walker's axe, ready to cleave the sphere in two.

TINK!

The sphere resisted and leapt away from the force of the blow. Several flying arms came in and engaged themselves to the belt of machinery at the sphere's center. Soon, Bellathauser's sphere, over-large like an egg resting on a framework of toothpicks, had a working set of arms and legs.

ZZZZZZZZ...

ZZZZZZZZ...

Wheel destroyed the arms and legs, but, in a flash, they were discarded and replaced with other arms and legs, Bellathauser rebuilding herself as fast as Wheel and Kat could put them off. It dug the Anatameter out of the smoking ruins of the spider. With it tucked under her arm, Bellathauser turned to run, to escape out the hole in the floor and be gone.

ZZZZZZZZ...

Wheel sheared off one leg.

ZZZZZZZZ...

And then the second. The sphere toppled.

Kat was on it, swinging with Walker's axe. She hit the sphere, making a small crack, toppling the top-heavy assemblage over. Bellathauser raised her arm and fired a flashing red pulse. Kat leapt away, the beam burning the wall behind her.

Bellathauser fired again.

Kat leapt aside again.

It was a standoff: Kat's speed against Bellathauser's hideous technology; a terrible game of chicken.

Flying arms came in, seeking Kat's throat. Wheel downed several with perfect casts of her disks. Bellathauser had enough of Wheel and her deadly disks, she directed her minions to concentrate on Wheel, to take her down once and for all. A final surge of flying arms attacked Wheel, many going down in pieces along the way, but a few got in, latching onto her silvery flesh as they had with Bird. More attacked and found their mark. Wheel went down and was pulled apart in a horrific display, the Ghrundids trampling in her remains. With Wheel gone, they turned to Kat. Kat hacked them out of the air with her axe.

Kat was tiring. A slash from Bellathauser's knives found their mark and Kat fell to the floor. The demon seized her by the throat and held her fast.

"Wendilnight!" she screeched in triumph. Bellathauser raised her knives to kill Kat.

THUMP!

Bellathauser looked down. A MARZABLE dagger had hit her in the arm, disabling her knife. Stenstrom, still stuck, had managed to free his right arm. He waved up another MARZABLE dagger.

THUMP!

It lodged in the elbow joint. The robot could no longer move, and there were few Ghrundids left to replace the disabled ones. An arm came in to assist Bellathauser; Stenstrom skewered it out of the air with his daggers. Kat rallied, sensing victory. She raised her axe and brought it down, shattering the sphere, releasing stinking blue fluid within and the naked form of Bellathauser.

The demon struck, leaping like a demonic frog, claws reaching for Kat's throat.

A purple-tinged green globe hit Bellathauser in the back.

Hit by an NTH shot. She released Kat and fell to the floor, glistening from the fluid that had surrounded her.

Kat went to Stenstrom's side and helped free him. The place around them was crawling with the half dead and raging with fire. They picked up the Anatameter. It was back to its rather humble appearance, the green glow gone. With it in hand, he went to Bellathauser's lifeless body. He placed her hand firmly on its smooth face and turned the knob.

She reacted, eyes opening with fright and surprise, kicking out with Lady Gwendolyn's leg, and then was still.

With the knob turned, the Anatameter vanished, like it had never been there.

"Is that it?" Kat asked. "Is it over?"

"I have no idea. I hope so."

There came a rumbling and compacting as Bellathauser's horror realm began to close in on itself.

"Let's get out of here!" he said.

They ran out of the Hall of Many Faces to the open gallery beyond. An arm covered in red armor began clawing its way upward to attack. Stenstrom fired his NTHs and the arm fell away, insensate.

A Custard floated upward. Several shots brought it down.

"I'm going to burn this place, G! I'm going to burn it straight to hell where it belongs! Get 'em Buzzers!" Kat cried as the open hall erupted in fire, her previous-

ly placed StT's doing their deadly work. A Custard trucked around hopelessly blazing, as did two Tomatoes. Their armor spewed out fire-retardant material, but Kat's Silver tech flames would not go out.

Sprouting Silver tech wings, she guided them both to the ground floor. The forward part of the ship near the Hall of Many Faces was now an inferno; Kat's StTs had done their work. The walls lurched and compressed inward, everything Bellathauser had made coming apart. Ghrundids of all clans capered about, burning. An Avocado jumped into their way. Stenstrom hammered it with NTH shot and it slumped over. A few StTs were dropped onto its body and the remains caught alight, the flames climbing high into the gallery.

They passed out of the gallery area and Kat threw up a Silver tech wall, sealing in the Ghrundid clans. Many fists beat on the wall from the other side. Many armored feet kicked. They were being consumed by the irresistible flames, being turned into Revantors, as Crowe had called them. Then, silence: as everything crumpled up and collapsed.

They worked their way upward to the aft of the ship, struggling with the angle, Kat having to mostly carry Stenstrom. They found the hole Kat had made previously and bounded up the stairs to the surface of rainy Gelt. She sealed it with a Silver tech cap and then, as Sygillis of Blanchefort had once done, leveled the ground and filled in the hole; forever, this time.

They stood there, trying to cope with the horror of what they had been through. Both fell into the mud, too fatigued to stand.

Eventually, Kat spoke: "Thanks Walker, thanks Bird, and thank you Wheel. Most of all, thank you Paige du Long of Moane. Couldn't have done it without you. Can we go home now, G?"

9—Lunch by the Sea

In the weeks after Gelt, the universe never ended. Life continued as it was, whatever damage Bellathauser had done was healed. It took some time getting back home, taking a slow, primitive transport off Gelt that meandered its stumbling way across the cosmos, visiting every backwater outpost and crap stand it could find. The long trip sitting in the dingy, can-like interior of the transport helped wash away much of the terror of what they had seen. It helped get the fiery images of disembodied creatures and dying Silver tech friends out of their heads.

During the voyage, Kat practiced making StTs—her Belmont Buzzers—without using the squash. She struggled, eventually able to make a cockroach-like shape in silver, but it was too big, had no life; it couldn't move and fly and do all the incredible things Paige du Long's StTs could. She cradled its unmoving form in her arms like a dead infant.

"Buzzer no buzz," she said, trying to make light of it. It was frustrating knowing what was possible with Silver tech and not being able to create it by herself. StTs would be the first thing she would ask Countess Sygillis to teach her.

They befriended a commoner family traveling to Hoban. Kat was good with their children, smiling as she played with them, coaxing laughter out of them. He was so proud of Kat.

Eventually, they arrived at Hoban. They bade their new friends goodbye. From there, they took a better transport home to Kana in just a few days.

After a time of rest, Stenstrom took Kat to their favorite cafe in Tyrol village by the sea, so close to the jetty they could occasionally feel spray from the surf tickle their faces.

"You know, after all the places we've been, after all we've seen, this little cafe is my favorite, here with you by the living sea," Kat said.

"I agree."

"I'm getting all sorts of invitations from your sisters for all sorts of things. I don't know what to do with them all. The cooks told me to just burn everything, haha."

"Just look them over, select the functions you wish to attend and politely decline the rest. Please don't ignore any of them, and I wouldn't advise burning the notes at this time."

Kat stirred her piping hot soup. "I was hoping, next week, we could go to St. Edmunds, check in on A-Ram, see how he's doing."

"I think that sounds fine. I would wager he and a reformed Lady Alesta are well on their way to falling in love."

"I hope so. What about Ottoman John and Melazarr? Do you think there's any way to get word to them?"

"Not officially. Vain is an enemy city with no formal lines of communication with the League. I still have a few friends at the Fleet. We can probably back-channel a communication out to them one way or the other."

"Great." Kat looked around. "And what about Carahil and Paige? I really miss her. I'd like to return to Xandarr and see how she's doing."

"I miss her too. Let's give Xandarr a little time to bloom, then we'll return."

Kat aimlessly stirred her soup. "Hey, G, there's something I've been wanting to ask you."

"What is it?"

"Paige du Long of Moane."

"What about her?"

She pushed her soup bowl aside. "I think she's still alive. I know Atha told us she was dead, but I don't think so. At one point, I thought I was seeing what she was seeing. I thought I saw the three mountains in the Street of Knowledge. It's confusing, having someone else's thoughts in your head. I don't know if she's living in Vain with a bought squash, or if she's one of those poor people in those Verti-Hovi parks, but I think we owe it to her to at least try to investigate, see if she needs help."

"All right. When we make contact with Ottoman John, we'll see what we can do."

They continued their meal, savoring their mutual closeness, laughing, discussing their plans for the manor. The subject of children came up. They agreed to wait a year, do a little traveling, see the League, visit Xandarr, then have their first child. "If we choose to have a girl, let's name her 'Paige', in honor of Paige and of Paige du Long," Kat said.

"I was going to suggest the same thing."

Kat laughed.

As they talked, a soft voice filtered in over their shoulders. "Bel?"

Standing several tables down were a pair of familiar figures. It was A-Ram in his blue Calvert suit and Lady Alesta, long black hair pinned up, wearing her resplendent green Pilgrim of Merian robe. No tattoos, no elongated eyelash or demon tongue; just the woman in her natural beauty.

It was the two of them, from another universe, who had guided both Stenstrom and Kat. They stood there, all smiles, beaming as they looked at Kat like proud parents. "Sorry we were delayed. We wouldn't have missed helping you for anything," A-Ram said. Stenstrom stood and shook A-Ram's hand. He was so different from the version of himself that inhabited this universe.

"Lady Alesta, well met," he said, bowing.

"Hi, Bel," she said, rising up and kissing him on the cheek.

They turned to Kat. "We were hoping you would invite us to sit and join you for lunch," Alesta said. A tear fell from her eye. "We've ... been so eager ..."

Kat dropped her spoon and slowly stood. In breathless joy she stepped toward them, her hands clasped together at her midriff. She said nothing, a few hushed sobs coming from her open mouth as she approached.

Her angels ...

She stared at them, they stared at her; nobody saying anything. Stenstrom, hat in hand, stepped back, allowing them to have their moment. Kat raised her hands, reaching out to touch them, to feel their skin against hers. Her hands felt the warmth of their cheeks, she savored their touch.

They were real. They were here before her, not alternate versions, but the real people she had so longed for.

Tears falling from her face, Kat fell into their embrace, touching her angels at long last.

Fin
RDG--August 2016

ABOUT THE AUTHOR

Ren Garcia, the author of the League of Elder Series, graduated from the Ohio State University with a degree in literature. He enjoys playing volleyball, urban exploration, taking pictures of clouds, and ice hockey. He lives in Columbus, Ohio, with his wife and their four vivacious little wiener dogs. You can visit Ren's website/on-line glossary at:

https://www.thetempleoftheexplodinghead.com

ALSO BY REN GARCIA

The League of Elder Series:
Sygillis of Metatron
The Hazards of the Old Ones

The Temple of the Exploding Head Trilogy:
The Dead Held Hands
The Machine
The Temple of the Exploding Head

The Belmont Saga:
Sands of the Solar Empire
Against the Druries

Turns of the Shadow tech Goddess:
The Shadow tech Goddess
Stenibelle
Kat

The House of Bloodstein Series:
Perlamum
Mentralysis

Non-Fiction by Ren Garcia:
10 Weeks at Chanute

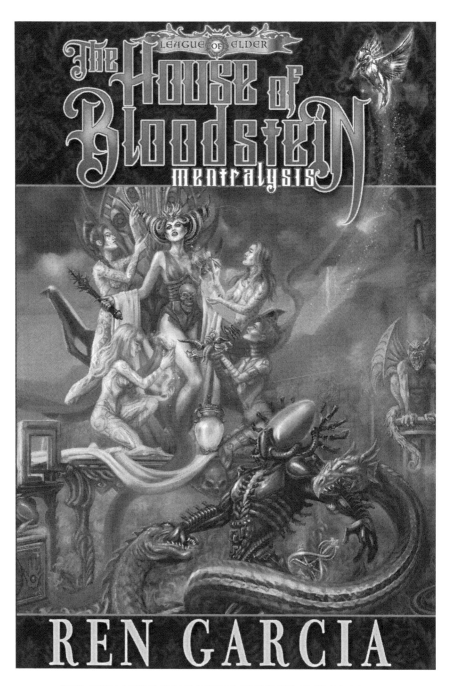

DEATH AT THE HANDS OF THE IMMORTAL
Book 11 in the League of Elder Series.
Foolish is he who dares to possess the Ultimate Object, for misery will
be his only reward

Shandahar is a cursed world. People will live and die. Wars will be fought, kingdoms built, discoveries made. For centuries, history will proceed apace... and then everything will come to a grinding halt and start all over again.

A prophecy. Spoken by the renowned seer, Johannan Chardelis, there is a divination that tells the coming of someone who can stop the curse.

The snag? They have failed four times already.

Enter a world swirling with mystical realms and bloody battles, with enchanted forests and crowded cities where things are not always as they seem. Enter the World of Shandahar.

Found within these pages is a wonderful assortment of tales and adventures from some of the most memorable people in the world of Shandahar! Come and meet Sirion as a young lycan hunter, Thane before he became corrupted by the greatest of evils, Sorn as a young rogue tempted by love, and Dartanyen before he meets up with the Wildrunners! You will meet some new people too, and experience the depth and richness Shandahar truly has to offer!

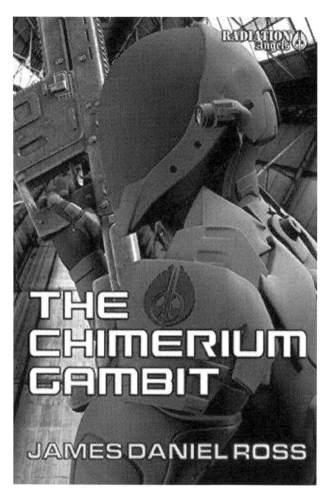

They Say You need three things: Honor, Integrity, and Courage.

What you really need is the nerve to fly half a billion light years, touch down on alien soil, and fight in a major land war… every other week.

When the enemy sets foot on your soil, when civil unrest or revolution raise their bloody hands to the stars, when governmental factions leave words behind and reach for guns and knives and bombs, there is little that the aerospace navies can do. This is when planets contact mercenaries, the last scions of professional ground troops.

Led by their Captain, Todd Rook, The Radiation Angels must wager their fortunes, their friends, their very lives on a plan that will make them rich beyond kings, or ensure their painful demise: The Chimerium Gambit.

46402343R00182

Made in the USA
Middletown, DE
31 July 2017